THIS *Hallowed* GROUND

DONNA E. LANE

Unless otherwise noted, all Bible verses are from the King James Version (KJV), Public Domain.

This novel's story and characters are fictitious. Certain historical events and historical figures are included for realism; however, when accounts of historical figures are given, they are fictionalized. With the exception of these historical figures, any resemblance to persons living or dead is entirely coincidental.

Reader alert: This book contains scenes of war and graphic violence.

ISBN: 978-1-7342675-4-9

Cover art by Wyndagger
wyndagger@gmail.com

ACKNOWLEDGEMENTS

I would like to thank my critique group and critique readers: Kimberly McKay, Chloe Flanagan, Tabitha Bouldin, Naomi Craig, Lisa Renee, Sara Beth Williams, and Connie Mitchell—for your invaluable feedback, your willingness to wade through these many pages, your insights, and your support.

I would like to thank the person who said I would never be able to write in first person present tense and shouldn't even attempt it—I don't remember your name, but I appreciate your challenge. We will see if you were right.

Most of all, I would like to thank my husband, David Lane, for his willingness to answer endless questions on the Civil War, share his knowledge of American history, read chapter after chapter and rewrite after rewrite, and tolerate being ignored for endless hours as I buried myself in my computer to research and write this book.

This book would never have happened without you all.

DEDICATION

To my husband, David.

My split-apart.

For your many years of love, patience, support, and belief in me.

PART ONE

The Last Full Measure of Devotion

CHAPTER ONE

Death surrounds me, bodies piled atop each other like cut wood, wedged between the boulders, strewn like debris after a storm near the base of the larger Round Top. Seven times, the Yankees pressed us up against those devil boulders. Seven times we pushed them back. But what of the price we paid?

When the 11th Georgia drove down Plum Run Valley, we thought we would have another day like Seminary Ridge. The Yanks fell back from our advance. The fighting was fierce, for certain. Fire rained down on us from above, off the two round hills, but we prevailed all the way to the base.

It is sorrowful ground we hold. We lost so many. So many. It has me a-wonderin' about Pa's conviction that you fight for your land, no matter the cost.

"The Good Lord promised a land tae Israel, and He fought beside them for the land, as the Good Book reads, 'For the Lord hath driven out from before ye great nations and strong," and 'He tis that fighteth for ye, as He hath promised ye.' What the Good Lord dae for Israel, He gonnae dae for us, dae ye ken, boy? Tis the Good Lord what give us this land, and tis the Good Lord what telt us tae keep it." Pa doesn't brook any argument with the Good Book.

Ma was more straightforward. "The Good Book say, 'Thou shalt not kill' to be sure."

"Yer aff yer nut, woman. Have nae ye read the rest? The Good Lord Himself kilt nations for Israel, tae defend their land."

"Aidan be a child still!"

"A'most seventeen. Auld enough tae shoot." Pa poked my chest. "Ye fight for yer land, boy, and let nane take it from ye." He had the last word on that argument, so here I am.

7

It's dark now, but the crack of musket fire still echoes between the rocks on all sides of me. The air smells of copper and rotten eggs and burnt earth, and my eyes burn and water like little Bobby Creel just flung handfuls of red dust in my face. It's much like I imagine hell.

The Alabama boys pushed all the way up the little hill, but the Yankees charged down like rabid dogs with fixed bayonets and captured our boys. Now, my orders are to stay behind and fire at will on any soldiers coming from that hill. Truth be told, I don't much feel like firin' at anyone. So much death.

The rest of the 11th was to skedaddle back across the fields toward Seminary Ridge. I reckon I will be joinin' 'em soon, once they have had time to clear the wounded. Assumin' a Yank don't get me first.

I can still hear moans from the mounds of bodies. Hard to imagine something worse than breathin' your last under a pile of mortifyin' corpses.

Pa fell back with the rest. At least, I'm hopin' he did. I lost sight of him when we neared the devil stones. I pray he ain't moanin' somewhere under the dead or walkin' himself toward the heavenly gates. Losin' Pa would do Ma in. She begged him not to go.

"Tis not yer fight, Liam MacAlister. You have no slaves and wouldna ever. Tis a wicked business."

"Ah dinnae fight for no *tràill,* woman. The *gòrach* Yankees be invadin' to take our land!"

"I see no Yankees on our mountain."

"Ye dinnae see them on the mountain noo, dinnae mean ye willnae see."

"Och, you aul gobdaw! I cannot speak sense to ya."

"How no? Ah ken what loss dae to a body long afore noo."

Ma sighed. "I know you have." And no more was said, for Ma understood. The MacAlister clan's land had been taken by the English in 1746, and his family had suffered and starved for decades, until finally they were forced to emigrate because of that loss. The vow to protect your land at all costs had been passed down through the generations of MacAlister's ever since.

"If ye dinnae have land, ye have *gun dad idir*," he used to say. You have nothin' at all.

We fought for this little piece of land—fought hard, bayonets and knives and hands and fists, scratchin' out eyes, beatin' heads with rocks, whatever it took. War turns men into wild animals, no mistake. It was a bloody mess, and for what? For a pile of boulders and a rocky hill? And now, we are pullin' back, so it was all for naught. I wonder what Pa would say now?

The full moon lights the field beyond the boulders as if it were dusk instead of nearer midnight. I must make it back through the boulders and across that field to get to my brigade. The Yankee line will be to my right as I cross the field, but I don't know how far away they are. I just hope no one's lookin'.

My rifle over my shoulder, I crouch low and crawl and skitter from boulder to boulder until I reach the edge of the open field. The tall grass would've provided cover for me, except for the terrible tramplin' it took during the battle. Now it is flat as a hoecake and I am laid bare like the foundations of the world at the rebuke of the Lord, at the blast of breath of His nostrils. Oh, dear Lord, please protect me. But why would He? The Good Book says no killin', and I've killed— many times over.

Takin' a deep breath, I scamper as fast and as low as I can toward the ridge. The edges of my vision gray, and the ridge wavers like seein' distant mountains through layers of fog. The distance to the ridge seems to grow with each step I take. Time slows to a crawl. I hear the occasional ping of a shot nearby, but I don't know if they are shootin' at me or at the Confederate line.

A puff of dirt blossoms in front of me, and I hit the ground. That answers my question. After a few minutes of kissin' dirt, I raise my head enough to gauge how much farther I must run and decide to swing wide left in hopes of gettin' beyond the reach of their fire. No more crouchin'. I'm a rabbit runnin' from a fox. I bolt full speed in a wide arc left to the clipped rhythms of more rifle fire. When they decide to stop wastin' ammunition on me, I finally breathe again, and soon I reach the blessed cover of trees.

After a brief kneel for a prayer of gratitude, I creep through the undergrowth, careful to avoid sticks and pinecones and stay on the carpet of pine straw and dead leaves. You never know where a Yank might be lurkin'.

The night is silent as the grave now. I guess they don't have anyone else to shoot at that they can see. Still, I don't want to get careless. Creepin' quiet-like through the woods is something I do well. I been huntin' since I was big enough to tote a rifle. I guess that makes me good at shootin.' I'd rather be good at just about anything else right about now.

Truth be told, I was never of a mind to be a soldier. I wanted to be a teacher, or maybe a preacher. Secretly, I agreed with Ma on the subject of killin'. But Pa said, "A man has tae defend his ain land and folk."

The trees and darkness are thick, and my eyelids are startin' to droop. I guess a body can only take so much horror before it says, "Enough." All I want to do is lie down in the soft leaves beneath a broad oak and sleep. But I keep hearing rustlin' in the underbrush, and I don't know if it's my boys or Yanks...or animals goin' about their business. Oh, to be a bear in its den. My bleary eyes can't make out where I am or where I'm a-goin' so I keep headin' in the same direction in hopes of reaching my unit—or what's left of 'em.

"Mac...that you?" The whisper off to my left causes my heart to crash into my throat, and I collapse to the ground and scuttle behind a trunk.

But wait...a Yank wouldn't call me Mac. "Who's there?" I hiss back.

"It's Will. Will Hatcher. And Josiah."

Will. Relieved, I stand and move slowly in the direction of the whisper. "I'm a-comin'. Don't shoot me."

Will just about crushes my bones when I find 'em. He keeps muttering, "Thank God. Thank God," under his breath.

Josiah settles for a hand clasp. "You made it."

"Where's the unit?"

"Don't know. We got separated. Trying to get back to them now."

Will tugs my arm. "C'mon. We gotta find where they camped before the sun comes up."

Will and Josiah lead me like a stray pup through the trees until finally we see some dim firelight flickering on a rise up ahead.

Josiah's hand is on my chest. "Careful. They might think we are Blue Bellies."

"Is it our division?"

"Could be." Will marches forward, hands raised. "Don't shoot us. We ain't Yanks."

I'm surprised when we get little notice and few greetings. The mood in the camp is grim. Will, Josiah, and I wander through the clusters of exhausted soldiers, lookin' for familiar faces. I don't see my Pa anywhere.

"Major McDaniel." Josiah points down the far side of the rise.

Major McDaniel stands over a small fire surrounded by a large group of soldiers sittin' and crouchin' all around him. "Some of ours might be there." We skid down the hill and join the soldiers from Anderson's division, hopin' to find a few of our boys who survived.

We catch Major McDaniel mid-speech. "...and with Colonel Luffman wounded, I sent part of the unit forward with several of the other Georgia divisions as replacements for Wright's Brigade of the 3rd Corps, which was decimated this day in their courageous advance on Cemetery Ridge. They will lend support to General Pickett's division. You will remain here under my command to protect their flank. I understand General Longstreet is pushing for a flanking maneuver then straight on to Washington, but General Lee wants to keep pressing our advantage."

What advantage? I guess General Lee wasn't there amongst the devil stones to see our boys get whupped.

"So, we must be ready to deploy on a moment's notice. Take some rest while you can. The morning will bring a critical hour for us, whichever decision wins the day."

So, Pa must be with Wright's Brigade. I scan toward the trees below Seminary Ridge, the hard-won land we hold still. If Pa is there, I have to go. But how?

Will, Josiah, and I wander amongst the clusters of soldiers, lookin' for whatever scraps of food we can find. As we finally settle down with our meager meals beside a smoldering fire, Josiah points toward more stragglers coming into the camp. "They will be dividing us up and organizing us soon. We best find a unit who will take us in."

"We need to catch up with the 11ᵗʰ." I gesture toward the line of trees.

"We will never find them. The whole of the 1ˢᵗ and 3ʳᵈ Corps are in those woods. We are better off staying here under McDaniel."

"I can't. My Pa went with Wright's Brigade. I need to find him."

Will shrugs. "I agree with Josiah. How're we gonna get there before the fightin' starts?"

"I'm a-goin'. You can stay here if you want."

Will looks to Josiah, who shakes his head. "At least wait until daylight. You will never find your Pa in the dark."

His advice seems sound, so I stretch out, and before I know it, Will is shakin' me. The bright sun is like knives in my eyes. "C'mon, Mac. Get up. They're sendin' us out."

The fuzz in my head makes it difficult to think. "No. No, I have to find my Pa."

"You are really going to go it alone?" Josiah heaves a great sigh. "You know you will be walking through the middle of the battle."

"I know."

"Very well. Go on, then, but I believe it is a mistake."

I refill my canteen from a barrel, shake Josiah's hand, clap Will on the back, and set off across the expanse between me and my Pa. I run at first, rememberin' Will's certainty that I'd never make it in time. I reckon I caught some energy from hopin' to find my Pa, but it sure ain't lastin'. I'm not gonna be able to keep up this pace. I slow to a quick march—until I'm about to drop. The sun is high in the sky by the time I get within shoutin' distance of the trees, but the best I can manage is to trudge. I can't see through the trees for the shimmer in the air from the risin' heat. The trunks look like giant stalks of wheat ripplin' in the breeze, but with puffy green tops instead of golden. They remind me of the story of the blind man Jesus healed with his spit, who at first saw persons looking like trees a-walkin' round.

My hand slips through the opened buttons of my gray jacket to touch the tacky oilskin wrapped around the leather-bound book strapped against my breast. I need God's help if I'm gonna find my Pa. I stop inside the edge of the tree line to kneel. "Heavenly Father, Thou knowest all things. I ask Thee, please, help me find my Pa. Bless my eyes to see. In the name of Christ Jesus, our Lord, Amen."

The woods are a-swirl with noise and chaos. No one seems to know where anyone else is or where they're supposed to be. "Can you point me to the 11th Georgia?" I ask over and over again. "Where might I find Wright's Brigade?" Finally, I resort to, "Which direction for the 3rd Corps?" That question gets me more than a shrug or a shakin' head. Some sergeant finally points toward the center of the line.

On and on I go, weavin' my way through milling masses of soldiers. I keep gettin' shoved back and aside and commanded to join forming and reforming lines, so I seem to make little forward progress. Commands are shouted with no sign of response. I hear the murmurs of the soldiers. "I don't hardly think that position can be carried." "Tell my Mama I done my duty." "...seems a fool's errand." "I feel the angel of death upon me." "They's gonna get us all kilt." "...out in the open like that...them holdin' the high ground." Lookin' across the field toward the ridge, I understand what they're sayin'.

Pa is gonna be on that field. I have to get to him before he goes. I have to be with him. But the lines are forming up, and the generals are callin' for the men to take positions. I'm too late.

The booms of artillery begin to shake the ground. Boom after ear-shattering boom, down the line the cannons fire, belchin' smoke and flame, whistlin' metal through the air toward the Yankee line, only to return to the start and have a go again. Smoke shrouds the field. I can hear the screams of men and shrieks of horses from across the chasm between us. Little blossoms of fire sprout up along the Yankee lines.

Some gruff ol' coot grabs my arm and shoves me forward with a growl. "Git yo'self in line."

"Yessir. I'm lookin' for..." But the ol' man turns away, shakin' his head. After he's out of sight, I duck away and begin my search again, but the masses are so thick and bunched up now, it's hard to move, and if I step farther into the trees, someone's gonna accuse me of desertion.

The cannons thunder until my ears bleed. Several men on horseback pound along the line of trees, wavin' swords and screamin' out, but I can't understand a word of it. It brings to my mind the Lord God's challenge to Job: "Hast thou an arm like God? Or canst thou thunder with a voice like Him?" I guess we decided we'd try.

My chest feels thick with the weight of this moment, in our thinkin' we have the right to decide who lives and who dies, and then believin' we are righteous and just in our reasons for killin'. How God must be weepin' in the heavenlies over our foolishness. It's like the Good Book says: "In the greatness of his folly he shall go astray."

I want to go home. I love our mountain, the rolling green carpet flowin' toward the valley, the sparkle of white water dancin' over the rocks in our stream, the pale blue of the distant hills stacked one behind another like sentinels standing guard over our land. In comparison, this place seems washed out, like the colors have faded in the blisterin' of the sun. The dirt's all brown and parched and dry—I don't think it'd grow much else besides wheat. The scrub brush is thick and prickly, and those devil rocks, they're the height of five men and no life on 'em. I understand why Pa wants to defend our land. It is a thing of beauty, the artwork of God. But I can't say I agree it's worth killin' for.

Ma always said, "Live yer life accordin' to the ways of the Lord, and all will go well with ya, to be sure." Since I can recall, I sat at her feet ev'a mornin', readin' the Good Book. She'd pound those words into my head and have me repeat 'em until I got 'em all right. Then, ev'a night, we'd sit by the fire and talk about what I'd learned that mornin' and how I'd used His words durin' the day. And I'd better have an answer for her, or my rear'd be so sore I'd be standin' to sleep.

She taught me to read usin' the Good Book. When most boys was learnin' field plantin' and cow milkin', I was strugglin' over words I'd ne'er heard before. But she was always there to explain their meanin', and soon it started to make sense to me. Then, of course, Pa would have his turn with me, and I'd be out workin' in the fields from the heat of midday 'til sundown. Ma and Pa had an arrangement. My time was hers first, then Pa could have me. She was gonna teach me to read, and that was that. She didn't put her foot down about much, but on that one, she wouldn't bend. Of course, I didn't really get a say in it.

Her Pa was a preacher. In fact, Pastor Connolly was still preachin' at the little church by the river when Pa and I left for the war. Ma'd learned to read usin' his Good Book, so she figured if it was good enough for her, it was good enough for me. She told me more times than I can count that the Lord told her I would serve Him my whole life, and that's why she put her foot down with Pa. She wanted to make sure I was ready. I don't think she counted on me soldierin' though. Neither had I. But here I am.

The throng of soldiers presses against me. I'm at the center of the line, so I guess I'm amongst the 3rd Corps, but I still don't see Pa. The cannons have lulled from their constant pounding, and the men on horseback are before us again, calling out for us to head straight toward the stone wall and to the trees beyond. Then, with a bugle blast, we're movin' beyond the cover of the trees and out onto the slopin' field. It isn't long before the Yankee cannons start to ring out. I find myself marchin' in step with their boom-boom-boom.

Our cannons bellow an answering call, their iron balls hurtlin' over our heads toward our goal. Still, we trudge forward. The field is wide, and it takes some time before their cannon fire starts to hit us, then the howls of those hit add to the strange cacophony.

I'm pressed against the soldier in front of me so I know which way to go. The field is blanketed in thick smoke. Somewhere on my right, a cannonball levels several of our boys like corn stalks after the harvest. My stomach roils and I wonder if I'm gonna wretch right onto the back of the boy walkin' in front of me. I hear boys behind me scream as a ball thumps the ground and a flash of heat sears my back, then another strikes, and another, rainin' down around me like summer hail. The clamor chases all thought from my head.

Then, musket blasts join with the cannons' thrummin', and boys are droppin' like flies. All around me, folks are yellin' and screamin' and cryin', and I notice all of a sudden that I am yellin', too. It's strange how a body does things without realizin' it, like my sister twirlin' her hair until the ends break off, and Ma yellin' at her to quit and she don't even know she's a-doin' it. What a thing to think on right at this moment. I think I may be off my nut.

We come upon a wooden fence, and there's nothin' for it but to climb, but it's a fool's errand for certain, and as soon as a body raises up over the fence, the Yanks pick 'em off like squirrels out on a limb. By sheer luck, I make it over the fence, but those few of us who make it crouch low because the fire over our heads is fierce. Between the dead bodies and the afeared livin', we create quite a pile along that fence. I crawl out of the mass of bodies and inch my way closer to the stone wall, which is finally in sight.

Out of the dense white smoke, streams of boys come a-runnin' toward me. Whatever lines we had are long gone, and it looks like the front is breakin' down. But I see this one general, sword lifted high in the air, screamin', "Come on, boys! With me! Charge! For your homes! For your lands! For your sweethearts! For your wives! For Virginia!"

I stand, and brayin' like a donkey in pain, I point my rifle into the smoke and follow the general on a dead run. I'm barely aware others are running all 'round me—and fallin'—but I keep going, because that general is hollerin' like someone callin' in the pigs, and if he is keepin' on, so can I.

He reaches the wall and climbs over it, and I see the Yanks fallin' back as our boys stab and slash with their bayonets, stackin' up bodies in rows between the wall and the copse of trees. But a new round of Yankee troops comes roaring forward, and about the time I reach the stone wall, the general falls, and our boys collapse under the relentless blue wave. As if by silent assent, we turn tail and run, walk, hobble, or crawl back toward the battered fence.

As I stagger across the wrecked field, I see that brave general collapse inside my mind, over and over again. Along with the image, I hear, "Why? Why? Why?" It's like my brain is stuck, like it won't jump on to another thought. Just the wounded general and, "Why?"

A brigade of soldiers is runnin' across the field from the left flank, firin' into the Yankee lines, and at the front of the line, there he is. There's my Pa. Wright's Brigade. "Pa! Pa!" I scream and wave my arms over my head. I see his eyes widen as he sees me, and everything slows to a crawl. I hear a hollow pop echoin' as if my head is in a bucket, I see Pa's mouth reform into an O, and I watch in horror as a red stain blossoms on his gray coat like one of Ma's roses as he collapses to his knees. "Pa!"

The rest of the brigade keeps runnin', providin' cover fire for our fleein' boys in retreat, but Pa doesn't move. He is starin' at his chest, but he looks up at me as I get close, then he falls back. "Pa!" I slide down beside him and cradle his head in my lap. "Pa, it's me. Aidan."

"Aye." His voice is little more than a croak.

"Don't you die on me, Pa. Don't you die. You know Ma'll kill me if you do."

He turns his face to mine. "Aye. Tell yer Ma...tell her...*tha mi duilich*. An tell her..."

He coughs and blood spurts from his mouth, then he takes in one last, wheezin' breath, and leaves me with a final gurgle of air bubblin' through his blood.

I am sorry. That's what I am to tell Ma. I am sorry. I don't know exactly what he means. Sorry he left? Sorry he died? Sorry he didn't listen to her? Sorry for everything? I am left without knowin' what else he wanted me to tell Ma, but I know what I'm gonna say because it's the only thing Ma would want to hear: *tha mi gad ghràdh*. I love you.

17

CHAPTER TWO

There's nothin' for it. I have to leave my Pa lyin' alone on the field, but I can't bear it. Wounded men are streamin' away from Cemetery Ridge, carried by soldiers who can still walk. The numbers of dead and wounded are staggerin', beyond my mind's ability to comprehend, like the count of the stars or the breadth of eternity. Men grab my shoulders and pull my arms as they walk by, trying to dislodge me from my Pa, but I'm frozen, as if time stopped and I will be livin' at the moment of Pa's death for the rest of my life. I am stiff, rigid beneath their hands, and they soon move on, away from the risk of continuin' enemy fire.

"Get up, son." I look up into the kindly eyes of a sergeant. He drapes his arm around my shoulders and gently pulls me to my feet. I become aware of tears streamin' down my face. "Are you wounded?"

Wounded? Yes. I am broken. My chest is ripped open and my heart crushed and pulled out. Don't you see? I have a gapin' hole in the center of my very soul. I glance down at my Pa, starin' blankly up at the sky, and the whisper of a thought flitters across my mind: *He is with Me.*

"No, Sergeant."

"Then come along, son. Nothing you can do for him now." The sergeant ushers me forward a few steps, then he is off to follow his retreatin' men, and I am on my own.

The sky darkens, and the gatherin' clouds glow amber from the lowerin' sun hidin' behind 'em. All I know to do is return to the last place I saw the remains of my unit, to see if I can find Will and Josiah. I follow the stragglers back to the woods, figurin' I will make my way toward the flank at daybreak. Inside the tree line, to my surprise, I find a congregation of our boys flockin' around General Lee, who is astride his gray horse, repeatin', "It is all my fault."

19

A tiny flicker of anger sparks up and clenches my chest. The general has given me someone to blame that my Pa lies dead and left to rot on the fields of Gettysburg. The other boys are screamin', "No! No!" but I want to snatch him down from his horse and scream my ever-present intonin' question in his arrogant face: "Why? Why?"

I remember Major McDaniel sayin' Longstreet wanted to flank the Federals and go on to Washington. If Longstreet had prevailed, my Pa would still be alive. The flame of anger twists and wrenches my gut, rippin' the hollow hole in my chest open wider. A moan escapes my lips against my will. I want to fold myself in two, to clutch my chest and hold in my insides before they pour out on the ground, to keep myself from beatin' General Lee senseless, to hold in the wail buildin' up in my throat. Instead, I walk away.

Ma would tell me to forgive. I know her, and if she were standin' right where I am, next to the man who caused her husband's death, she would offer him both forgiveness and love. I know the Good Book says to forgive. They are some of the first verses my Ma made me memorize, right along with the Lord's prayer: "For if ye forgive men their trespasses, your heavenly Father will also forgive you. But if ye forgive not men their trespasses, neither will your Father forgive your trespasses." But my anger will not abate, and I can't find it in my heart to forgive the man. I guess the Father will have to hold that against me.

The sky opens up, as if the Good Lord Himself is weepin' over this day. Officers try to regroup the troops, warnin' to watch for the Yanks to counterattack, but they do not come, and nightfall finds soldier and wounded alike left to lie in the mud without food or fire to warm us.

The next mornin', my trek to rejoin my unit is a slog through torrents of rain and ankle-deep mud. My insides are as cold and wet and thick as the mire. My thoughts rattle around like spirits in an attic, blank-eyed and mindless in their movements. I'm walkin' with some other Georgia boys, sent to dig trenches and construct earthworks to protect the flank, but I guess none of us feel much like talkin'.

I come upon some boys diggin' up shovelfuls of mud, and I think I spot Will amongst them, although he looks fairly like the rest of the lot, covered in muck from forehead to foot. Still, I want to see if it's him, so I walk up behind him. "Will?" My voice sounds barely a whisper to my ears, but the boy turns toward me, his teeth gleaming white in the midst of the filth coatin' his face.

"Mac! You're alive!"

Not really, no. I'm a spectre, a shell of who I was when I last saw him. "Yes."

"Did you find your Pa?"

I can't say it. If I say it aloud, it'll be true. "Nah."

Will turns back to his diggin'. "Some fight, eh? We almost had 'em."

The general, his sword raised, clamberin' over the stone wall, screamin' for his Virginia boys to attack, fallin'—I haven't the heart to tell Will we never had a chance. "Yes."

"We'll take 'em next time."

I'm not sure there'll be a next time, hopefully not anytime soon. Will doesn't seem to understand just how many we lost. "Sure, Will."

"Did you get any of 'em?"

Did I? I can't seem to remember. "Where's Josiah?"

"Dunno. We got separated durin' a skirmish with the Blue Bellies. Grab a shovel."

"I think I'll go look for Josiah. Make sure he's well."

"Suit yourself."

I wander farther down the line of soldiers, but I don't see Josiah. I spy some boys through the sheets of rain workin' a-ways up the hill, so I tramp up the rise to see if he's with 'em. They're sharpenin' spikes to add to the abatis before the earthworks, and Josiah is one of them.

"Josiah." I lift my hand.

"Hey, Mac. I'm relieved to see you."

"You, too."

"Will and I were worried you might have been part of the charge."

21

"I was."

Josiah's face darkened. "A horrible business."

"It was."

"We could use your help."

I nod and sit beside the pile of wood across from Josiah, pull out my hatchet, and start carvin'. After a long silence, Josiah lays down his axe. "What was it like, walking across that field under fire?"

I shake my head, and Josiah lifts his brows and nods. I suppose he understands not wantin' to talk about something so raw. At least he understands it was horrible.

Josiah retrieves his axe. "I hear the plan is to return to Virginia, across the Potomac through Hagerstown. I fear if the Yanks were to come against us now..."

"I know." So much death. So much loss.

We work in silence. The runoff from the rain flows in rivulets down the hill to fill the newly dug earthworks with water. Those boys are fightin' a losing battle, tryin' to pile up mounds of mud, all the while the rains wash it away. Somewhere deep inside, I awaken to the realization that our efforts are for naught. We will leave these battlements behind of a mornin', and if the Yanks don't attack this day, our labors are a waste, like all the lives lost walkin' across that open field and up that ridge to that stone wall. Tears spring in my eyes.

Josiah glances at me, concern etching lines across his brow, but he doesn't speak. He always was the wisest among us. Appreciation wells up in my empty chest for Josiah's friendship and strength. It's strange—I'm not one for emotional displays, but I'm findin' myself swingin' from one extreme to another, and I can't seem to help myself showin' it. Pa wouldn't be pleased.

"Yer too much like yer Ma," he'd say.

"No, Pa, I wanna be like you!" I'd growl and huff and storm around actin' like a big man until he finally laughed.

"Awright, then, boy. Ye be a braw laddie. Git on wit ye, noo." At that, I would run into his open arms. Arms I will never feel again.

I work my hatchet into the wood like I'm cleavin' a chargin' bear, and the spike breaks off. The others stare, but Josiah reaches across and hands me another piece with an understandin' smile. He's a good friend.

"Be quick about it, lads. If the Yanks are comin', they'll be comin' soon." A sergeant strides across the space between us and the boys diggin' the earthworks. "Look lively." Water runs off the brim of his hat like the waterfall near the top of Pa's beloved mountain, the place we'd go on a stiflin' summer's day to wash off the sweat and dirt of hard work or hard play before enterin' Ma's kitchen, lest we get her switch across our legs.

Josiah stands and collects a large pile of the spikes to carry down for the abatis. For some strange reason, I can't bear him leavin' my side, so I get up, too, pick up bundles of spikes from the other boys, and follow him down the hill. I stay glued to his side and find his calm presence helps me, and the work of finishin' the abatis distracts me from my rampant, chaotic thoughts.

Once the earthworks and abatis are complete, the sergeant returns to position us along the line. We're crouchin' down in 6 inches of water and sinkin' in a quagmire of muck. I cling to Josiah like a possum hangin' from a limb. Will settles beside me on the other side. "Protect the flank, no matter the cost," the sergeant instructs us. "Longstreet and his men will be comin' down that road in the mornin', and our job is to cover 'em."

"Where'll we be a-headin'?" one of the boys calls out.

"Hagerstown. We've a rough climb over South Mountain to get there. Then we cross the Potomac into Virginia."

I hear grumblin' up and down the lines. The thought of goin' back to Virginia seems like failure to those of us who fought at Manassas, Sharpsburg, and Fredericksburg to get to Pennsylvania— which is all of us still standin'.

I don't think it will be possible for any of us to sleep, but fatigue and shock set in, and I drift off sittin' straight up until Josiah shakes me awake. It's dead dark, but I hear the clink and thud of marchin' soldiers, the creak of leather, and the snorts and clops of horses, and I know the rest of the army is headin' toward us. But other than the occasional crack of sharpshooter fire, they appear to walk past us unmolested.

The sheer weight of the waste envelopes me like the mud fillin' my boots. We spent a day diggin' trenches we will abandon as soon as the main army passes by. We spent three days fightin' and dyin' for ground we are about to forsake. My Pa died—no, if I go there, I'll lose what little hold I still have on my mind. But a resolve starts to churn deep within my gut. My Ma was right all along. Killin' is wrong. The Good Book commands, "Thou shalt not kill." It is waste. I close my eyes and clench my fists before my face and swear, no more killin'. No more waste. No matter what, I will not take another life, so help me, God. If they make me shoot my rifle, I'll fire it into the air. And yes, Lord, if I have to, I will die before I kill anyone else.

Will punches my side. "You awright?"

I grit my teeth and shift my rifle so the barrel points toward the tops of the trees. "I'm well."

Will shrugs. Josiah glances at me but lowers his eyes from my glare, and the three of us sit in heavy silence until Major McDaniel calls for his troops to fall into place at the end of the line.

Soggy and rank, we slog through sheets of rain along a road that soon becomes a path not much wider than a deer track. I am only vaguely aware of puttin' one foot in front of the other. My eyes stay focused on Josiah's broad back. It's my only grip on reality. The day wears on, and another cavalry unit joins us, saying the Yanks have finally begun their pursuit. The officers charge up and down the lines, urging us to make haste. They say our one hope is to beat the Yanks over the mountain and establish a hold on Hagerstown. I don't care one way or t'other. Will pushes me from behind, but the reason I quicken my steps is to keep up with Josiah. I don't want to lose him in the blinding rain.

The slope begins to increase, but we get no rest, no break from the frantic pace. I'm like Pa's ol' mule being driven up the mountainside, draggin' the plow after him to break the ground. I feel sorry for that ol' mule and wonder where he is and what he's doin'. I wonder how Ma's gotten the fields laid in and how she's gonna harvest 'em with just my sisters to help her. I mean, she's a tough woman and can hold her own, but the thought of Elspeth, Caitrin, Anice, Maisie, and Ma draggin' that mule and pushin' that plow tightens my throat. I should be there, not here, wastin' lives and time.

My eyes mist over, but I can't help but smile thinkin' about my sisters, all with fiery red hair like mine, and dispositions to match, except for Maisie, who is as sweet and gentle as a lamb with hair like golden fleece. Maisie, who runs to me every time I come in from the fields, her arms up, with a smile that shines brighter than the sun, and all for me. Caitrin and Anice, the inseparable twins, with their own language and a bond no one else is allowed to enter. Elspeth, who I swear if she had been born in another time and place would've been a princess, the way she carries herself, sashayin' this way and that, head high beneath her long, flowing mane of red hair, which she is quick to toss with contempt to match. I miss them, even Elspeth.

How am I gonna tell Ma and the girls about Pa?

Darkness shrouds us as we reach the base of South Mountain. I fully expect the Union army to run up our tail, so nervous are the commanders, but I hear nothin' in the darkness save the nickerin' of exhausted horses and the grunts and groans of battered men. The rest is brief, and we are soon roused to begin the march through the pass.

The trail is windin' now, and steep, and the mud is thick. The rain continues to pelt us, but we dare not stop. Scouts report the Yanks are on the other side of the ridge, crossin' over through another pass, tryin' their best to beat us to the Potomac. But I'm worried. I've seen the stream rushin' down our mountain like a river after a long, hard summer rain, so I can only imagine what the Potomac River is gonna look like after this downpour. And we have to get soldiers, horses, munitions, and supplies, the whole train, across that river with the Blue Bellies right behind us—or on top of us.

I'm used to climbin' up into the hills, and our mountains are a lot like these, but many of the lads are from flatter lands further south, and they're strugglin' to keep up. Even Josiah is pantin' and heavin', and we're less than halfway up the trail. "The way down'll be easier." I whisper, so as not to embarrass him in front of the boys. He gives me a sheepish but grateful smile.

I guess the officers sense we are laggin' because they call for another halt. I want to read the Good Book while I got the chance, but I'm afeared the rain'll ruin the pages, so I close my eyes and try to recall a verse or two, somethin' to comfort me. Only one comes to mind. "Yea, though I walk through the valley of the shadow of death, I will fear no evil, for thou art with me; thy rod and thy staff they comfort me." I asked Ma how a rod and a staff were any kind of comfort. "Liken to a shepherd," she said. "You mean the Good Lord beats His sheep?" I asked. She shook her head and said, "You will understand, one day." I'm sorry to say, I still don't understand, although I do feel like I've taken a beatin'.

"I'm plum tuckered," Will says, scrubbin' rainwater off his face and out of his eyes.

Josiah grunts his agreement and looks like he's fallin' dead asleep sittin' straight up.

"We've a ways to go still." I crane my neck to spy the crest of the trail, but it's shrouded in clouds.

"This whole thing is a misery." Standin', Will shakes himself off like a dog. "I can't stand much more."

"Best sit while you can."

"Sit in mud, stand in rain. What difference does it make?"

"It might make a difference to you before we get to the top."

Will shrugs. "Makes me no never mind. Misery is misery."

Josiah pipes up. "My feet feel raw. I'm afraid they're going to be mush before we reach the Potomac."

I look at my sodden, mud-caked boots and wonder if I'd be better off walking barefoot.

Will points to his battered brogans. "My shoes is fallin' apart."

"When'd you last get new ones?" I ask.

"Had these when I come."

We are a pitiful lot. What's left of us.

I can't tell how long we've been walkin' because the sun is as covered up as the mountaintop, and the sky hasn't lightened any since the early dawn. I guess I'll figure what time it is when the sky goes black. As it is, it's hard to see anything even in the day.

Dear Lord, when is this rain gonna end? How much hardship is enough? My only comfort is knowin' the Yanks are walkin' in the same muck and mire and sufferin' in the same downpour; otherwise, we haven't a chance of beatin' 'em to the river. And Lord, I'm a-prayin' we do beat 'em and cross ahead of 'em so I am able to keep my promise to You without gettin' myself killed.

At the call to move out, I struggle to my feet and trudge back into line. As I slog along, I recall Pa witnessed the Cherokee bein' marched out of Georgia. He was a boy, a couple years younger than I was when I joined the Confederacy. It was one of Pa's first experiences after his family emigrated, and the horror of it never left him. When I asked him about it, the blood drained from his face, and all he said was, "Ah widnae treat an animal meant fur slaughter thon way." Then he would close his eyes, shake his head, and raise his hand as if to push me away. I knew better than to ask him again. Later, Ma pulled me aside and said, "Yer Pa suffers for those poor folk still. Always remember, 'Therefore all things whatsoever ye would that men should do to you, do ye even so to them.' Say it." I repeated the verse, and Ma nodded once, then closed her eyes. "Twas a wicked business." Now, I understand, havin' a little taste of what Pa witnessed.

Cavalry scouts return and the pace is quickened, tellin' me we must be fallin' behind the Yanks. The word is passed down the line that we'll be marchin' through the night. The mood around me seems to change from despairin' to determined, but I can't say I share their renewed spirit. Quite the opposite. I want to lay down in the mud and give myself over to death. I might, too, had my Ma not drilled it into me that life is a gift from God and what a sin it is to waste it. Waste. Like this whole war. No wonder we're sufferin' in this endless rain. God must be bawlin' his eyes out over the waste.

We finally reach the crest and start the downward trek, which lifts everyone's spirits a right considerable. The cavalry is sent along an easier path toward Williamsport, along with much of the munitions and wounded, while we wind down and down, walkin' much quicker than before, so that by the time the sky begins to lighten, we can see the base of the mountain up ahead. I fairly sprint to the bottom, such is my relief.

Word is passed down the line that the cavalry has been attacked on the pass, so instead of the planned rest, General Lee calls for us to quick march straight to Hagerstown. Thunderstorms pummel us as we hurry the last leg of our retreat. No one speaks. I don't hear a single complaint. I think we all know the importance of beatin' the Yanks to Hagerstown and gettin' across the Potomac before they can organize an attack. We are hoary and haggard, separated from our cavalry support and supplies, and with more than a third fewer numbers than at Gettysburg. We wouldn't stand a chance.

As we march into the town, I hear cheers erupt ahead of me. The Yanks are nowhere to be seen. General Lee is quick to establish a line of defense, stretching from the outskirts of Hagerstown along the Potomac, near where the cavalry established positions after expellin' the Union cavalry from Hagerstown and pushing them back to Williamsport. My unit is sent southwest and told to hold the position near Fallin' Waters and wait for the cavalry to join us.

But as we near the river, my heart sinks. The waters are racin', and the pontoon bridge is destroyed. Fordin' the river is not an option. Major McDaniel sends a runner to inform General Lee in Hagerstown about the pontoon bridge, then sets some of the boys to collect what supplies they can find while the rest of us establish our line. The night passes without incident and I am finally able to sleep, a blessed relief after the two-day forced march.

Food is scarce, since the supply train went with the cavalry to Williamsport, so the morning brings hunger—and more rain. The river is runnin' fast and deep, floodin' in some places. Engineers arrive with the dawn to rebuild the pontoon bridge, but their task is nigh unto impossible in these conditions. Our task is to protect them, and the bridge, from any Yankee saboteurs.

Day after dreary, wet day passes, and still no Yankee attack. I start today the same as every other day since we arrived, with a prayer to stop the rain and a plea to hold back the Yanks. My prayers are fifty-fifty so far. We hear the cavalry had a rough go in Williamsport but held off the Union cavalry tryin' to advance on our position and forced them back toward Boonsboro. I hope our cavalry joins us soon. They'll have food and ammunition, both of which we are sorely lackin'.

Finally, the engineers report the pontoon bridge is repaired and the waters are beginning to recede. Once again, Major McDaniel sends a runner to inform General Lee, and we settle in to await the arrival of the main body of the army. As darkness blankets us, and another round of rain sets in, I hear the distinctive sounds of marchin' men. The army floods into Fallin' Waters and begins the perilous crossin' of the Potomac.

But in the wee hours before dawn, I hear another sound, the thrummin' gallop of horses approachin' from our southwest. Is it our cavalry, comin' to join us for the crossin', or is it the Union cavalry, spoilin' for a fight? I cradle my rifle against my chest. It's loaded but will not be fired, no matter who rides around that bend.

Lee sends a division to reinforce our position, which tells me I'm in for a fight. Our backs are to the river, Josiah on my left, Will on my right, their guns leveled and ready to fire. As Union soldiers and cavalry pound into view, firin' toward our boys crossin' the Potomac, Josiah and Will fire. I do nothin'. I made a promise to God. No more waste. No killin'.

Will elbows me as he reloads. "What're ya doin'?"

To deflect his questions, I raise my rifle. Up and down the line, our boys are shootin' their muskets, killin' enemy soldiers, but still, I refuse to fire. Their cavalry hits our flank and thunders up our line. The line breaks. Persons are runnin' in every direction, both Union and Confederate alike. I see Josiah runnin' toward the Yanks, bayonet raised, and for some reason, I'm compelled to run after him, even though I am committed to my vow before God. I hear Will howlin' bloody murder behind me. Josiah jabs his blade into a screamin' Yank, shoves him off, and clashes metal against metal with the next one. I realize I'm standin' still oglin' when Will screams my name. "Mac! Mac!"

I turn to see him a few feet away, wrestlin' with a Yank on the ground. Everything around me seems to still. What was chaos and racket on every side a moment ago is narrowed down to one action—Will against the Yank. All I can hear is Will callin' me, callin' and callin'. Will clouts the Yank in the face, and the Yank punches back, over and over again until Will's head is reelin'. The Yank rolls on top of Will, lifts his knife to plunge it in, then jerks back, his eyes wide, and falls on top of Will. I spin around, and there's Josiah, holdin' his musket, the barrel smokin', and I realize Josiah saved Will's life. Josiah is starin' at me, his eyes hard, his mouth hangin' open in disbelief. He must've seen me standin' there, watchin' but not actin' to save Will, and he can't believe it. Neither can I. But he doesn't understand—I made a vow.

Behind Josiah, I see an enemy soldier approachin', but I can't seem to move or even open my mouth.

Will screams, "Behind you!"

Josiah turns, just in time to catch the downswing of the Yank's gun with the barrel of his own. They grapple, and Will, still strugglin' to get out from underneath the dead Blue Belly, screeches, "Help him!"

Josiah is in danger. I have to move. I lift my rifle, knowin' there is still a round in the barrel. Will screams, "Help him!" and somethin' inside me rips in two, as easily as if I am made of thin cotton cloth. I wrench my finger onto the trigger. Josiah falls to his knees beneath the weight of the larger Yank, and I have a clear shot. A clean shot. I know I'm good enough to take him. I can save Josiah. I try to will my hand to move. Will screams again, "What's wrong with you?! Help him!" My friend is gonna die if I don't fire. But I'm paralyzed.

Josiah thinks to lunge forward and grab his enemy around the knees. The Yank falls with a thud, and Josiah jumps on top of him, hands around his throat. But the Yank manages to shove Josiah off balance and kicks him in the chest. Josiah lands on his back, and the Yank is on him again. The Yank claws at Josiah's eyes while Josiah pounds frantically against his chest.

I catch some movement beside me. It's Will, finally out from under the Yankee's body, rushin' up to help Josiah. He wraps his arm around the Yank's throat from behind, howlin' as he uses his own weight to pull the Yank off Josiah, but the Yank lands on Will's legs, and they tumble to the ground in a tangle. Josiah jumps up like a shot and grabs the enemy around the waist, jerkin' him off Will. When the Yank rolls back to his feet and stands, I see the glint of a knife in his hand. Covered in mud, the three circle each other like male wolves in a standoff for dominance of the pack. The Yankee swipes at Will, who yelps and staggers back, then he lunges for Josiah.

The rifle is heavy in my arms, cold like the decision I can't make—life for life. Suddenly, as if someone is raisin' shutters coverin' my mind, I hear once more the clash and bedlam of fightin' all 'round me. Death is everywhere. It's Gettysburg all over again. As if the chaos of battle is a spirit that leaks into my eyes, nose, and mouth and through my skin, something takes over my body. My finger squeezes the trigger. I am so unprepared for the action my body seems to take with a will of its own. that the blast of my rifle makes me stagger and almost fall. I watch in horror as the Yankee soldier comin' at Josiah stops short, looks down at his belly which is gushing red, and falls.

Josiah runs to Will, whose chest is sliced open, heaves him over his shoulders, and runs toward the river. Again, my body moves without thought, and I find myself runnin' after my two friends. We splash into the river and wade through the rushin' waters, followin' lines of our boys makin' their way across the Potomac, Josiah holdin' Will up out of the water. Balls whistle over our heads. I glance back to see Union cavalry surround what's left of the division Lee sent as reinforcements.

I see a horse without its rider, strugglin' against the current, her eyes wide with panic, so I grab the bridle and drag her closer to Josiah. "Put Will on!" I'm not sure he can hear me over the sounds of the battle and the rushin' water, but Josiah turns and slings Will across the horse's back. Together, we pull the horse the rest of the way across the river to the safety of the other side.

After we drag ourselves onto the shore and into the trees beyond the bank, Josiah pulls Will down from the horse and checks his wound. "I need something to stop the bleeding." He doesn't look at me. I'm not even sure he's speakin' to me. He shrugs off his jacket and rips strips of cloth from his shirt, then ties the strips together and wraps the makeshift bandage around Will's chest. "Help me get him on the horse."

My body is numb. I don't believe my hands and legs are gonna work, but I reach out to help my friend. We manage, with Will's help, to sit him on the horse, then we lead the horse, followin' the streams of soldiers pourin' from the river, to the site where General Longstreet is reorganizin' his armies. There are so many wounded, most more serious than Will, so we have to wait for one of the doctors to see to his wound.

The silence between us is deafenin'. Josiah won't, or can't, look at me still. Will lies there glarin' at me but says nothin'. I know they must see me as a coward. I see myself as a coward, too, but not for the same reason they do. To me, a coward doesn't fulfill his vow. A coward backs out on a promise. A coward abandons God's will at the moment of greatest testin'. Yes, I am a coward. And a murderer. I don't deserve to live.

CHAPTER THREE

"I don't understand, Mac. Why did you wait so long to shoot?" Josiah and I are sittin' alone on a rise, waitin' on the doc to finish with Will. He's decided to speak to me, but I'm not sure how long that'll last. I have no answers for him that he can understand, so I stare at the grass and shrug. "We fought side-by-side at Fredericksburg, Sharpsburg, Manassas—Devil's Den, for heaven's sake! We always stood shoulder to shoulder. What's changed?"

All I can do is shrug again. Josiah is a good friend, but that doesn't mean he can grasp the torment in my heart. I haven't even told him about my Pa. How can he ever comprehend the muddle that is my mind?

"How can we ever trust you again?" Josiah is not one to be put off, and his tone is gettin' testy.

My body takes over again, and words blurt out before I can stop them. "You shouldn't trust me. Why would you? I'm not worth trustin'. Oh, why don't you leave me alone?"

"Very well." Josiah stands and brushes the mud from his trousers. "Have it your way." His forceful stride and clenched fists show me how angry he is.

I watch him as he collects Will, who from a distance looks none the worse, and the two put their heads together—to discuss me, I suppose. Yes, Will glances my way, so I am the topic of their conversation. His glare could light kindlin'.

So, as I deserve, I'm completely on my own. Pain tries to well up in me, but I shove it deep down like I'm buryin' a skunk to get rid of the stank. When I stand, I turn my back on Josiah and Will and make another vow—I won't bother them ever again.

I wander amongst the nameless soldiers, wonderin' which ones will die tomorrow, which the next day, which next week, and which ones, if any, will make it home. I'm resigned to my fate. Death awaits me soon, and I know I will die alone. I wonder if Ma and my sisters will

33

ever hear what happened to Pa and me, or if they will be left in a perpetual state of empty hope. The Good Book says, "Hope deferred maketh the heart sick," so I offer a brief prayer for God to let them know our fate. Maybe He will answer this one since it's prayed in love for another. He surely hasn't been answering any of my other ones.

Major McDaniel calls for his men to gather 'round, but I wait until I see where Will and Josiah sit before I join, placin' myself at angles and on the outskirts of the group so they can't see me. "We've been assigned to Wright's Brigade…"

That's who my Pa was with when he…stop. No more thinkin' about Pa. I can't afford to let my thoughts betray me again.

"…and ordered to move ahead to Manassas Gap to hold the pass until the rest of the army can move through and join our forces near Richmond. This is a tough assignment, but General Wright told General Lee that our Georgia boys will deliver." His proclamation is met with shouts and cheers—not by me, but everyone else seems proud to be chosen. To me, it's a death sentence, so I don't feel much like shoutin'.

"We've got a rough night and a long march ahead. Get some food, then gather your things. We'll be off at dark."

Everyone wanders off in groups, murmuring about the task before us, but I remain by the fire. I have no interest in food, and I have nothin' to say, so why move? I'll be movin' soon enough.

I remember Ma, sittin' in her rocker by the fireplace, readin' her Scripture. The fire roars and crackles, and Ma brings the book closer to it to better see the tiny words on the page. I'm on the floor in front of her, listenin' as she reads and explains the words. Her words float on the air and settle on me like balm.

"Be careful for nothing; but in every thing by prayer and supplication with thanksgiving let your requests be made known unto God. And the peace of God, which passeth all understanding, shall keep your hearts and minds through Christ Jesus. Finally, brethren, whatsoever things are true, whatsoever things are honest, whatsoever things are just, whatsoever things are pure, whatsoever things are lovely, whatsoever things are of good report; if there be any virtue, and if there be any praise, think on these things."

I remember, sittin' there before that fire, feelin' such a peace, like I'd never felt before. It flooded through me like a wave and filled me and warmed me like the fire had leapt from the hearth and pressed itself into my heart. The peace of God. I don't have that kinda peace anymore. What would my Ma say to me if she were standin' here? I can fair hear her. "You don't know peace 'cause you don't give yer whole heart to God. You worry 'steada prayin', and you think impure thoughts. That's yer problem, the Good Book say." So it does.

In the hideous mire of this place, what is pure? What is true? Where is justice? Where can I see loveliness or virtue? What can I praise? I can't see anythin' but darkness and waste all 'round me. Maybe God has abandoned me. Of course He has. Why wouldn't He? I'm a murderer.

"For He hath said, I will never leave thee nor forsake thee." My Ma's voice rings in my ears, and I can't deny the Good Book says it. So, why is He so hidden from me now? Why won't He take away my pain? Why doesn't He help me? It's almost worse, knowin' He sees my agony and does nothin', than if I believe He has abandoned me. But every time I try to accept I'm all alone, a heaviness weighs on me, like I'm bein' pressed down by unseen hands.

My innards feel like snakes coilin' 'round and 'round each other until they're a writhin', hissin' mass. I want to shake my fist at the sky and curse His name. I want to tell Him it feels like He doesn't care a whit for me. I want to say to Him what I said to Josiah—just leave me alone.

I bend my face to my knees and clutch handfuls of hair. "Please Dear Lord, spare me this torment! I don't know what to do. Help me. Help me, please."

I realize I'm moanin' aloud, so I wrap my arms over my head. I don't wanna think about what others are thinkin' of me. We have to sort this out, the two of us. I need answers. I'm Jacob, grapplin' with

God. I'm Job, demandin' an explanation. I don't want to need Him, but, Lord help me, I do.

My whole life, He's been there, the cornerstone like the Good Book says, the anchor that keeps me from driftin' off in the wind, the one thing I'm sure of. Why now, when I need Him the most, is He silent? Something stirs in the deep places in my heart, a question I can't bear to ask. I don't want to voice it, 'cause it means it's real. But I must. I have to know. I have to reach Him, or I'll never again get up off this here ground.

"Why'd You take Pa?" Somethin' breaks in me with the askin', and I'm as withered as a dead vine, scooped out like a melon after breakfast. The relentless ache crushes me.

I don't know how long I've been sittin' balled up in a knot in front of this dyin' fire when somethin' almost like a soft touch brushes on the back of my neck, and I hear, "Peace I leave with you, my peace I give unto you: not as the world giveth, give I unto you. Let not your heart be troubled, neither let it be afraid."

I unwind myself real slow-like. Am I losin' what's left of my mind? The voice didn't sound like me, or Ma. But I did hear it. I know I did. And I still feel it, somehow, in that empty place in my soul.

Like that day by the fire with Ma, peace and warmth flow through me. My hands unclench. My shoulders lower and my head lifts. And I can imagine a place where this war ends, and I walk out of it still whole, where life continues separate from the darkness and death of this place, where hope lives, and love is still possible.

I see the shinin' faces of my sisters and Ma's tender smile. I even see her tears when she hears about Pa, but still, her smile lives on. I don't know exactly how to work these things out, but I believe they're possible with God, and I'm willin' to try, with His help.

"Thank you, Lord. Thank you for answerin' my cries. Please, tell me what to do. I feel so lost. Show me the way."

The Lord and I sit in silence a while longer. A soothin' touch caresses the desperate ache in my chest. It doesn't make it go away, but I sense it doesn't need to go away, that the pain is an important and necessary part of the love I have for my Pa. His touch gives me a small measure of comfort to mingle with the hurt. "It's so hard, Lord."

"Likewise shall also the Son of man suffer."

I look around at the darkness of this place—the misery, the ever-present death—and realize Jesus experienced the world in the same way—the ugliness, the hatred, the violence, and even death.

"The kingdom of heaven suffereth violence, and the violent take it by force."

He knows, and He understands. A new awareness dawns in my spirit and washes over me like a spring rain on a cool mornin', and the flood of weepin' comes, unbidden but oh, so needed. My shoulders heave as the tears pool on my mud-crusted woolen trousers. But these cries carry with them blessed relief. I'm not alone. He understands.

"On your feet, soldier." I turn to see a sergeant stalkin' by. "Get to your unit."

I wipe my cheeks, surely smearing them with grime, and push myself to my feet.

"Yessir." I kick some dirt on the remains of the fire and go in search of my unit. I finally spot them, congregatin' with the other Georgia boys, already shruggin' on their packs and readyin' their guns. Josiah and Will are among them.

Do I explain to them what happened on the battlefield, tell them about my vow and the reason for it, and apologize? I haven't even shared about Pa. Would that matter to them, or are they gonna despise me no matter what? Do I ignore them and hope they ignore me? The momentary peace I felt sittin' by the fire listenin' to God scatters like birds before a runnin' hound dog, and the snakes start wrestlin' in my gut again.

Will sees me, and a frown creases his brow. Heat rises up my neck and spills onto my cheeks. He elbows Josiah and shoves his chin toward me, so Josiah turns and meets my eye. With everything in me, I want to cry out, "I'm sorry. I didn't mean it. I'm so sorry," but neither my feet nor my mouth'll move. Josiah lowers his head again. Well, that's it then. They want nothing to do with me.

But then he looks up and walks toward me, his steps slow and deliberate. If not for my frozen feet, I'd run to the hills. He pauses a few feet from me, starin' at the ground, his mouth a thin line cut into his face. When he finally looks up, I blanch. I'm something akin to a fish, with my mouth openin' and closin' as if I'm gulpin' for air. Then, his mouth slash breaks and widens into a calm smile, and my throat clenches. He holds out his hand.

I can't believe it. The kindness, the generosity, the forgiveness. I've n'er seen the like. My feet finally come unstuck, and I fair run to his side and grasp his offered hand in both of mine. I can't help myself, though—a handshake isn't enough, so I wrap my arms around him and hold on like he's a rope and I'm swingin' from a cliff. I can feel his chest hitchin' beneath my hold, and I realize he's chucklin', and I can't help but laugh, from relief, from joy, and from deep gratitude.

I manage to choke out a couple words. "I...I'm sorry." My tears threaten to flow again.

"Who can make sense of all this? I know I cannot."

I pull back, my hands grasping his shoulders. "Josiah." I pause, knowin' full well if I say what I'm thinkin' of sayin', it will be real. Final. "I..." My throat closes over the words. "I saw..." I can't say it.

"Yes, it has been horrid for us all, the things we have seen. I do not know how any of us have survived."

I nod. "My Pa...he died." The words choke me. "At Gettysburg."

Josiah's face melted in sorrow. I love him in that moment. "You saw him die." His whisper is not a question, but a realization. I nod once and close my eyes against the emptiness.

"I cannot imagine." He sighs and embraces me again, this time pullin' my head onto his shoulder. "I am so deeply sorry."

"That's why...why I couldn't shoot. Why I almost let those Yanks kill you and Will. I just couldn't...couldn't do anymore killin'."

"I understand."

"It's all such a waste!" The words pour from me in a rush, like venom from a snake. "What're we dyin' for? I don't want no slaves. I

38

don't believe in slavery! The Good Book says there is neither bond nor free. All Pa wanted was to be left alone, to work his land, to raise his family. Is that too much, too much to ask? Now, he'll never see..." My voice hitches as the tears flow hot and furious. "Never see his daughters grow up. He won't know his grandchildren. He'll never again work his beloved land. And for what?" I wave my arm around. "For this? I don't want none of it!"

Josiah stands patiently, listenin' and waitin' for my torrent to wear itself out. My chest heaves, and my breath comes out in short, watery gasps. Still, Josiah waits. Finally, I whimper, "I just wanna go home."

"I know. I do, too. But we must finish what we started, one way or the other. Come, now. Come with me and join the others." He encircled my waist with his arm and ushered me toward the unit. "Between the two of us, I believe this war will not go on much longer." He sighs. "I feel we have lost with the defeat at Gettysburg."

So many lost. So much death. I see the general once more, his sword raised in the air, screamin', "For Virginia!"—and fallin' beyond the wall. I see the bodies litterin' the field like blossoms from a crepe myrtle after a strong wind. I see my Pa's eyes bulge and his mouth fall open as he crumples to the ground. I see the Yankee soldier look down in shock as his belly opens up like a red rose blossomin' in the sun. Oh, my Lord, why?

"But we must go on." Josiah straightens his back and lifts his head. "We must fight the good fight."

I don't understand his words. I can't see one single good thing about this fight.

General Wright is speakin' to the whole brigade as we arrive. "...assigned the task of going ahead of the main body and protecting the retreat by holding Manassas Gap. Should the Union attack, we must defend the pass at all costs and protect the flank. Form up, men. Let's move out."

Like ants followin' after a trail, we march out single file. That's it. I understand now. I'm nothin' more than a worker ant. I have no individual value. I have no life beyond the brigade. I only have my task. I march without thought, one foot in front of the other in an endless drone of thuds, movin' through dense wood and across ridgelines. The darkness presses in on me. The weight of my pack bows my back, and the rifle slung over my shoulder grinds a raw rut in my skin. I remember what Josiah said about his feet, so I look down at his shoes as he marches in front of me. Can he feel his feet? I can't.

At some point on the march, I realize I haven't eaten. The hunger cramps my belly, but still I march on, still mindless, still meaningless, and still lost. None of that matters. All that matters is the task.

The night wanes, and we march on. The sun rises high into the sky, and we march on. The sun hides behind the mountains, and we march on. For four days straight, Will walks behind me without sayin' a word to me, but on the fifth day, as we finish off our one helpin' of food, he leans in and says, "Sorry 'bout yer Pa."

Josiah musta told him. "Thanks." It's all I can muster. But from then on, Will acts like nothing ever happened, and we are friends once more.

Six days and seven nights we march, stoppin' only for brief rests and for meager rations. On the mornin' of the seventh day, General Wright positions us along the heights overlookin' the Gap, and we wait for Meade's soldiers. We don't have to wait long. An entire corps comes toward us. There's nothin' for it—vastly outnumbered, we have to stand our ground, because General Lee is bringin' our boys south, and if the Yanks take the pass, Lee will be cut off.

Despite the fierce fightin' all 'round me, I'm numb. I fire, reload, and fire again like a machine—aimless, hopin' my stray rounds don't find a target—until the Yanks overrun our lines, and I'm forced to resort to knife and fists. We beat them back. They regroup and beat us back. And it happens all over again. Bodies pile up on both sides, and still we fight.

Just as it seems like we're gonna lose the pass, another division comes up in support and pushes the Yanks back. The fightin' gets more vicious as both sides dig in and try to gain ground, but the Yanks still outnumber us, and after hours of sloggin' and batterin' against each other, they start pushin' us off the heights. Wright calls for the retreat, and we surrender the Gap to the Union army, scamperin' to meet up with General Lee.

Exhausted and depleted, we reach Front Royal as Lee is movin' out, and we realize we have succeeded in holdin' off the Yanks long enough to secure Lee's retreat. I don't have the time, the energy, or the inclination to celebrate, though. All I can muster is a worker ant march, one foot in front of the other in endless succession. The battle is a dispassionate blur for me. I barely recall it except for the blood and noise. Why do battles have to be so loud? Why don't we do like the Israelites and Philistines, and select a warrior to stand for the nation instead of the cracks of rifles, the booms of cannon, and the yellin' and screamin' and gore? It's simple—sling a rock and it's done and over.

Our farm is quiet, especially in the early mornin'. You can hear birdsong, of course, and the distant moos of the cows grazin' on the hillside and the occasional nicker of a horse, but other than that, the air is as soft as rabbit's fur. A short distance from the house, the stream splashes over rocks with a gentle hum that lulls you to sleep at night. And even though these mountains we're crossin' are part of the Blue Ridge, this God-forsaken land feels harsh and as hard as a saber's edge. Their heavy silence stifles me like my head is wrapped in burlap.

Ma loves the early mornin'. She's up before the roosters, collectin' eggs for breakfast, then sittin' on her porch in her rocker overlookin' the range in rows of different shades of blue and gray, beyond the valley. The steam rises before her face from her hot tea or coffee. She always closes her eyes with a thank you on her lips before she takes a drink. She says her best conversations with the Lord are on that porch.

When Pa comes through the door to go care for the cows, that's her signal to whip up the eggs. On good years, we have fat back to go along with the eggs. Then she makes her biscuits, soppin' with butter 'n honey. It's enough to make your teeth hurt. Ma has two rules about breakfast—ever'body eats together, no matter what chores need doin', and we begin of a mornin' with thanks to the Lord for giftin' us with another day.

Those words still hold special meanin' to me, thinkin' of the day as a gift to be treasured instead of something expected and taken for granted. Even more so now that Pa...but I'm not appreciatin' these days, am I? It's hard to appreciate misery, I guess. But that gets me to thinkin'. I'm still here. Josiah's still here. Will's still here. Ma and my sisters are home waitin' on me to come back. In the middle of a war, I guess that's a lot to be thankful for. I vow I'll start tomorrow and every day after with Ma's prayer of thanks.

CHAPTER FOUR

I spend the rest of July, all of August, and into September on a series of long hikes and short train rides to Tennessee. Food and other supplies are scarce as hen's teeth, so me and Josiah and Will take to huntin' for food along the trails when it's safe. The long journey without fightin', along with the comradery of my friends, helps start my heart a-thawin'. Over time, Will comes to know the rest of the story I shared with Josiah, and he responds much as Josiah did, with warmth and forgiveness.

I keep my vow to begin each day with Ma's prayer, to good effect. I'm lighter and more alive. Something about comin' back into my country and gettin' closer to my home helps, too, even though I can't go visit 'em. I can almost breathe the change in the air.

When we get on the first train, we're told if we want to write letters home, they'll try to deliver 'em. I'm torn. Ma would want to know about Pa. But I don't want to tell her in a letter instead of face-to-face. It seems cruel to hear such news by impersonal mail. Knowin' Ma, she's already sensed what happened anyway. She's like that. So, I decide not to write to her.

For me, the days roll like the hills, some risin' to touch the clouds and others fallin' deep into the valley's mist. Josiah and Will are pretty good about sensin' when I'm in a valley, and they mostly leave me alone those days. I do a lot of talkin' to the Lord those days, too. On the up days, we talk and even joke around and tease each other. Laughter. That's something I thought I'd never do again. But Will is such a cut-up, always keepin' Josiah and me in stitches. What I'm discoverin' is laughter is a very short step away from tears.

I think about Pa all the time. Memories come unbidden, with tears followin' right after. What I can't bear is when my mind tricks me into seein' Pa's face as he's shot and hearin' his last words. Those are valley days.

On the high days, my memories go toward times at home with my family—workin' the fields with Pa, carryin' water in from the well for Ma, splashin' with my sisters in the stream, eatin' meals together where the talk is always rich with humor, deep discussion, and conflict, readin' Scriptures by the fire, and prayin' before bedtime. These memories comfort me like a familiar friend and help me reconnect with what matters most to me, and after a few weeks of visitin' these memories, my goal becomes to survive the war so I can see my Ma and sisters again. I know they need me, and I surely do need them.

It makes me laugh—and cry—to think of Ma and Pa together. They were always fightin', but no one ever doubted how much they loved each other. Ma's a feisty woman, and Pa is—was—as hard-headed as a goober hull. A Scot marryin' an Irish woman—well, fights were bound to happen. It made for some very interestin' scenes around our house. I don't know how Ma is gonna be without Pa. She centers her life around him so much, and me and the girls, of course. With him gone, how will she get along? I hope it doesn't break her spirit.

Their gettin' married almost got derailed by ol' Pastor Connolly, who wasn't keen on his only daughter bein' with a Scotsman. Pa won him over with sheer determination and perseverance, and a little bribery—Pa offered to tend the Connolly livestock whenever the pastor was away on the mission field. Granda was also favorable toward Pa's bein' a landowner and how hard he worked. Work ethic meant a lot to the pastor. So, eventually, Granda relented and allowed Pa to court and marry Ma. Of course, Pa had to convince Ma, too, and she was none too easy to convince. But Pa wasn't gonna take no for an answer. I think Ma secretly relished how hard he was willin' to fight for her hand and drew it out a bit for her own enjoyment.

Their fights started soon after, the first big one bein' over where they were to marry. Ma insisted on her Da's Methodist church, but Pa's church in Scotland rejected Methodism as heresy. That didn't go over very well with the pastor. Ultimately, Pa relented and became a Methodist.

I see them all around the fire—Pa, standin' behind Ma's rocker, regalin' us with ever' detail of the story, arms flyin', imitatin' Ma's voice by squealin' like a stuck pig—Ma, wavin' her hands before her eyes to dry her tears from laughin' so hard and to cool down the blood rushin' to her cheeks—the girls sprawled on the floor, hootin' and hollerin' at the thought of Ma as a "heathern" (as Pa described her). I see it all as if it is happenin' before me, and all I can think is, *Never again.*

Never again will we all be together, laughin', tellin' stories, teasin' each other. Never again will Ma and Pa have one of their battles of the mind they both reveled in fightin'. Even the memories of those times are tainted, awash in a film of sadness like a pond covered with scum. No, this war doesn't even leave my memories unscathed.

As we move through Tennessee, we hear the news that General Bragg has been driven out of Chattanooga, and we are to hurry to Georgia to reinforce his lines and retake the city to regain control of the railroad. So, another overnight march with no stops and no rest. We hightail it through the Tennessee River valley overnight and cross into Georgia the evenin' of the 19th of September.

Heavy fightin' had taken place on the 19th, and our side, while holdin' their own, had not been able to dislodge the Yanks, and there were heavy losses on both sides. On the morning of the 20th, General Longstreet orders us to assault the Union line. I've honestly never seen anything quite like what is takin' place at Chickamauga Creek.

The line is stretched far and wide, with the most men on one field of battle I've seen since Gettysburg. Our brigade is given the left, but the chaos of the battlefield makes it hard to know what's what. Still, we do our best to come against the Union flank, and to their misfortune, as we're comin' toward the line, the Yanks appear to be tryin' to reorganize. So, the general calls for the attack, and we're able to break through their line—a huge victory. But that's when the fightin' begins in earnest.

Josiah, Will, and I, and the rest of our brigade, find ourselves with the Yanks on all sides. The musket fire is so close, it makes my ears ring, and cannons boomin' in the distance explode with a belch of fire and hot wind and ash in my face. Smoke is everywhere. I can't see where I'm goin' or who's around me. Everywhere, runnin', screamin' figures from both sides create a mélange of brutality and chaos.

The terrain is tough with lots of trees, so advancin' is slow, but with clashes of metal on metal and blasts of musket fire, we are able to push the Yanks back. After I fire my weapon above their heads, I use the butt of my rifle to strike the enemy soldiers down, and I don't feel bad about it. At least I'm not killin' them when I knock them down, or out.

Beside me, Will is slashin' his way through the Yanks with his bayonet when I hear a howl. I turn, and through the smoke I see some Blue Belly has shoved his bayonet into Will's stomach. Will is hangin' like a marionette on a string from the bayonet, eyeball-to-eyeball with his attacker, and even as he yelps in pain, he is poundin' the Yank on the head with his musket.

This time, I'm not paralyzed. I dive toward Will and shove the Yank back, pullin' his bayonet out of Will's belly in the process. My mind leaves me, and I start beatin' that Yank until his face is bloody, mangled pulp. I don't think anyone coulda stopped me from beatin' him to death, but when Will falls to the ground beside me, I forget the bleedin' Yank and tend to my friend.

Blood is flowin' from Will's belly wound too fast. I know he's gonna die if I don't get that pumper to stop. I rip my jacket off and press it hard against Will's stomach, while he bellows. "Mac! Mac! They got me. Oh, they got me good."

"I have you. I'm here. You ain't gonna die on me, you hear me? I have you."

Will is writhin' on the ground. "It hurts! Mac, it hurts somethin' awful. Make it stop. Please, make it stop."

"I'm tryin'."

Out of the corner of my eye, I see another Yankee soldier runnin' toward us, musket raised, and I know if he fires, I'm dead. So, without really thinkin', I pick up Will's bloodied bayonet and launch myself at the Yank like I'm explodin' from a cannon. He fires as I ram the metal deep into his chest. Smoke from his musket stings my eyes, but his shot goes wild from me hittin' him, and at the end of it, he is lyin' on the ground bleedin' out, and I'm still standin'.

I don't even take a second to consider what I've done. I leap back to Will's side to find Josiah there, holdin' Will's head. But when he looks up at me, I see the pain in his eyes, and I know Will is done for.

I kneel beside my friends and grasp Will's hand.

"What's gonna happen to me, Mac?" His voice is already far away, more like an echo down a valley than a cry.

Josiah looks at me, expectant, but I don't know what to say. Lyin' to him seems wrong, even cruel. I open my mouth once to speak, but nothing but a squeak'll come out. Then, my tears start to fall, and when I open my mouth again, I hear my Ma's soothin' voice in my head. "All this pain and toil will fade away into darkness, and you'll climb a staircase up, up, up all the way above the clouds, and at the top you'll see a beautiful gate made all from pearls and jewels, and it'll be open for you, Will, and Jesus'll be standin' there with His arms wide open, and He'll bring you into the gate, and on the other side, you'll see the most beautiful sight a man could hope to behold, all crystal and shinin' gold everywhere you look, and the light'll be so bright it'll almost hurt your eyes at first, but then you'll see His throne, gleamin' in the light like a second sun, and on the throne you'll see Him, and He'll welcome you into His Kingdom where you'll never again feel any pain or sorrow, and there'll be no more death. And then Jesus'll take you to your very own house..."

"Stop, Mac." Josiah paused, then heaved a deep sigh. "He's gone."

I look down at Will's face and see a gentle smile gracin' his lips.

Josiah and I pick Will up and pull him back away from the fray, which has already moved farther forward as our boys are pushin' the Yanks out of Georgia. A litter bearer comes to take the body away, so Josiah and I, without a word, run forward to rejoin the battle. We don't have time to grieve, and I don't have the inclination to stir up all those feelin's again. But feelin's have a way of demandin' you deal with 'em.

It's like being outside your body a-watchin'. Whatever that is, that sense of being disconnected from your own reality is the strangest thing I ever felt. I'm numb, yet I'm vaguely aware that tears are streamin' down my cheeks, and I'm wailin'. How strange, to feel while not feelin' anything. One thing I know—I no longer care if I kill those Yanks. It may be against God's Word, and it may be waste, but I just don't care anymore. I realize I've decided they deserve to die. Now, in the disconnected watcher part of my mind, I know that's a horrible thing for me to believe, and an even worse thing for me to act on, but when I look at them, I see devils, not men. My feelin' mind becomes the judge and jury and executioner, all the while my watchin' mind is sayin', "Judge not, that ye not be judged."

Soldiers are fallin' all around me, and on some level, I realize it's me doin' the killin', but my hands have an existence all their own, separate from my ability to decide. They're rippin' and slashin' and poundin' flesh, burstin' skulls, and clawin' eyes and ears and face and neck like a wolf at its prey. I'm completely mad. Worse, I know I am. I'm standin' by, observin' a stranger who lost his senses, and I'm doin' nothing about it.

The boys on either side of me, Josiah included, start yellin' like me, and then they start actin' like me, pummelin' those Yanks and leavin' 'em bleedin' in the dirt. We're a pack of wolves on the hunt. Blood and death are left in our wake.

The Yanks start to run, and we set out to chase 'em, but the general calls for us to hold our position to wait for the rest of the line to catch us. Josiah has to restrain me. I'm a rabid dog, and havin' acquired a taste for killin', I want more. The watcher part of me thinks someone really should put me down.

But waitin' for the rest of the army calms my frenzy and my bloodlust. I allow my two minds to come back together, and when I look back across the field we just took from the Yanks and see the bodies piled everywhere, then I look at my hands and see the blood and flesh of others up to my elbows and soakin' my clothes, I can't hold it anymore. I run to a tree and heave up my guts.

Josiah is by my side in an instant. "All is well, my friend. You are good." I appreciate his attempt to soothe me, but his words fall on deaf ears. Nothing is well, and I am anything but good. My savagery is an abomination in the eyes of the Lord. I am everything He despises—hatred, lust, pride, wrath—murder. I have witnessed the dark side of my soul. I cannot abide it. I want to rip it from me, tear my skin and reach inside my chest, grasp the wretched thing, and crush it in my fists, or fling it to the ground and stomp it like a snake. But all I manage is another heave of bile, and still my soul burns within me. I have visited hell and become a demon. There is no hope for me now.

Josiah pulls me back to standin' and puts his arm around my shoulders. "Come with me, my friend. Let us return to the men."

I have no awareness of movement. It's as if Josiah is my mind tellin' my body what to do. As we approach the brigade, the men break out in cheers. I wonder if they've received some news of the Yankee retreat, until I notice they're all starin' at me. Wright, the brigade commander approaches me and shakes my limp hand.

"Well done, soldier. Well done." More cheers. Are they congratulatin' me for my murderous rampage? Are they cheerin' my descent into hell? Are they praisin' my demon? I can't make sense of it. I can't make sense of anything. "There will be a commendation for your good work here this day."

When I don't say anything, Josiah speaks for me. "He...is overwhelmed with gratitude. He thanks you, sir."

"Single-handedly routed the Union from their positions. I have never seen the like."

"Yes, sir. We are all very proud of Mac."

In the distance, I see the bulk of the army marchin' up, but the Yanks have already fled out of reach. The brigade commander leaves to make his report to General Longstreet, and the boys in our brigade flock around me. I'm like someone who's disturbed a hornet's nest and the hornets are all over me. Every touch of a hand in congratulation stings.

Josiah seems to sense my discomfiture and guides me away from the well-wishers toward the creek. "Are you quite well? You look as pale as a spectre."

I moan and lean against my friend. "I'm sick. Sick at heart. Sick in my soul." Now, the tears come again in a flood. "What have I done?"

"Here. Let us clean you up." Josiah hums a hymn I recognize but can't place as he splashes water over my arms and rubs the blood into the cool water. Gently, he bends me down and cups water in his hands to trickle on my neck and down my back, then he wipes my cheeks and forehead. "There. Much better."

"Is Will really dead?" My question is more of a plea.

Josiah sighs. "Yes, Mac. Will is gone."

I have an impulsive thought. "Baptize me."

Josiah's head jerks back. "What?"

"Baptize me. Please. I need God's forgiveness."

"Mac, I cannot. I am not a priest."

"I don't need a priest. I'm not a Catholic, I'm Methodist, and the congregation is the church for us. You can. Please, I beg you."

Josiah looks doubtful, but he finally walks with me out into the creek. "What do I say?"

"Say, I baptize you in the name of the Father, and the Son, and the Holy Ghost, Amen."

"I baptize you..."

"Wait. No, you have to wash my head with the water. Like this." I scoop up some water and run my hand over my head. "See?"

Josiah nods, cups water into his hands, and ladles it over my already-wet hair. "I baptize you in the name of the Father, and the Son, and the Holy Ghost. Amen. There. You are forgiven."

But my soul still burns with shame and the horror of what I've done, so I know the truth. I can never be forgiven. The shock of this revelation sends a cascade of ice through my chest. I can feel my heart harden beneath the piercing, frozen spikes.

I glance at Josiah but can't bear to hold his eyes. "Thanks." I can barely hear my own voice.

"Come, let us go to the fire before you catch your death."

As we walk through the clusters of soldiers, their stares pierce my back, and I hear their judgments. They're askin', "What kind of man does those horrible things?" It's the same question I'm askin', but I'm only askin' it 'cause I don't wanna face the answer. I'm not a man anymore.

Time passes, but I have no idea how long. I'm too numb from the cold inside me to sense anything around me. I'm vaguely aware of movement. At one point, Josiah whispers that the Yanks have escaped back to Chattanooga, and we're goin' to Chattanooga to retake the town, but I can't make sense of what he's sayin' or what it might mean for me. More movement. I'm like one of the herd of pigs that ran off the cliff in Scripture. That's right, they were possessed of demons. Legion, that was the name. Am I now called Legion?

If my Ma is prayin', which I know she is, I hope the Good Lord spares her. She has a way of knowin' things from Him before it can be known. I never could get away with anything as a child 'cause He'd always tell her, but I hope this time, He keeps my secret. If she finds out what I've done, the anguish will kill her for sure—one more death on my conscience.

We're marchin' again. The rhythmic hymn, "Come We that Love the Lord," plays in my head, mockin' me. The Confederacy believes the Good Lord is on their side in this war. In winnin' this battle by evil means, have I turned His face away from us, such that now we are destined to lose? I find I don't care about the outcome. No one is winnin' in this abomination. I see again the strewn bodies across the expanse of the field we left behind, both blue and gray, knotted and piled in grotesque displays of the depraved nature of man, and I come to experience true hatred for the first time in my life—hatred for war, hatred for the men whose arrogance got us into this, hatred of myself most of all.

The night passes, but no joy cometh for me this mornin'. Instead, the risin' sun exposes me. Once again, I can see the stares of my fellow soldiers, with what seems like fear in their eyes. I can't blame 'em.

In the distance, I can see the telltale signs we are approachin' the town of Chattanooga. Our leaders start to spread us out, focusin' our strength to block roads and rails. The cannons and mortars are pulled into position overlookin' the valley. We fortify positions atop Lookout Mountain—our orders are to control the Union supply lines and the Tennessee River, which means the general's plan is to hold the Union armies under siege.

So, we wait. Days become weeks. We are low on ammunition, and food is rationed, so the boys encourage themselves by talkin' about how hungry the Yanks must be. Josiah and I take night watch over the river. I prefer the darkness and isolation.

One foggy night, I think I hear something, so I poke Josiah. "Do you hear that?"

"What?"

"Sounds like...oars in the water? Small splashes?"

We sat in silence for several minutes, then I hear the sound again. "There. Did you hear it?"

"No, but we best tell someone, just in case."

He slips off to make a report. I can't see movement on the river for the heavy fog hangin' in the valley, but I continue to hear the occasional slosh and ripple of water. I guess it could be a breeze down in the valley stirrin' the water, but there's nothing on the mountain, and I know from livin' on a mountain my whole life that winds are usually stronger up high. I squint to try to make out any sign of Union forces. No moon combined with the fog makes it impossible to see anything on the river or movin' through the valley.

Josiah returns without new orders, so we continue our watch. Before sunrise, we see flashes and hear the cracks of musket fire in the valley. The skirmish doesn't last very long. When our relief doesn't come, I realize something serious is happenin'. As the mornin' fog lifts, Josiah points down toward Brown's Ferry. "Union soldiers. Our boys have pulled back."

"We lost the high ground."

"That means the end of the blockade."

By that afternoon, we watch as a column of Yanks march straight through Lookout Valley to Brown's Ferry. Supplies are sure to follow. We are recalled to the main body, and Longstreet orders our brigade to go to Wauhatchie Station to hold the communications line through there.

On the way to Wauhatchie, our scouts run up on Union soldiers standin' in the open on the road. Longstreet calls for the attack around midnight. We surprise the disorganized Yanks and overrun their positions, takin' the station, but it isn't long before they counterattack, and I'm caught up again in the chaos of hand-to-hand fightin'. All I can do is claw and scrape to survive, but this time, the ice in my heart chills the fury I felt at Chickamauga. My body won't move like I want it to, more like a possum than a wolf, freezin' in place and hissin' instead of attackin' outright, protectin' myself instead of goin' on the offensive.

In the middle of the battle, I hear the call to retreat, and I gladly run back toward Lookout Mountain with the rest of my brigade. Weary, low on ammunition, and discouraged, we wait for the generals to decide what to do next. To my surprise, Longstreet's corps is sent to Knoxville to try to regain the rail supply line, and we are once again on the march, this time in the cold and wet southern November.

We run into the Yanks at Campbell Station, which delays us reachin' Knoxville, but we manage to chase the Yanks back behind their defensive positions. And once again, we set up a siege. For twelve days, we try to keep supplies from getting into Knoxville, but as it becomes apparent that we are failin', Longstreet calls for the attack.

I keep hopin' time, distance, and circumstances will improve my mood, but I'm still as hard as stone and as cold as this late November mornin'. To keep my demons in check, I decide I will not engage in hand-to-hand fightin', so I ask instead to take a position above the battle as a sharpshooter, something I haven't done since Gettysburg. This way, I have a good excuse for my misses. Fortunately, they're always lookin' for good sharpshooters, and my reputation means I can pick my assignment.

From a perch above the battle, I watch my friends advance, retreat, and advance again, only to be repulsed and driven back outside the town to set the barricade again. I remain in my overwatch position, still preferrin' solitude. Some might've suffered with the cold, no fire to warm me or tent to shield me—but not me. I embrace it like a familiar friend, a welcome and just punishment for my crimes.

Several days later, from the southwest of town, I spot a division of Union soldiers approachin', over 20,000 strong, so I scurry down to make my report, and Longstreet decides to make a hasty retreat north to rejoin the Army of Northern Virginia.

We face several battles along the long, arduous march north, but I can't figure the point of 'em. It seems to me every time we take a position, we leave it the next day, with more death the only result. Finally, we find quarters at a little town called Russellville and wait out the winter.

I have plenty of time with nothin' to do but think and remember. I get very good at pushin' away anything resemblin' pain or grief. Shame, however, I nurture like I'm growin' a crop. I weed out mercy and chop down grace, all the while I'm feedin' and waterin' condemnation and plowin' my heart for more self-loathin'.

The worst of it is when I think of my Ma. My imaginin' of her disappointment feeds my shame more than anything else. The seed of a thought begins to grow—I'm never gonna go home again.

CHAPTER FIVE

We are marchin' across Virginia when we hear General Lee is engaged with the new Union General, Grant, along a tributary of the Rappahannock River, a location I know very well. Longstreet double-times us overnight, tellin' us, "You have been resting all winter. Now, it is time to fight."

We arrive at the battlefield to find the Confederates outnumbered and in collapse, dense woods, thick undergrowth, stiflin' smoke, ragin' fires, and a haggard General Lee tryin' to rally his men to attack. Longstreet rushes in and pulls General Lee back out of the line of fire, then steps forward to lead his troops in a bold counterattack against the Union left. There'll be no hangin' back for me, no shootin' from a distance, no controllin' my demons. Like at Devil's Den, we're fightin' the Yanks and the terrain in close quarters.

Maybe it's the memory of Devil's Den resurfacin' in me, or maybe I've had the whole winter to thaw, but the hatred I've nurtured starts to erupt in me like boilin' water overflowin' onto a cookfire. Blinded by the smoke and my own rage, I crash through the undergrowth with a howl, firin' my first shot, then clubbin' heads with my rifle and slashin' throats with my bayonet. It's hard to see who I'm cuttin' but that doesn't stop me. I'm in the grip of the demons again, and nothin' I do halts their ruthless rampage.

I find a spot behind a large tree and reload, then shoot a Yank runnin' past me. I reload and fire again, again and again, but my demons are restless and soon drive me from my cover and into the middle of the Yankee lines. Water pours from my eyes, but not tears like before—the stingin' smoke from the fires all 'round me is the cause. I have no remorse for the bodies in my wake. I'm a musket ball, propelled forward to seek flesh and bone with no thought of the consequences. The yells of other boys in gray all 'round me and the screams of the wounded add to the din of mortars rippin' through the tree limbs and the cracklin' of the inferno gobblin' up the woods. To my right, I see a young Confederate soldier in flames. He flails his arms and bats at his clothing, but he collapses, and the fires take him. Dimly, I'm aware this sight is a horror, but I feel nothing. It dawns on me that I have truly descended into hell. Charred bodies litter the ground, Yankee and Confederate, indistinguishable from one another, wounded and unable to escape as the flames encroach and consume them. Yes, the pits of hell.

The slashes with my bayonet are automatic and continuous. I keep pressin' forward, and the Yanks keep comin' in a seemingly endless stream. I have no idea where I am—for all I know, I'm behind enemy lines, but I still see my boys nearby, so I know I'm not completely lost—at least not in that way.

A Yankee soldier even younger than me grabs me and wrestles my rifle from my arms. I grapple him around the head like I'm holdin' a calf for brandin' and push his face into the thick ash coatin' the ground. He coughs and sputters but manages to turn on me, and I find myself on my back. I see his eyes, wide and white in his sooty face. I'm fair sure if he found his voice, he would be squealin' in terror, but right now, he's mute as he chokes my neck. I bring my knee into his gut and see the air rush from his mouth in a puff of smoke, then I wrench his hands off my neck and gasp in a breath of my own as he rolls off me, his knees to his chest. I crouch over him and whip my knife to his throat. His eyes catch me, a wordless pleadin' with me for mercy. I have none to give. My hesitation is brief.

As I stand, a searin' pain rips into my back and strikes bone. I turn and find myself face to face with a Yank, holdin' a bloody bayonet. With a roar, I launch into him and jab my knife deep into his chest. As his last breath gurgles through his lips, I struggle to get to my feet, usin' my rifle like a crutch to push myself off the dead Yank, but the stabbin', burnin' pain in my back is unbearable, and I collapse back to the ground.

Crawlin' is almost as painful as walkin', but I've seen enough burnin' wounded to know I've gotta move. I haven't seen Josiah since we arrived at the Wilderness, and I know no other names to call out for aid, so I grit my teeth, grind the butt of my rifle into the ground, and lurch up on my one good foot. It's as if my right leg is useless from the hip down. I can't make it work right, so I drag it along, my rifle actin' as my other leg as I limp in what I hope is the direction of field headquarters. I can feel a wet flow drippin' down the back of my right leg. As long as I'm strainin' to walk, I'm makin' the blood flow worse, which means I don't have much time before I'm goin' down again.

The stabbin' pain changes to a deep ache, and with every step the ache worsens. How far did I run into the Yankee lines? Am I goin' the right way? Nothing is certain in this dense smoke. My vision begins to gray around the edges, and my head could float clean off, but I keep goin' because I must. Musket fire and mortar shots continue 'round me, but to my ears, the noise sounds hollowed out, like an echo through the valley at home.

I don't wanna die here in this godforsaken place, my body left to rot or burn and no one knowin' what happened to me. I wanna rest on my mountain on the fields before my home. I start to pray and ask God to help me make it home, but before I can get the prayer out, I remember—I can't ask the Good Lord for anything. I am overtaken, given over to a reprobate mind, so there is no hope for me. Still, I slog on, determined to make my own way home since the Good Lord won't help me.

The smoke is gettin' thicker, so thick I can't see anything but gray. Everything swirls 'round me. I'm tellin' my legs to move, but I can't feel them walkin'. Then, something presses against my arms and pulls hard. I struggle against whatever it is and try to cry out, but the grip is strong, and my voice fails me. Something flat slaps my back and the spinnin' feelin' gets worse, like my whole body is hoverin' in mid-air. The gray darkens. I try to say, "I'm hurt," and my lips are movin', but my breath catches in my chest. Everything goes black.

The next sounds I hear are moans and screams of agony. I pry open my eyes to find seemingly endless rows of wounded, some sittin' but most lyin' on the ground like me. I touch wetness beneath me, and when I lift my hand, I see red drippin' from my fingers. "Help me." My voice is nothing more than a squeak. My tongue feels swolled and stuck to the roof of my mouth.

"Help." No one looks my way. My head is swimmin'. My heart feels like a flutterin' bird, and I can't seem to get my breath. Once more, gray creeps across my eyes, but this time I'm pretty sure it's not smoke.

Jostlin' rouses me. The first thing I realize is the sky is dark. Then I notice, in an odd, sorta detached way, that I'm very, very cold and thirstier than I've ever been in my whole life. They move me into some kinda structure, maybe a barn, and plop me down on a table. I hear voices yellin' commands and loud grindin' and crunchin' noises. The air smells like copper and excrement. I try to move, but I can't. I try to call out, but again my voice fails me. I'm sinking like I used to do at the swimmin' hole, driftin' down under the black water to soundless oblivion.

When I resurface, I'm not at the swimmin' hole. Confusion and fear wash over me like icy rain. Where am I? What's happenin' to me? What I can only guess are hands turn me over, and I sense more than feel the hands proddin' my back. Why can't I feel anything?

Someone standin' over me moans. "Another bloody bayonet wound. Nasty business. Impossible to close. I must tie this off before I can attempt to close the wound."

Wound? Someone shoves a leather strap in my mouth like a bit in a horse. And then I feel again, a sharp, bitin', searin' pain that burns through my hip and down my leg, and I wish for the oblivion I left behind. Then, something pierces deep inside me, and I holler like a stuck pig. Did Jesus feel pain like this? How did He endure it? Strong hands hold me down and try to keep me still, but I'm squirmin' from the agony. I can't help it.

My whole right leg feels like it's been dunked in a mountain stream full of snow melt. I can't move my toes. Panic rises in my chest. Is he gonna cut off my leg? I've heard the surgeons are butchers, taking limbs willy nilly. I try to scream, "Don't cut it off!" but all that comes out is a garbled howl.

"Be still, son, it will be over soon."

If he takes my leg, I don't wanna live. How will I live? What will I do? What will Ma do, and my sisters? I'll be useless. I can't lose my leg. I try again to beg him to spare it, and he finally seems to understand.

"I'll not be taking your leg, son. Quiet, now. Be still."

The air rushes from me, and I'm able to stop wigglin' so much as he pokes something sharp through my skin and pulls on the wound over and over. A few more prods and pulls around my hip, and it's over.

"Take him out," the doctor barks, and I rise off the table, jostled about and taken outside to lie on a makeshift hammock, surrounded again by other wounded soldiers. The throbbin' ache in my back and down my leg is painful but tolerable, especially when I look at the many soldiers without an arm or leg and realize they'll be that way for the rest of their lives.

I don't know how long I've been lyin' here or how long I've been out. Light is returnin' to the sky when a couple of men lift me and carry me to a wagon. I'm piled in with at least twenty other men and taken away. I'm strangely disconnected from this process and oblivious to the sufferin' around me, as if I am a dumb cow bein' taken for slaughter, and the men with me are cattle instead of fellow soldiers. Behind us and in front of us, I can see more wagons filled with more men, until the road is filled as far as I can see.

"Where're we goin?" I ask the driver.

"Fredericksburg."

The wagon bounces and grinds along the battle-pitted road, and the soldiers with me are cryin' out most of the way, at least, those who remain conscious. As we near Fredericksburg, I am shiverin' despite the warmth of the May mornin'. The driver stops the wagon before an old tavern, and one by one we're carried into a dark, musty room filled with smoke and bodies and stained with blood.

A kindly woman wraps me in a blanket and hands me a flask of water. "Here, now, drink this up." I gulp the water, but it won't seem to go down my throat, and I start chokin' on it. She pats my chest. "Slowly. Drink slowly."

The flask is empty, most of the water drenchin' the front of my shirt. "More." I sound like a frog squattin' in a pond, singin' for his mate, and I'm not sure she understands me at first, but she takes the flask and refills it. Her straw-colored hair is escapin' the scarf she has wrapped around her head, like hay lifted by the wind, and her eyes have the haunted, haggard look of someone who has seen many horrors and had little sleep. I feel pity for her.

"I'm sorry." My voice is a croakin' rasp and speakin' causes me to fall into a coughin' fit.

She smiles gently and gestures for me to drink. A kind of love for her swells in me that seems well out of place in this nightmarish scene. "Do you need anything else?"

"No, ma'am."

She touches my forehead and frowns. "Oh, my, you're burning up." She scurries away and soon returns with a tall man wearin' a bloodied apron. "He's fevered," I hear her sayin' as they approach.

The man feels my head. "Where is your wound, young man?" I point to my backside, so he circles me and lifts my shirt. As he carefully unwraps my bandage, he clucks his tongue against his teeth. "Miss Samuels, would you get this young man a clean shirt, please?"

"Yes, doctor." Sweet, gentle Miss Samuels rushes off again.

"Let's get this filthy thing off you." The doctor cuts my shirt up the back and slips it down off my shoulders. My shiverin' worsens in the open air. "I'm afraid your wound is showing signs of infection. Your surgeon has done the best he could, given the circumstances and the fact that it is a bayonet wound—difficult to stitch closed—but we must get you to a hospital so the wound can be cleaned out and resewn. You've also lost a lot of blood which weakens you." He pokes around near the wound, and I can't help myself—I yelp like a beaten pup. He pokes some more, deeper this time, and I cry out again. Tears spring to my eyes. "I'm afraid you may have a pelvic fracture, too. The bayonet may have broken your right ilium."

I don't know his words, but I get the gist—a broken bone means I can't walk. "Why does my leg feel cold and numb?"

"The bayonet may have damaged the nerve going down into your leg. Over time that should improve. I'm more concerned about the pelvic fracture and the problem of infection. You are going to need some time to recover. I'm going to send you to a hospital in Richmond where they can better treat you and aid your recovery. In the meantime, drink a lot of water and keep warm."

Miss Samuels returns with a white cotton shirt, some more water, and another blanket. "Let's replace his bandage, Miss Samuels," the doctor says as he walks away.

She places a wad of something soft against my back, then she winds cloth strips around me to hold it in place. She is so kind as she holds the shirt up for me, slowly slips it over my arms and up on my shoulders, and buttons it for me, her face hoverin' near mine. Her smile is like sittin' in the sun on a spring day. I want to touch her soft, pink cheek, with its tiny hairs glistenin' in the candlelight, but I'm too embarrassed of my filthy hands, so I content myself with watchin' her as she moves away to tend to another soldier. She is as graceful as a cat, her simple cotton skirt swishin' against the dirt-coated floor, her hands soothin' the young man's brow as he cries out for his Ma. She leans close and whispers to him. After a few minutes, his cries cease, and I wonder at the magic comfort of her touch, until I see her cover his face with a sheet, and I realize she has only eased his passin'. My heart aches for her. So much pain. So much death. How can she bear it?

Two men come to carry me to a waitin' wagon, but I don't want to leave. As they tote me out, I stare at Miss Samuels, tryin' to memorize the elongated shape of her face, the golden color of her eyes and the crinkles that pop up around them when she smiles, and the curves of her bodice and hips. She is a singular ray of hope in a black world. I don't want to lose sight of it. She catches me gawkin' at her and offers me a brief gesture and a smile as I'm carried through the door. Miss Samuels. I vow to remember her always.

The wagon ride to the train terminal is blessedly short. Hundreds of wounded soldiers are stacked like cord wood in the train car I'm in, so I have no place to lie down. I lean against the back corner, away from the open door, and pray I don't fall on someone. But as the train starts to move, it becomes apparent I'm not gonna be able to balance myself—plus, I'm as weak as a kitten, so I beg the men around me to make enough room for me to sit, as painful as sittin' is for me. One soldier who's lost an arm to a surgeon uses his good arm to help lower me to the wooden floor. As best I can, I put my weight on my left side, but my whole right side is burnin' like I'm caught in the fires of the Wilderness, like so many were. Before too long, I'm too woozy to hold my head up.

When I awaken, it's late in the day. I apologize to the young soldier who helped me sit, as I've apparently been sleepin' against him the whole trip, but he's nice and doesn't seem to mind.

"Where're you from?"

"North Carolina. You?"

"Georgia. My name's Aidan MacAlister. Most folks call me Mac."

"I'm Walter. Walter Wright."

"Your humble servant. Sorry 'bout your arm."

Walter shrugs. "Nothing to be done for it now. I'm lucky to be alive."

Walter is as white as my shirt, so I see the truth of his words. "Here, take a turn and lean against me for a while."

He offers a wan smile and sighs. "Thank you."

I give him my shoulder. His shallow, ragged breaths soon steady and deepen, and I know he's asleep. My mind wanders, and I wonder what happened to Josiah. In my mind, I see Miss Samuels, with her sweet smile, her gentle hands, her mussed hair, her kindness to the dyin' soldier. Then, the images grow dark, and I see Will fall, his shirt covered in blood. I see the grisly scene of burned bodies at the Wilderness. I see the general at Gettysburg screamin' "For Virginia!" and leapin' over the stone wall. I see Pa, his mouth hangin' open and his eyes wide. I can almost feel his head in my arms. A violent shiver runs through my body, so severe that poor Walter almost bounces off my shoulder. Ma and my sisters float through my mind. I imagine Ma faintin' dead away when she hears the news Pa is gone.

My head feels all fluffy, and my heart is patterin' like hummingbird wings again. The fire consuming my back and leg has expanded to my face. I know I need more water—Miss Samuels told me I have to drink water—but I can't remember where I put the flask she gave me. "Walter, you got any water?" But Walter is dead to the world.

The noise of the train rollin' down the rails seems so far away now, like I'm sittin' on the bench down by Smith's Hardware and hearin' the train run through on the outskirts of town—a low thrum fadin' into the distance—instead of ridin' on the train itself. My lips are dry and cracked as if I've been workin' outside on a hot, windy day. A wave of nausea surprises me, fillin' my mouth with thick spit, but I manage to swallow it down. It does nothin' to quench my thirst.

Time for me slows to a sluggish limp, movin' in jerks and starts of awareness followed by periods of long, vacant daze. I'm in that daze when the train rolls to a stop in Richmond. I become aware that Walter is shakin' me and tryin' to pull me up with his one good arm, but I'm dead weight and no help to him. His voice sounds like he's talkin' to me underwater. I have the strange sensation of drownin' and try to flail my arms to pull myself to the surface, but it's too far away, so I let myself sink down, down, into the black.

Ice pours over me, and I scream. When I open my eyes, I see a man and a woman fussin' over me, and I see a bucket of ice poised above me.

"No!" I screech, but the bucket tilts, and the ice showers down across my body.

The man leans close to my face. "We must lower your fever immediately. Don't fight us."

"Hurts." My breath comes in quick gasps. I shiver uncontrollably. The brightness of the room burns my eyes. Everything is an agony. Is this torture for my many sins?

The woman pours water in my mouth, but I cough and sputter most of it up. She tries again. I don't want to choke, so I turn my head and clench my lips tight.

"You must drink," she says.

"Miss Samuels?" I'll drink for Miss Samuels. Anything to please her.

"Drink it."

I turn back to her and open my mouth to receive her cup, but instead of Miss Samuels, I see only dark hair twisted in a prim knot, a hawkish nose, and a stern mouth. Where did Miss Samuels go?

"Hold him still." The doctor's voice is gruff and commandin'. I must be thrashin' about, but I'm not aware of it. Strong hands lock me down against the bottom of the metal tub. The ice stings, then burns my skin, and I holler again, but they offer no relief.

The nurse pours water in my mouth, and this time I try to swallow it, but my thickened tongue causes most of it to dribble out of the sides of my mouth. She keeps pourin'.

My body numbs to the ice, which is meltin' to freezin' water, but the shiverin' keeps gettin' worse. I try to reach for the sides of the tub to pull myself out, but my hands won't work. When I try to speak, I sound like someone talkin' with a mouth full of caramel. My thoughts are as jumbled as my words sound. What're they doin' to me?

"Enough. Get him out." The disembodied hands pull me from the tub and drag me to a table where they dump me face down. "I have to clean and cauterize this wound. Samuel, heat the rod for me while I debride it."

Is he talkin' to Miss Samuels? I can't see her.

"Here, take this strap. This is going to hurt." Once again, a leather strap is shoved between my teeth. I know what that means, so I start to buck again. "Hold him still."

But I'm a wild horse who won't be ridden. The doctor calls for more hands, but still I'm floppin' across the table with every ounce of strength I can muster. He ain't gonna stab me again. No sir.

"For goodness sake, hold him down!" The hands clamp down on me and press me against the table, and the doctor starts cuttin'.

"Wha ya doin'?" I bellow the question between my gasps and screams.

"I have to reopen your wound. It must be cleaned out to rid it of foreign material in the wound, such as torn pieces of your clothing that were pushed into it with the bayonet and filth the surgeon failed to clean out before he sewed you up. Then, I must cauterize it to stop the infection. We are saving your life."

Cauterize? What does that mean? I don't think anything can be worse than the first surgeon's pokin' and proddin', but I'm wrong. The doctor is stickin' something deep into the wound, something that feels hard and cold, and the pain explodes through me like a mortar screamin' across the sky and lightin' the trees aflame. I think I might bite clean through the leather strap. My shrieks are continuous as he wallows his instrument inside me.

Then I see who I suppose must be Samuel comin' with a red-hot poker in his hand, like he's preparin' to brand me. I writhe under the firm hands holdin' me down, but there's no escape. The poker disappears from my line of sight. Two seconds later, indescribable pain shatters the core of my very soul, and I am no more.

CHAPTER SIX

I awaken in a white room, surrounded by a curtain of white mesh, filled with wanderin' figures in white and rows of metal beds covered in more white mesh. Is this the line to get into heaven?

"Doctor." A woman's voice floats from behind me. "He's back with us."

"Well, young man, I'm glad you rejoined us." I recognize the voice of the gruff doctor, but he doesn't seem harsh anymore. In fact, his smile is quite pleasant. "You gave us quite a scare."

When I try to respond, my throat feels like it's been scrubbed like a cowhide, and my mouth seems full of cotton bolls. I manage a weak croak. "How long?"

The doctor's smile fades to a grim line. "You've been with us three days. We need to get some water and food in you, but you will need to go slowly, sips at first and small amounts of soup." He beamed. "If you can do that for us, I am quite sure you can make a full recovery."

"Hurts."

Furrows creased his brow. "The wound still hurts?"

"Back. Leg."

"Have you tried to walk since your injury?"

"Can't."

"Hmmm. The wound was extremely deep. The blade may have reached your pelvis and chipped your pelvic bone, or even fractured it."

"Hit bone. Fracture. The other doctor said...illimum?"

"Ilium. I see. As soon as we get your strength up, we will try to get you out of bed. That will tell the tale if you do indeed have a bone fracture. If so, I'm afraid that will mean a lengthy recovery period of several weeks. But do not concern yourself. First, we need to get you upright as soon as possible to prevent the development of pneumonia, so the nurse will bring you some soup. Remember, eat and drink slowly."

Three days. I find it almost unbelievable that I've lost three days of my life to oblivion. Walter's observation that he was lucky to be alive flits through my mind, and throw a thank you toward heaven, even though God and I are not on very good terms. Walter. When the nurse brings my meager meal of lukewarm broth and water, I ask, "Someone came in with me. Walter Wright." I have to pause to catch my breath. It's astonishin' how weak I am. "Where is he? I'd like to thank him."

The nurse's genial face melts into a frown. "I'm afraid Mr. Wright didn't make it. Was he a friend of yours?"

The shock of another loss settles over me like a cold bath. How is that possible? He was in much better shape than I was when I got here. "How?"

"He developed sepsis at the amputation site. It took him quickly. There was nothing more we could do."

I can hear Walter saying, "I'm lucky to be alive," and an overwhelming sense of humility tinged with shame fills my heart. So many are dead, so many who deserved life so much more than I do. So why am I still here? I have to believe it is for some reason, some greater purpose, because the thought that it is a random occurrence, the injustice of such a thing, enrages me beyond bearing. Everything my Ma taught me says God is the One Who spared me. Why? Why take Will and Walter and Pa, and maybe Josiah, and thousands of nameless young men who will never have a chance at a full life, but not take me? Is it because He still wants to pull me out of the teeth of hell and set my feet back on His path? Even after all I've done? Is there hope yet for the likes of me?

This time, my prayer is from my heart. *Heavenly Father, I don't understand why Thou hast spared me, but I know it is by Thine hand I am still here, so I thank Thee. I repent of my horrible deeds and dedicate myself to Thine service from now on. Please, if Thou canst find it in Thine heart to forgive me, the worst of sinners, and even if Thou cannot, I praise Thy Holy name. Amen.*

I think of Jesus' parable of the two men prayin' at the temple, one a Pharisee thankin' God he was not like other men, all sinners, and the other who smote his breast and begged God for mercy, so I strike my chest with my fist and repeat the Scripture words in a whisper: "God, be merciful to me, a sinner." Then I struggle to sittin' and slurp up some broth, my will set toward gettin' better so I can do whatever it is God has for me to do.

The next few days in hospital are a blur of learnin' to walk with crutches, buildin' up my strength, and prayin' with the other boys who are willin'. Finally, the doctor tells me he needs my bed, so my rehabilitation will continue at the home of a wealthy Richmond family who volunteered to take in wounded soldiers. I must admit, I'm a little uncomfortable at the thought of stayin' with a rich family. They'll think me a poor rural boy with no learnin' and no sense, and they might be afeared I'll steal from 'em, so they'll be careful about me. So, when the cart comes to carry me to the Richmond house, I'm a mite hesitant to leave. I move amongst the beds and speak to each one of the men with words of encouragement and strong hand clasps, then I linger to thank the nurses. The orderly stands, impatient, in the hospital doorway, until I can't put it off any longer. With a quick prayer for strength and one last goodbye all around, I hobble on my crutches out the door and down the steps and pull myself onto the small wooden cart.

My nerves don't improve with the journey as the horse turns down a street lined with massive homes covered in brick and fronted with columns holdin' up sweepin' porches. About midway down the street, the driver pulls the reins and stops the cart before a broad lawn leadin' to an elegant two-story home that reminds me of drawin's my Pa made of castles in Scotland. Round turrets stand sentinel on both ends, and the gray stones used to build the house give it a solid and somewhat dismal feel.

The driver gestures for me to get off, which takes some doin' as I try to navigate usin' my crutches to balance and jump down without fallin'. I figure I must look quite the sight. The drive is long and curved, covered in stones. I make my way slowly toward the grand front stairs,

69

then limp on one foot up the stairs to the double door. I stand there, knowin' I should knock, but I can't quite make myself do it.

The doors fly open, and a lovely middle-aged woman with golden curls piled on her head sweeps through them, her silken hoop skirts buffeting the doors and swooshin' around her like a ringin' bell. Behind her, three girls line up like steppin' stones, each one in frills and lace and flowers.

"You must be the young man they sent over from the hospital. Welcome to our home. I am Mary Monroe, and these are my daughters, Ruth, Ester, and Elizabeth, my youngest. Ruth is 14, Ester is 12, and Elizabeth is 7."

"Aidan Connolly MacAlister, at your service, ma'am. Ruth. Ester. Elizabeth." I nod at the girls. They could be my sisters—except without the red hair. These girls all have blonde curls like Maisie.

"Well met, Aidan. Won't you come in?"

"Thank you, ma'am."

"I hope you will make yourself at home here with us, Aidan."

"Yes, ma'am." I hobble through the door and stop short. The open hallway includes a curved staircase, marble floors, and finery the likes of which I've never seen.

"Now, don't you worry about those stairs. I have set up a place for you to sleep in the library, right through here. Did you bring any things with you?"

"Things?"

"Clothes, necessities?"

"Um, no, ma'am, I don't have any things."

"I see. Well, my husband has some clothes I am quite sure will be adequate for you. I will see to that now."

I expected, with a house as grand as this, Mrs. Monroe would have some servants, but so far, none have appeared. As Mrs. Monroe hurries up the staircase, the girls hover 'round me, clearly curious.

"What's wrong with your leg?" Ruth, the oldest, is the first to speak.

"Well, I was stabbed in the...um, back, and the bayonet broke a bone in my...well, back. So, my leg won't work right."

"Why did you get stabbed in the back?" Ester chimes in.

"Well, let's see, that's a long answer. I've been fightin' in the war..."

Ruth interrupts my story. "Our Daddy died in the war."

"Oh. I didn't know."

Then, Elizabeth speaks, her voice like tiny bells. "He isn't coming back."

"I'm sorry to hear that."

"He fought for Virginia. Who did you fight for?" Ruth reminds me a little of Elspeth, a bit more pushy and haughty than her sisters, but still very sweet.

"Um, the same side as your Pa."

"Good. I wouldn't want one of those Yankees staying at our house."

"My Pa died in the war, too."

"I'm sorry." Elizabeth takes my hand and squeezes it.

"We have that in common."

"Girls, leave Aidan alone now. I'm sure he is very tired and needs his rest." Mrs. Monroe skips down the steps, an impressive feat in those skirts, and hands me several shirts and pairs of trousers. "Hopefully, these will fit you."

"Ma'am, these belong to your husband. Are you sure you want to..."

"He won't be needing them anymore, so yes, absolutely. You take them."

"But..."

"Not another word about it." Mrs. Monroe beams a broad smile. "Ruth, would you show Aidan his room?"

"This way." Ruth lifts her head in the way of the eldest and marches through some doors and down a hall to a large room filled ceilin' to floor with books on every wall. "This is my Daddy's library. You'll sleep over there." She points to a golden silk-covered divan.

I gulp and stumble. "No. I can't possibly..."

"What's wrong with it?" Ruth folds her arms across her chest with a frown.

"It's...too fine. I'm afeared I'll dirty it."

"Mother says you are to sleep there." That was the end of the discussion, as Ruth turns and stalks from the room. I hope I haven't insulted her too badly.

Mrs. Monroe has left folded blankets on the end of the divan, and a feather pillow for my head, but I can't bring myself to sit down, so I limp around the room, lookin' at all the books. Many appear to be law books, so I guess Mr. Monroe must've been a lawyer or judge, but he also has collections of famous literature, and I'm gratified to see several leather-bound Bibles. The Bible my Ma gave me to carry into battle is long since lost, fallen among the bodies during my frenzy at the Wilderness. Shame tries to creep back over me, but I shake my head and dismiss it, lookin' up at the ceilin' to give thanks once again for the Lord's forgiveness and provision. At least I'll have a Bible to read while I'm stayin' here.

Someone taps on the door, and Mrs. Monroe pushes her head in the entrance. "Dinner will be served soon. I hope you feel up to eating with us."

"Yes, ma'am. Thank you, ma'am."

"Aidan, you are very courteous, and I appreciate the fine example you are setting for my girls, but it might be easier if you called me Mary."

"My Ma's name is Mary," I blurt out.

"Oh, my, what a happy coincidence."

"She wouldn't be too favored of me callin' you Mary."

"Why in the world not?"

"She'd call it disrespectful, and she'd box my ears for it, too."

Mrs. Monroe laughed, and I can hear where Elizabeth gets her bell-like voice. "Well, I promise not to box your ears. I would appreciate you calling me Mary, so we can become good friends while you stay with us."

"Yes, ma'am...um, Mary. Most folks call me Mac."

"Ah, for your last name, MacAlister."

"Yes, ma'am."

She clucks her tongue, laughs again, and leaves, callin' over her shoulder, "Dinner will be ready soon. I'll send Elizabeth to fetch you."

"Thank you, Mary." Her laughter rings down the hallway.

I realize after she's gone that I shoulda talked to her about the divan. Instead, I decide to use the blankets to make a pallet and sleep on the floor. I look down at my hands and clothes, and realize I need to wash, but I don't know where to do it. I'm a fish out of water, floppin' around legless and not knowin' how to breathe in such a fine home. Maybe I should go back to the hospital.

Elizabeth runs in a few minutes later. "Dinner is ready. You can follow me." She runs from the room, not realizin' I'm not much in a position to run anywhere, so I do my best to follow the sound of chatter, and after only one mistaken turn, I walk into the dining room. The walls are paneled in dark wood, and maroon velvet drapes hang over the windows. Silver candlesticks dot the table, and a chandelier hangs from the ceilin', lightin' the room as bright as day despite the dark decorations. The chair at the head of the table is empty. The girls line one side of the table, and Mary sits across from them. She has set a place for me next to her, so I limp over to my seat and breathe in the aroma of baked chicken and fresh roasted vegetables, and even a potato with real butter. I've died and gone to heaven.

"Who will give us the blessing?" Mary looks expectantly at her girls.

Ester is the first to speak. "I will. I will." She folds her hands, and the rest follow suit, so I clasp my hands and lower my head. "Dear Jesus, we love you so much, and we thank you for this good food, and we thank you for bringing Aidan to us and keeping him from dying in the war, and please take care of our daddy there with You in heaven. Amen."

I've never heard such a heartfelt, personal, warm, gentle prayer. I don't think I ever thought about talkin' to God like you talk to a friend, but that's what Ester did. She didn't question why God would take her daddy and spare me. She embraced it with childlike faith and the open arms of love. Maybe I'm supposed to be here after all.

I dig into my food but find I'm too quickly full. Fearin' what might happen if I push it, I lean back and hope no one notices I've stopped eatin'. I'm terrible disappointed, too, because the food is the best I've had since I left home, and I don't want it to go to waste.

"Are you quite well, Mac?" Mary touches my arm, concern etched in her face.

"Yes, ma'am. It's just that...I haven't been eatin' so good for a long time, and..."

"I see. Of course, you're not used to such rich food."

"Well, I'm not used to so much food."

Her laugh makes my heart feel alive again. Between Mary's kindness and joy and Ester's prayer, yes, I'm sure God has brought me to this family. I just hope, somehow, I have something to offer them to pay them back for all they have already done for me.

The girls clean off the table, and Ruth offers to save my plate for later, in case I get hungry. I thank them, feelin' rather useless sittin' while three young'uns do the work. But fatigue is beginning to overtake me, and I find myself noddin' off in the middle of Mary's light conversation.

"Now that dinner is done, perhaps it would be best for you to retire. The doctor does say you need your rest."

"Yes'm." My words sound sluggish, even slurred to me, but Mary doesn't react. Without being obvious, she gently takes my elbow to help me stand, then walks with me to the library door.

"Do you have everything you need?"

"Yes'm." I can't even think about what I have or what I may need. My brain is a muddled fog.

"Would you like to wash up?"

Oh, that's right. I did want to wash. "Where?"

"Let me bring some water in for you. There's no mirror, but that doesn't deter most men." Her giggle trills like a bird's song. "I can help you if you need help."

I blanch at the thought. My Ma hasn't helped me wash up since I was 5 years old. I'm not gonna start now.

"No'm. I can..." Suddenly, I feel dizzy and grab the doorframe to keep my balance.

"See, now, you have pushed yourself too much. Oh, and it's my fault, inviting you to sit with us at dinner, making you traipse up and down my halls. I am so sorry, Aidan. We'll wash up in the morning. For now, let me help you to bed."

"But, ma'am..."

Mary shook her head firmly. "No more talking for tonight. We will have time a plenty to share stories and get to know each other. For now, let me help you, because I refuse to stand by and watch you fall." She grasped my arm again, this time more firmly, and guided me to the golden divan.

As she reaches to lower me down, I pull back. "Mary, this is too nice for me to use. I've been sleepin' on the ground, so anything is an improvement over that. A pallet on the floor will do me nicely."

"Heavens, no! I won't have a guest sleeping in my house on the cold floor." She pressed down on my shoulder, and I obediently sat. "Besides, no one has been in this room since my husband passed. That divan is going to rot away from disuse if you don't sleep there. Point of fact, he never used the bloody thing anyway. He was always curled up in his leather..." Her voice breaks as her eyes roam to an oversized, well-oiled leather chair behind the impressive corner desk, made of the same dark wood used to panel the dining room.

I reach out and take her hand. "Mary, I..."

She pulls her hand from mine and swipes under her eyes, then forces a grim smile.

"No, I am well." She sighs. "I do not usually come in here. I don't want to upset the girls, and they don't like it when I cry."

75

"Please sit with me for a few moments. To collect yourself." I gesture to the seat beside me.

"You need your rest..."

"I am restin', see?" I make a show of leanin' my head back and closin' my eyes until she sits beside me.

We are quiet, allowin' each other to remain in our own thoughts, until Mary dabs the tears from her cheeks. "My husband's name is—was—Alexander Barclay Monroe." Her smile is soft and bittersweet. "He was a Scot, too, you know. His family emigrated in 1746, so he no longer had a trace of the accent, but he was proud of his Scottish heritage and still wore the colors and coat of arms of the Monroe clan. He would be proud that we are helping a fellow Scot during your recovery."

"When did he die?" My voice is quiet, reverent, as I recognize this rare moment of vulnerability for this fine woman.

"At Sharpsburg."

"I was at Sharpsburg, too. Many good men died there."

Mary glances up at me and nods once, then looks again to the leather chair. "He went by Barclay—I think he thought the name Barclay Monroe sounded more elegant, you know? More appropriate for a governor, which was his aspiration—but I always called him Alex. It was something only the two of us shared." She shook her head as if to chase away her thoughts. "It's been almost two years. One would think I'd..." Her voice lowered to a hushed whisper. "He was a well-respected man, a wonderful father who adored his girls, and the only husband I will ever want." Her sigh shudders in her throat.

I wait in silence. If she has more to share, I want to offer my presence and my solace to her, but she appears spent and soon sits forward, her hands pressin' against her knees. "My girls will be wondering what became of their mother." She smiles. "Make good use of this divan, Aidan MacAlister. Sleep well." She pushes herself up to standin', but her gait is much slower, almost wanderin' instead of the purposeful strides I'm used to seein.' "Good night."

I spread one blanket over the divan as a feeble protection for the rich cloth, position the soft pillow against one arm, and pull the other blanket over me as I settle down on my left side. As sleep takes me, I imagine those three girls, bright and gigglin' and full of life, rushin' into this library to leap onto their father's lap and disrupt his work. I see him belly laughin' at their antics, throwin' them into the air one-by-one and catchin' them as they squeal with delight. I see Mary standin' in the doorway, leanin' there with her arms folded and a knowin' smile that treasures the richness of the love they all share. And when I dream, I dream of my sisters and me, runnin' circles in the yard and jumpin' into the pile of October leaves, Pa chucklin' with delight even while he complains about havin' to rake the pile again, Ma with her arm around his waist and her head leanin' on his shoulder, with the exact same knowin' smile.

CHAPTER SEVEN

My days fall into an easy rhythm revolvin' around food, readin', playin' games with the girls, and talkin' with Mary. We take turns sharin' our stories from before the war. I tell her all about our mountain farm and about my ma and sisters—Elspeth's prissy demeanor, the twins' private language, and Maisie's gentle heart, so much like her Elizabeth. We marvel at their similarities to her girls and imagine them becomin' fast friends one day. Mary shares more about her Alex, who sounds like a strong man, not as stern as my Pa but just as lovin'.

Once a week, she takes me by carriage to the hospital, where the doctor examines my wound and tests my progress by havin' me walk without crutches. At first, my leg won't hold my weight. The numbness down my leg remains a hindrance to walkin', almost as much as the severe pain in my back. The doctor encourages me to get my strength up, claimin' it may help my overall healing, so Mary and I take to circlin' the block every day. I hobble on crutches, and she patiently glides beside me with her voluminous skirts floatin' like a cloud around her. Our conversations durin' our walks help distract me from the pain. The more I learn about Alex and their life before the war, the more I feel the weight of her loss and the pain and grief she and the girls must be endurin'.

I also begin to learn a little about her current circumstances and future prospects. Apparently, Alex planned well for her provision, but with no new income, she wants to be prudent with her finances. However, the maintenance and upkeep of the large house and property are her greatest concern. I don't ask if she owned slaves. It doesn't seem like a proper question. What I know is now she is on her own to manage everything, and she finally admits to me that she feels overwhelmed. The girls are a help, but they are young, and she doesn't want to rob them of their childhood.

Hearing her concerns adds to my guilt. I increase her burden and can do very little to contribute or repay her kindness. When I mention my concerns, she dismisses me with a wave of her hand and assures me that my company more than makes up for any extra work. "I have to cook for four. I might as well cook for five. After all, I'm used to it." Her smile always holds a tinge of sadness when she speaks of her husband, even indirectly.

One evening, I'm rockin' on the massive, wraparound porch and overhear some voices behind the house. Concerned, I pull myself up on my crutches and make my way toward the back to find Mary ladelin' up stew into an assortment of bowls, cups, and tin cans held out by a mass of raggedly dressed persons gathered at her back door. I watch the processional for a few minutes, then quietly return to my seat. She joins me some time later, and I notice her eyes are red with gray smudges beneath them, and the creases beside her mouth seem deeper.

After a few minutes of heavy silence, I'm compelled to say something. "What's wrong?"

In the dim light provided by the candles near the front windows, I can see her quick glance and wry smile. "I do not suppose you will accept it if I say, 'Nothing.'"

"Well..."

"Just like Alex." I barely hear her whisper, then she clears her throat and leans forward in her rocker. "I feel such compassion for all the persons suffering because of this war; yet, I can do so very little."

"Seems to me you're doin' a lot."

She looks at me, her question in her eyes.

"I saw you feedin' those folks out back."

"Ah." She closes her eyes and leans back. "It isn't a drop in the bucket."

"Who are they?"

"Some are Confederate soldiers like you, wounded, but they cannot return to the army, and they have no way to provide for themselves. Some are runaway slaves, or freed men who cannot find work. And some are women with children who lost their homes when their husbands died in the war. All of them are starving."

"That's very kind of you, to feed them."

"The numbers grow every day. I suppose the ones who come tell others, and they pass it on to still more. Soon, I'll not be able to feed them all."

"Let me help you. I can sit and spoon up stew."

"Thank you, Mac, but the issue is having enough food for them all. I had to turn many of them away tonight. Resources are becoming more and more difficult to acquire, with the army requisitioning so much to meet the soldiers' needs while the Yankees are destroying our farmlands. I fear I will have to start turning them all away or I will not be able to feed my own children."

I sit rockin' with her, watchin' the tears slide down her cheeks to leave wet splotches on her blouse. A growin' wariness in me about what she's doin' forces me to break my silence, even though she won't want to hear what I have to say. "You know, it's a crime to aid runaway slaves." I have to strain to hear her whispered reply.

"I am aware."

"And?" She continues to stare at her lap, so I answer for her. "And if you are in prison, who will take care of the girls?"

"I will not get caught."

I find it hard to argue her twisted logic, so I try another approach. "And when things get harder for those folks, which they surely will, and you aren't able to feed them anymore, what's to stop them from takin' what they want by force?"

She appears genuinely surprised by my question. "They wouldn't."

"Mrs. Monroe, they would, and don't you be tellin' yourself otherwise. Men will do things they wouldn't normally dream of doin' when they're starvin', or when they see their children starvin'. Think of what you'd do to protect your girls."

"I won't believe it. I cannot."

"You must. This isn't the time for blind faith in the good will of others."

"I put my faith in God."

I snort. "And look what happened to His own Son."

"That's quite enough, Aidan MacAlister." She bolts from the chair like it's on fire, turns her back to me, and marches into the house.

It's clear I've stepped over a line she can't abide, although I know what I said is true enough. Seems to me being a follower of Jesus doesn't guarantee you much of anything but sufferin', just like He suffered. But Mary seems to believe my observation is disrespectful, maybe even blasphemous. I know I need to apologize for my offense to her, but right this minute I'm too angry. How can she be so...so naïve? Does her lack of common sense come from a life of privilege, or is it arrogance? She's puttin' those precious girls at risk. Doesn't she realize that?

I'm seconds from stormin' into the house and lettin' her have it when Ruth steps onto the porch. "Mac, come quickly. Mother is crying, more than I've ever heard her, and we don't know what to do. Did she say anything to you?"

Guilt wrenches my gut in a vise. "I'm afeared it's what I said to her." After they've been so kind and generous to me, I throw her generosity back in her face as an accusation. What's the matter with me? "I'll come make it right."

I follow Ruth into the house and hobble painfully up the sweepin' staircase, with her help, to stand at Mary's door. Ester and Elizabeth are waitin' by the door, tears on their cheeks. I can hear Mary's sobs through the heavy door, so I tap gently, dreadin' her reply before I speak. "Mary, it's Mac. May I come in?"

Seconds pass. "Please go away." Her voice sounds pained and bereft of hope.

"I'm so sorry, Mary. I spoke out of turn. Please forgive me."

"Please leave me in peace."

"The girls are worried. Please, let us come in. They want to comfort you. So do I."

"I need...I just need a few moments alone. Please."

I don't know what else to say. I'm certainly not gonna barge into a woman's bed chamber, and I'm worried I'll only make things worse, so I put my arm around Ruth. "Let's let her be for a bit, then we'll check on her a little later."

"Mother needs us!" Elizabeth's cries are growin' stronger, as is the sick feelin' in my stomach.

Ester grabs my hand and pulls it to the doorknob. "Do something!"

Ruth is more perceptive. "What did you say to her to upset her so?"

"I kinda made a sarcastic remark about God."

All three girls gasp at once. "You didn't!" Ester lets go of my hand like it's a red-hot poker.

Ruth folds her arms and lifts her head. "Mother would never allow such talk in this house."

"I can see that."

"You made her cry." Elizabeth's innocent accusation hurts the worst of all.

"You're right, I did. And I'm terribly sorry for it."

The door swings open, and Mary, her face blotchy and eyes puffed, steps through, her arms open to her girls. They flock to her side and bury their faces in her skirts.

I open my mouth to apologize, but she speaks to the girls before I have the chance. "Girls, Mac didn't do anything wrong. He meant nothing by what he said, and everything he spoke to me was from a heart of love for the three of you."

"Then, why are you crying, Mother?"

"Oh, my dears, I don't know. So many things. So many reasons. I miss Father. He..." Her voice catches for a moment in her throat. With a hard swallow, she continues. "He would know what to do." She shakes her head. "Mac is right. I'm walking blindly ahead with no idea what is going to happen or what the consequences may be for you, and in doing so, I am putting you in harm's way. I feel...so...so lost."

"We will help you, Mommy." Elizabeth's bright assurance seems to lighten the moment, as Ruth and Ester echo her words.

"And Mac will help you, too." Ruth takes my hand and pulls me closer to their little cluster. "You'll help, won't you, Mac? You won't leave us, will you?"

Now, a wash of tears rises in my throat. I can't promise them I'll stay. At some point, I have to go back to my unit. I can't imagine the kind of pain they've gone through with their Pa not returnin', and gettin' all attached to me probably isn't the best thing for them since I must be leavin' them, too, not to mention the fact that I'm a good six years older than Ruth. But truth be told, if not for my Ma and sisters, I'd gladly stay and help them see this through.

"Now, Ruth, we talked about this. You know Mac must return to the army as soon as he is able, to finish fighting for Virginia, like your Father."

"But he isn't leaving yet."

"No, he isn't, and I'm sure you are all very glad of it. As am I." She looks at me, her reddened eyes sparklin' with sincerity. "He's already been more help than he knows."

I'm awkward and fumblin', so I say nothing, but my heart swells with a feelin' I can't describe.

"There, now. See? All better." Mary smooths her cheeks and beneath her eyes, then brushes her hands together as if to dust off the feelin's her tears represent. "Who wants tea cakes?" The girls squeal. Tea cakes, so I've learned, are a special treat, usually reserved for company and rarely shared with the children. They clamber down the stairs, their concerns forgotten.

Thankfully, Mary remains by my side to help me navigate my way down. It's a laborious process. Halfway down, as we stop so I can rest and regroup, she says, "What possessed you to climb these stairs in your condition?"

I'm huffin' and puffin', so it takes me a second to respond. "They asked."

Mary's melodious laugh echoes off the walls and down the staircase, and with that, all things are right with us again. We resume our daily walks and our communal meals, and we add the new activity of servin' soup together from the backdoor to whomever comes for aid. As expected, the numbers continue to increase. On those nights, Mary lets me be the one to tell them when the supplies are exhausted. It seems to spare her heart for me to bear the bad news. I try to tell those who've received to allow the ones who didn't receive to be first in line the next night, but it's nigh impossible for me to keep track, and I'm sad to say the strongest ones with the least need are first in line more often than not. As I told Mary, man's nature is not on its best display when they are hungry. So, I decide to start each night with the children, and then the widows. That way, the ones the Good Lord told us to feed are being fed.

Over the next few weeks, I'm finally able to put down the crutches, with the doctor's approval. Our walks become slower and for shorter distances, with more frequent stops to recover because I fatigue very quickly. It feels like my right leg has forgotten how to work. Even after a short walk, my muscles ache, but I can tell the pain in my back is gradually improvin'. The numbness has all but gone away. It isn't long before the doctor is suggestin' I may be ready to return to my unit sooner than he expected.

"But Doc, I'm still limpin'. What good will I be for the 11th?"

"There's nothing wrong with your hands, is there? You told me you're a sharpshooter for your unit. So, sharpshoot."

"I'll slow them down."

"They aren't moving much right now anyway. As I understand it, everything is stalled at Petersburg."

"Petersburg. That's awful close by."

"Around 25 miles away."

My heart sinks. What's gonna happen to Mary and the girls if the Yankees break through to Richmond? Suddenly, the pressure to rejoin my unit intensifies. "Are you clearin' me to return?"

85

"I want to give it another week, then we'll see if you've continued to improve."

I decide to push a little harder on my walks, and I enlist the girls to help me work on my leg strength. I sit in a chair, and little Elizabeth sits on the lower part of my leg, and I lift her up into the air and back down like a teeter totter. The pain is excruciatin' at first, but I grit my teeth and tolerate it by imaginin' Yankee soldiers stormin' in the front door and doin' who knows what to Mary and the girls. Somehow, I have to keep that from happenin'.

I notice Mary is quieter than usual at dinner. I try to lighten the mood by teasin' and jokin' with the girls, but I'm not able to draw her in, so finally I ask. "Is somethin' wrong?"

She gives me a wan smile. "I'm well. Just tired."

I don't question her, but I don't believe her, either. Later that night, I pull Ruth aside. "Do you know what's troublin' your Ma?"

"I think she's worried about you leaving us to go back to the war. We don't want you to go. What if...what if what happened to Daddy happens to you? What if we never see you again?"

"Ruth, you know I have to go back."

"Why? Why can't you stay with us?"

"I have an obligation to fulfill. But more than that, I want to protect you and your mother and sisters, and the only way I know how to do that is go back and fight against the Yankees."

"You can protect us here."

"I'm one man fightin' against many if I stay here, but with my unit, we all fight together and that makes us stronger. We stand a better chance of stoppin' them."

"But what if the worst happens? Who'll protect us then?"

"Don't you worry about that. I'm not gonna let anything happen to you."

"How can you say that? Daddy wanted to protect us, and he never came back."

"I know. But I'll come back, I promise."

Tears spring up, and she balls her fists and slams them against my chest, then runs upstairs to her room. Dismayed, I wander out onto the porch to calm myself in the coolin' night air and find Mary sittin' there cryin'. I don't mean to startle her, but she jumps when the door closes behind me, then quickly turns her face away from me. "I thought you had gone to bed." I hear her snufflin' as she gazes toward the north—the direction of Petersburg. Has she heard somethin' or is she tryin' to hide her tears?

"Are you worried about the Yanks?"

She sighs. "I overheard some persons at the hospital talking about the Confederates digging in at Petersburg to keep the Union out of Richmond." She glances up at me. "If they come here..."

"You're worried what's gonna happen to you and the girls."

She doesn't speak for several minutes. I sit in the rocker next to her and reach out to touch her hand, but she pulls back from me. "I see how hard you are working to get ready to return to your unit, and I understand it. The girls will miss you...honestly, I'm going to miss you, too, when you leave us. It has been nice having a man in the house again."

"I want to get back so I can fight and keep the Yanks out of Richmond—and away from you and the girls."

She gazes at me, pensive. "Will you make that much of a difference? You're just one man among thousands. But here, you make a big difference. To all of us."

My chest feels like it's rippin' open. I don't know how to think or what to do. Beyond the recuperation from my wound, these four months have healed me in ways I didn't think possible. My heart is softened again. Hope peeks its head up, hope that my life won't have to be one of bitterness, rage, and shame. Will going back reopen those old wounds and harden my heart? Will I lose myself again? But I can't abandon my brothers in arms or renounce my commitment to the cause. How can I be two places at once? If only the doctor would take away my choice and tell me I'm not well enough to return, then I could be here for this beautiful family who have been so kind and accepting toward me.

"I'm sorry, Mary, but the doc is sayin' I'm almost ready to go back."

"I know."

"He said likely next week."

Silence descends except for the singin' of the tree frogs and chirpin' of the crickets. Her rocker creaks against the boards of the porch. There's nothin' for it. As much as I'd rather take Mary and the girls away with me to Georgia to start a new life, far away from the threat of war, I have to return and fulfill my obligation. "I hope you understand."

She nods once but doesn't speak again. Finally, I murmur, "Goodnight," and limp my way to the library. But as I curl up on the divan, I'm surprised at the emotion chokin' my throat and the tears that wet my pillow.

The next few days are tense and awkward for me. The girls range from playful and high-spirited to clingy and tearful. Mary is stony silent. No one talks about my leavin' which is fast approachin', until the night before I'm scheduled to return for my last hospital check.

"I want you to take one of the horses." I'm lyin' on the divan, tryin' but failin' to fall asleep when Mary startles me from the doorway.

"I...I can't take your horse. You and the girls might need it."

"No, please take it. You can ride to your unit in Petersburg, which will be much easier on your back, and you will..." Her words seem to stick in her throat. She closes her eyes and swallows hard. "You will have a way to come back to us." She manages to squeak out the last words, then flies from the room, slammin' the door behind her.

Needless to say, I don't sleep two winks that night. The next mornin' at breakfast, Mary is calm, even warm again. She takes my hand across the table. "Mac, you mean the world to us, I hope you know that. It has been such a joy to have you in our home." The girls are smilin' but their eyes are glistenin'. I wonder if their mother told them to let my last day with them be a happy one. "You are like the son I never had. I hope you will keep in touch with us from time to time."

"I promised the girls I'd come back, so I'm comin' back. Perhaps, dependin' on what happens with the war, you might consider comin' with me to Georgia. You and the girls would be welcome there."

Mary titters and waves her hand. "Oh, I don't think I could ever leave our home, but thank you kindly for the invitation."

Ruth opens her mouth to protest, but a stern look from her mother stops her words in her mouth, and she resumes her stiff smile.

"My meeting with the doc isn't until this afternoon, so we can play some if you want." Elizabeth and Ester cheer and scramble from the table, but Ruth is more reserved and ladylike, pushin' back her chair and foldin' her napkin on the table.

"Mother, may I help you clear the table?" So, she is already assumin' the role of the other adult in the home. My heart aches for her, knowin' she's losin' the rest of her childhood to this war.

Elizabeth, Ester, and I roll in the grass and tussle about. They enjoy beatin' me in chase and wrestlin' and pretty much anything else we play, since I'm still movin' half speed. I let them pin me and tickle me until they're tired, then we lie together on the lawn findin' animal shapes in the clouds. It doesn't seem long at all when Mary calls me from the front porch.

"Mac, I think it is time."

I have nothing to pack. All the clothes I've been wearin' belonged to Alex, so I change into the white shirt and ragged gray trousers I wore when I arrived, now clean and neatly folded, and I leave Alex's clothes folded on the divan.

As I walk to the front door, Elizabeth and Ester run up to me and swallow me in their arms. At first, Ruth is reserved, imitatin' her mother's demeanor, but as I walk out the door, she cries out and rushes to my side, grabbin' me in a vise grip. I stroke her soft, blonde hair and whisper reassurances of my return and her safety.

Ruth releases me, and Mary accompanies me onto the porch. "You will take the horse." She says it as a statement, but I can hear the question in her voice.

"If it brings you peace."

She breathes a deep sigh and smiles. "It does."

"Then, I'll ride her. But I promise, I'll bring her back to you."

"Very well." She reaches into the folds of her skirt and pulls out a book. "And please take this with you to replace the one you lost." She holds out a beautiful leather-bound Bible with gold letterin' on the front cover.

At this point, I know better than to refuse her. I take the precious book as if it were a crystal vase. "I'll keep it safe and bring it back."

Mary clutches my arm. "Keep yourself safe, for the sake of my girls."

"I will." I open my arms, and she falls into my embrace. Her arms wrap around my back and her head buries on my shoulder. We hold each other for a few moments, then she pulls back, wipes her eyes, and nods once. There is nothing else to say.

Ruth walks to the barn behind the house and brings out the saddled black mare that Elizabeth named Blossom, a tall, strong horse with a shiny coat and a long, thick mane and tail. I know she will serve me well. I rub her neck and whisper, "I'm gonna take good care of you." Then, I swing myself onto her back. As I ride away, I turn and wave to the little family watchin' from the doorway, and I hear Mary yell, "Aidan MacAlister. You come back to us."

"I will. I promise." I pray I'm right.

CHAPTER EIGHT

As expected, the doctor clears me to return to duty. The doc tells me the Union has pushed forward near the James River outside Richmond and suggests I connect with the Confederate defenses there. So, Blossom and I travel the now short distance to the Confederate line on the high ground outside Richmond. I'm appreciative I don't have to travel far, because my back is painin' me something fierce. Blossom is a gentle horse, but bouncin' in the saddle is an agony, so we walk most of the way. As I approach the lines, I start my search for the armorer to issue me a new rifle.

The camp is in chaos. Scouts have spotted the Union army gatherin' across the James, and they outnumber us two to one. I look for an officer who can direct me, but everyone is busy scramblin' to shore up our defenses, so I am on my own. As I wander along the trenches and breastworks, a feelin' of dread washes over me, rememberin' sittin' in the trenches after Gettysburg with Will and Josiah, knee-deep in water and mud, waitin' for the inevitable Yank attack that never came.

My chest tightens, but this time, I resist the urge to close down and harden my heart by lettin' my mind go to little Elizabeth bouncin' on my knee. She is the reason I'm here. I think of Mary pressin' her Bible into my hands, and Ester playin' with me in the yard. I recall Ruth's powerful hug goodbye, and her beggin' me not to leave. Her family is who I'm here to save. I must remember that.

Finally, I see a tent some distance from the line that looks like it might be the armorer. Sure enough, a clerk meets me at the front of the tent, takes my information, and gives me several chits, one for a rifle, bayonet, and ammunition, one for a new uniform coat and trousers, and one for some rations. I receive my rifle and pouch of ammunition at the counter, 50 rounds, which allows me only a few rounds for sightin' in my rifle, then they direct me to the Sutler's village nearby to purchase my uniform and supplies.

All they have at the Sutler's are uniforms taken from the dead, not surprisin' given the state of things, so I pick out a coat without obvious holes in it, and a pair of gray trousers that are less hoary than the ones I'm wearin'. The coat is a bit big, but I don't mind. It allows for good range of motion for sharpshootin', plus it leaves me plenty of room to store my new Bible.

I move well back from the line and start the process of sightin' in my rifle. Fortunately, this one is in pretty good shape, so it only takes a few shots to get used to it. Now, I've got to find someone in charge to tell me where they want me to go. Once again, I wander the line of defenses, lookin' for an officer.

A voice calls out to me. "Are you cavalry?"

I understand his question, since I'm leadin' Blossom behind me, and my uniform is unidentifiable. I decide I'm not gonna answer his question directly. "I'm a sharpshooter."

"General Hampton is at the left flank."

"Thank you, sir." I don't know who General Hampton is, but at least I have someplace to go to get some information.

The far-left flank is a flurry of activity, with cavalry and army units workin' to fortify defenses. "General Hampton?" I ask soldiers nearby. They gesture toward a tent set off some distance from the battlements. Blossom and I make our way through the scurryin' soldiers to the tent, only to discover it empty. Uncertain what to do, I decide to wait by the tent for the general's return; however, a junior aide carryin' a satchel filled with papers comes back before I see the general.

"Who are you?"

"Aidan MacAlister, sir. I just returned to duty from a severe wound at the Wilderness, and I was directed to see General Hampton."

"Cavalry officer?"

"I'm a sharpshooter, sir."

The aide looks confused for a second, then returns his attention to his papers. "Report to Major General Fitzhugh Lee." He scribbles a note for me, then waves me away, pointin' toward the cavalry congregatin' near the end of the line.

As I make my way back to the line, I rub my horse's neck.
"Well, Blossom, it looks like you're about to be pressed into service."
I'm thinkin' she and I are both pretty nervous at the prospect.

Major General Lee, or who I assume is Lee, is sendin' some of
his cavalry officers out on patrol. When he sees me, he frowns. "You're
late, soldier. Mount up."

"Um, General...Lee, sir...um...I am a sharpshooter from..."

"Ah, I see. So, they finally sent me a sharpshooter for support.
Very well. We are fortifying defenses for the left flank. It is fairly certain
the Yankees will attack across the James soon, and we must not lose the
flank. If we do, we lose Richmond."

"Yessir."

"That cannot happen. Do you understand?"

"Yessir."

"Find a position on higher ground where you can fire over the
heads of our troops, and when they attack, take out as many of their
soldiers as you can."

"Yessir."

"Son, I cannot afford to send men to relieve you, so you are the
final line of defense on the far left. Do you understand?"

"Yessir."

"Very well. Go. Kill as many of those baseborn mongrels as you
can. And Godspeed."

I mount Blossom and scout the surroundin' area for some good
ground where I can set up. I find some high ground with a copse of
trees where I can tie up Blossom, and I pull together some branches
and underbrush near the edge of the wood to create a hide overlookin'
the river. Then, I settle in to wait.

I figure if the Yanks don't attack before nightfall, they won't be
comin' 'til the mornin', so once the moon is high, I spread out my coat
on the ground and let myself sleep for a few hours, until Blossom
startles me with a blow through her nose. It's still dark, but the horizon
is startin' to lighten enough for me to make out movement in the
distance on the river. "Good girl," I whisper, and crawl into position in
my hide. Sure enough, there they are. The Yanks are crossin' the James
and comin' to hit our center where we're weakest.

They're still too far for me to hit anything, but I wonder if our soldiers are aware they're comin'. Should I fire to alert them? As I'm about to fire, I hear some shouts comin' from the camp, so I turn my attention again to the approachin' Yanks. Just as reported, their numbers are great, much more than we have. I see General Lee send one of his horsemen gallopin' toward the north, I suppose to report to the elder General Lee about the troop movements. From what I see, he's gonna need reinforcements in the center.

They've come within range of my rifle, but I don't want to fire too soon and give away my position before they are engaged with the main body of our force, so I wait until I hear shots from our boys. Then, I start lookin' for officers. Knowin' I have less than 50 shots to take, I wanna make 'em count.

I try to think of the soldiers as a covey of quail flushed from the reeds. Otherwise, my hands shake, and I can't aim true. I see my Pa and me lyin' in the tall grass, waitin' for our ol' Samson to stir the reeds near the stream. Then, with a whoosh, the quail soar into the air, and Pa and I stand and shoot one after the other mid-flight, and they tumble to the ground. Quail, that's what they are. They flock toward my boys. And I drop them one by one.

But I only have one rifle, and I only have a few rounds left, and my boys are collapsin' back past New Market Road. "Blossom, we better hurry and get down there, or we're gonna get cut off." I pull back out of my hide, gather up my meager belongin's, leap on Blossom's back, and race down the backside of the hill toward the road. I'm vaguely aware of a pain shootin' from my back down my leg, but I can't afford to pay it no mind. I gotta beat the Yanks to the road and my boys.

I make it across the open ground with the Yankee right rushin' up my tail and catch up with the retreatin' cavalry. "What're you doin'? Stop! We can't let 'em have Richmond!" But my screams are lost in the din of musket fire and artillery. Blossom is fast and seems undaunted by the blasts and mortars rainin' down around her, and I push her to get me to the front of the line. In my heart, I know, as if the Good Lord Himself has revealed it to me, that if the Yanks overrun us here, Richmond will fall.

Still, my boys are runnin' before the Yankee aggression. The panic closin' my throat suddenly transforms into rage, my familiar demon, that darkness within me, and I rein up Blossom with a howl. We turn in a cloud of dust as the other horses rush past us. I pull my rifle out of its scabbard, attach the bayonet, and scream, "Attack!" Blossom and I are off to face the Blue Bellies, alone if need be. I made a promise to Mary to keep them out of Richmond, and I'm gonna keep it.

I become aware of other horses runnin' beside Blossom, and more turnin' to join us as we gallop back toward the river. My yell echoes around me as others take up the call. Then, I see the ground troops rally and turn to face the Yanks, and the fight is on.

Blossom bursts headlong into the Yankee line, tramplin' men beneath her hooves as I slash my bayonet right and left. All around me, my Confederate brothers are clashin' with the boys in blue, and we're regainin' ground. We push them back until they turn and run, and our commanders call us to stop and dig in.

We did it. We stopped them. Cheers ring all around me as everyone celebrates our halt of the Yankee advance. Hampton and Lee are quick to reorganize the troops and start rebuilding breastworks, but Lee takes the time to ride beside me for a piece and congratulate me on rallyin' the troops.

"Well done, soldier. We were close to a rout. Did you spot an opportunity, a weakness in the Yankee line?"

I don't know what to say, so I decide to nod to whatever he suggests. My hands are tremblin'.

"Very well. We are fortunate indeed that you recovered from your injury in time to join us for this battle." He looks into the sky, presses his lips together, and shakes his head. "Yes, well done. Well done."

With the fever of the battle dissipatin', the ache in my back and the fire coursin' down my right leg reach a new level of intensity. I try to swing off Blossom but find I can't make my leg lift high enough, and when I try going off the other side, my right leg won't hold my weight in the stirrup. I wonder what kinda damage I've done, or if I'm sore from the abuse, and it'll pass. I coax Blossom away from the troops and under a tree with a limb low enough for me to grab. There's nothin' wrong with my arms, so I pull myself up out of the saddle, then lower myself to drape awkwardly across the saddle and, inch by inch, slide to the ground. As I touch the ground, a sharp pain explodes in my lower back.

I wrap my arms around Blossom's neck and bury my face in her mane. "Thank you, girl. Thank you." The sobs begin. I'm glad I walked her far away from the other soldiers before the dam broke. She stands, still and calm, waitin' for my heavin' shoulders and gasps to quiet. I love this horse.

My brain won't stop runnin' the scene, over and over again, face after face fallin' before me. All someone's brother, son, father. Just like Pa. Just like Alex. How much longer, oh Lord? The rippin' in my chest is back, and I wonder how many more tears my heart can withstand before the scar tissue refuses to heal.

I can't let myself think this way. I have to focus on my goal—protect the Monroe family and get back to my Ma and sisters. I have promises to keep. I swallow down the flashes of trampled bodies, the sliced and slashed faces and chests, and my turbulent feelin's, and put them all away in a box deep inside, far out of reach. Blossom blows through her nose and bobs her head, but I'm not sure if it's a warnin' or approval. "Sorry, girl. I gotta keep movin'."

But when I try to take a step, my leg collapses beneath me. I have to use Blossom's saddle to pull myself back up. The numbness in my leg has returned. The pain in my back is excruciatin'. "Looks like you're my crutch, girl." With my arm across her saddle, I hop beside her as she walks back to the herd of cavalry horses at the left end of the Confederate line.

A couple'a soldiers notice me limpin' along and come to my aid. With one under each arm, they carry me to the medical tent, but I already know I'm a low priority compared to lost limbs and gapin' wounds, so I use the opportunity to grab a bedroll, and holdin' onto Blossom, I hobble away to an isolated spot within a clump of trees to sleep.

Additional troops start floodin' into camp. I guess Fitz Lee's requests produce results. So, I know my presence isn't gonna be missed on the front line. I'm hopin' whatever I might've done to my back will resolve with a good rest. I conveniently ignore the fact that my first injury took weeks to heal, choosin' to believe the bone isn't broken again. At any rate, I already know seein' the doc is a waste of time.

Supplies of all kinds are limited, and we're lucky if we get one small meal a day. This time, however, I can't hunt for myself to supplement. I find myself dreamin' about Mary Monroe's overflowin' tables. Ammunition is limited, too. I ask the soldiers who helped me to the medical tent to scrounge me some rounds, because I'm all out, and it's hard for me to do it for myself. They seem more than willin' to help me. It's from them that I hear the first hints of my new nickname— Fourth Horseman. The name is both sickening and appropriate.

Fortunately for my back, after one failed ground attack, Lee has us diggin' in and holdin' our position, and the Yanks don't seem too interested in engagin' with us again, so I'm able to rest for over a week before anything else happens. By then, the pain is manageable, and I can ride and walk—even if it is with a severe limp. As far as I'm concerned, no one need know a thing.

General Lee the elder finally calls for another offensive, once again against the Union right flank at Darbytown Road and along New Market Road. Blossom and I and the rest of Fitz Lee's cavalry take on the Union cavalry, routing them off Darbytown Road, but the offensive stalls on New Market Road, and we are forced to return to our original defensive line.

As if this offensive sets a pattern in motion, October becomes a series of back-and-forth assaults near Darbytown and New Market Roads. Each Union attack against our defenses fails. We attack them at Fair Oaks and capture over 600 prisoners, but we can't dislodge them from their positions either. Cold weather and limited supplies force both sides to settle in for a long winter wait.

The cold doesn't help the ache in my back, but the long rest does. Blossom and I are able to wander into the woods behind our lines and set some squirrel and rabbit traps. Unfortunately, the pickin's are slim, but what I do catch, I share with the two soldiers who helped me when I was down. I don't ask their names, and they don't ask mine. It's strange, but I guess none of us want to form friendships anymore. Too much loss.

Sometime in late March, information trickles down the line that the army positioned near Petersburg has broken through the Union lines at Fort Stedman and successfully captured the fort, but our excitement is short-lived as we hear the Yanks have closed the gap and we are retreatin' and takin' heavy casualties. Our defenses are stretched thin already, with some places manned by single soldiers more than 5 feet distant from their nearest support. To shore up the line farther north, Lee pulls from our defenses, leavin' us weaker still.

I can almost feel the change in the air. We are desperately hungry, weakened by winter illness and desertion, and the Yanks appear to be gearin' up for a major assault against us. Fitz Lee calls his cavalry to action, sayin' we are instructed to rush to General Pickett's aid and defend the South Side Railroad from a Yankee offensive. So, Blossom and I charge through the woods and beyond the end of our line, hurryin' to reach Pickett's corps. Drivin' rain makes our journey difficult, but we arrive early the next mornin' and set our defenses at Five Forks.

Within hours, we are attacked by a Union cavalry unit. The skirmish is brief but intense. The ground is poor, and the hard rain makes the footin' terrible for the horses. Blossom manages well despite these conditions. I, on the other hand, am feelin' unwell, almost like I'm outside my own body and I'm watchin' the fight from a distance. She takes care of me, however, and I take out some Yanks in close quarters fightin'. We're able to hold off the Yankees until Pickett's troops arrive that night.

Rain continues the next mornin', and I'm relieved to be spared from more action, since I still feel ill. But that afternoon, Fitz Lee sends us to attack the southern ford, and for the first time, we face men firin' at us one after the other without havin' to stop and reload. There isn't much we can do against such weapons, so we are forced to withdraw. The only thing that saves us is the comin' of night. I guess the Yanks don't want to follow us in the dark, but they miss a good opportunity to finish us off.

My fevered mind imagines all kinds of scenarios, none of them endin' well for our side. My dreams are haunted by visions of gettin' overrun and trampled by Union cavalry, of our defensive lines washin' away like mud durin' a hard summer rain, of Mary standin' in the door of her home while Yankee soldiers run across the lawn and up the stairs to crush her beneath their feet, of those soldiers settin' her house aflame with the girls still inside. My tortured sleep doesn't allow me to rest, so the next day, I'm even worse.

In the end, it doesn't matter. Everything happens in a swirl of confusion that bein' in my right mind wouldn't change at all. No one can find General Lee or General Pickett.

Pickett. Disaster seems to follow him wherever he goes. We receive different orders from two different commanders, and none of the orders make a lick of sense. It's almost as if the craziness goin' on in my brain has infested the entire Confederate army. The Yanks are more than happy to take advantage. Our line collapses under attack, then we regroup only to collapse again. I see whole units throwin' down their arms, others runnin' from the battle. Every single Union division seems to be convergin' on Five Forks.

The missin' General Pickett finally shows up and asks us to hold back the Yankee attack long enough for him to get through to his men. A few of the men agree, so I turn Blossom and follow them through the Union lines under fire, with Pickett hidin' between our horses. Unable to return to our previous position, we race toward Hatcher's Run and the South Side rail line, hopin' to help stop the Yanks from capturin' the supply line.

The fevered pitch and confusion of the battle mirrors my inner world. My eyes won't tell the difference between our boys and theirs. I can't feel my hands to hold my weapon. Poor Blossom is runnin' to and fro without any guidance from her reins, as I'm tryin' to find someone who knows what they're doin'.

Finally, Fitz Lee gathers up what's left of his cavalry. "I have ill news, men. The Yankees have broken through. The railroad is lost. We are instructed to hold the flank at all costs. President Davis and his cabinet have fled the capital. General Lee and the Army of Northern Virginia are retreating. Petersburg is in the hands of the Yankees, and

Richmond is soon to follow. Our job is to protect the rear of the army during their retreat."

That's all I need to hear. I pull Blossom's reins, crouch low over her back, and whisper, "Go home." Movin' as one, we race from the battlefield, south toward Richmond. I have to reach Mary before the Yankees overrun the city.

CHAPTER NINE

The race is on. The bulk of the Confederate Army is already movin' out of Richmond or desertin', and the Yankee army is maybe two hours away, if I'm lucky. My head spins in a blur of trees and smoke, and the beats of Blossom's hooves match the poundin' in my head. Even the air seems to be burnin'; the night sky is alight with it. I urge Blossom to go faster, faster, as I hold onto her neck for dear life.

I'm numb to pain, existin' in another place where I look down from afar and see Mary and the girls waitin' at their door, hopin' to see me comin' down their street instead of a line of Blue Bellies marchin' with guns ablaze. The force of my will melds with Blossom's power, as if I am inside the horse and she is in me. I can sense her taut muscles pulsin' within me. They ripple like water disturbed by a skipped rock. Her lather and my sweat form a single stream.

Time ceases to have meanin' for me. We press hard and fast for what seems like hours, but I don't appear to be any closer to the city. I know if I don't let Blossom rest some, she'll give out on me, but I can't bring myself to stop or even walk for a bit. My senses tell me I should be there by now. Are we lost?

An explosion of orange and dense smoke billow in the distance. Fires in Richmond? How can that be? I know the Yanks are still behind me. Who woulda started a fire? I lean close to Blossom's ear. "Come on, girl, you can do it. Mary's in trouble." I don't know if she senses my urgency or understands the meanin' of my words—either way, she stretches out her stride and pushes herself, swift as a rush of snowmelt under a noonday sun.

I can sense the hollow thumpin' beneath me shift to a ringin' of metal against stone, and I know we've reached the city. We're soon blinded by the thick smoke, but Blossom presses on, almost like she's goin' on pure instinct and memory. I have nothin' to use to cover my mouth, and it isn't long before I'm coughin' and wheezin', addin' a lack of air to my already exhausted state. As we near the center of town, we are surrounded by flames that lick the sky from the warehouses linin' the street. Blossom is understandably skittish, rearin' her head back and fightin' the reins as burnin' pieces of timber and ash rain around us. Still, we press on.

The flames are spreadin' quickly and have already reached the main street. Mary's home is so close. What if it's burned already? I can't let myself even consider what that means. We turn down her street, and my heart seizes and locks my throat. Houses on both sides of her street are ablaze. I urge Blossom forward, even though I don't want to face what I might find. But when we round the final curve, for the first time since Lee's announcement, I am able to take a deep breath. Her house stands. Blossom, as if sensin' Mary's presence, bolts down the cobblestone street and races across the lawn. I leap from her back before Blossom digs her hooves in the turf to halt, and I race up the steps, heedless of anything except Mary and those precious girls. "Mary! Ruth! Ester! Elizabeth! Where are you?"

"Here!"

The voice—Ruth's voice—seems to be comin' from behind the house, so rather than enter, I race around the porch to the back where I find the girls soakin' quilts in buckets of water.

Ruth screams, "Mac! You came!" as Ester and Elizabeth drop their waterlogged quilts and grapple my legs as if they're afeared I'm fixin' to leave 'em again.

"Where's your Ma?"

Ruth points to a rickety wooden ladder leaned against the end of the house. I trace the ladder to the roof, and there Mary is, peerin' over the edge. "Help us!" Ruth lifts up a sodden quilt, and it dawns on me what's happenin'.

I grab Ruth's quilt and scramble up the ladder, handin' the heavy fabric to Mary. She drags the quilt to the roof's peak and spreads it across the tiles beside three more wet quilts.

"Mary, you've managed to stave off the fire so far, but we can't save the house. The Yanks are comin'. They'll be here soon. We gotta go!"

"Go?"

"Leave. We gotta leave Richmond. Now!"

"No..."

"Mary." I hold out my hand. "Please. Come down."

"Our home!" I hear her plaintive cry, and my heart breaks for her. Still, reality looms, ominous and unrelenting.

"There's nothin' for it. If you stay here, you all die."

After the briefest pause, Mary gathers up her skirts and makes her way gingerly down the roof to me. Sparks and soot are fallin' all around us, so it's moments before her roof catches up. I climb down before her, watchin' carefully to make sure she doesn't fall. When she reaches the bottom, she runs to me and embraces me, but we don't have time for such things. I hold her at arms' length. "Get all the food you can and a change of clothes—something durable—for you and the girls. There's no time for anything more. We gotta get outta here."

"But..."

"Ruth, can you hook up your horse to the cart? I think it'll fare better than the carriage for where we're goin'."

"I can do that."

"Good. Go quickly. Ester, Elizabeth, go help your Ma."

Out of the corner of my eye, I can see smoke risin' from the roof. I grab Mary's arm. "The house is catchin' up, so you gotta make the girls hurry and get their things downstairs before the upstairs is taken."

Mary stands like a statue, starin' at her roof. Her pale, soot-smeared face, her wide, wet eyes, and her slack mouth say she's gonna need my help, so I pull her behind me and run into the house. "Girls, get upstairs and pull out some clothes and bring them downstairs as quick as a bunny."

Ester and Elizabeth scamper upstairs, and I follow, with Mary laggin' behind me. "I'm gonna take a couple of things from Alex, if that's acceptable."

"Um...uh...yes. Yes, of course." Something about speakin' seems to pull her out of her shock, and she hurries to her armoire and selects a few articles of clothin' for herself. I pull a couple of shirts and a couple of trousers from a dresser while she runs to Ruth's room and grabs some clothes for her. We meet the girls on the stairs.

"Look, Mother, I thought to bring a nightgown, too." Elizabeth is beaming, she's so proud of herself.

"How smart of you! I did not bring a nightgown or robe. I suppose I could..."

"No! Look." I point to the ceiling, where fire is drippin' down. It looks like yellow-orange boilin' water as it bubbles across the ceilin' above us and creeps down the walls.

"Oh, my!"

"Cupboard!" I gather up all the clothes and race down the stairs with the armload, Mary and the girls on my tail. Mary bolts into the kitchen while I take the clothes out back, where Ruth is hitchin' up the wagon. I throw our things in the wagon and rush back in to help Mary with the food.

She is collectin' things into cloth sacks when I return. "Mac. I have some money..."

"Your Confederate money ain't gonna be good no more."

"Yes, but Alex purchased gold coins for us, coins he knew would have value, no matter the outcome of the war."

"Gold coins?"

"Yes, quite a number of them."

"Where are they?"

"In the strongbox in his study."

I don't recall a strongbox, so I step in and take over packin' the food. "Can you carry the strongbox?"

"Um, I believe so."

104

"Go. Girls, start carryin' these sacks to the wagon out back. Ask Ruth to help you get them in the wagon."

Elizabeth drags one of the sacks onto the porch and down the back stairs, but Ester hesitates. "Mac, shouldn't we cover up the food with something? It seems to me persons might be tempted to hurt us if they are hungry, and they see our food."

"Good thinkin', Ester."

"But all our quilts are soaking wet."

"Any other sheets or blankets?"

"They are all upstairs."

I try to picture the house as I remember it, seein' if I can think of anything that might be bulky enough to cover our supplies. "Curtains. Ester, run into the sittin' room and pull down the curtains from the front windows. Can you manage it?"

"I can do it, Mac."

"Go, then. Hurry. But if the fire's anywhere near that room, don't you go near it."

"I won't."

A loud metallic sound scrapes slowly down the hall. Mary returns, grindin' a large, metal box sealed with a thick lock across the wood floor. She is puffin' and blowin' as she drags the weight of the box behind her. She drops it at my feet with a thump. "I thought it would be wise to bring Alex's pistol." She hands me a Colt and pouch of ammunition. "It was his prior to the war, and his commander was kind enough to return it to us after he..."

I receive the pistol like a precious heirloom and secure it in my jacket. "Wise. We'll need it, I'm afeared."

"Where is Ester going?"

"She thought to get curtains to cover up the food to hide it from strangers. We'll need to hide that box, too. Anyone sees that is gonna steal it for sure."

"I will help her."

"She can manage. Here, you carry this load of food out. I'll bring the strongbox."

105

I heave the strongbox onto my back and tote it outside to the wagon. When we return to the kitchen for another load, I'm surprised Ester hasn't brought the curtains, so while Mary is gatherin' another sack of food, I hurry to the sittin' room. To my horror, the flames have consumed the whole staircase and a large part of the hall. The heat bakes my face as I run through the flames down the hall toward the doorway. "Ester! Ester, where are you?"

I hear a small, chokin' voice. "In here."

Fire has overtaken the doorway to the sittin' room, and Ester is inside. I mouth, "Ester." Sound sticks in my throat. I try to push past the flames roarin' around me, but the searin' heat is too great. "Oh, dear Lord, don't take Ester to you because I sent her to get those stupid curtains! You can't take sweet Ester. I won't let you! Please, Lord. Please, no."

The thought of the curtains reminds me of the windows, so I rush out the front door and down the porch. I can see Ester through the windows, huddled under the torn-down curtains in the corner as the flames eat their way closer and closer to her. I pick up Mary's rocker and throw it against the window, shatterin' the glass. A blast of hot wind and fire vomits from the openin' and forces my eyes closed. Blinded, I crawl through the window, oblivious to the shards of glass scrapin' my arms. Ester is coughin' furiously, so I follow the sound.

As I inch my way across the room, a loud, shatterin' crack reverberates above my head, and I look up in time to see a burnin' beam saggin' from the ceilin'. I dive across the floor as the beam breaks loose and crashes to the floor in an explosion of sparks and flames. Ester is close. I crawl toward the sound of her wheezes, usin' my hands to feel for the lump of curtains and child. There! I have her! I gather her in my arms, curtains and all, but our way is blocked by the fallen beam.

I close my eyes, since they're useless to me anyway, and picture the room where I spent so many pleasant weeks with this family. The gold brocade settee, the two wing chairs, the writin' desk and bookshelf, tables...I set the image in my mind, hold my breath, and circle around the beam, hopin' I don't fall over something and tumble with Ester underneath me. Debris is fallin' on all sides. I scramble the final few steps to the window as the rest of the ceilin' crashes down. As I push her through the window, flames are lickin' at my legs and back. I don't care. All that matters is Ester. When she is safely on the porch—safe at least for the moment—I beat my legs and stomp the ground to stanch the fire long enough for me to crawl out the window.

I pick her up again and rush her onto the lawn, far away from the now-engulfed house. I stomp the spots where embers have landed on Ester's curtains, then roll on the grass to extinguish the fire on my shirt and trousers. Ester is whimperin', so I know she's alive. Relief washes over me like a cold rain.

"Oh, dear Jesus, thank you, Lord." But what of Mary and Elizabeth? "Stay here, Ester. Don't move." Runnin' around the house, I breathe again when I see Ruth and Mary sittin' at the front of the wagon, Mary holdin' the reins, and little Elizabeth in the back amongst the piles of clothes and food. I wave them forward, then rush back to Ester.

When Mary sees Ester in her ball of curtains, she leaps down from the wagon. "Ester, are you well? What happened?" She collects Ester in her arms.

"The fire blocked her in, but she's safe now." I point to the house. Mary turns and her face contorts in horror as the upper level of her lovely home collapses onto the lower level and the whole house is consumed.

"We barely made it," she whispers.

"Let's go. We gotta beat the Yanks outta town, or they'll take us for Confederate sympathizers, or worse. Can you drive the wagon?"

"I am able."

I take Ester from her mother and lift her and her curtains into the wagon. "Elizabeth, can you help Ester spread the curtains on top of all of your belongin's?"

"I will, Mac!"

Tears glisten on Mary's cheeks in the firelight. "Very well. May we have just a moment to say goodbye?"

"Say goodbye on the road. We don't have time to waste." She doesn't know what I know—that the Yankees are right behind me, and we've spent too long here already. I mount Blossom while Mary pulls herself onto the wagon, then I grab the bridle of Mary's horse and lead them across the lawn and onto the street.

Homes on both sides of the road are in flames, so we have to watch for embers and fallin' debris as we make our way through the dense smoke. Flames in the town behind us shoot high into the air. The conflagration is spreadin' by the second. I'm under an intense pressure to hurry, but I know if I push too hard in these conditions, it could lead to a disaster like a lost wheel or an overturned cart, so I try to balance speed with caution, against the urgin's of my heart. Mary's horse is wild-eyed and shakes his head, tryin' to back up. I hold on tight. Through the roarin' of the fire, I listen for the sounds of musket fire or the distinctive noises of a marchin' army, but it's hard to hear beyond the tumult around us.

"Mac!" It's Ester. I drop the bridle, turn Blossom, and rush to her side.

An ember has fallen into the bundle of curtains, and the red-orange hole is slowly expandin' as a tiny flame erupts. I jump into the wagon, causin' it to dip and almost overturn, but it rights as I pound on the burnin' curtains. "Well done, Ester. I'm glad you were watchin'." Her smile beams white from her blackened face.

I jump back onto Blossom. "By the way, what's the horse's name?" I figure if I can call him by name, he might stop bein' so feisty.

"I named him Brutus." Ruth answers from the front of the wagon.

"Hmm, well—that's a perfect name for him, far as I can tell. Here we go, Brutus." I catch his bridle and start down the street again, but he's no easier to manage.

"Look at the end of the street, Mac." Mary points to a collapsed buildin' blockin' the exit to the main road south out of Richmond.

"I see it."

"What are we going to do?"

I scan the area for other routes around the roadblock, but I find it hard to see anything through the smoky haze. Mary's flushed face is crestfallen. "We can make it around. Somehow." I urge ol' Brutus forward. The fires press closer to us the farther we go, and even Blossom starts to get nervous. Her coat shimmers in the fire's glow, slick with sweat, just like all of us. She tries to back away from the obstacle, but I push forward.

"There." I see a pathway behind the fallen buildin' that I believe may eventually take us to the main road. It will be a tight fit for the wagon, though, so I take the reins from Mary and move Blossom in front of Brutus, single file. "Everyone, hold on." We move at a snail's pace next to the still-burnin' structure. Everything in me wants to run, to push Blossom into a gallop and get past the fire that's cookin' me like a turkey, but if I do and the wagon wheels get caught on something, we lose everything—our food, our clothes, Mary's coins, and maybe the children. So, I hold Blossom in tight check and inch us down the narrow path. Elizabeth and Ester hang over the sides of the wagon and call reports out to me if they spy objects in our path.

Sure enough, we're able to circle behind the burnin' structure and loop onto the main road, but to my dismay, the road is clogged with residents of Richmond, some in carriages, some on foot, some on horseback, all leavin' a dyin' city. I push my way into the slow-movin' caravan, then pull Brutus and his precious cargo onto the road beside me.

As we slog along the road, for the first time since I returned to Mary's house, I'm aware of the ache in my back and the sharp pain goin' down my leg. To distract myself again, I use the opportunity to plan our next moves. "Where do you want to go, Mary?"

Her blank stare tells me what I need to know. "Do you have anyone you can stay with? Relatives or friends somewhere outside the city?" I know Richmond won't be safe again for a long time.

"My mother's sister and my cousin live in North Carolina."

"Oh? Whereabouts?"

"Hendersonville. It's a little town in the mountains. They are Union supporters." She casts her eyes down, as if embarrassed they support the other side.

"Tell you the truth, you'll be safer someplace with Union supporters. I have a feelin' us Confederates are gonna have a rough go for quite a while."

"Then, you must stay with us."

"No'm. I gotta go home and take care of my family. But I can take you all the way to Hendersonville, if you like, to make sure you're all safe and cared for."

"I would be most appreciative."

"They won't take it out on you 'cause your husband fought for the Confederacy, will they?"

"I doubt they know, but even if they do, family is more important than affiliations."

"Well enough, then. Have you been there before?"

"Not for quite some time. They have never even met my girls. I'm afraid I will not be much help to you with navigation."

"Don't take much to know we need to head south. Seems like everyone's got the same idea as us. We'll follow the pack a ways."

"Are you concerned, with so many?"

"I'm worried about the Yanks catchin' up to us more than the folk around us. They ain't gonna be friendly for sure. Is there another road outta town?"

"This is the main one. Lesser roads will be rougher, and likely just as crowded. Once we reach the outskirts, hopefully the way will clear."

"At least we are not so close to the fires," Ruth says. I can see the scaldin' on her face and the fear in her eyes.

"Just make sure you keep movin'."

"Mac, I am worried for the poor we have been feeding. What will they do now?"

"They're likely amongst these folk around us."

"I am afraid they will starve."

110

"You're such a kind-hearted soul, Mary." I lower my voice and lean close to her. "But you need to know, many's gonna starve in these times. Don't be givin' away your food, or you'll be one of 'em."

Mary pales but nods her head in agreement. I'm satisfied she's takin' my warnin' seriously.

I spot a group ahead movin' with more speed, so I start pushin' around some of the slower folk to catch up to them. They appear to be helpin' each other by formin' a sorta wall of riders, almost like a wedge plowin' a trench in the ground. The crowd is partin' like the Red Sea before Moses to allow the riders through, and I wanna be one of them. I move Blossom in front of Brutus and pull him and the wagon through the masses between us and the riders, careful not to trample anyone along the way.

It's a rough go, but we finally catch the group of riders. I come alongside the far-right end. "I see what you're a-doin'. Can we help?"

"Sure, more's better, as long as you don't slow us down." The man eyes the wagon.

"We'll keep up."

"Them that's walkin' are cloggin' up the streets." The man looks up and down the ragged remnants of my uniform. "Soldier?"

"Yessir."

"Most of the soldiers left Richmond yesterdee." I can tell he's a suspicious sort.

"I was at Petersburg."

His frown deepens. "Deserter, then?"

"No sir, I stayed until they said the soldiers were leavin' Richmond. I had to come an' get my—uh—family before it was too late. I fought all the way up to the end."

"It ain't over yet, boy. Lee's gonna gather the troops and come back to Richmond, victorious. You joinin' him at Danville?" His eyes narrow.

I don't want to discuss war tactics with this man who obviously isn't a soldier. I know he won't like my response anyway, so I nod and turn my attention back to shorin' up our line. It's eerily reminiscent of

111

walkin' across the field at Gettysburg, shoulder to shoulder in a long line, which in hindsight proves a failin' strategy when the enemy holds the high ground. In this case, though, it seems to be workin'. At least there ain't nobody shootin' at us...yet.

With our new allies, we begin to make some real progress, and we're soon outside of town. Most of the crowd appears to be headin' due south, followin' the Richmond and Danville Rails. This seems folly to me. Since the railroad is so important to both the Union and the Confederacy, I expect fightin' to continue over the rails. I also understand that the Confederate army took the trains to Danville when they left Richmond, so to me that means the Union will follow them. I don't wanna be anywhere nearby when they meet again.

I turn back to the man next to me. "Where you headed?"

"To Danville, of course, with General Lee and the army."

"The Yanks'll be comin' after 'em, you know."

"Lee'll protect us."

I'm not gonna argue with the man, who is obviously an ardent Lee supporter. "My family is headed to North Carolina to join up with family there. The western mountains. Do you happen to know a road that gets them there?"

"Sorry, friend, I can't hep ya."

"Thanks anyways. And thanks for lettin' us join your group for a spell."

"Shore 'nuff." He offers me one final glare, then he and his fellow riders head south beside the rails.

"Will we go with them?" Mary seems quite tense, more than she was amongst the fires.

"I don't think it's wise. The Union soliders'll be followin' the Confederates straight down that rail line."

"Oh, my." Her eyes are dartin' left and right, her breath comin' in short gasps.

"We need to head more toward the southwest, I believe."

"Yes, of course."

Something is terribly wrong, but I can't figure it. We're through the worst part. If we can find the open road, we'll be safe again. "What's wrong, Mary?"

My question unleashes a flood of tears the likes I've never seen from her.

"Mother?" Ruth caresses her Ma's arm.

Ester wraps her arms around her from behind. "All is well, Mother. Mac is with us."

Now, Elizabeth starts wailin' and I'm getting frantic. "What is it, Mary? What's got you cryin' so?"

"Everything is...gone. Gone." She's wailin' like Elizabeth. "Alex. Our home. Our friends. Our town. Our country. Everything is destroyed. It will never be the same again."

"No, I s'pose it won't."

"How can I bear it?"

"We bear what we must. My Ma always says the Good Lord giveth and the Good Lord taketh away. Blessed be the name of the Lord."

"What does that mean?" I'm taken aback by her venom.

"To me, it means whatever happens, we gotta always remember the Lord is good. It also seems to me the Good Lord ain't afeared of sufferin' and wants us not to be afeared of it either."

"Surely, you're not suggesting this war was the Lord's will."

"I'm not sayin' that it was. I'm sayin' the Lord brings good things outta sufferin' like He did for Joseph. And Jesus."

"What good comes from this horror? Only death and loss." The weepin' starts again.

"I've seen plenty of both. And it does seem an awful waste to me. My Ma never wanted me to fight 'cause she didn't believe in killin' under any circumstances, so if not for my Pa I wouldn't be here. But I am here. And 'cause of it, I've lost my Pa and my good friends. I've killed folk, to my great shame. Now, I'm lookin' to the Lord for how He's gonna turn it for good."

Mary's face softens, and her eyes turn from fiery rage to compassion. "I forgot. I'm sorry. I know you have suffered, too."

"Maybe me bein' here to help you and your girls is part of my redemption."

"Oh, I do hope so. I apologize for my outburst. Girls, I apologize to you as well. I let my emotions get the better of me and forgot myself. Elizabeth, come here, child."

Elizabeth climbs into her mother's arms, followed by Ester. Ruth leans against her Ma. "Like Ester said, all is well. As long as we have each other."

Ruth is behavin' so grown-up, now. My heart aches for her, but I'm proud of her all the same. "We best be goin'. We want to be far away from Richmond when the Yanks come after our boys."

"Which way, Mac?"

The risin' sun to my left tells me our direction. "That road up ahead looks well-enough traveled and appears to turn toward the direction we want to go. We will keep goin' southwest until we find someone who can give us better directions."

"When may the girls take rest?"

"If they can sleep in a movin' wagon, they can rest now, but we'll keep goin' as long as the horses can manage it."

"Very well." Mary sighs, but I see she has stiffened her back and collected her emotions for the long journey.

After we ride a ways down the new road, well out of sight of the other refugees, I stop the horses. "I need to change these clothes. If we get stopped by either side, I'm likely to be hanged as a spy or a deserter." I hop down from Blossom, and grunt as the pain shoots up my back. I limp to the wagon, and with Ester's help, I pull out a pair of Alex's trousers and a nice white shirt. Then, I hobble over to a grove of trees, hide myself, and change. Once I'm done, I bury the gray trousers and jacket under a pile of leaves and return to the wagon.

I hand Mary the Bible she loaned me. "Keep this safe for me."

"I shall."

"If anyone asks, we're family. Do you understand, girls? I can be your son or even a nephew, whatever you think best."

"We will say son." Her eyes shine as she declares I am her own.

"We have a brother!" Elizabeth and Ester whoop and holler, but Ruth remains aloof and serious. I understand. She's carryin' a weight she's never had to carry before, of bein' responsible for her Ma and sisters.

"And as your new brother, I'm the man of the house now, so you'ns have to listen to me and do what I say."

The girls fall over in gales of laughter, and I know just where I stand.

CHAPTER TEN

Twenty-five grueling days pass, twenty-five days of ridin' through the night hours and tryin' to sleep on the hard ground durin' the day, skirtin' around towns to stay out of sight, hidin' from marauding Union and Confederates soldiers, dodgin' other travelers tryin' to survive, like us. We never know exactly where we are or if we're goin' the right way, but we keep plowin' forward. We're careful with our food supplies, which have lasted us so far, and we've been able to find adequate water. But life on the trail isn't easy for anyone, certainly not for young'uns. Mary and the girls are exhausted from lack of sleep, discomfort, and fear, my aches and pains are only gettin' worse, and I'm wearin' down from havin' to stand guard while they sleep and lead them when they're awake. Many a night, I've fallen asleep in Blossom's saddle, and the horse has been our only guide.

We are in North Carolina, now, which seems to boost everyone's mood. Everyone also feels better 'cause we start travelin' in daylight. We find the ridgeline and travel parallel to it for a ways, hopin' to see something that will point us in the direction of Hendersonville. One elderly couple we pass on the road mentions Buncombe Turnpike, sayin' Hendersonville can be found near this byway, but when we ask how to find the Turnpike, they can't say.

My experiences durin' the war taught me well how close you feel with those who go through great hardship with you, and how quickly those bonds form. Mary and the girls and I are spendin' all our time together, facin' constant danger and sharin' in our difficulties, so we become terribly close. I love these girls with all my heart and see Mary as a second Ma. I begin to wonder if I'm gonna be able to leave them behind in North Carolina. One night by the fire, I share my thoughts. "Mary, what if you and the girls come on to Georgia with me. I can't think of a good reason for you to stay with your aunt over comin' with me."

"They are family, Mac."

117

"But so am I. Remember?" Her laugh lightens my heart.

The girls start pushin' on her, too, sayin' they want to stay with me, but Mary won't relent. She says she feels obliged to connect to the only family she has left.

We take to tellin' funny stories as we travel to keep our spirits up. I tell her about the time I jumped out of the barn loft, and my pants got hung on a nail, and I hung there until my Pa came in from the fields and found me, and how when Pa unhooked me, he dropped me straight away, saying, "Thon'll skelp sense intae ye." The girls are tickled by this one.

Then, Mary tells me about the first time Alex came a-courtin'. He picked her up in the same wagon we are usin' now, and when he helped her into the seat, the old mare lifted its tail and...she left the rest of the story to my imagination, but she says she had to change her dress, and poor Alex was mortified and almost didn't ask if he could come a-courtin' again.

"You mean you almost didn't marry Daddy?" Elizabeth's eyes widen like two little full moons.

"Oh, I do not believe anything could have stopped your father, once he set his mind on something, not even a wild horse." Mary's laughter rings bittersweet.

Mary lets me start an evenin' Bible time, where we sit close to the fire, and I read the Scripture to the girls and ask them questions like my Ma did with me. The girls are very smart and show a good grasp of Scripture. Every evenin', Ester begs me once again to choose a story of God's love for His children, which are her favorite stories. It isn't hard for me to find many such stories to read. I honestly believe I'm more encouraged by our lessons than they are. Reading those stories reminds me nightly of God's love, which the war almost made me forget.

As we move deeper into North Carolina, we see an increasin' number of Union soldiers, some in small roving bands and some whole units, which slows us down quite a bit, since we have to hide until they are well out of sight. No one wants to go back to ridin' through the night, so I scout before we move through an area, which slows us down even more.

This scoutin' expedition takes me through some beautiful country, reminiscent of my home's blue-gray mountains, stately trees, and spring blossoms coverin' rollin' green fields. My mind wanders to the farm. It's been so long since I've seen my sisters' faces—four endless, horrific years. I wonder what they'll look like when I return home. Elspeth, now old enough to marry—might be married, in fact—it's hard to imagine it. In my mind, Elspeth is still Ruth's age. Caitrin and Anice are a little older than the age Elspeth was when I left home, so they're young ladies, no longer little girls. Will I even recognize them? And my sweet Maisie, my little love. Will she remember me? I bet Ma has aged more than the four years I've been away, from worry and sickness of heart. Oh, how I long to see them all, to hold them in my arms. I haven't really felt homesick since I first hobbled up the steps of the Monroe house, but today, the ache in my chest feels like someone shot a musket ball clean through me.

Up ahead, I see a clearin', so I slow Blossom and move as quietly as we can through the trees. I see movement, but it doesn't look like soldiers marchin'. As we near the open space, I spot a wagon and a couple of horses passin' each other on what appears to be a road. I watch as folks drive livestock down the road toward the east and wagon loads of vegetables toward the west. Is this the Buncombe Turnpike? I observe from my hidin' place for a good while, but I don't see any soldiers from either side, so I risk comin' out onto the road.

Approachin' a fancy-dressed young couple with an infant ridin' east in their wagon, I wave in salute. "Excuse me, sir, ma'am, could you tell me what this road is called?"

"Certainly, sir. This is the Buncombe Turnpike that runs from Tennessee all the way into South Carolina."

"Does it go through Hendersonville?"

"Yes, it does. Is that where you are heading?"

"Yessir."

"Have a care, sir. I hear, just a few days ago, a corps of Union soldiers came through Hendersonville and occupied the town. The word from the town is the Yankees were brutal to the residents and caused a good deal of destruction. You may meet some of those men should you head that way."

"Have you run into any soldiers on your journey?"

"No, sir, not on this leg. Of course, hearing the news about Hendersonville's troubles, we bypassed that town, and we've seen no soldiers on the road today."

"Thank you kindly, sir."

"You are most welcome. Best wishes on your journey."

"Same to you, sir. Ma'am."

Elation at findin' the road runs headlong into disquiet at the news about the Union soldiers. Are they still in Hendersonville or have they moved on? I consider goin' on down the Turnpike into the town to see what I find there, but the thought of leavin' Mary and the girls alone, possibly overnight, with the chance of a corps of Yanks discoverin' 'em provokes me to go and fetch 'em first.

I turn Blossom and we race back through the forest. I don't notice the beauty of my surroundin's this time. All I sense is a warnin' in my spirit to hurry. I am still some distance away from our camp when I see a lot of movement around the site where I left the wagon and its precious cargo. I fight the urge to gallop into our camp guns a-blazin', choosin' instead to move quietly through the trees until I can see exactly what I'm facin'. When I'm still far enough away that I don't think I'll be heard, I jump off Blossom and tie her to a limb, then creep up to the camp.

Five men, Union soldiers or deserters by the looks of 'em. One of them pulls Ester from the wagon. Two more hold Ruth and Mary down on their knees, their fingers pressed against their throats. Little Elizabeth is still in the wagon, cryin' her eyes out and callin' for her Ma. A man on the other side of the wagon growls at her to shut up or he'll give her something to cry about, but Elizabeth keeps on wailin'.

The last man is pawin' through our things. "They got food!"

"Look for valuables," the man glowerin' over Elizabeth says. "Lady, you got any valuables in here?"

"Answer the man." The soldier holdin' her neck tightens his grip.

"We have nothing. Just food and a few clothes." My chest swells over how brave Mary is bein', and I make a quick vow that these men'll pay dearly for scarin' her and the girls so. Quietly, I slide Alex's pistol from my trousers and take aim.

"Hey, Joe, can I have my way with her when you're done?"

"Sure you can."

"The older one is likely unsoiled. I want her."

He will die first. I take aim and fire, and the scoundrel drops like a sack of flour. I shift to the one they call Joe and send a bullet through his eye, then seek the one who asked permission for Mary, but he's runnin'. My tree cover serves no purpose now, so I race out after the two runners, firin' as I chase. I fire twice at the closer of the two runners. The second shot gets him in the leg. I have to sprint a good ways to get close enough to fire at the second runner. My first shot hits his left shoulder. To make sure he don't keep runnin', I fire again and take him in his lower back. My pistol is empty now, but I race back to the camp to find the last man standin' over Mary, his knife pressin' against her throat.

"Put down you weapon, or I slit her throat."

I lift my hands above my head, pistol in hand. "Careful, stranger." I keep walkin' a steady pace closer to him. "You don't wanna hurt the pretty lady."

"Stop right there. Put it down." He grabs a handful of her hair and slides the knife closer to her exposed neck.

I drop the pistol but keep inchin' my way closer. Elizabeth cries out, "Mac!" I lower my finger to my lips and nod once to reassure her.

The man I got in the back calls to his companion, "Kill her!"

"Nah. I'm gonna take her and make him watch."

I keep sidlin' up, bit by bit. "You know, two of your friends are dead and two are badly wounded." I wonder if he realizes his predicament. "What're you gonna do now? If you cut her, I'm a-gonna kill ya, but if you drop your knife and run, I'll let you go, so think hard about what you're gonna do next."

"I ain't lettin' her go. She's the only thing keepin' me alive."

"Maybe, but I'm of a mind to let you go if no harm comes to her. So, you decide." Just a little closer. "What will it be?"

"Get on your face!" He makes the mistake of wavin' his knife toward me. I make a show of crouchin' down like I'm goin' to the ground, then I launch myself at him and bowl him over. We roll away from Mary and tumble down an embankment in a ball of flailin' arms and kickin' legs. Somewhere durin' the fall, he drops his knife. We come to a stop with him on top of me, and he starts pummelin' my face. While I pound on his ribs and back, I slide my feet up underneath me and use them to gain leverage. As he's rarin' back for a knockout blow, I flip him on his back and just like that, I'm sittin' on his chest, holdin' his arms flat on the ground beside his head.

Blood drips from my nose onto his face. He's mewlin' and squirmin' like a cow stuck in a briar. When I release one of his arms to wrap my hand around his throat, he reaches for my right eye and gouges at it with his thumb. I rear my head back out of his reach, then press down on his throat with both hands. He's scratchin and clawin' at my arms, but I don't care. I'm not wastin' anymore time fightin' the man. I throttle him until he's blue.

I pull myself back up the embankment, pickin' up his knife along the way, and find Mary clutchin' her girls to her chest, all of 'em weepin'. I limp slowly to the injured soldiers.

"Turn away," I call behind me. Mary covers the girls' eyes and lowers her head over theirs. Without a single thought of mercy, I bend down and cut the throat of the man who was gonna violate Mary. Then, I go to the man I shot in the leg.

"Who steals from a woman and young girls? What kind of men speak of takin' a mother in front of her children? What sort of animal would want to violate a child? You don't deserve to live."

"I never. That was them what said it. It was them!"

Disgust roils through me in a scaldin', bitter wave. This man doesn't deserve my mercy. But then again, I don't deserve God's mercy, do I? Still, if I let him live, he's like to send others to come after us, and I won't risk Mary and the girls. So, I cut his throat, wipe the blade on his trousers, and walk away. I feel nothin'.

I know Mary and the girls will be shaken after their experience, but we can't stay anywhere near this place. If we're discovered near dead Union soldiers, we'll be hanged. I go straightaway to get Blossom, then ride back to where Mary and the girls are still in a cluster. "Get in the wagon. We need to leave this place."

Mary pauses only a moment. "Come, girls." Her voice is quiet but isn't tremblin' like I thought it might. "Let's go, quickly now." She lifts Elizabeth into the wagon while Ester and Ruth clamber onto their places, then she steps to her seat, takes up Brutus' reins, and nods to me without makin' eye contact. Her face shows no expression, but in my heart, I'm afeared she now despises the sight of me.

I ride in front of the wagon, reloadin' Alex's pistol as I lead them through the trees toward the road. I want to share the good news with 'em that we're almost there, but I don't think I can bear it if Mary refuses to speak to me, so I ride along in heavy silence. The girls are uncharacteristically quiet, too. Even Elizabeth isn't makin' a peep.

The thought crosses my mind to pray. A deep shame bubbles in my stomach at the thought, like a thick shadow is cloakin' my words, but then I remember what my Ma taught me about the wayward son. "But when he was yet a great way off, his father saw him, and had compassion, and ran and fell on his neck, and kissed him." Do You, Lord? Do You have compassion on me, Your son? Or am I beyond all hope and beyond Your reach? Will You forgive me, Lord? Hot tears well up into my throat, but I swallow 'em down to keep 'em from reachin' my eyes. My chest aches from the knot of balled-up emotion throbbin' in counterpoint to my heartbeat. Oh, Heavenly Father, free me from this torment.

Lord, I don't want Mary to see me as someone dangerous, who she's afeared to be near her girls. Please, don't let her despise me, now that she's seen what I am. Don't let the girls be scairt of me. Don't let things change between us. I don't think I can stand it if they do.

My prayers fall upon an unnatural silence. It's as if even the wind and the birds know my guilt and have turned their faces from me. Has my shame so drowned my prayers that the Lord won't hear my pleas? Do I stand condemned before His throne? An intense feelin' I've never had before floods through me, an emptiness in my soul, like someone turned on the spigot and drained me and all that's left is a hollow shell of a man. Am I nothing now, Lord? Have I lost You, too?

I'm a little child alone in the woods, out of sight of his home and family, wanderin' in the darkness without hope of bein' found, callin' out to his Pa to come and find him, but his Pa doesn't answer. A desperate, afflicted feelin' grips my gut, and spit fills my mouth as I struggle to keep from retchin'. Then, it's too late. I leap from Blossom, scamper behind a tree, and vomit it all up—the shadow of shame, the knot of tears, the terror, the anguish, the hollow emptiness, the desperation, all come pourin' out in a gout of bile. And I hear a gentle whisper in the wind— *What you have done is not who you are.*

I swish some water around in my mouth from my canteen, spit it out, wipe the drops from my lips, and drag myself back to Blossom, who has remained stalwart, guarding the wagon.

"Are you ill?" I glance at Mary, whose concern is etched on her face. Relief falls like a cool shower on a July afternoon. Perhaps she doesn't hate me.

"I feel better."

She nods once and offers the slightest smile.

"We're not far from the road, and Hendersonville is only a short ways down the road from here." I'm glad I have some good news to share.

She closes her eyes, and I wonder if she's offerin' a prayer of gratitude. "We are almost there." Her sigh reminds me of the whisper in the wind.

"I think we can make it by nightfall." I pull myself onto Blossom. "Are you ready?"

"Yes."

I glance at the girls and notice they are all curled up in the wagon and appear to be sleepin'. "Hopefully, we won't have any more troubles."

"Yes." She pops the reins, and Brutus takes off. This time, I ride by her side, but we only speak when I have directions to give her.

It's late afternoon by the time we reach the road. Again, I watch for soldiers for several minutes before we venture out onto the Turnpike, but I'm hopin' the presence of other travelers, our civilian clothes, and three children will discourage any soldiers we see along the way from disturbin' us.

The mood seems to lighten as we near our destination, so I risk startin' a conversation. "Do you know where to find your aunt and cousin in Hendersonville?"

"I hope they live in the same home." She gives me a wry smile. "And I hope I remember how to get there."

"I need to tell you, someone I spoke to on the road comin' from Hendersonville said the Yankees were there and brought a lot of destruction with them."

Mary shuddered. "Oh, my poor aunt. I hope they didn't lose their home, too."

I don't tell her the part about the Yankee brutality toward the residents. Maybe she won't need to hear that part. "I hope you can still recognize the town."

"It has been a while."

We ride in silence again. I imagine she is considerin' what she might do if her aunt no longer has a place where she and the girls can stay.

The sun dips below the mountains surroundin' us, colorin' the treetops, the ridgeline, and the sky with a golden shimmer that fades to rose. Finally, in the distance, we see the flickerin' lights of the town. We move slowly, cautiously down the streets. It's strange—no one is out and about, even though it's a beautiful spring evening. I look to Mary for some sign of recognition or direction, but her head is on a swivel, her eyes wide in the semi-darkness. Burned out buildings line the main street. What I assume was once a courthouse stands in ruins. No taverns or eatin' establishments appear open.

"Who can we ask after my aunt?"

"I don't know." I point to a low, wooden building with bars on the windows. It looks for all the world like a jail, so I gesture toward it. "Maybe there's a sheriff?"

We pull in front of the building, and I jump down from Blossom and knock on the door, but no one answers. "Well, if it is a jail, no one's in there. Let's try knockin' on the first home we come to with candles lit inside."

We amble on down the street and come upon a fair size home with light in the windows. "Let's try here."

"I believe it may be best for me to be the one to knock on the door. They may feel threatened by you, given recent—um—events." Mary gathers her skirts and climbs down from the wagon, but I'm not about to let her knock on the door alone, so I stand behind her as she raps several times on the rough wooden door.

A scowlin' man holdin' a pistol up in plain sight cracks the door. "What do you want?" I guess it's because of the times that folk seem to think rudeness is acceptable. Mary isn't flustered.

"Good evening, sir. I am from out of town, here to visit my aunt, Mrs. Caroline Bennett. Could you please direct me to her home?" She gives the gruff codger a sweet smile.

"Bennett. I know of a Marcus Bennett."

"He is my cousin, Caroline's son. Do you know where I might find him?"

"He lives out a ways from town." The man gestures loosely toward the southwest.

"Hmm. I do not believe it would be wise for us to travel into the mountains in the darkness. Do you know of a hotel in town?"

"There was one." The man growls. "Them Yankees destroyed it."

"I understand they were here recently. Are they gone now?"

"They moved on a few days ago."

"Such a shame."

The man murmurs some obscenity under his breath, bids her goodnight, and closes the door in her face. Mary turns to me. "This may be more difficult than I thought."

"Well, we've been campin' out all along, so one more night ain't gonna do us harm."

"We can leave the girls sleeping in the wagon. They are so exhausted, I imagine they will sleep quite a long time. But we can't simply plop down to sleep in the middle of the main road in town."

"No'm. Seems to me the best thing to do is start headin' toward the southwest, where he said your cousin is livin'. That way, we're at least part way there."

The grimace on her face tells me she's as tired as her girls, but she hauls herself back on the wagon, and with an air of resignation,

126

picks up the reins. I hop onto Blossom and lead Brutus in the general direction indicated by the less-than-helpful man. Once we're outside town, we find a clump of trees, park the wagon, unhitch Brutus and tie him and Blossom up, then pile up some straw and leaves as best we can to make a pallet of sorts and lie down.

Before too long, her breathin' slows and deepens, and I'm left alone with my thoughts. I can't help but wonder at what's become of me. In four short years I've gone from a carefree boy who cries when his Pa slaughters a pig for winter to a cold, heartless killer who cuts a man's throat while he's pleadin' for his life. Who am I now? What am I? How can I face my Ma after what all I've done? Will I ever be able to find peace again? The terrified face of the Yankee thief rises up like mist before my eyes. No, I don't s'pose I will.

The strange, still whisper on the breeze speaks again. *Find peace in forgiveness.*

Forgiveness? I don't understand. The man certainly can't forgive me. I'm afeared God won't forgive me, 'cause the Good Book says, "For the wrath of God is revealed from heaven against all ungodliness and unrighteousness of men, who hold the truth in unrighteousness," and "God gave them over to a reprobate mind." Where do I turn for forgiveness, then? The breeze makes no reply.

CHAPTER ELEVEN

The next mornin' brings drizzlin' rain. Our little group huddles under the soggy curtains to eat a meager meal of smoked ham and leftover biscuits before we set out on a search for the Bennett farm. Our first stop, a small farmhouse near the road, reaps no more information. We move on to the next house, nestled in the side of a hill with a long, windin' drive leadin' up to it. These folk know the Bennetts and are able to direct us to the right path to take, not too far up from their farm goin' off to the left. We turn on the windin' path and make our way up the hill. In the distance, a stately home sits atop a ridge overlookin' the valley below.

"This is it." Mary's relief is palpable. The girls, who have been strangely quiet, begin to chatter with excitement. Mary moans. "Oh, I look a sight." She tries to smooth her hair, which hangs in wet strands across her brow, but it's futile.

"I don't s'pose it's gonna matter much to your aunt and cousin that you're wet and dirty from travelin' when I imagine they're worried sick if you're still alive. They woulda heard by now about Richmond fallin'."

"You are right, of course. I'm being silly." Still, she wrings rainwater from the girls' clothes and pats them down before she walks up the steps and knocks on the front door.

A tall, square-built man with shoulder-length sandy hair who appears to be a little younger than Mary answers the door. "May I help you?"

"Cousin Marcus. It's Mary. Mary Monroe."

His face lights with recognition. "Cousin Mary! What a wonderful surprise!"

Mary gestures to her girls. "These are my children, Ruth, Ester, and Elizabeth."

"Well met, young ladies."

Ruth curtsies and speaks for the girls. "Pleased to meet you, sir."

"And this is Aidan MacAlister. He is a young soldier who helped us escape Richmond when it was overrun."

Marcus' face darkens. "We heard the Confederates burned the city rather than have it fall into Union hands." He grasps my hand. "Thank you, sir, for helping my cousin and her children in their time of peril. Were you part of the occupying force?"

I realize Marcus believes I'm a Union soldier. Mary gives me a warnin' glance, so I hedge on my story. "Yessir, I entered Richmond that day."

"Well, now that Lee has surrendered and the war is over, those rebels can finally be put in their place. I owe you my thanks. Come in, come in all. Mother will be so relieved."

As he's talkin', all the blood drains from my face. This news is the first I've heard of Lee's surrender. A wave of nausea and dizziness washes over me. The war is over, and we've lost.

"How is Aunt Caroline?"

"I'm afraid the struggles brought on by this war have taken their toll on her. I will take you up to see her as soon as I announce you, and she has the chance to freshen up a bit." Marcus escorts us toward the large, formal sittin' room but stops in the doorway. "What am I thinking? You will want to freshen up, too, no doubt, after your long journey. How thoughtless of me. Mary, you and the girls come with me straightaway so you can change into some fresh clothes."

"I'm afraid all our clothes are in the wagon and are quite soaked from the rain, so these will have to do. But we would like to wash up if we could."

"Yes, of course. Right this way." Mary and the girls follow him down a long, narrow hallway toward the back of the house. He returns a few moments later. "If you'll follow me, you can clean yourself up in my bedchamber." He eyes me up and down. "It will be a tad large for you, but I might have something you can wear if you'd like."

"Thank you kindly, sir, but no, I wouldn't want to put you out."

"It's no trouble. No trouble at all."

I don't feel much like makin' myself beholden to this stranger who, if he knew who I was, would throw me out of his home, so I shake my head. "My clothes will dry well enough. All the same, thank you."

"Very well, right this way." We climb a steep staircase and walk to a large room at the end of the hall. "Were you wounded in the war?"

He's noticed my limp. "Yessir."

"Ah. What battle, may I ask?"

"At the Wilderness, sir."

"Terrible business." He hands me a small towel, gestures toward a pitcher and basin, bows slightly, then leaves me to my ablutions.

My hands shake as I pour water into the bowl. The war is over. My mind won't seem to accept it. I splash water on my face, but it doesn't help the strange sensation, like if I touch the basin my fingers'll go right through it or like I'm walkin' both inside and outside of myself at the same time. I'm a spectre, a shadow. It's truly over.

Which means, when I killed those thieves, they weren't my enemies.

The thought hits me like a fist in my stomach. I remind myself they threatened Mary and the girls, but the truth is, they weren't Yankees tryin' to take my land anymore, they were just men stealin' our food. Pa's reasonin' for killin' no longer applied to them. And I killed 'em anyway, which makes me a murderer, pure and simple. If I ever had any hope of receivin' God's forgiveness, it's flown from me now. A black sickness settles over my heart, an anchor chain pullin' me down into the depths where I'm to suffocate and die.

I go through the motions of washin' my face, neck, arms, and hands, stilted in my movements. I refuse to look at myself in the round mirror hangin' over the dressin' table. Otherwise, I might lose the tenuous control I do have. Time moves in rushes and stops. I find I have to keep lookin' at my hands to see if I'm actually here, or if I've transported to the world of the dead, to my own personal hell.

A flicker of realization flashes before me—the war bein' over is actually a good thing. No more killin'. No more waste. That much is true, but who can say what the consequences of the rebellion will be on the Confederate states? The losers will certainly suffer retribution in some way. How will the Union mete out punishment on us?

I have no sense of how long I've been standin' in Marcus' room, but I know I can't stay hidden in here forever, so I shuffle out the door and down the stairs to the sittin' room, where I find Mary and Marcus seated on the divan, talkin' quietly. The girls are playin' some game of cards together in the corner. As I slide into a nearby chair, I hear Marcus say, "Yes, and thank the heavens that Lincoln is dead. His plan to forgive the South would've emboldened them further, and there would be no end to this war."

Abraham Lincoln is dead?

"Marcus, you cannot mean it. The man left behind a wife and children. No matter whether you appreciate his politics or not, you shouldn't wish a man ill."

"All I'm saying is Andrew Johnson has the right idea. He will hold the Confederacy accountable for their actions, which is by rights. They have cost us all dearly. You, of all people, should agree with me. You lost everything."

"My husband willingly fought and died for Virginia. Do not disparage his name or his purpose." The edge in Mary's voice makes the hair on my neck stand up. If Marcus upsets her, cousin or not, I will stop him, whatever it takes.

"I understand Barclay felt obligated to fight for his state, but you must admit he was misguided. If he had stayed out of it, you would still have your husband, your children would still have their father, and you would possibly still have your home. He was a fool to fight for the rebels."

Suddenly, Ruth jumps up, throws her cards down, and runs from the room. Ester and Elizabeth stare after her, their mouths agape. Mary is off like a shot, boltin' after Ruth. I find myself standin' over Marcus, unsure how I got there, with my hands pressin' on his shoulders. "You arrogant, insensitive..."

"Stand down, sir."

"How dare you speak before them in such a way? Disparagin' Mary's husband and his brave sacrifice in front of her children."

Marcus pushes my hands off his shoulders and stands. Towerin' over me, he glares down his nose and pokes my chest. "I will remind you, sir, you are a guest in my home."

"And I remind you, Mary is your kin. You speak to me any way you want, but you won't speak to her in that manner again, or you will answer to me. Am I clear?"

"Get out!' Marcus snarls, lifts me up by the front of my shirt, and shoves me to the front door.

"Mac!" Ester cries out as Marcus flings open the door and pushes me onto the porch. I trip, tumble down the steps, and sprawl on the dirt. The door slams behind me.

What do I do now? I don't want to leave Mary and the girls with such a man, defenseless against his hateful rants and who knows what else he may be capable of doin' to them. But he and Caroline are her only kin. What if she won't come with me? It's clear I'm not welcome here. Who knows what Marcus will do if he learns I'm a Confederate soldier—turn me in? Have me hanged?

I stand and brush the mud from my clothes, leavin' streaks of red clay on my white shirt. Havin' nowhere else to go, I wander over to Blossom. She raises her head from munchin' on the wet grass and nuzzles me, so I rub down her coat and murmur to her about Marcus and his ilk.

Mary flings open the front door, and spottin' me with Blossom, she bounds down the steps and runs to my side. "Whatever did you do?" She wraps her arms around my neck.

"I told it plain."

"Marcus is in a tizzy. He is saying you cannot remain at his house, not one moment longer."

I pull Mary back and hold her at arms' length. "Come with me, Mary. Now. You have a home with my family in Georgia. You don't have to stay here. Please."

"Mac, I..."

"Think about your girls. Do you want them growin' up around someone who is going to speak critically about their father? Who shoves s stranger down his front steps?"

"Aunt Caroline is in a bad way. I don't know how much longer she will live, and if I stay, I can help ease her last few weeks or months before she passes."

"While Marcus poisons your girls against their own father."

"I know Marcus to be an obstinate, opinionated man, but he won't harm my girls."

"How can you say that? He just did!"

"I can handle Marcus."

"And when he decides to kick you out, too?"

"He would never. Aunt Caroline would never allow it."

"I can't leave you and the girls here, knowin' you're at his whim and mercy."

"Do you want me to speak with Aunt Caroline and see if she will speak to Marcus on your behalf? It is her house."

"But Marcus is clearly the one in charge."

Mary's eyes are like round pools, wide and quiverin' with grief. "Will you leave then?"

"Marcus is not leavin' me much of a choice, is he?"

"The girls will be devastated."

I pick up Mary's hands. "You know I don't want to leave you, not like this. Please reconsider comin' with me to Georgia."

She shakes her head. "My aunt needs me, and even if Marcus isn't especially pleasant or kind, he is my family."

I turn my head away. "I reminded him of that fact, right before he shoved me out his front door." I pat Blossom on the back. "Well, ol' girl, I guess it's goodbye."

"Mac, she was a gift to you."

"She was loaned to me, to carry me back to the front. I can't pay you for her—I have no money."

"Well, she is a gift now."

"I can't accept such a gift."

Tears are now streamin' down her cheeks. "Wait here." She scurries to the wagon and rummages through our remainin' supplies. When she returns, she has a sack filled with food, the change of clothes I brought from Alex's dresser, the embossed Bible, and Alex's pistol. "Here, take these with you."

"Mary, I'm not gonna take Alex's pistol. It's one of the last things you have of his. And his Bible. You need that to keep up our readin's with the girls. And you'll need food more than I do. I can always hunt along the way."

"If you insist on being difficult, these things are loans. When you are able, when everything gets back to some semblance of normal, you come back and find us. That way, I can be sure we will see you again. And when we do, you can return them to me."

Despite my anguish, I can't help but chuckle. "The food, too?"

She coughs out a laugh. "Mmm, you can repay me for the food when the time comes. But return Alex's pistol, the Bible, and Blossom."

"And Alex's clothes."

"Well and good, his clothes, too."

"I promise. Now, you make me a promise."

"If I am able."

I take her hands again. "Promise me you won't tell Marcus or Caroline about Alex's gold."

"My goodness, whatever for?"

"I don't trust Marcus not to take it from you and use it for his own ends."

"That's quite a larger promise than I asked of you."

"Do you trust me?"

"I do, but..."

"Then do this one thing for me. Please. Hide the strong box. Lie about what's in it, if you must. But don't tell him you have it."

"How, then, can I use the gold when needs require it?"

"Get a coin while he is away and take it to town to exchange for whatever you need. Or take it to the local banker and exchange it for Union money you can use to buy what you need."

"I would feel like I am deceiving my family, and since they are offering me a place to stay, it feels wrong."

"Mary." I squeeze her hands. "You are a kind and trustin' person. You've never had to deal with folk like Marcus because Alex always took care of you. I know in my spirit Marcus cannot be trusted."

She pulls her hands away, and an uneasy silence falls between us. Mary toes the ground and wrings her hands. The silence lengthens. Her steady stream of tears continues unabated. I can't seem to find my words.

Finally, she looks up and sighs. "I will do as you say."

"Promise me?"

"I promise."

Such a profound relief washes over me, I'm faint from it. My tears match her own. "Thank you."

"I do not want to see you go." Her voice quavers. "My girls are going to be so sad."

The ache in my chest intensifies to a sharp pain as if someone is plungin' a knife deep inside me. The girls are losin' another person. How much more can they take? My throat works like a frog's until I'm able to croak out a question. "May I say goodbye to them?"

"Of course. I will bring them out to see you off." Her breath hitches on her last word. She walks to the house all hunched over, lookin' for all the world as if she's carryin' a two-ton weight on her shoulders. When she returns, she has her three girls in tow. All four are cryin.'

Why don't I swallow my pride, apologize to Marcus, and beg him to let me stay? It would be worth it, for their sakes. I can hold my tongue and get along with the man, surely. Doesn't the Good Book tell me to love my enemies?

Elizabeth breaks free from her mother's grasp and runs into my arms. "Mac, don't leave us."

My heart melts. I glance at Mary. "I'll beg Marcus for forgiveness and ask if I may yet stay."

But Mary shakes her head. "He is adamant. Given your response to his comments about Alex, he suspicions you are also a Confederate soldier, and he is...well, ranting about having let a rebel set foot in his home. He will not accept your apology, nor will he allow you to stay, unless to turn you in to the local authorities. I am afraid there is nothing we can do."

I run my hand down Elizabeth's golden hair. "Sweet child, I wish I could stay. But you heard your mother. I can't."

Ester wraps her arms around my legs. "Don't leave us."

Ruth remains next to her mother, her arms across her chest like she is keepin' her heart from fallin' out. Unlike her sisters, her voice is quiet. "Don't go, Mac. I don't like it here."

I start to say I don't like it one bit, either, but I catch Mary's eye, and she frowns and shakes her head. "I'm sure everything is gonna be well with you. You're with your family, now."

"You're our family!" Ester's distress is palpable.

Elizabeth echoes her sister. "Mother said you are our brother."

"Mr. Marcus and Mrs. Caroline are blood family."

"But you taught us the Bible says whoever loves God is family."

I can't argue Ester's point. "We'll always be family, too." I'm at a loss for how to help them understand what I myself can't explain, so I change my approach. "Listen, girls. I made a promise to your Ma. I told her, one day, I will come back to you. You see, your Ma is lettin' me keep Blossom for a spell, and your Bible, and your Pa's pistol. So, I have to come back so I can return what I borrowed to your Ma."

This seems to brighten the younger one's faces a bit, but Ruth isn't moved. "How long?" She squeezes her arms tighter around her chest.

"I—I don't know exactly. But I always keep my promises."

"Mac must check on his family, a long way away in Georgia. After that, if everything is well with them, maybe he can come back to us."

"We're his family!" Ester's death grip on my legs makes it impossible for me to move.

Mary comes to my side and gently tries to pry Elizabeth from my arms. "Tell Mac goodbye and wish him well on his journey."

"No." I've never seen Elizabeth be anything but sweet and lovin', so her petulant outburst is a surprise.

Ruth, ever puttin' on maturity beyond her years, reaches down to help Ester. "Come, Ester. Mac must go now."

"But I don't want him to go."

"I know. None of us want him to go, but we must say goodbye anyway."

"Goodbye, Mac. Don't forget us."

"Ester, I could never forget you. Ever."

"And you'll remember your promise?" Elizabeth looks up from her clingin' hug.

"I will fulfill my promise." I place my hand on my heart. "I promise before God."

Elizabeth's eyes grow wide. "He promised God, Mother."

"He did indeed." Mary smiles at me, but the sadness on her face seems to age her in a way the smile can't touch. She collects Elizabeth in her arms, while Ruth holds Ester's hand, and they stand in a cluster like they are bracin' against a storm. My little family. Please, dear Heavenly Father, keep them safe and let me see them again one day.

I turn toward Blossom, packin' Mary's precious gifts into the saddlebag. Behind me, I hear a chokin' gasp, and I turn in time to see Ruth racin' toward me. I envelope her in my arms.

"I love you."

"And I you. I'll miss you so much."

She lowers her head and backs away. "You best keep your promise."

"I will." With one final glance toward Mary, whose tears are flowin' again, and a wave to Elizabeth and Ester, I grab Blossom's saddle and hoist myself up. I try to make my way down the long hill without lookin' back, but I can't manage it. At the last curve, I look back, and my heart shatters. Mary is on her knees, and the girls are draped over her like all their spirit has been sucked right out of them. I can hear their cries.

The sounds fade as I round the curve, but the sick feelin' in my gut remains. What have I done?

CHAPTER TWELVE

Blossom and I make our way back to the Turnpike and turn west toward Asheville, keepin' with the farmers and artisans takin' their goods to market and hopin' I blend in with them. To say my heart is heavy wouldn't come close to describin' it. Maybe for the first time in my life, I'm completely alone. I'm also lost. I hope someone in Asheville can point me in the direction I need to go to get home.

Home. The thought of home is the only thing keepin' me movin' forward. Otherwise, I might lie down and never get up.

I want to make haste, but the one thing I do know is home is far away, which means I need to spare Blossom and let her rest and eat frequently. The delays gnaw at my gut. It takes two full days to get to Asheville, longer than I hoped. The food Mary packed for me isn't gonna last more than a couple more days, but there's nothin' for it. Although there are shops a-plenty in Asheville and farmers along the road, I have no money with which to buy what I need, so I'll have to rely on huntin' to survive, once I get into the mountains.

Like we found it in Hendersonville, folk in Asheville are reticent to speak to strangers. They're holed up in their homes for the most part, and the ones out and about refuse to meet my eye. I'm able to get some directions from a shopkeeper to a byway that crosses the Turnpike and goes southwest all the way to Murphy, North Carolina, but no one can tell me more. That'll have to do. At least I've heard of Murphy, and it isn't terribly far north of our mountain. I let Blossom rest up outside of town, then the next mornin', we set off down the road I hope takes me toward my home and family.

It's slow goin' through the mountains, as I knew it would be. My savin' grace is the warm weather. If I were fightin' against the winter cold, the rough terrain, and hunger all at the same time, I might not make it. But as it is, circumstances are in my favor. I'm able to catch game or fish here and there, bein' that it's warm, and there are even some berries and such I can pick along the way. I guess I'm lucky—as long as I don't run up on any rovin' bands of Yankee soldiers. The war might be over, but the soldiers 'round these parts sure ain't actin' like it.

The road runs through a few towns—Waynesville, Webster, Watauga Gap—which I have to skirt around, not wantin' to be spotted in case any soldiers remain there, which slows us down. My wound hinders our progress, too. I get to achin' something fierce and have to stop and rest more than I want. And times when I could walk Blossom to give her a rest instead of stoppin', I can't bear it for long. If anything, the pain keeps gettin' worse. I can only hope I'm not doin' myself a permanent injury.

The weather favors me, but my own memories and thoughts turn against me, fillin' my heart with shame and anguish and bitterness. Marcus becomes a primary focus for my rage. I imagine him doin' all sorts of unspeakable things to Mary and the girls, fuelin' my certainty that I never shoulda left 'em there.

As time passes and my loneliness intensifies, my anger spreads like the fires in Richmond to include everyone from my Pa to General Lee himself. Josiah, the only friend from the war I have left, has forgotten all about me, and I'm certain Mary is relieved I'm gone, enjoyin' a peaceful and easy life with her aunt and cousin. The girls have forgotten me just like Josiah has. Even my sisters have been gettin' on with their lives all the while I've been away. Who knows what I'm gonna find when and if I do make it home? What if Elspeth is gone away, married to some man I've never met? What if Caitrin and Anice don't want to have anything to do with me, bein' older and more interested in other things besides playin' with their brother? What if Maisie doesn't remember me at all?

And what of Ma? Will she ever forgive me, once she finds out what I've done? I can't lie to her—she knows it immediately when I do and can usually guess the nature of the lie. It's like she and the Good Lord conspire together against me to bring my worst actions to light. No, she won't forgive me. She can't. And it'll break her heart.

Speakin' of the Good Lord, I ain't heard nary a whisper on the wind since I left Mary and the girls behind. He's abandoned me, too, like everyone else. Maybe Mary and the girls are the only reason He has been talkin' to me. That's well and good, as far as I'm concerned. Of all

140

those who've betrayed me, His is the worst of all. He didn't protect Pa, who believed and trusted that God was on our side in this war, and then He didn't help the Confederacy win the war, either. He didn't save Will. He didn't save Walter Wright. How many others died because He withheld His hand? Yet, I'm still here. Why? Why spare me, someone possessed of evil, a murderer, the worst of sinners? The wind remains silent. Savin' me from what I deserve may be His biggest betrayal of all. Now, I'm left to live with my disgrace, abandoned and utterly alone.

I vow to leave Mary's Bible tucked away in my saddlebag. I'm bein' plum foolish to think not readin' the Good Book is gonna punish God somehow. If anything, it punishes me—and maybe that's the point. If He won't see fit to do to me what I deserve, I'll do it to myself.

While the flames of my rage grow ever higher, the heat inside my body grows as well, as if my anger has set a fire within me. The ache in my back has spread everywhere, even behind my eyes. My head pounds with the beat of my heart, and my breath struggles to reach past my throat. I find myself slumpin' forward in Blossom's saddle, and only the startle from almost fallin' off her rouses me.

Dark thoughts come upon me, especially at night, thoughts of usin' one of the shots left in Alex's pistol to end my own sufferin'. Thoughts of not eatin' and lettin' myself wither away with no one the wiser—another casualty of war. Thoughts of huntin' for Yankees instead of game, and once I stir 'em up, lettin' 'em kill me. Thoughts of findin' a black bear in the woods and wrestlin' it until it bleeds me dry. But ever' mornin' I get up and plod on. Why, I can't figure.

I'm crossin' the Little Tennessee River when I see up ahead an entire company of Union cavalry comin' toward me out of Franklin. I duck off the road quick-like and down into some woods beside the river to wait out their passin', but I decide then and there, goin' through Franklin and Murphy is too big a risk. So, I leave the road for good and make my way through the mountains, tryin' my best to keep pointed toward home.

I keep count of the days with scratch marks on the leather strap of the saddlebag. The day I figured I'd be comin' near my home, I'm still wanderin' in the mountain wilderness, so I figure I'm lost sure as the world and may never find my way out of these mountains. All I can do is keep goin', though.

The voices in my head keep gettin' louder until my head is a wasp's nest, paper-thin and heavy with buzzin' and stingin'. Makin' it worse, I'm havin' a hard time catchin' game. I can't recall when I ate last. I can't remember when I've rested Blossom or if we've been walkin' too long.

It's strange what goes through a feller's head when there ain't nothin' but silence to keep him company. Voices I don't recognize are tellin' me to die and be done with it or thankin' me for all the horrible things I've done. Is that the darkness within me talkin'? Pa's voice is yellin' at me in Gaelic words I don't know or can't recall.

Strange. I can feel Ma's switch against my legs while she quotes from the Good Book: "My son, despise not thou the chastening of the Lord, nor faint when thou art rebuked of him; for whom the Lord loveth, He chasteneth, and scourgeth every son whom he receiveth. If ye endure chastening, God dealeth with you as with sons; for what son is he whom the father chasteneth not?" Is it Ma's switch, or are the shootin' pains up and down my leg from my wound—or something else?

My head swims. My eyes are bleary. The trees start to look like they're dancin' around me. I can hear them laughin' at my plight. Fiddle music echoes in my head, the same song over and over until I scream for it to stop. Did I scream out loud?

I lean over Blossom and wrap my arms around her neck. "I'm not gonna make it, girl. You go on home, now, when I die. Find Mary. Go back home." I stay there, my head restin' on her mane. After all, it doesn't matter if I lead her. For all I know, I'm goin' round in circles.

I mighta slept for a while, but I can't say for sure. When I sit up again, my whole body feels numb and tingly-like, and my throat is closed up tighter than the lid on Ma's jars of pickles.

When I try to speak to Blossom, all that comes out is a grindin' croak. "Where are we, girl?" She is ploddin' her way up the side of a grassy hill, which makes me wonder if we've stumbled on a farm, since the hill is cleared. But when she reaches the top of the hill and I peer down into the valley, I see a river and a town situated on its banks. What river, though?

I decide to risk goin' down the hill into the town. If I get arrested, they might take me to a doctor. I might even sleep. I keep Blossom on a tight rein as we make our way down the hill, but as we clomp down the dirt streets toward the river, recognition dawns on me like the risin' of the sun after a night of storms.

I've been here before! This is Murphy, which means this river is the one our little stream flows to from our mountain. It flows right past my Granda's church. Pa and I have taken a boat upriver to Murphy many times. All I have to do is follow its banks, and I'll find home. My excitement pushes back the fuzzy feelin' in my head.

"Home, girl." I pat Blossom's neck and cough a deep, raspin' bark, followed by a wheeze when I try to breathe in. "We're almost home." I know it'll take longer to walk it than it does to paddle it, but there's nothin' for it—I don't have a boat or money to buy one, and I wouldn't leave Blossom anyway. So, when we reach the river, we both take a deep drink, then we turn south and follow its windin' path until the sky is streaked with golden orange.

I want to push through the night to get home, but Blossom is well lathered and hangin' her head, which I know means it's time to stop. "We'll have one more sleep on the trail, girl. Just one more. Then we'll be home."

I wipe Blossom down as best I can, then curl up beneath a tree in a bed of pine straw. The sounds of the rushin' waters soothe me, and I have the best night's sleep I've had since my last night stayin' in Mary's home.

The mornin' sky dawns rosy red, which means rain's a-comin', so I hurry and saddle Blossom, take her to the river to drink her fill, wash my hair, face, and arms in the river so my Ma won't switch me for not washin', pull myself onto Blossom's back, and head down the river as fast as we can safely go. Sometimes, I let Blossom step into the cool water to walk, thinkin' that might refresh her in the summer heat. She seems to like it.

The day wanes, storm clouds gather, and I begin to wonder if I made a promise to Blossom that I can't keep, for I don't see any little farmhouses dottin' the hills in the distance or any other signs of life.

Did my childish mind not realize how long the trip took? Did we take a wrong turn? I know I don't need to spend another night out in the pourin' rain, so I apologize to Blossom and push on, drivin' her and myself beyond our limits. Then, the clouds open up, and it's hard to see where we are or where we're a-goin'. Lightnin' flashes above us and thunder rumbles quick on its heels. The lightnin' is close.

I look up into the heavens. "Lord, You'll not bring me this close to home only to thwart me reachin' it, will Ya? Haven't I had enough sorrow and troubles? Can't You let this one thing go right?"

Blossom paces beneath me, her wide eyes rollin' up to scan the clouds. She shakes her head and spews rainwater in my face.

"I know how you feel, girl." Still, I click my tongue and push her forward. "Please, Lord, just a little help." The wind drives the rain in our faces. I'm drenched and shiverin', even though it's not cold. I bend down again over Blossom's neck to let her body warm me and to try to keep the rain from my eyes, but it's futile.

"Look, girl." Up ahead, at a bend in the river, I can barely make out a dark shape. "Is that a house?" The building appears misshapen in the heavy rain, almost like it's lopsided. As we approach, my heart freezes within me. I recognize this area. This is where Granda's church is supposed to be, but I see no steeple, no cross, and no whitewashed boards linin' the walls. This hulk is blackened and smushed, like a giant stepped in the center of it. Yet, I know I'm right about the place.

I turn Blossom away from the river and trudge across the muddy ground to the burned-out buildin'. "Yankees have been here."

My own croakin' whisper sounds strangely disconnected to me, like it's the voice of a spectre from the graveyard carried on the wind. I hop down and pick my way through the rubble, kickin' at pieces of timber and pawin' through ash to see if I can find anything I recognize. With some relief, I recognize I haven't seen any human remains. So, the Yanks burned the church when no one was in it. At least that much is a relief, but my heart breaks for Granda, who built this church with his own hands. Now, nothin' is left of his labor but charred wreckage and scorched earth.

"What kind of folk burn a church?" Blossom has no reply. Suddenly, the significance of what I've found dawns on me in brilliant, terrifying clarity. "Yankees have been here." Sayin' it aloud again makes it real. "Ma." The word is only a breath snatched away by the wind and rain, as panic claws up my throat. I hobble back to Blossom and swing one leg over her, kickin' her before I'm secure in the saddle, urgin' her to hurry, hurry. I've got to get to my Ma and my sisters.

At least now I know where I'm a-goin'. We follow the river to where our stream joins in, then start up along the stream. I push Blossom to gallop, but she's slippin' and slidin' on the loose, wet ground, muddy beneath her hooves as she struggles to pick her way up the hill in the drivin' rain. I'm like a swollen stream beatin' against a beaver dam, strainin' to explode past the obstacle to rush ahead down my path, but nothin' I do can make Blossom go faster.

My mind floods with question after question. What if the Yankees found our farm? What if they burned our house like they burned Granda's church? Where would Ma take the girls if the house is gone? What if I can't find 'em? I'd seen plenty enough what Blue Bellies are capable of doin' to women and young girls. What if they hurt Ma or Elspeth or the twins—or sweet, innocent Maisie. I can't bear the thought.

I urge Blossom on. We're so close now. Just two more turns 'round the hill and...my heart plummets to my stomach.

There it is. A stone chimney standin' like a silent sentinel over the remnants of our house. Nothin' else is left. Nausea grips me as I leap from Blossom and run to the debris, heedless of the searin' pain in my back. My frantic, scramblin' search uncovers no bones, which is a relief of sorts, but now I don't know what to do or where to look for my family. The barn. It still stands, although the barn door is off its hinges and hangin' open with frayed rope danglin' from the header. I find the barn barren, emptied of all the feed and grains, all our livestock gone, and our farm tools and implements missin'.

I have to pull myself together so I can think. I sit on the barren dirt floor of the barn, my head in my hands, tryin' to breathe through the watery tightness in my chest and the dread cloggin' my throat, but I can't make my mind stop racin' like a bunny escapin' a fox. Blossom wanders into the barn and nuzzles my neck. "Where are they, girl? Where would they go?"

145

Somehow, the comfortin' touch of her velvet nose calms me a bit, and I'm able to come up with three places to look for 'em—in Morganton, the closest town, where we get our supplies and do our business—at Granda's house—and at Mr. Johnson's shack at the base of the hill.

Mr. Johnson is a freedman who showed up at our door one winter's night a few years ago, freezin', starving to death, and beggin' for food. He offered to work for food, but Ma would have none of it. Mr. Johnson shared our supper that night and for many nights after, while durin' the day, he and Pa worked together to build him a one-room shack on our land. They built it by a feeder stream, so Mr. Johnson would have plentiful water for himself and his crops.

Ma and Pa also gifted him that acre of land and some seed to get him started that spring. Since then, Mr. Johnson, a kindly man, had offered to help Pa and me on occasion, as we helped him when it came harvest time. He is my first stop, since I'll be goin' by his shack on the way into town. I pray he knows where to find Ma and the girls.

The rain has let up as I make my way down the hill. I guess Mr. Johnson sees me comin' 'cause he comes out on his porch to meet me. His face is creased with worry, his thin shoulders stooped, and I'm afeared he has bad news to share. To lighten his burden I say, "I already saw my home." I swing down off Blossom, limp to his step, and take his hand in greetin'.

He studies the ground and shakes his head. "Union soldiers," is all he says.

"I figured."

"Ye back from the war?"

"Yessir, just got back."

"Sorrowful."

"Yessir."

He looks up, his eyes pained. "Yer Ma."

"Where'd she go?"

"I's a-knowin' but I's not wantin' to tell ye."

"Why?"

146

"Com'on, son." He shakes his head again, then wanders behind his shack to climb back up our mountain a ways. I follow behind him, my horror growin' as we go, 'cause I think I know where he's headin'.

"No..." The groan escapes my lips before I have a clear thought behind it.

Mr. Johnson walks on in stony silence, a form of reverence I s'pose, because Mr. Johnson truly cares for my Ma.

We approach the little graveyard on the hillside where Pa and Ma buried their three children who died when they were still little. Fingers of ice crackle up through my insides, as if I might shatter like a skim of ice on a pond. Five new graves. Five. All five.

Wet grass smashes into my face. Hands on my back and shoulder. My arms suck down into thick mud. Images flash in my mind. Gettysburg. Trenches. Bodies. Hot burnin' in my throat from my own screamin', but I can't hear it. A metallic taste fills my mouth, then watery bile pours out of my nose and mouth. My guts are gonna come out. All five. One question rises in me like a copperhead liftin' its head from the water.

"How?" I can smell my bitterness.

"Nawsir." He shakes his head vigorously.

"I wanna know."

"Nawsir, you ain't hearin' the likes of this from me."

"Who else, then?" I cough and spit, but when I try to pull myself to my knees, dizziness makes the earth turn upside down, and I'm back on my face, this time in my own vomit.

"Better ye n'er did hear it. Keep your memory of 'em as ye left 'em."

"At least tell me how you know?"

Mr. Johnson groans. "The soldiers come. They found my shack first and believed I's a slave. I told 'em, nawsir, nobody on this here mountain keeps slaves, I's a freed man, but they didn't believe me."

"So, they wanted to punish Ma for having a slave."

"Mostly they wanted to hurt any folk from hereabouts and wanted me to watch 'em. I believe they thought I'd like it, but when I's yellin' for 'em to stop, stop, they put one of them rifles to my head and make me go down on my knee. And watch."

"What did they do, Mr. Johnson?"

He shakes his head again.

"Please, sir. I have to know. I don't know why, I just know I have to. Otherwise, what I'll imagine will torment me."

"Son, your imaginin's ain't worse." He looks down on me, lying' in a puddle of vomit in the mud, and tears well up in his eyes. "Awright, then." He closes his eyes and swallows hard. "Oh, Lawd, forgive me for what I's 'bout to do. He says he's gotta know, Lawd. I believe 'tis wrong to say, but Ye say be truthful, Lawd. So, I's askin' Yer forgiveness." He stands in silence, as if he's waitin' for permission from the Lord to speak.

I struggle to my knees. "Mr. Johnson?"

He clears his throat. "First, they tied up yer Ma and stands her o'er yonder." He points toward the barn. "She's a-cryin' and beggin 'em to do whate're they must to her but leave her daughters be. She's a-callin' on the name of the Lawd and pleadin' the blood a-Jesus o'er 'em. But it don't matter. Them Yankees took the girls, one by one, right there in front of yer Ma. And they made me watch, too."

"Took 'em?"

He raises his brows and gives me a meaningful glance, then his face crumples in grief, and he closes his eyes again.

"You mean they...my sisters? Elspeth? Caitrin? Anice?"

Mr. Johnson clutches his chest, rocks, and moans but won't confirm what I already know in my soul is true.

"Even Maisie?"

Nothin'. If my Maisie had been spared, I know Mr. Johnson would want to tell me so.

"But not Ma?"

"Nawsir. Yer Ma..."

"What did they do?"

"After they... after what they done, they take a rope and they...hang her in the barn door, right there in front of them babes." Now that he's gotten the worst of it over, he rushes through the rest of the story. "Then they shoot the girls, one by one, in the head."

I thought I knew misery when I held Pa as he died, when I watched life leave Will's eyes, and when I left Mary and her girls behind. I imagined I finally understood what Jesus meant when He said, "My soul is exceedingly sorrowful even unto death." I thought I had nothing left in my soul already, but I was wrong. The emptiness, the searin' black agony, doesn't compare with anything I've ever felt before. It's as if those Yankee soldiers have sawed off my four limbs and ended the torture by cuttin' out my heart. I'm no longer a person—I'm a dry husk. I'm cold ashes. I'm a dead, hollowed-out tree, left to rot from the inside-out, turnin' to stone. Soundless tears stream down my face. I can't imagine a reason for me to ever move again.

"I buried 'em proper." Mr. Johnson sounds almost apologetic, like my tears are an accusation. "I said some words, too. Miss Mary was a fine Christian woman. A mighty fine woman."

I want to thank the man, but I'm afeared if I open my mouth, something in me is gonna burst open like an explodin' mortar, so I stay as stiff and rigid as a corpse. Maisie's face tries to float up before my eyes, but I stuff it down into a gapin' hole like it's a poisonous snake and clamp a stone seal over it.

I'm vaguely aware that Mr. Johnson is shufflin' back down the hill toward his shack, leavin' me on my knees, alone with the graves and the ghosts.

PART TWO

That These Dead Shall Not Have Died in Vain

CHAPTER THIRTEEN

The sun lowers behind the mountain, and the sky dims to charcoal with a crimson glow along the ridgeline. Draggin' myself to my feet saps what's left of my strength, so my walk back to the barn is slow and labored with several stops to catch my breath. My mind is as still as an undisturbed lake. I can't let myself think. I can't face what's happened—I won't.

I walk past the frayed rope hangin' from the doorpost, now knowin' its use, but I won't see it. I can't bear it. Blossom waits patiently for me in the barn. I take her bridle and lead her into what used to be a stall for our now-stolen horses. Scrapin' together some remnants of hay and straw around the barn floor, I drop what I can find at her feet, and she munches gratefully. Then, I curl up in the corner and beg God for sleep to take me.

I startle awake in the deep darkness to realize my own screams have roused me. Blossom sniffs at my ear, but I brush her away and renew my desperate plea for sleep, my only escape. This time, sleep eludes me, and my barriers begin to crumble. I gather myself around my chest like a caterpillar in a cocoon, tryin' to hold everything in—and failin'.

Blossom watches as I tremble and shake with wrenchin' sobs. My anguished weepin', once it starts, refuses to let me go. I pound the dirt, first with my fists, then with my head, but I can't stop the wailin'. Then, I'm rollin' around on the ground like a snake writhin' on a hot rock.

The next thing I realize, the sun is peekin' through cracks between the boards, and Blossom is nowhere to be seen. Her absence is the only thing that gets me off the ground. I hobble to the door, past the rope again—that thing is comin' down. Right now. I grab it and yank and pull, finally hangin' on it with my whole weight, but it won't budge. I have no tools left and nothin' to stand on to untie it. Frustration overtakes me in a wave, and I become a screamin' wildcat on its prey, flingin' myself against the door frame to try to break the wood, beatin' my head and pullin' my hair, howlin' and cryin' to the sky, then fallin' in a heap and clawin' at the ground as if I can unbury the dead.

I awaken again to find the sun is high in the sky. I lie in the bakin' heat to sweat out what's left of my fever, and my coughs start loosenin' up in my chest, but my mouth feels full of sand and cotton, so I struggle to my feet and make my way to find water.

Blossom is standin' next to the stream, her nose down in the water. Our stream. The memory of Maisie and me in the water rises unbidden, then the other three girls join us, and we swim and wrestle and splash, full of glee with not a worry in the world, and I crumple to the dirt again, bawlin' like a hungry bairn.

"When they needed you most, where were you, huh?" My question accuses me, condemns me for waitin' in Richmond, despises me for takin' Mary and her girls to their relatives instead of comin' straight home. "If you'd been here, you would've stopped 'em. You could've saved 'em."

Self-loathing eats a hole in me that nothing can ever fill. I consider bashin' my already battered head against a rock in the stream and hopin' the water carries me under, but a new feelin' stops me. Bitter rage bubbles up from the deep places toward the One who is supposed to protect His children.

"And You. Where were You?" I shake my fist at the sky and demand He speak. "They never hurt a soul, narry a one of 'em. Ma knew your every word and followed 'em all. If anyone deserved protection, surely it was Ma. And her children were innocents. They didn't deserve this." I kick the water like a poutin' child. "No one deserves this. Tell me why!"

The whisper is as silent as a tomb. Not a breeze stirs the heavy air.

"Answer me. You took Pa. You took Ma. You took Elspeth and Caitrin and Anice and Maisie before their lives even began. I wanna know why. Why them? Why not me?"

Nothin'.

I bellow my rage, poundin' my chest. "Why didn't You do something?!"

Blossom turns her head and stares at me. "What're you lookin' at?" She turns back to her drinkin'.

Ma used to tell me, "No matter what comes, 'tis the Good Lord Who redeems."

I always thought her words sounded nice, but I never fully understood what she meant. Now, as my anger burns against the One she trusted with her whole life, I consider her words anew and wonder if she was tellin' me something important, something I need for a time such as this. No, unless He can raise my family like Lazarus, nothing He might do is gonna matter to me.

"So, is Ma right? You got a redemption for this, too?" I shake my head. "I can't see it. I can't even imagine it. No, you ain't got nothin' for me. And...I ain't got nothin' for You, neither. You and I are finished." As if to seal my dismissal, I bend over the water and scoop handfuls in my mouth, then douse my head and neck, baptizing myself into a new, empty, and loveless life.

"C'mon, girl." I grab Blossom's bridle, feelin' weak-kneed. "Let's go back." I lean against the horse for support and hobble up the hill to the barn.

The next days exist in a fog of cat naps, nightmares, and dazed starin' at nothin'. Blossom wanders in and out of the barn, I guess findin' grass or hay stubble to eat, but she always makes her way back to me. I've not eaten in some time, but I can't make myself put out the effort to hunt for food. It doesn't matter, anyway. Nothing matters anymore.

Every couple a days, I wander to the stream to get some water. The exertion leaves me spent. Sometimes, I stay by the stream and lie there the whole day, listenin' to the water run, but what used to bring me joy and peace now reminds me of tears as if the land itself is in mournin'. My own tears join with the stream's flow.

Soon, I become too weak to make the trek to the stream. I'm relieved, honestly. As if she smells death on me, Blossom takes to stayin' outside the barn, and I'm totally alone. Now, it's a matter of waitin'. The days smear together in a swirl of light and darkness.

Through a gray haze, I hear an echo. A voice? "Pa?"

Hands are pullin' at me, makin' me sit up. "No..." Wetness touches my lips, on my forehead, in my mouth and throat. Again.

"Drink."

"Leave me be." My grunt sounds like it's comin' from a great distance, like the voice.

"Drink, son."

I try to focus through the fog at the blob loomin' over me and swat at it to push it away. Now, soft, wet lips nudge my face. Blossom. She came back.

Wet cloths are wrapped across my head and behind my neck. Fingers poke something in my mouth. Bread, I think. Or maybe potato, I'm not sure. My tongue pushes it back out.

"Eat, son. You gotsta eat somethin'."

A sip of water, then more bread. Another piece, and another. This time, I swallow. I don't want to, but I do. I try to turn my head away, but something is holdin' me still. More water, then another piece. Darkness takes me.

I don't know how long I've been out, but when I wake, I see ol' Mr. Johnson sittin' beside me, dozin'.

"Mr. Johnson?" I croak.

He startles awake. "There you is." He lifts a cup of water to my lips, and I drink greedily. "Go slow, son. A little at a time is all."

I nod. "It was you?"

"Yessir, 'twas."

I close my eyes and nod.

"Blossom done it. She moseys down to my farm and brings me back up, and there you is, lookin' like death itself. What are ye thinkin', son? Not eatin'. Not drinkin'. Yer Ma'd tan yore hide fer such foolishness."

He's right, she would. If she were here to do it. I moan and turn my face away.

"Nawsir, you sit yourself right up and takes some mo' water and food. Awright, now."

I'm too weak to argue, so I take his broken pieces of dried meat and his morsels of bread and chew them deliberately before I swallow. I have to admit, the water on my cracked lips and goin' down my parched throat is a relief.

"No arguin' from ye, now. Blossom's gonna carry you to my farm and you're gonna stay with me 'til ye get yer strength back."

I recognize it'll be pointless to argue. I'm too weak to stop him from whatever he decides to do to me, so instead of fightin' him, I do my best to help him as he lifts me up onto Blossom's back.

"Lawd, you's as thin as a rail, son."

"How long?"

"Been mor'n two weeks since I seen ye."

Blossom walks slowly, and Mr. Johnson keeps his hands on me to hold me on her bare back as I slump over her neck. When we reach his farm at the bottom of the hill, he carries me in his arms like a bairn to his bed. I suppose I sleep, because the next thing I know, I wake to warm broth bein' ladled carefully into my mouth.

Days pass in a rhythm of small, warm meals, a lot of water, and sleep. For some reason, my nightmares don't plague me in Mr. Johnson's bed. For that, I'm grateful. He even gives me sponge baths and brings me a chamber pot when I need it, like a dotin' mother carin' for a sickly child. Finally, he decrees me strong enough to walk outside. I have a moment of dizziness when I first stand, but it passes, and I'm able to make it out to the stream—and the outhouse—on my own.

Sittin' by the stream replenishes more than my body. For the first time since I saw the newly dug graves on our hill, I have something akin to a will to live, not quite a desire but at least enough strength to make myself eat without Mr. Johnson forcin' me.

Before too long, I take to helpin' Mr. Johnson collect in some of his crops and hunt for some rabbit. He and I talk each night, him sharin' some of his wisdom from his many years of struggle and his many losses when he was a slave. I discover he was separated from his wife of eight years, and his children were sold away one by one from the plantation where he worked the fields. He told me of his bitterness toward the plantation master, and how that bitterness almost killed him.

"But it wasn't the master who tried to kill me. 'Twas the ugliness in my own heart done me in, or close to it. Weren't 'til I forgave the master that I's set free."

"How could you forgive him? He sold your own children."

Mr. Johnson shakes his head. "Ye still don't understand, son. He sinned against me, sure he did. But I carried his sin like it was my own instead of his. And the burden almost broke me."

"How'd you do it? How'd you forgive?"

"That's a question you gotta search out for yourself."

"I can never forgive 'em. I don't wanna forgive 'em."

"Suit yourself."

But the conversation plagues me. Something my Ma always said keeps ringin' in my ears. "Ye forgive because ye be forgiven much." I see my own sins piled high and deep and wide as the dead bodies at Gettysburg and Chickamauga and Chattanooga and the Wilderness. I remember the murdered bodies of the Union thieves—and the horror on Mary's face.

Since the war, I haven't believed, not once, the Lord would forgive me for my many sins. I see them as much too heinous to forgive. Is that why I'm so sure I can never forgive what happened to Ma and my sisters? Accordin' to Mr. Johnson, I'm carryin' a burden that doesn't belong to me. But what about the burden that is mine to bear? What would he say if he knew what I'd done?

The next night, I ask him about the rest of his story. "How'd you come to be a freedman?"

He smiles. "One day, the master takes ill, and all the other slaves run off 'cause he can't do nothin' to stop 'em, but I come to the big house ta take care of him. He doesn't think he's gonna live, but I sit by his side day and night, carin' for him, same as I did for ye, and he starts to get better. He's so grateful, he frees me and give me my papers." He looks down at the table. "I ask after my wife and children, but he don't know where they is. He tries to help, sendin' messages to them that took 'em, but they's been sold again by then. I do know they were split up. I guess my boy and my girls got ol' enough to work like they's grow'd."

"I'm sorry."

158

"I spent a long, long time lookin' for 'em everywhere I could think to look. I traveled far and wide, but there's no sign of 'em. I was starvin' from my wanderin's when I finally came to yer doorstep, and yer Ma and Pa took me in."

"Have you searched anymore since then?"

"Nawsir. I know they's free now, and grow'd, so I hope they finally have a good life."

Finally, the day comes when I know I must return to my own land. It's time I start to rebuild. I know it's what Pa and Ma would want, so I shake Mr. Johnson's hand, thank him for savin' my life, climb on Blossom's back, and ride up the hill to the barn. As I approach the top, I brace myself to see the cursed rope, hopin' I won't break down again, but it isn't there. Mr. Johnson must've cut it down when he was carin' for me at the barn. I whisper another word of thanks in his direction.

One of the benefits of weeks of rest is my back seems almost fully healed. I paw through the rubble that was my home but can't find any useable pieces of wood.

"Well, girl, I guess the barn is gonna be our home for now, until I can figure some things out." No supplies. No tools to cut wood. No seed. And worst of all, no money to buy any of the things I need to rebuild. "I guess I'd better find a way to earn some money. Let's go into town and see what's happenin' there."

First, though, I wash my clothes in the stream and hang them out in the sun to dry. No need to go into town lookin' like some bum seekin' a handout. I take supper from the bundle Mr. Johnson sent with me, then settle down to sleep, determined to find some answers tomorrow.

The sun finds me at the stream again, bathin' to ready myself for the trip to Morganton. I don't know what I'm hopin' to find there, but there's no doubt I need some way to earn some money if I'm going to rebuild our farm. I saddle Blossom, and we make our way down the hill and through the valley until we reach Morganton. Burned out homes along the outskirts of town prepare me for what we find downtown. The courthouse is gutted. The farm and feed store, the general store, the livery—all destroyed by fire. Just like in Hendersonville, no one is out on the streets.

A few homes remain untouched, so I knock on the door of the first home still standin'. No one answers. I try again and again, with the same result. Either no one is in town anymore, or they're all too afraid to answer their doors. The boardin' house near the square still stands, so I knock on that door. A haggard woman, her grayin' hair pinned loosely on top of her head, pokes her head out the door.

"What?" Her voice sounds like metal scrapin' on wood.

"Hello, ma'am. My name is Aidan MacAlister, from the MacAlister farm on the mountain beyond the river."

"What d'ya want?"

"I recently returned from the war, and I thought I'd come to town to look for someone I know. Can you tell me what happened here?"

"What d'ya think?"

"Well, the Yankees burned my farm, too, and...killed my Ma and my sisters. Why did they spare your house?"

She leans close to me and whispers. "They're stayin' here."

"Who is?" My face grows hot, my chest tightenin'. Surely, the Yanks are not still here.

"Them carpetbaggers. The government sent them...to manage the town durin' reconstruction. Them, and the scalawags."

"Manage the town?"

"They've taken over everything. And I have to feed 'em and serve 'em like regular guests, even though they ain't payin' me a red cent."

"Are they here to help us?"

She barks out a harsh laugh. "Help us? No, they're here to steal from us and tax us to within an inch of our lives."

My heart runs icy cold. Taxes. I have no money to pay any taxes.

"Truth is, if the Yankee soldiers didn't use this place for their headquarters while they were here, they'd have burned it down. And if the carpetbaggers weren't needin' a place to stay, they woulda stole this place from me, too."

"Where's the rest of the town?"

"Most of 'em left after they burned us out. A few of 'em tried to pay the taxes, but the government men kept demandin' more, and when they couldn't pay anymore, they took their homes. They're gone, too."

"Who's stayin' in those houses?" I point to the ones still standin'.

"Them scalawags took 'em all. They say Yankees are comin' down and are gonna buy up the houses—and the land. Have you paid your taxes on your farm?"

"No'm, I have no money."

"Then it ain't your farm no more." With that, she slams the door in my face.

Not my farm anymore? I can't lose Pa's land, too. It's all I have left of my family. And Pa will haunt me for sure if I let his land go. I have to find a way to pay whatever taxes they impose. But how? There ain't any work in this town, that much is clear. Where can I turn?

Pastor Connolly. My Granda doesn't have much money, but he may have some he can give me. But, where is he? The parsonage next to the church is also burned to the ground. Where'd he go? I risk knockin' on the boardin' house door again, and the woman, her eyes wild, her brow furrowed in folds, sticks out her head.

"What now?"

"Do you know Pastor Connolly, from the Methodist Church on the other side of the river?"

"No. Now, go away." She slams the door again.

Surely someone in this town knows where to find my Granda. I wander farther down the street, lookin' for habitable houses or someone walkin' about, with no success. Turnin' down a side road into what used to be a neighborhood, I spot some homes toward the end of the lane still standin'. I hurry to the first home, a large, two-story structure with columns somewhat like the Monroe home, and when I knock, a man who looks somewhat familiar opens the door. His eyes dart left and right as he smooths the stray strands of hair down across his baldin' head, then rubs the back of his neck.

"Yes?"

"Hello, sir. My name is Aidan MacAlister. From the mountain." I point in the direction of my farm.

The man offers a wan smile. "Liam MacAlister's son."

"Yessir. You knew my Pa?"

"He and I do...business together. He passed? In the war?" I nod, and he sighs. "So many good men." His voice trails off, then he clears his throat. "I am...was...his banker. Before the war." The man scans the road behind me and rubs his neck again.

"Is that right? What's your name?"

"Mr. Griffiths. Samuel Griffiths."

I can't believe my ears. "Griffiths? Do you have a son named Josiah?"

His eyes narrow. "I do. Why?"

"Is he alive?"

"He is here right now."

My heart slams in my throat. "May...may I speak to him?"

He frowns. "What is this about?"

"Josiah and I...we served together. We fought together in the war. We became good friends."

Mr. Griffiths's face softens. "Well, I'll be. How did you find him?"

"I didn't knock on your door lookin' for Josiah. I've been tryin' to find someone who knows my Granda to tell me where he is, that's all. But..Josiah was...is...we are close. I would surely like to see him."

"Who is your grandfather?"

"Pastor Connolly, the pastor at the Methodist Church across the river."

"They burned that church."

"Yessir. Do you happen to know where my Granda went?"

"I am sorry, no, I do not know."

"Oh. Well, thank you anyways. Do you think I could see Josiah?"

Mr. Griffiths hesitates—why, I can't imagine. He glances over his shoulder, looks past the top of my head up the road again, rubs his hands together, blinks, then stares behind him for several seconds.

"What's wrong, sir?"

"I...I will need to check with Josiah..."

"I'll wait." Something is definitely wrong.

Mr. Griffiths shuffles through the main room, down a hallway, and disappears. He is gone for several minutes, and I begin to wonder if he is hopin' I'll give up and leave. What could possibly be causin' him to act this way?

Finally, he returns, his lips tightly pressed and his eyes downcast. "Josiah will see you."

I follow Mr. Griffiths down the hall. We enter a darkened room where I see a form in a heap of quilts on a bed beneath a single window with closed shutters. His head is propped on several pillows, his eyes wide and sunken in shadow, his bones pronounced above hollow cheeks. I barely recognize him. "Josiah!"

"Mac." The cracked whisper sounds strained—eerie, like I imagine a spectre would sound if it spoke.

I move to the bedside and sit on the edge, holdin' up my hand. "It's so good to see you." He doesn't take my hand. "Josiah, I'm sorry. I lost sight of you at the Wilderness, then I got injured, and I never...well, I'm glad I found you now."

Josiah stares blankly at the wall across from his bed but doesn't respond.

"What happened to you at the Wilderness?"

Nothin'. The silence is uncomfortable, as is the need to fill it. "I know, the Wilderness was horrifyin'—men burnin', chaos and death everywhere. I don't like to think about it either. I took a bayonet in the back—it broke a bone, too. I'm just now gettin' better."

"You are thin."

"You are as well. I guess the war took a lot out of both of us. But...the worst of it...was when I came home..."

He blinks and turns his eyes to meet mine.

"What the Yankees did...they did...horrible, unspeakable things...to my sisters." My words stick in my throat like sap, and the silence between us lengthens. His blank eyes bore into me. I imagine accusation there.

"Tell me what happened to you?" My question lies flat and lifeless, like his face.

"Finish."

"What?"

"Finish your tale."

I swallow the thick lump in my throat. "They...hung...my Ma. While my sisters watched. Then they...shot...murdered my sisters." Unwanted tears drip on my cheeks.

"I am sorry." It comes out more like a groan than words.

"My whole family is dead. Pa, Ma, the girls...and I can't find my Granda either. I came here to try to find him, to see if anyone knows where he is."

"Ask Father."

"He doesn't know."

"Mmmm."

"Now I hear the Yanks may take our land, too. I'm hopin' if I can find my Granda, he may have some money to help me pay what I owe in taxes."

Josiah shakes his head slowly. "It will not be enough."

"Why? What do you mean?"

"Ask Father." He gestures with his head toward to door, then closes his eyes. I guess he's askin' me to leave, but I don't want to go.

"Won't you please tell me what happened to you?"

"Go."

"Josiah, please..."

He turns his head away. In the semidarkness, I see the slightest shimmer next to his right eye, and I know I've pressed him too hard. I stand and take my leave, but I'm not willin' to leave this house 'til I get the whole story. Mr. Griffiths will tell me, even if Josiah cannot.

I find Mr. Griffiths sittin' alone in a rocker near his front window, starin' out at nothin' on the lane. "Mr. Griffiths, tell me what happened to Josiah."

He looks up, his eyes dazed and glassy, then gestures for me to sit. "He did not tell you?"

"Nosir."

His sigh shudders like lake water fleein' a skipped rock. "At a place called the Wilderness..."

"I was there."

He lifts his brow. "A musket ball fired at close range—shattered the bones in both his legs." He sighs again. "He was taken by the

164

Yankees to their field hospital—where he lay outside, waiting to be seen. You see, they were seeing to their own first. By the time they got to him, they had no choice but to amputate—both his legs." He pauses to let me absorb this news. "Then, as if that was not enough, they took him to a prison camp. He remained there for the rest of the war, in deplorable conditions. When he was released and sent back to me, he was emaciated, unable to eat, ill—I did not believe he would long survive. Thankfully, he is still with us. I guess we are all more resilient than we believe."

My own circumstance fades to nothing. Why had I even mentioned it to Josiah? How heartless must he think I am?

"He does not sleep, really. When he does, he wakes screaming. We keep his room dark because any light makes his head pound. I fear he has given up all hope. I must force him to eat. Other than that, he lies in that bed—and wastes away."

"I didn't know."

"I am surprised he agreed to see you. He has refused to see anyone, even family, since his return."

"Should I go back in and talk to him? Now that I know?"

"He does not want your pity."

"No—no, of course not. I want to encourage him, to remind him he's still alive."

"Perhaps another day." Mr. Griffiths breathes another tremulous sigh and resumes his glazed stare out the window.

"Mr. Griffiths, may I ask you something?"

"Hmm?"

"Why were you so nervous when I came to your door? Was it because of Josiah?"

"You have not been around long enough to hear the rumors."

"Nosir."

His mouth flattens to a thin line. "You see, I am what they call a scalawag, a betrayer of his own. A Yankee sympathizer."

"You, sir?" I can feel the knife edge of my rage rumblin' in my gut.

Misery etches across his face and ages him before my eyes. "That is what they say. When the Yankees came through, I opened my home to them. I made the bank's information fully available to them. I helped them find and steal resources and collect taxes...well, you see."

"I don't understand, sir. Why? How could you? After what they did to Josiah?" My rage blossoms in hatred, and I can understand why he is nervous openin' his door. If not for Josiah, I might kill him myself.

His head slumps to his chest. "I had no choice. They were going to burn down my house if I did not help them. I knew they needed my information—the deeds to land and so forth—and I bargained with them for the sake of my son."

"For Josiah?" I truly can't fathom what he's sayin'. Josiah would never have wanted this.

"Josiah needs constant care, food, a safe and quiet place to recover. If we were living on the street, he would not survive."

"You betrayed your neighbors to keep your house?"

"For Josiah's sake."

A roilin' flame sears through me. "You gave them the deed to our farm?"

"Yes, they have it. They plan to auction all lands with unpaid taxes as soon as the men arrive from up north."

"And if I can't pay the taxes?"

"The land will go to the highest bidder."

"So, you get to keep your house, but we lose everything." My flat voice doesn't betray the deadly intensity of my fury. My demon is scratchin' and clawin' to make its way out.

"I did it for my son."

Mr. Griffiths' defiant whine fails to pierce my heart, which stews with a desperate desire to exact revenge. The demon pushes to burst forth in its full glory and ravage this man cowerin' before me, but a whisper freezes me in place. *To what lengths would a man go for the sake of his son that he loves?*

I see my Pa liftin' me in his strong arms after I fell off a horse he'd forbidden me to ride, holdin' me tight against his chest, his worry rollin' off him in waves as he rushed me into the house, callin' for Ma to come quick. He never punished me for disobeyin' him. He only held me as I cried, repeatin' over and over that he loved me, and all was well. I see myself standin' beside him, holdin' his hand as he knelt beside the grave of his infant boy who died from the scarlet fever, weepin' like I'd never seen him cry before. I know the answer. My heart won't allow me to voice it.

To what lengths did I go for you, whom I love?

A crushin' humility floods through me, washin' the demon back down into the depths from whence it came, and I know in that moment that I can say I'm finished with God, but it don't matter none. He ain't done with me.

I don't want to waste time being angry with Mr. Griffiths. I see now, in the same situation, I might have made the same choice. The whisper echoes inside me. *To what lengths did I go for you, whom I love?* Whatever it takes, I reply. Whatever it takes.

If I'm gonna save Pa's land, I have to get money, and fast. "Can you give me a loan, Mr. Griffiths?" I have little hope, but I have to ask.

"The bank is in their hands now." He looks at me, his eyes pained. "Why would they give you a loan? They prefer to take your land."

I'm a rabbit backin' into his hole before a hungry wolf. "How much time?"

"Honestly, I do not know when the men are coming. All they told me is the land and remaining homes with taxes outstanding will be auctioned off when they arrive."

"What will you do then?"

He grimaces. "Oh, I have paid my taxes. I had some gold saved, and I managed to get it from the bank before..."

Gold. Mary. Could I ask Mary to help me? Would I? Would she? She needs that gold for her children—I couldn't. But I can't lose the farm.

"Do you know how much the taxes are on our farm?"

"No, son, I do not."

"How would I find out that information?"

"You would have to go to the bank and speak to the—man in charge there."

"You don't still work there?"

He coughs out a bitter laugh. "Only if they need to use me for some dastardly scheme."

167

The land my Pa loved so dear, the land he died for, is slippin' away from me. If I don't find some money before the out of towners arrive, it will be lost forever. I can ask Granda, if I can find him. But no one seems to know where he is. I can ask Mary, but I don't believe I can live with myself if I do. I can ask the Yank for a loan, but he has no reason to give me one and every reason not to. I'm pressed against the back of my hole, and the wolf's teeth are closin'.

CHAPTER FOURTEEN

To my surprise, Mr. Griffiths invites me to stay the night with them rather than ride back up the mountain to sleep in the barn. He promises to allow me some time to talk with Josiah the next morning, so I agree to remain. I lead Blossom to his stable behind the house, take off her saddle, rub her down, and give her some hay, then I walk back to the house and settle in the room next to Josiah's where Mr. Griffiths prepared a bed for me.

As described, the night is filled with screams and howls and sobbin'. My heart aches for Josiah. Although I don't have the severity of his experience or his kind of loss, I at least understand, more than his father, why the nights are so terrifyin'. I've had my share of screamin' wakeups, too.

The wind whistles through the eaves of the large house, but I don't hear the whisper again. I'm mad at myself that I'm listenin' for it. I wouldn't call it prayin', but I do remind God that He and I still have a problem, to which He, of course, doesn't reply. But learnin' of Josiah's circumstances has changed things for me, somehow. It's like I am seein' through a different set of lenses, like the colors were gray and dark before, and now the lenses are lighter, the colors brighter.

The next mornin' dawns clear, and I decide Josiah and I are gonna go outside. I don't see Mr. Griffiths anywhere, so I amble into Josiah's room. "Good mornin'."

As I expect, he doesn't reply.

"I thought you and I might spend the mornin' outside, before I have to head out to search for my Granda."

Josiah moans and turns his head away. "No. I cannot."

"Sure you can. I'll fix up a place for you and tote you on out. As skinny as you are, it won't be a problem."

"No!"

169

"Why not? It's not too hot yet, it's a beautiful mornin'. You've been stuck in this room too long. You need some air."

"The sun..."

"Well..." I look in his armoire and find a dusty wide-brimmed hat. "Here you go! This'll shade your eyes."

"NO!"

I'm not so easily dissuaded. "You're as pale as a ghost. You need some light." I reach to pull back the covers, and Josiah screeches like a wounded animal, grabs them, and pulls them up to his throat. So, I lift them again, faster this time, and yank them back. The stumps of his legs, cut off above the knee, are wrapped in brown-stained gauze. I look him in the eye. "We're goin' out. Now, you can cooperate, or you can fight me, but I'd suggest cooperatin'. My Pa raised me to be especially hard-headed."

Josiah's head rests on his chest, his eyes hooded and blotches of red on his cheeks. I can barely hear him when he speaks. "Everyone will see."

"So, let 'em see! You fought bravely on their behalf. They should be throwin' you a parade. If they don't understand that, who needs 'em?"

"It is a hideous sight."

I reach down and place a hand on each arm, so my face is aligned with his. "Now you listen here. Look at me." Josiah cuts his eyes up furtively for a second or two before slumpin' farther down in the pillows. "You're alive. Don't you ever forget that. You're still alive, and just 'cause you ain't got all your legs, that don't change nary a thing 'bout you. You're the same person, with the same kind heart and the same strength that got Will and me through some terrible, impossible times. Or don't you recall?"

He doesn't respond, so I take that as permission to continue.

"You're alive when others ain't. So, stop actin' like you're dead already. I'm gonna lift you up, now. Tell me if something hurts."

I plop the hat on his head, gather him up in my arms, along with the bundle of coverlets and quilts, and carry him down the long hall to the front door. As I thought, he don't weigh no more than a bairn.

Mr. Griffiths has returned from wherever he was, and when he sees me carryin' his son, he yells out from the kitchen. "What are you doing?"

"I'm takin' this young man outside to get some fresh air."

"Put him down! At once!" He scrambles into the main room, where I'm standin' with Josiah and his quilts, about to open the front door. "Stop!"

Josiah is moanin' in my arms, but I'm not sure if it's from pain or humiliation that his father is yellin' at me.

"Nosir. I'm takin' him out, for his own good. He's been too long in the shadows, hidin' from life and feelin' sorry for himself. So, I'm takin' him, and you should join us. Stop skulkin' about and face the day." With that, I sling the door open and march outside. Mr. Griffiths follows, scurryin' around Josiah like a little rat, twitchin' and fiddlin' and squeakin'.

I carry him onto the slopin' lawn and drop all but one of the quilts. "Mr. Griffiths, take some of these quilts and make a pile to give him a soft place to sit." He fusses with the quilts, all the while scannin' up and down the lane for people. When he's finished, I set Josiah down gently, then wrap the last quilt around his stumps. "Now, then. That's better."

Josiah groans and covers his eyes. "My head hurts."

"You'll get used to it."

"Enough of this. He's in pain, can't you see that?"

"I know he's in pain. We're all in pain! That don't give us no right to bury ourselves afore we're dead." My own recent bout with despair flashes in my memory. "You see, when I found out my Ma and sisters were dead, and how they died, I did just like you. I climbed in a hole and laid there waitin' to die. But a good friend picked me up and carried me out of my hole. He showed me, even though my family was gone, I still have my life to live. He taught me about forgivin' those who done them wrong, so I don't carry a burden that ain't mine to bear. And I saw that God wasn't done with me yet, or I'd be home with my family already. It ain't like He hasn't had plenty a chances to take me, and He didn't. So, I'm gonna live. And now, it's my turn to carry you out."

"You do not understand."

"Sure I do. I got my legs but everything else is gone—everything that matters. You don't think I'd trade my legs for the chance to be with my Ma and sisters again?"

Josiah withers under my glare. I realize my own words are strengthenin' my resolve. There's a reason I'm still here. God has something for me to do, and I'm a-gonna do it. Whatever it takes. Whatever it takes.

Finally, Josiah meets my gaze. "You are right. I have no reason for self-pity. I am alive. I still have my father. Others fared much worse than I."

"And some are no longer with us."

"I'm sorry, I'm quite ashamed of how I've acted. I never asked you what happened to you at the Wilderness. I suppose I was too caught up in my own plight to ask about yours. I long feared you were dead."

"It's awright. I was injured, too, stabbed in the back by a bayonet and broke a bone in there. They sent me to a field hospital, then on to Richmond to the hospital there. After a spell, they sent me to someone's home in Richmond to convalesce, a real nice family. Once I was some better, they commandeered me for the cavalry, so I fought at Petersburg, then I helped that nice family evacuate from Richmond when the Yanks overran it."

"I'm glad you were there to help them."

The corners of my mouth turn up in something akin to a smile. "She has three girls. Just like..." My voice and my smile fade away.

"I'm so sorry."

"That's enough about that. Now, we need to figure some way for you to get around. Mr. Griffiths, you got a garden cart in your stable?"

"I am not sure. I will go and see."

"And I'm gonna need a wooden chair. And some tools."

While we wait for Mr. Griffiths to return, I share with Josiah some of the wisdom I learned from Mr. Johnson while he cared for me. We talk about purpose and meanin' in life, about hope, and finally about forgiveness. "I'm sure you're angry. Is it with God? With the Yankees? Who?"

"Honestly, I have not cared enough to be angry. Like you said, I wished to die."

"Do you care now?"

"I feel a little better. I suppose I do, yes."

"I'm still workin' on forgivin' them that killed my Ma and sisters. What they did to 'em..." My throat closes around the words.

"I am truly sorry, Mac."

My breath makes a high-pitched whistle comin' out. "Maybe it's my fault." I'd had this thought, but never voiced it aloud before now. "Maybe all the killin' I done...this is the price."

Josiah touches my arm. "I do not believe God works like that, punishing someone else for our sins."

"But that's just it. Who's punished by their dyin'? They're with Jesus, if you're to believe my Ma. And surely if anyone is with Jesus, it's her and my sweet sisters who never hurt nobody. I'm the one still here, and this life is misery upon misery and ain't lookin' to get no better soon. So, is this my punishment? For all the killin'?"

"I believe in God's grace."

"I do, too, but the Good Book also says, 'Whatsoever a man soweth, that shall he also reap.'"

"Mac, God did not kill your mother and sisters. The Yankee scum did that. He did not kill your father, either. A Yankee musket ball killed him."

"So, you ain't mad at God? About your legs?"

Josiah cocks his head and glances at a passin' white cloud. "No, I do not think I am."

"Are you angry at the Yanks?"

173

He presses his lips to a thin line. "Yes. But more for what they are doing to my father than for what happened to me." He sweeps his hand across his lap. "This...this is just a consequence of war. What they are doing to my father and the people of this town—it is thievery, plain and simple."

"We need to fight 'em."

Josiah chuckles. "I am sure they will listen to a cripple and a pauper."

"We have to try."

"How?" Josiah sighs. "You cannot fight without any weapons. We have no leverage—no money, no power, nothing even to offer them they might want that they have not already taken by force."

"Your pa has money."

"None that he will use for anything other than our survival."

"I'll find a way. I must. I can't let the Yanks have my Pa's land. The land is why he went to war. It's why he died. I won't let him die in vain."

We sit in silence, watchin' light and shadow flit across the lawn as the sun and clouds play hide and seek, until Mr. Griffiths returns with a large garden cart, a wooden chair I recognize as bein' from his dinin' table, some wood, and a heap a tools piled high on the cart.

"Here is what I have."

"I believe I can make it work." I set about cuttin' the legs from the chair while Josiah lounges and dozes in the warmth of the sun. I use a brace and bit to drill holes on the bottom of the cart, then fasten the chair to the inside of the cart with wood screws. "There you have it. A makeshift wheelchair."

Mr. Griffiths squeals in delight. "Wonderful!"

"Once your stumps heal, you can make yourself a wooden leg and use crutches to get around. But this'll do in the meantime."

"Thank you, Mac."

"You're welcome."

The sun is high in the sky, and I'm impatient to head out to find my Granda, but Mr. Griffiths insists on providin' me lunch. Rather than carry Josiah back inside, he proclaims, "We will have a picnic." He scurries in the house and soon returns with biscuits, ham, and tomatoes, and beams as he watches Josiah gobble up the food, perhaps for the first time since he returned home.

Filled to the brim and satisfied with my efforts here, I take my leave of Josiah, promisin' to visit again very soon. Accordin' to Mr. Griffiths, the newly constituted military governance for the town headquartered themselves at the bank, since it's the only large building left standin' after the Yankees finished their burnin', so he suggests headin' to the bank first, to see if anyone there can tell me about my Granda or perhaps answer my questions about how to reclaim my farm. So, I collect Blossom, and we head back to town to the bank.

I wriggle in Blossom's saddle as we make our way slowly down the lane and back out to the main street. My whole future seems to hang on what these men are gonna say. I've never felt so powerless in my life, not even when I was under enemy fire durin' the war. At least then, I could shoot back. But fate is out of my hands now, clutched in the vise-like grip of people who see me as their enemy.

"We mak' oor ain fate," my Pa used to say.

Ma would argue, "Tis the Good Lord makes our paths straight, not us."

Looks to me like the Yankees are choosin' my path, and neither I nor the Good Lord have much a hand in it.

The bank is quiet when I enter. I don't recognize either of the two men in there, one in the office I suppose used to be Mr. Griffiths' office, and one behind the counter. I choose the one at the counter, hopin' he will be someone more like me.

"Excuse me, sir, I have a couple a questions I'm hopin' you are able to answer. Could you help me?"

The man didn't look up from his papers but waved his hand toward the office. "Speak to Captain Germain."

"Thank you, sir." I walk across the lobby and stand outside Captain Germain's office and repeat my speech.

"Come in." He sounds either fatigued or very bored. He motions me to a chair across from his desk. "What do you need?"

"Well, sir, first, I understand you may be holdin' the deed to my land, and that my land might be auctioned off sometime soon."

"Are you delinquent on payments or taxes?"

"I don't know, sir. I just returned from..."

"Which side?"

I'm aware many of my neighbors believed in the cause of the Union, so his question doesn't surprise me. "I fought for the Confederates."

He smirks. "Name on the deed."

"MacAlister."

"Remain here." The captain disappears through a door at the back, leavin' me to my anxious twiddlin'. When he returns, he is carryin' several documents, which he plunks down on his desk before me. "Your taxes have not been paid since 1863." His tone is accusatory.

"As I said, I have been away, but I'm willin' to pay what I owe. What accommodations can be made for me to make payments?"

"None. The full amount is due if you do not want your land to be auctioned."

"How much is owed?"

"105 dollars."

I can't believe my ears. "105 dollars? My Pa told me our land is worth about $400—at least it was in 1860. It can't have increased that much in value in five years."

"We don't tax based on value. We tax based on reparations for costliness and hardships caused by your rebellion. Be thankful it is not more. 105 dollars. Due now."

"I don't have 105 dollars. Sir, can you allow me to work off the debt in some way?"

"Sure, you can give me 105 dollars. Or say goodbye to your land." He gathers up the documents from his desk and stands to return them to storage.

"Wait. Sir, I do have another question."

He rolls his eyes. "What now?"

"I'm lookin' for my Granda—um, grandfather. He is the pastor of the Methodist church across the river that was burned. His parsonage was also burned, and I don't know where he went. Is your office where I would report someone missin'?"

"Now, why would I know where your grandfather went?"

"I thought since you are a military authority, you might be the ones addressin' crime."

"No crime has been reported."

"Or maybe keepin' an eye on Confederate sympathizers?"

"Only if they cause trouble." His glare told me I was quickly fallin' into that category.

"Any idea how I might find him?"

"No, son, I don't know how you might find him." His sneer drips with disdain.

"Thank you anyway, sir." I stand to leave, but he stops me at the door.

"Don't forget to bring the 105 dollars around. Before it's too late." I suspicion it's already too late, but I nod and walk out behind him.

I wrap my arm across Blossom's saddle. "Now what, girl?" She chuffs and wiggles her ear but has no suggestions to offer. "I guess I'm back to knockin' on doors."

I spend the rest of the afternoon doin' just that, with no success. The option of contactin' Mary and askin' for help begins to look more attractive to me, but my pride and my deeply ingrained sense of what's right wars against the need to save the farm. One side of my mind works a quick estimate of how fast Blossom and I can go to Hendersonville and back, and if I will return in time, while the other side of me rails about takin' food from the mouths of bairns, ones that I love. "You'll pay her back," side one insists. "How, with no job and no prospects?" side two argues.

As I'm troddin' down the main street to leave town, a young man approaches me with his hand raised.

"Yes, sir?" I recognize him as the man sittin' behind the counter at the bank.

"I overheard you're lookin' for ways to pay off your tax debt."

"You from these parts?"

"I'm from outside McCaysville, up the road yonder ways. They sent me back here 'cause they thought the local folk would have less trouble with one of their own instead of an outsider. I don't see that workin' too well, though."

"Well, if they'd treat people decent, they might not have such problems."

He shrugs. "I can't help what those above me do."

"You could stop helpin' 'em do it."

"Listen, I wanted to give you some information the captain failed to tell you. The Union army's real depleted, and they're lookin' for soldiers to join up, particularly cavalry." He nods to Blossom. "They're needin' folk to fight out West against the Indians. Maybe if you was to join, they might forgive your debt."

"Join the Union army?" Today is one shock on top of another.

"Soldierin' is soldierin'."

"I never wanted to fight in the first place. I sure ain't gonna fight for them that killed my family."

"I'm sorry. I thought, seein' as how you're desperate and all, it might be a way out for you."

"Well, I appreciate the thought, but I can't see myself wearin' the uniform of the men who killed my Pa and my Ma and done..." I can't say it. "...and...my sisters."

"Just a thought."

"Thank ya kindly, but I'll not be fightin' anymore. I'm done with killin'."

His grimace tells me he's done his share. "Good luck, then." He lifts his hand and walks away, his shoulders slumped and his head down.

I have a brief flash of sympathy for a man havin' to treat his own neighbors like enemies and rabble, and my conscience pricks me. I shoulda been nicer. He was only tryin' to help. I wonder if I've forgotten how to be a normal, amiable person. Ma'd correct me if she was here to do it.

But as I walk up the long hill out of the valley, the young man's words swirl like a tornado in my mind. I try to shove them away, but they won't stop comin'. I couldn't raise $105 in five years by workin', and that's if I could find a job to hire me. Mary has a chest full of gold coins, each one worth $100—but how could I ever pay her back? Goin' to her for help moves the problem from one place to another, it don't solve it. And what if, in those years I'm in her debt, she gets in trouble and needs the money back, and I can't raise it—it'd be my fault her children starve.

I've spent two days searchin' for my Granda with no leads on his whereabouts, but even if I find him, I already know he ain't got that kind of money. $105 might as well be a million and five. I don't have a way of gettin' either one. So, it comes down to this—losin' the land my Pa died to save or fightin' for the side that violated and shot my sisters, planned to violate Mary and Ruth, hung my ma, and shot my pa. How much exactly is this land worth to me?

"Ye fight fur yer land, boy, and let nane take it frae ye." Pa's words resound in my ears.

My very soul rips in two, wrenchin' a cry from my lips against my will. "What do I do now?" Who am I askin'? In my desperation, am I reachin' out to the Good Lord again? Am I willin' to make my peace with Him? "What do I do now?" I sob, my cry quiet, mournful, somber—even humble.

The wind ruffles the leaves gently as I pass under them, whisperin'. *To what lengths did I go for you, whom I love?*

"Whatever it takes," I whisper in reply. Whatever it takes.

CHAPTER FIFTEEN

Sleep won't come for me this night. My decision is made, but my mind won't let it rest. I keep goin' through it over and over again, tryin' to find an option that doesn't make me join sides with them that I consider my sworn enemies. And along with my own frettin', now that I've reached out to God in desperation, He won't stop His whisperin'.

For if ye forgive men their trespasses, your heavenly Father will also forgive you.

"Why? Why would You forgive me?"

For by grace are ye saved through faith, and that not of yourselves; it is the gift of God.

"But I've broken Your commandments."

All have sinned and come short of the glory of God; being justified freely by His grace through the redemption that is in Christ Jesus.

"But I hear You sayin' You won't forgive me unless I forgive them that took my family."

He that is without sin, let him first cast a stone.

My frustration explodes in a surprisin' fury. "What do You want from me?"

After several moments of silence, I hear, *Blessed are the merciful, for they shall obtain mercy.*

I blow out my breath in a rush. "Please. Leave me be."

This is my commandment. That ye love one another as I have loved you.

My heart hangs heavy in my chest like I've swallowed an apple whole, and it got stuck on the way down. It's hard to breathe. "And I forgive because I be forgiven much, like Ma said."

I want to ask Him if He does love me, or if He still loves me like He did when I was a child, but I'm afeared to hear His answer, so I hold my tongue. But the whisper isn't finished with me yet.

181

As the Father hath loved me, so have I loved you; continue ye in my love.

A strange peace washes over me, quietin' my mind and freein' the knot from my heart. "Yea, Lord. I do love You." Sleep comes quickly after that.

I wake before the day dawns, all my questions put to rest, my heart settled, and my mind determined. My first task is to pay a visit to Mr. Johnson. Blossom and I find him already at work in his garden.

"Mornin', Mr. Johnson."

"And a fine day 'tis."

"Yessir. Mr. Johnson, I have a favor to ask of you."

"What can I do for ye?"

"I'm goin' to Atlanta, and I need you to keep an eye on my farm while I'm away."

"Happy to do it."

"You can plant crops if you want."

"Plant crops?"

"I may be gone for some time..."

"What are ye doin' in Atlanta?"

"I'm signin' up for the US Cavalry to fight in the Indian wars out west."

Mr. Johnson stops his diggin' and rests his arms across the handle of the hoe. He stares at me but says nothin'.

"It's my only hope of keepin' the farm. Ma didn't pay taxes for two years, and now that the Yanks are runnin' the county, they've set the tax so high, I'll never be able to pay it. So, I'm gonna ask to trade my service for forgiveness of the taxes. But I gotta make the agreement before they auction off the farm."

"If they take your land, they take my land, too. That right?"

"Yessir, I'm afeared so."

"Are ye sure, son? Fightin' again? Killin' again? Ye said..."

"I know what I said." I look to the ground at his feet. "There's no other answer that I can see. And I'm not even sure they'll agree once I get there. But it's the best chance we got."

182

He nods once. "Well, then...while ye be gone, I'll watch over the land for ye."

"It could be years."

"I ain't goin' nowhere."

"Thank you." I stare solemnly at him. "Don't you let them force you off your land."

"I won't. Nawsir."

I reach down and shake his hand. "Take care, Mr. Johnson. And thank you."

"Ye come back, ye hear me?"

"I'll do my best."

"Ye got my prayers."

"And you have mine."

He grasps my hand in both of his and doesn't seem to want to let go. Honestly, I don't want to let go, either. I look back up the hill toward the barn, out of sight beyond the rise, then I scan left and right, to try to commit my land to memory. This last look will have to sustain me, potentially for a long time.

"Wait here, son. Let me get ye somethin' to take with ye." He rambles to his shack, returnin' a few minutes later with a sack filled with dried meat, a few apples, and some beans and squash. "That should do ye a while."

"Yessir. You're a good friend."

"Take care, son." His eyes look watery to me, but he manages to show me his crooked teeth in some semblance of a smile. I can't return the smile, and I can't speak again either, for my tears are too close to the surface and threatenin' to fall. So, I turn Blossom toward the south and head out, Mr. Johnson's sack swingin' from the saddle.

We stop at the stream to take a drink and collect some water for the journey, then we retrace our steps to Morganton to tell my McCaysville neighbor at the bank my plan before we start on the trail to Atlanta.

When I enter the bank, the young man sits at his post, as I'd hoped. He looks up and smiles in greetin', so I come to the counter. "I changed my mind. Gonna take you up on the offer to sign up in exchange for payin' the taxes."

He raises his brows but nods and stands and gestures for me to follow him. It looks like I'll have to deal with Captain Germain again, which don't please me none, but I swallow my pride and shake his hand.

The young man speaks for me. "He's askin' the taxes to be forgiven if he serves in the Cavalry."

Captain Germain looks me up and down., then pulls out some paperwork. "Five years. Minimum."

I blanch, swallow, and nod once.

"You'll be fed and given a uniform, but you won't be paid. Your pay will come to cover your delinquent taxes."

"I understand."

"If you don't serve all five years, the land reverts back to the U.S."

"Yessir."

"And if your service doesn't cover all the taxes after five years, you'll have to come up with the difference in a timely manner or continue in service for additional years."

I smell a rat, but I say nothing. In other words, they can demand I serve however long they want, and I'll have no recourse. But if I want to keep my land, what can I do? They have me trapped like a fly in a spider's web.

"Sign this agreement to serve. Right here."

I sign my name before I can change my mind.

"Take these papers. Go to the garrison at this address in Atlanta. See a Colonel Wilcox and give him your papers. He will take care of it from there."

"How do I know you'll keep your end of the bargain? Where's your signature on the paper? Where does it say my service is payin' my taxes?"

Captain Germain frowned. "Are you questioning me?"

"Yessir. I don't want to spend five years of my life fightin' to come home only to have my land belong to someone else."

He slams one of the papers in the stack he's holdin' onto the desk and points to a paragraph. "Do you read, son?"

"Yessir, I do."

"Then read right here."

The paragraph outlines the agreement to serve and includes mention of erasing my debt. "Very well."

"You'll need to get your attitude right before you get to Atlanta. Colonel Wilcox will brook no disrespect."

"Yessir."

"Take the papers and go."

"Yessir." I take the stack from him, pick up the important piece from his desk, salute as I learned to do in the Confederate army, and turn to go. The young McCaysville soldier at the front desk reaches out his hand, and I take it gladly. "Thank you for your help."

"Maybe I'll be seein' you again."

"I hope to be back." I lean close and whisper. "Try to keep 'em from stealin' everything and runnin' everybody out of town."

He presses his lips together. "I wish I could say I can do something about it, but...well, I'm a soldier, not an officer."

"Do your best to watch out for 'em anyway."

He shrugs. "Take care of yourself."

I lift my hand and leave the bank, tuck my precious papers in my saddle bag, and mount Blossom to start the long trail to Atlanta.

I can't say how many times I second-guess my decision along the trail and threaten to turn back, but needless to say, I experience many sleepless nights and anxious days before I finally see Atlanta—or what's left of it—in the distance. A pall hangs over the city, not just the heavy feelin' of loss and devastation, but the yellow-gray smoke from cook fires and camps. I have never seen such complete desolation. The air itself feels thick and burnt. There ain't a single tree as far as I can see— not a one—anywhere 'cept behind me. It's how I imagine the Egyptians felt after Moses and his ten plagues consumed their lands.

Findin' a particular street in a destroyed city is far from easy, but with so few structures remainin', at least my choices are narrowed a right considerable. When I find the garrison, I hesitate outside, because I know once I commit, there is no going back. Five more years of my life will be spent at war, fightin' for a side I despise, for a cause I abhor, against a people I sympathize with. But I'm not allowed to remain in my thoughts for long.

"Are you looking for something, son?" A Union officer walkin' up to the garrison jolts me from my reverie.

"Um, yessir." I dig in my saddlebag for my precious papers. "I come from Morganton up in north Georgia, from Captain Germain. He gave me these papers and told me to report to Colonel Wilcox here."

The officer makes a sour face. "Germain," he mutters under his breath. Well, it's nice to know I'm not the only one.

"Yessir. I'm reportin' to serve in the Cavalry. In the West."

The officer pats down Blossom's haunches. "Fine horse."

"Mighty fine, yessir."

"How'd you come by such a fine animal?"

I guess he's referrin' to my ragged clothes and generally unkempt appearance. "She was a gift, given to me by a family I saved during…" I stop myself before sayin' Richmond. I don't want to reveal just yet that I served with the Confederacy.

"You served in the war? Cavalry?"

"Yessir."

His brow creases. "Confederate?"

So much for tryin' to leave out that information. "Yessir."

"And now you want to serve with the Union?"

No. No, I really don't. "Yessir."

"Did you see the error of your ways?"

I heave a deep breath. "Honest, sir, I don't have any money and I owe a lot of taxes and I can't lose my farm. It comes down to that. I ain't got no choice."

"Very well. Come with me."

I follow him inside the bustlin' buildin', back to a desk behind a line of men. "Remain here." He walks forward to the soldier behind the desk and whispers something to him, then disappears through a door. I can only guess that all these men are waitin' to be processed and reassigned to the West.

Once again, my heart begins to pound and flutter. I'm sweatin' like I'm standin' out in the July sun at noon. My breaths come in short gasps, like I'm tryin' to breathe underwater.

"It's not too late," I tell myself. "I can leave. I can turn around and walk out. They don't have me yet." I recall I once managed to trap a giant black bear out in the woods. His desperate, roarin' howl expresses better than my words what I'm feelin'. My leg is caught in a vise with teeth bitin' down into my flesh. Every step forward in the line is a misery, and short of eatin' through my own leg, there's no way out.

Truth be told, I can't leave, because leavin' means losin' Pa's land, and I won't let that happen as long as I have breath. There's nothin' for it. So, I drag myself forward, the property of the trapper now, and hope I don't get turned into a rug or a blanket or a coat before it's said and done.

The corporal at the desk takes my papers, gives them a cursory glance, and stuffs them in a file. I open my mouth to ask for Colonel Wilcox, but the corporal interrupts me. "Colonel Wilcox said you have your own horse, is that correct?"

Ah, so the officer was Wilcox. "Yessir."

"Fine, fine. You'll be assigned to the 2nd Cavalry Regiment. Take this to the back to receive your orders and transportation information."

Time becomes like the water runnin' over the rocks in our stream, a blur of rushed words and proddin' hands, one after the other, bouncin' me from place to place. I'm forced to swear an oath of allegiance to the United States, given more papers to sign, stripped and checked head to toe, then they issue me a heavy wool uniform, a hat, and a new pair of brogans. Once I put on the uniform, I'm told I'll be headin' to a place called Fort Laramie. The sergeant instructs me to collect my horse and bring her 'round for inspection. After they take

Blossom from me, I'm handed a stack of vouchers for meals and herded like cattle with a cluster of Blue Bellies behind the building toward the rails, where I end up on a railcar with fifty or so boys and a few grizzled ol' men. Blossom, to her chagrin, is shoved into her own car with other horses, her handlers feelin' the sting of her hooves more than once as they try to force her into her stall.

I'm in the tight, itchy blue uniform, which is the height of betrayal and terrible uncomfortable to boot. I can't imagine ridin' Blossom in this thing, so I look around to see if one of the bigger boys has a uniform that's too big for him. In the Confederacy, we freely traded clothes, I guess 'cause there wasn't really one set uniform for all, so it didn't matter much. But no one in my car looks big enough, so I bide my time. Maybe when I get to Fort Laramie, they'll give me something more comfortable.

The swirl and tumble that brought me here now slows to a lazy pace, leavin' me plenty a time for my thoughts to run wild like skitterin' chipmunks goin' to ground. I'm caught up in something, and it's gettin' away from me. But when I try to stop and think, I can't capture my own thoughts to make sense of 'em. I scan frantically through the deep places in my mind to try to find something to hold onto, some place to set anchor, but everything is a blank. I have no family. My home isn't really mine and won't be for five years. The deeper my search goes, the more the darkness closes in 'round me. Thick, chokin' fingers close on my throat, and to my shame, my eyes fill up. I'm truly alone in a desolate world. Everything that matters to me, everyone I've ever cared for is gone.

Everyone except Mary and her children.

That's it, then. I'll hang onto Mary and Ruth and Ester and Elizabeth. I promised them I'd come back. I have to keep my promise. So, I'll imagine their smilin' faces of a mornin', and I'll say goodnight to' em at bedtime.

When I'm bored and lonely, I'll talk to them like they're sittin' behind me on Blossom or ridin' in that ol' buggy. I'll imagine ridin' up on Blossom after five years to screams of delight and hugs of joy—

although they'll be very different in five years. Ruth'll be about the age Elspeth was when she...no, don't think about that. Think about the girls. Think about Mary. That'll have to be enough to keep me alive for five long years. I have nothing else.

The train car is smelly, dusty, and stifling hot, but still much nicer than the ones I rode in for the Confederacy. At least we have a bench to sleep on instead of the wood floor. I have no idea where I'm goin'—don't have a clue where Fort Laramie is—so I don't know how long we'll be ridin' the rails. Most of the other men in my car are assigned to Fort Fletcher. In fact, I'm the only one goin' to Fort Laramie. That, plus the fact the others figure me to be a Johnny Reb, as they call me, leaves me isolated on my bench while the other soldiers congregate and share stories. The older ones tell their war stories, while the younger boys listen, rapt, at their feet. I find it very interestin' to overhear their war stories from the Yankee point of view. They even call the battles different names. It's likely I coulda faced some of these same men across the battlefield, maybe even killed their friends. Such a strange thing.

We stop three times a day for water, and while the water for the engine is replenished, we're allowed to use our vouchers to get food. Still, I sit alone. I imagine I'm gonna have to get used to bein' alone right quick like, 'cause it's becomin' apparent Johnny Reb is not really welcome in their army.

Durin' the first long day and night of travel, all I have is time to think, and my mind becomes another enemy, revisitin' horror after horror against my will. Pa dies a hundred times in my arms. The vision never leaves me of Ma frantically clutchin' the frayed rope encirclin' her neck, eyes bulgin', her face turnin' red and then blue, hangin' in the doors of the barn. I see sweet little Maisie's golden-haired head explode with the shatterin' impact of the Yankee bullet. When my mind brings up Elspeth lyin' on her back beneath a sweaty, dirty Yank, I want to beat myself senseless to stop the parade of images tormentin' me. Instead, I try to sleep, but sleep won't come.

The second day, the tired, grumpy soldiers become bored and bolder. At least their harassment and name-callin' distracts me from my internal torture. I know better than to respond, havin' been taught by both my parents that it's better to respond with calm acceptance than angry rebuke when verbally attacked.

"Words dae nae harm, 'less ye allow them," Pa always said.

"A soft answer turneth away wrath," Ma would often quote.

So, I do my best to ignore their peckin' at me like a buncha riled hens, and they soon get bored with me, too, and return to their story-tellin'. The young soldiers start askin' about the Indians we'll be fightin', so some of the ol' timers tell tales from their time in the Indian Wars against the Navajo, Cheyenne, and Sioux before the start of the war.

"I fought against them red devils in the Nebraska Territory in '54. They attack us unprovocated, kilt more'n thirty of us. I tell ye, them heatherns are crazy wild and savage in a fight. They'll rip yer scalp right off yer haid for no reason, given half a chance. Their screams alone'll send shivers right up yer spine. They ain't human, I tell ye. They're animals."

I remembered my Pa's description of the Cherokee, broken and starvin', bein' marched like cows to the slaughter. Who exactly were the ones being less than human? Nothing in this soldier's story matched what my Pa described.

"Didn't you come onto *their* land?" As soon as I speak, I regret openin' my mouth. Pa also used to say, "Yer tongue wull be th' death o' ye, ye ken?" Often, he was sayin' this when he was switchin' me for back talkin' him or speakin' outta turn. I still haven't learned a thing.

The storyteller's eyes narrow. "What'd you say, boy?"

This time, I hold my tongue. Better late than never? But the ol' man isn't gonna let it be. He stands and wanders over to my bench at the front of the car. "You got somethin' ta say ta me?" I can smell his sweat and his rank breath as he leans into my face.

"Nosir. I was just askin'."

"You a secessionist *and* an Injun lover, boy?"

190

Again, I know it's time for silence, but I'm too hard-headed to stop. "I'm a fellow soldier in the United States Cavalry, sir."

"That right? I guess they'll let just about anybody in the cavalry these days."

"You one of them Galvanized Yankees?" someone from the back of the car asks.

I have no idea what that means, so I continue to stare down the older fella in my face.

"He's askin' if ye were a prisoner of war. Were ye?" The ol' man shoves his face even closer to mine. I can't help myself—I draw back from the rancid smell.

"Nosir, I am not."

"Why'ere ye fightin' for the Union then, Johnny Reb?"

"The war is over."

"Then head on home to yer folks, boy."

Blood rushes up my face as I burst from my seat, and my rage erupts in his twisted face. "I ain't got no folks, 'cause you Yankee scum killed 'em all." I shove him back from me. "You killed my Ma—hung her like a criminal on her own land. You stole the innocence from my three sisters, then shot 'em in the head. And you shot my Pa dead on the battlefield at Gettysburg. I ain't got no one 'cause of worthless animals like you!" I give him a final shove on the last word, then turn to sit on my bench, but he grabs my shoulder, spins me around, and punches me in the nose. I hear a sharp crack and blood begins to dribble outta one side.

The other soldiers jeer and encourage the ol' man to hit me again, but I'm on him before he can take another swing, poundin' him in the gut and chest, then wranglin' him 'round the neck like I'm turnin' a calf for a brandin'. He goes down with a thud, and I sit astride his chest, my hands locked on his throat. In the distance, other hands pull on my shoulders, but I refuse to let up. The ol' man is gaspin' and gruntin', and his puffed cheeks redden—much like I imagine my Ma's face doin' as she was hangin' there. I squeeze tighter.

"Let him go!"

191

"You're killin' him!"

Those words break through my demon haze. I don't wanna do no more killin'. So, I slowly open my clenched hands and lean back. Now the arms I felt before are able to pull me off the ol' man, but none of 'em dare to retaliate on the ol' man's behalf. They drag him back to the back of the car, and I'm left alone again with my thoughts.

The endless clack of the wheels against the rails becomes a kind of balm, makin' my mind go oddly blank, which is a blessed relief. The third and fourth days on the train trudge past without incident. My fellow passengers leave me alone. Even the ol' man is wary, cuttin' glances sideways at me when we walk off the car together at water stops. The daily rhythm of sleep and stop and eat and sit and stop and eat and sit and stop and eat and sleep becomes a numbin' counterpoint to the whoosh of the steam and the tick and clunk of the rails. On the fifth day, we hear the news that we are nearin' Fort Fletcher. The relief for the other soldiers is palpable. I don't share their joy.

We pull into the station and disembark. Farther down the track, I see them takin' the horses off the train, so I wander down to find Blossom. She's skittish as they try to pull her down the ramp, rearin' back her head, puffin' and snortin' and stampin' her hooves, her eyes wild, so I move forward and take her reins.

"All is well, girl. All is well. Come on with me, now." I rub her face and neck, and she calms some and walks down the ramp. "There you go. Good girl."

Other soldiers are pilin' onto wagons and carts for transport to Fort Fletcher, but I decide to follow on Blossom. We have a five-mile trek to get to the fort, and the goin' is slow behind the overloaded wagons. The creak of Blossom's saddle and thud of the wagon wheels against the dirt road replaces the sounds of the train fillin' my thoughts. Everything gleams a golden-tan—the sky and the wavin' grass—and the trees, such that there are, look more like scrub brush than the thick pines I'm used to. The land is absolutely flat, with not a single rise or indentation in sight. The endless expanse leaves me feelin' small.

Finally, our little wagon train arrives at the fort, and I'm directed to take Blossom to the stables for inspection and cool down. Then, I'm bustled to a small room at the garrison headquarters with a handful of folk destined for Fort Laramie and a sergeant tasked with introducin' us to the fort, settin' expectations for our conduct, and preparin' us for service. This day is set aside for issuin' our ordnance. I'm quite relieved when the sergeant issues me a second uniform that fits and an extra shirt, pair of socks, and undergarments. I'm given a rifle—a newfangled carbine, not like the one I'm used to carryin'—a bayonet, and ammunition. They also provide me a knapsack containin' a shelter half and a blanket, and a haversack with dish and canteen, fry pan and spatula, a mucket for boilin' coffee, a knife, and a comb, soap, and washrag. Since I'm cavalry, they also provide cleanin' tools and blankets for Blossom.

We're taken to a mess hall and fed, then shown our quarters. The soldiers destined for Fort Laramie squeeze into the back section of a barracks with almost no space between the beds. I'm tempted to sleep out under the stars, but our sergeant informs me that isn't allowed, which seems ridiculous, since we'll be sleepin' under the stars the whole way to the next fort, but I don't argue.

Once more, it becomes apparent that a Confederate soldier is less than a welcome member of the troop. My knapsack is dumped off each of the beds I try to claim closer to the center, where there is at least room to sit on the side of the bed. I read the handwritin' on the wall and select the farthest bed shoved in the back corner, store my gear under the bed, turn my face to the wall and try to sleep.

We're awakened before sunrise. At breakfast, cavalrymen are instructed to prepare their horses for a day's work, while the infantry is instructed to head to the fields for shootin' drills. I'm relieved to see Blossom, at least one friendly face around here, and she seems just as happy to see me. When I pull out an apple I saved from mess, she gobbles it up, then nuzzles my neck. We walk outside together, where I brush her and rub her down, don her new blanket, and put on her saddle. I can't imagine what kind of paces they mean to put her through—she's already proven an excellent horse in battle. But of course, they don't know that.

The sergeant has us gallop, perform tight maneuvers, finish a series of jumps, and ride headlong through smoke and the cracks of gunfire, surrounded by other horses. Blossom is smooth as butter, fluid in her movements and unshaken by the noises. The other soldiers may disdain me, but they're impressed by her performance during the drills. After we're done, a few even come up to her to look her over and comment about how well she did. I accept their fussin' over her, but I'm under no illusions that they'll treat me any different in the barracks. The line between us is clearly drawn and will not be crossed.

The next day, a few more men headed for Fort Laramie join us, bringin' our numbers to twenty. The days run together into a monotonous brew of drills and meetin's. We learn the company's bugle calls, go on mock "patrols" where we must respond correctly to each call, ride distances in formation, shoot and bayonet targets, and sit through endless talks about the strategies and tactics of our so-called enemies. Each night, after I read my Bible, I mark another day off my five years and add 40 cents to my ongoin' tally of payment against my debt.

When we're out on patrol, I relish my time alone with Blossom, although I'm sick at heart with missin' the woods, the stream, and my mountain. The scenery 'round these parts don't change much, no matter how far out you go.

The new fellers don't immediately reject me, and some of 'em seem nice enough, but I figure it won't be long before they fall into the typical pattern. My new nickname in the barracks is Johnny Red, because of my red hair. I'm not certain anyone even knows my name yet—surely, no one has bothered to ask.

While standin' out on the shootin' range one day, waitin' our turn, a boy, his face awash with freckles, and his head covered with a thatch of strawberry-blonde hair, asks me if I'm from Ireland.

"My Ma's family came from Ireland."

"How 'bout yer Pa?"

"My Pa was a Scot."

The boy wrinkles his nose. "A Scot and an Irish? Really?"

I can't help but smile as memories of my Ma and Pa in the middle of one of their verbal wars floats up. "It was about as you'd expect. How 'bout you and yours?"

"Irish Catholic, the lot of 'em." I can hear the lilt in his voice, and it reminds me of Ma. "Me name's Martin. I take it yer name's not really Johnny, eh?"

I smirk and nod. "You guess right. My name is Aidan, but most people call me Mac."

"What clan?"

"MacAlister."

"I'm a proud member of the Clan Ó Murchadha. Murphy be me last name now. Nice tae meet ya, Mac."

"Nice to meet you." I want to ask him doesn't he know who he's talkin' to? Isn't he worried about what the others will say or do to him? But I keep my own counsel.

"Ye have a fine harse."

"Yes, she was a gift."

"Quite the gift."

"I promised to return her after..."

"That's a trustin' lot, I tell ye true."

I shrug. "I don't think they expect me to return her, actually. They just said to return her, so I'd accept the gift."

"Mighty fine."

The conversation stalls. I've forgotten durin' my long periods of solitude, both durin' the war and since, how to talk to people. And since I can't exactly hand Martin an apple and nuzzle his neck, I stand, dumb and uncomfortable, while Martin shifts from foot to foot and stares at the line of men before us. It's almost a relief when we're called for our turn on the line.

The instructor comments on my skill with the rifle and urges the others to watch and learn from my example, which doesn't help me with the other men in my barracks one bit. Martin is the only one who congratulates me after I complete my rounds. He seems genuine enough, but I've learned things aren't always what they seem.

After the standin' shootin' is finished, the cavalrymen are sent for their horses. When we return, we take to the field and fire at targets from horseback, then we attach bayonets and stab straw dummies as our horses circle through the obstacle course. Once again, the instructor singles me out and has me do a second demonstration run for the others to watch. I can almost feel their glares on the back of my neck as I put Blossom through her paces. Jealousy added on top of resentment and bitterness is a deadly combination. I'm not lookin' forward to returnin' to the barracks tonight.

"Ye and yer harse put on quite a show." Martin sidles up from behind me. "Can ye teach me some tricks?"

"Sure, I can show you what I know."

"Tonight, then. After mess."

"Tonight."

I'm angry with myself for allowin' even a glimmer of hope for a friend to sneak in, for at dinner, Martin is sittin' with a group of fellers who were grumblin' about me earlier, and I'm once again sittin' alone. So much for genuine. No matter. As Ma always said, "Take ev'ry chance to do a kindness, ev'n for those who are unkind to ye. Dunnae let how they treat ye make yer choice of how to treat them. Let the Good Lord choose for ye instead." So, I'm a-guessin' the Good Lord would choose for me to help Martin become a better horseman.

It's near dusk when we ride out together. After I offer some pointers on how he sits his saddle and how to teach his horse to follow his slightest movement, he takes his buckskin mare through the course again. His mare is smaller than Blossom and should be able to take the turns easier, but she seems tentative as she approaches all the obstacles. At one point, she refuses a jump and almost throws poor Martin over her head.

I don't want to offend any worse than my bein' here already does, so I'm careful to ask for permission. "Would you mind me takin' her through?"

"Not a'tall. Maybe she'll respond better to ye."

"What's her name?"

"Honest, I haven't giv'n her one. I just met her this morn'."

"Ah, that explains it. All horses need a name." I smile at him. "That's all that she needs. She still doesn't feel like she's yours, that's all."

Martin jumps down, and I spend a few minutes strokin' her and lettin' her get used to my smell. She's a bit skittish, but that's not surprisin', given she's an army horse without a real owner. "Here, pat on her and talk to her, then tell her the name you choose for her." I pull some apple bits from my pocket and give them to Martin. "When she responds to you, give her a nice bit of apple."

Martin spends a few minutes rubbin' on her and complimentin' her, then he says, "Alright, then. Yer name is...Murphy."

"Perfect."

"'Tis not a girl's name, though. Maybe I should name her Buttercup."

I make a face. "I don't think she cares that Murphy isn't a girl's name. I think she cares that you're proud of it."

"Murphy. Do ye like it?" Murphy nuzzles him, so he gives her some apple bits, which she gobbles up appreciatively.

"So, now that she's properly named, let me give her a go through the course." I give her a few more pats, a sniff of my hand, and a piece of apple, then I hop on her back. I can feel between my legs that she's calmer, which is encouragin'. We start slowly. I walk her through the first obstacles, then we loop back around to go through again, this time at a trot. The whole time I'm talkin' to her, lettin' her know with my words and my knees exactly what I want from her.

"Well done, Murphy." I pat her neck and lean low. "Now, let's do the whole thing, shall we?"

Martin calls out to me across the field. "Ye talk to her like she's a person."

"I find horses are much nicer than most people I've met."

Rather than takin' offense, Martin leans his head back and guffaws as Murphy and I take off full speed and race through the course without a hesitation or a refusal. I bring her back to him and jump down.

"Your turn." I put the reins in his hands and lean close. "Be firm and confident. She's ready. She'll do you proud."

Martin and Murphy take off like a shot and barrel through the course, Martin whoopin' and laughin' aloud through most of it, and Murphy, for her part, seemin' to enjoy his pleasure and her success.

As they trot back to where I'm standin', Martin lifts his hand. "Thank ye, Mac. Ye be a good friend."

My heart warms a bit, but I'm quick to squash the feelin'. I don't want to let myself in for another terrible loss, whether through rejection or death—and both are very possible, even likely where we're a-goin'.

The next day we're told we will be leavin' for Fort Laramie on the morrow. Against my better judgment, I'm relieved Martin and Murphy will be comin' along. There are twenty-two of us in all headin' out the next mornin', led by a Captain Michael Norris Tucker and Lieutenant Horatio Bingham, both of 'em green as gourds, as best as I can tell. Captain Tucker, a tall, elegant man with thick, chestnut moustache and muttonchops, missed the war, being stationed at a fort in Nebraska for the duration, guardin' settlers along the Platte River. A full eight inches shorter than Tucker, Lieutenant Bingham is a squirrely lookin' feller with a hooked nose and golden curls. He is quick to let us know he is a graduate from the academy at West Point, quite recently I'm a-guessin'. By my estimation, both of 'em are rich folk, unaccustomed to real hardship or work. They lead our final briefin' in the afternoon.

After he goes over our itinerary and assignments, Tucker calls my name, asks me to stand, and comments on my skill in the field and my work with Martin, to my utter humiliation. "This type of excellence in performance, camaraderie, and spirit of unity is what we will need in abundance if we are to be successful in our campaign against the natives. MacAlister, I am raising your rank to Corporal. You will be the noncommissioned officer in charge of the day-to-day functioning of this unit. I am confident you will do an exceptional job of bringing the men together through your fine example."

I sit down as quickly as I can without being considered rude or insubordinate. I am most assuredly not confident in anything except the Captain just put a big target on my back. Martin punches my arm.

"Corporal Mac," he snickers.

"Have everything packed and ready to leave tonight before you turn in. We will leave at first light. Dismissed."

As I afeared, the men—all except Martin—glare at me as they file out of the small room. As if I'm not already set apart from them enough, now this. Martin, to his credit, hangs back and walks out with me, his eyes sympathetic. "Don'tcha worry none. The men'll come 'round."

I give him a dubious look, then we walk in silence to the mess hall. After I pick over my meal, my nervous stomach not cooperatin' with me in the least, I visit Blossom and give her a nice rubdown. "We've got us another long journey tomorrow, girl. You ready for it?" She nickers, and I offer her a sugar cube and some apple pieces. "What have I gotten us into, girl?"

Five long years, that's what. Five years of fightin' a people I have no quarrel with, who in fact I side with since the same people who took my land are takin' theirs. I still have no idea how I'm gonna navigate not shootin' at 'em in the middle of a fight, while not findin' myself court-martialed. I guess I'll figure that one out as I go.

I resist goin' back to the barracks—for more than one reason—so I take Blossom out on a short walk out the tall gate, then we take an easy ride around the outside of the camp. Thoughts of racin' on Blossom as far away from this place as I can get flutter through me, but a calmer voice reminds me of my promise and my debt. Savin' my land means more to me than my comfort and ease, so after once 'round, I go back through the gate, return Blossom to her stall, put out some hay for her, rub her down again, then walk—slowly—back to the barracks.

As I suspected, the men are talkin' real loud and boisterous-like about the Johnny Reb who thinks himself above them all. I don't know why, but I listen outside the door for a spell. I guess I want to torture myself or something. To my surprise, Martin stands up for me. Of course, he's drowned out by the others, but I appreciate his gesture of friendship.

When I walk in, the room falls into a thick, black silence. Hostile glares follow me all the way across the room to my cot in the back corner. I do my best to act like I don't notice, holdin' my shoulders back and my head high, like my Pa taught me. My back feels like Ma's pincushion from the stares borin' down on me from behind as I pack up my gear as ordered and climb into the cot, face turned toward the wall and scratchy blanket pulled up over my shoulders.

CHAPTER SIXTEEN

Bugle call sounds while it's still dark. Breakfast consists of hardtack and salted meat, then we stow our gear on the wagons, mount up, and head out as the sun peeks over the edge of the horizon. Captain Tucker estimates a journey between three and four weeks long, he says, dependin' on how the natives, as he calls 'em, behave. He talks about 'em like they're errant children instead of noble, brave warriors. I'm afeared we'll find out right quick that Tucker's estimation of them is what's in error if we run into a band of 'em on the way. If my Pa was impressed by 'em, I know they're deservin' of my respect.

Martin rides beside me, and I enjoy listenin' to his stories of his home in Boston. It's like listenin' to Ma, only with a deeper voice. He says he misses the city life, not used to sleepin' and eatin' in the outdoors. "Ach, me backside's bruisin'." He raises up in his saddle and rubs a sore spot.

"I imagine you'll be a-gettin' some sores and blisters afore too much longer."

"Got'em already," he moans.

"You'll get used to it."

"I dunnae think so." The poor boy looks sorely miserable.

Tucker calls for one brief halt a day for our daily meal of hardtack and salted meat, then at night we cook up beans, or stew, if it's been a good day. Fruit is nonexistent. I miss sharin' apple pieces with Blossom, who's forced to live off of what she can glean from the fields where we stop. I don't understand the logic in starvin' soldiers or horses that you're expectin' to stand in a fight, but I keep my own counsel. No wonder grumblin' gets worse by the day.

Several days into the journey, I decide to ask Martin the question that's been botherin' me for a while. "Martin, why're you nice to me, when I'm a 'Johnny Reb' as everyone else calls me?"

201

He turns his head aside and waves his hand. "Ach, yer no Johnny Reb tae me. We be brothers—Irish tae the core." His face goes serious. "Yer me friend. Besides, the Ol' Irish proverb say, 'A companion shortens the road.' Tis true, that one."

He's right, at least by my account.

The cold creeps in at night and sometimes lingers long into the day until the sun is able to catch its breath and re-bake the flat land beneath us. But as soon as the sun sneaks away, the heat evaporates like a July rain, and our bones start to ache. Our fires do little to chase back the frigid wind while carryin' significant risk of attractin' unwanted visitors.

The days become a repetitive drudgery in worsenin' conditions. Lieutenant Bingham becomes more and more sour as we go along, findin' fault with everyone and any little thing, as if we're at West Point instead of out wanderin' in the wilderness. His men are hungry, some sick from sleepin' out in the cold and some from the terrible food and no fruit, and he's worryin' himself about spit shinin' buckles and squarin' away our uniforms for inspection. The men take to callin' him Ramrod Bingham. They don't mean it as a compliment.

We are about three weeks in, afore our one stop for a meal, when our scout comes racin' up to the front of our line.

"Injuns!" He reports an Indian band, Crow by the looks of it, is headin' straight for us.

Tucker waves his arms. "Take defensive positions behind the wagons! Corporal! Take Murphy and Johanssen and ride out to ascertain their intentions."

Martin glances at me, wide-eyed and brows raised almost to his thatch of red hair. "Ascertain their intentions?"

"Figure out what they're after."

"As if we dunnae already know that." He fingers his fuzzy curls.

"Com'on." I prod Blossom into a gallop in the direction the scout points, and Martin and Johanssen trail behind me. We don't have to ride far. Because the land is so flat, we can see them in the distance, a plume of dust behind them lettin' me know they're ridin' fast.

Martin hisses at me. "D'ye hear that?"

I stop and listen. A faint, undulatin' yell rises on the wind. It reminds me of a chargin' line of Confederates chasin' the Yanks after their lines broke, and I'm pretty sure I know what that means. "It's a war party."

Johanssen backs his horse away from the ever-growin' cloud of dust. "Too many for us to fight." His words have the screechin' quality of someone in a panic.

"We might not have a choice."

Martin and Johanssen turn to ride back to our men, but I remain. There is something beautiful about the scene before me—something pure and even holy, in a way—men thunderin' forward on their horses to protect their land and defend their people, men without guns facin' men with rifles, boldly announcin' their approach without fear, certain of the righteousness of their purpose.

I wonder briefly if it would be possible to meet with them, to talk through their grievances and find a solution that would give them peace, but when they grow close enough for me to discern the streaks of red and black warpaint runnin' down their faces and chests, I turn and race after my companions to report to the captain.

Martin has made his report by the time I slide Blossom to a stop next to Tucker and Bingham. I notice the men have positioned the wagons to provide a barricade and some cover and are crouching behind them. Tucker's raised brows tell me he still wants my assessment of the situation, so I make my report.

"There's more'n thirty of 'em. They have no guns, only bow and arrow, but they are spoilin' for a fight, for sure and certain. I see no fear of us in 'em."

Tucker seems flustered, uncertain of his next move. Bingham's pompous commentary doesn't surprise me, but it certainly seals my view of him as a fool. "The cavalry should ride out and meet them in the open. They are no match for our well-trained soldiers. We can deal with them in short order and move the train along to our destination."

"Twenty-two of us, only twelve cavalry, against their mounted thirty or more? I don't like those odds on an open field." I know I shoulda kept my opinion to myself, but like Pa always said, "Ye dinnae ken when tae shut yer geggy."

Tucker's wide eyes dart from Bingham to me and back to Bingham. He hesitates a few beats too long, then raises his arm with a flourish.

"Bingham, you will lead the cavalry out to meet the heathens on the field. I will remain here with the rest of the soldiers to guard our wagons should one of the natives get through. We would not want them stealing our supplies, leaving us without food or water, or capturing our guns and ammunition."

Of all the foolhardy plans I've ever heard, this one sure steals th' cake. Suddenly, Bingham don't look so high-and-mighty. I almost feel sorry for him, but not quite since this stupidity is his idea. Still, his reticence is only gonna make the men more afeared, so I pull my rifle from the saddle holster and raise it above my head. "You heard the captain. Let's go."

The men mount and form up behind me. Lieutenant Bingham makes his way to the front of the formation, a sour grimace creasin' his face, like someone about to vomit bile. I don't wait on him to give the order 'cause I have my doubts it will ever come. At my click, Blossom's hooves pound the golden earth, and I race out to greet my death. At least it will come at the hands of a noble opponent. I can't call them my enemies, because they've never done me no wrong, and I harbor no ill will toward these fine men. As I ride out, a strange lightness floods me, a release of something I've gripped tight against my chest since I left home with Pa to join the cause. Something akin to joy rushes through me like a waterfall dousin' me after a hot day of plowin'. All the filth and stickiness in my soul is gone.

I give Blossom her head, and as if she senses the strange ebullience within me, she sails across the ground like Gabriel's winged horse. We leave the other riders in our dust. Throwin' my head back, I howl and whoop like a madman, racin' full tilt straight at the oncomin' riders.

My men fan out behind me, formin' a wave of horse and dirt and shadow deceptive in its size. To my surprise, the Indians rein their horses. I fire my rifle once over the Indians' heads, eject the cartridge, and fire again, still hollerin' like Ma callin' her pigs. I hear the whoosh and thud of arrows, one whistlin' by my left ear so close I think it mighta nicked my skin. Now, the men behind me are firin'. Horses are wheelin' left and right, dodgin' arrows, but I still run headlong toward the Indian warriors. I can hear the beat of my heart, poundin' out, "Take me. Take me," callin' to the warriors, or maybe to God, for deliverance.

I fire my final load, then, screamin' like a fox on the hunt, I lean close over Blossom, and we fly in amongst the scatterin' band. Their ponies are dwarfed next to Blossom's bulk. I swing my bayonet, catchin' an arm on the left and a bare side on the right, slashin' the face of a particularly majestic brave who rode straight at me. I have no awareness of where my men are or what's happenin' to them. The sounds of battle are muted. Everything moves at an unnatural pace, as if I'm Joshua, and God has stopped the sun and moon in its tracks. My consciousness is consumed by the glints off my weapon as it tatters skin, the shimmerin' beads of red drippin' from their wounds, and the strange silence inside my head.

Before I can turn to ride back through their lines, the Indians veer off and pound across the plains, away from my frenzy and the torrent of rifle fire from my men. Blossom stops, and I survey the ground on either side of me. To my great relief, no natives lie dyin' in the butchered grass. I swing 'round to find my men—all accounted for—heftin' their rifles over their heads, cheerin' their victory. But as I ride toward them, I begin to make out their cheers.

"Mac! Mac! Mac!" They aren't congratulatin' themselves. They're yellin' my name. I can't make any sense of this a'tall.

Lieutenant Bingham sits astride his horse beyond the cheerin' men, his face a mask of restrained fury. As the men gather 'round me, poundin' my back and reachin' to shake my hand, Bingham turns his horse and trots back toward the wagons, I suppose to make his report. The men and their horses are like a roarin' river Blossom and I ride all the way back to the captain, where a clamor of voices give account of my actions on the field. It's as if they're tellin' someone else's story, like I was watchin' it all happen instead of doin' it.

"Cap'n, you shoulda seen it."

"Mac rode straight at'em."

"Didn't give no heed to'em a'tall."

"Like they wasn't real to him."

"He scared 'em away single handed, I tell ya."

"I don't think he shot a one, but they ran away scairt all the same."

"It was like he was a wild thing, slashing his bayonet all around him..."

"Like a crazy man."

Bingham clears his throat to call for quiet. "The men performed admirably, Captain, as I told you they would. The natives were no match for our combined might."

A jeer and a snicker or two vibrate the air followin' Bingham's gloat, but the captain appears to ignore them. "Well done, all. Well done."

"'Twas Mac, sir. Mac won the day." I shoot Martin a witherin' glance.

"Yes, well done, Corporal. I'm sure we would all like to rest on our laurels, but I feel we must make haste and move on from this area. We do not want to tempt the natives to attack us again. Let us prepare to leave at once."

The men who hunkered down behind the wagons begin movin' them back to the trail while the rest of us refill our ammunition pouches, reload our rifles, and clean and store our gear. Within a few minutes, we are lined up and ready to continue our trek.

I ride up next to the captain. "If I may, sir."

"Go ahead, Corporal."

"I suggest sendin' out flankers to protect against the natives comin' at us unseen from the sides. They may regroup and try to come at us again, but I doubt they'd come at us head-on like before."

"Very well. See to it, Corporal."

I instruct two of the cavalrymen to swing out to the left and two more out to the right of the wagon train to watch for approachin' Indians. Martin and I hang back to cover the rear.

When we finally stop for the night, I notice the men treat me differently. For one, I'm not eatin' alone or with Martin anymore. They cluster 'round my fire, askin' me questions and wantin' to hear from me what it was like to run in amongst the natives like I done—how I managed it and what I was thinkin' the whole time.

All I can do is shrug and say, "I dunno" to their many questions. I find out Martin, on the other hand, is quite the storyteller. He regales the group with tales I've shared from the war, some of 'em partly true but most aspects are completely made up, then he goes on to give a description of my charge against the Indians in exquisite (and exaggerated) detail. I imagine by the time we reach Fort Laramie, the story will have grown and taken on the proportions of a Greek myth, with Blossom playin' the role of Pegasus, and I gallant Perseus who slew the Indian gorgon. I prefer the quiet times of rejection over all this acclaim. The last time this happened, if I remember correctly, I got stabbed in the backside.

The final week of our journey seems to go by quicker than the first legs. We don't run afoul of any more Indian scoutin' parties or war bands, which is a relief, but I believe the men are excited to get to the fort now, havin' something more to share than the mundane stories of bitter cold nights and starvin' days on the trail.

Another change I notice is, when the captain gives me a directive, the men are almost anxious to join me. Martin says they see me as their good luck charm, a talisman against the angel of death, and they want to go with me wherever I go. I don't believe in such nonsense, and it's a little unnervin' that they're relyin' on me to protect 'em, even if it is just superstition.

We're greeted at the fort with enthusiasm. Apparently, tensions are high with the natives because the Lakota and the Crow are both claimin' the land beyond the Powder River, and the Bozeman Trail goes through the territory under dispute, so soldiers from the fort have been tasked with protectin' those travelers headed to the gold mines up north and settlers goin' west.

We settle right into our lives at the fort. Along the trail, we wished for the comforts of Fort Laramie, but the reality is quite different from what we imagined. Winter is settin' in, so supplies are scarce and must last us until spring. Already gaunt from the weeks of hard travel, most of us are soon weak and sickly. Disease spreads like wildfire through the camp when there's an outbreak, and while I thought the Indians the biggest threat to us, men are more at risk of dyin' from illness, and we've not seen hide nor hair of the natives. It's such a strange thing, watchin' and waitin' for attacks that never come while wastin' away from lack of basic necessities.

On days when the snow isn't piled high against the gate, I offer to go out and hunt on the plains for game, which Captain Tucker is happy to allow, but apparently animals have more sense than humans, because game is as scarce as the food in our storeroom. I suppose to keep us busy, the captain still sends out patrols when we are able to leave the fort, but no Indians are ever sighted. A few men are sent to smaller outposts nearby to relieve solitary soldiers who've been guardin' those bases for weeks, sometimes months. Something in me longs to be sent to a solitary outpost, but Tucker won't allow it. He says he needs me here to keep up the men's morale and keep them in line. I can't say I'm doin' a very good job of either one.

I've never seen winter storms like the ones blanketin' the plains this winter. At home, the few times it snows, the snow is soft and wet, and everything is as silent as a prayer—nothin' like the howlin' winds and bitin' snow here. I swear it snows sideways more times than not, and the snow cuts into your skin like tiny, icy razors. You can't see an inch beyond your own nose if you're out in it. It's a misery for sure. If I didn't have to be here, I'd-a already headed south long since, and if I never see another snowfall again, I won't miss it a lick.

A single day seems to me to last a lifetime. When I mark off my list of days countin' up to five years, it appears the number of X's isn't growin' a'tall. The men's grumblin' ain't helpin' matters any. I believe the only reason the men don't leave like rats from a sinkin' ship is they're afeared of dyin' alone on the plains.

Martin fares better than I. He says Boston has these types of winters, too—I make a mental note to never travel to Boston—although he does complain from time to time about the snow blindness. Other than that, he maintains his good humor and jovial nature. It's annoyin', really. But I try not to put a damper on his good spirits 'cause he makes the men laugh with his fantastical stories, full of magic and leprechauns and fairies.

"You should be a writer."

He laughs. "'N what wid I write?"

"Your stories. The ones you tell by the fire at night."

"Ach, those stories already been told."

"Well, I'm sure you could make up some stories. You made up plenty about me."

Martin chuckles but offers no further comment.

I worry about the horses. We've already had a couple of 'em die—not sure if from starvation or disease—and I don't want to lose Blossom, but the fort didn't prepare well for the winter and the hay is runnin' out, too. Martin and I spend as much time as Bingham will allow in the barn with Blossom and Murphy, and on those infrequent days when the snow melts away, we take them out to forage for themselves.

It's in February when Tucker comes down with a bad case of winter fever. He's quickly confined to his quarters, 'cause no one knows if the winter fever is catchin', so a thick mantle of fear, heavier than the snow blanketin' us, settles over the fort. Men volunteer to leave for the outposts, but Bingham, now fully in charge, won't allow anyone to leave lest we spread disease further. I've come to like Captain Tucker a bit, so

I'm sorry for his sufferin', but it's Ramrod Bingham runnin' the fort now that has my stomach in a knot.

As the days pass, the captain worsens, his fever burnin', his coughs becomin' thick and wet, and his breaths labored. Bingham is on his high horse, orderin' men around like a rooster in a henhouse. And on top of that, he don't like me none, so he assigns me the worst duties, includin' cleanin' up the captain and tryin' to feed him. He thinks he's punishin' me for—well, for bein' me I guess, but he don't know I'm not afeared of dyin'. Death holds for me sweet release from my grief, eternal peace, and seein' my folks and my sisters again.

But God ain't got release for me, yet. The captain dies on the twelfth day. Since the ground's too hard to dig a grave, Bingham has me build a fire out behind the fort and burn the captain's body, still hopin' I'll catch the fever myself, I guess. But I don't. All this does is solidify the men's view of me as their guard against the angel of death, and they take to scrubbin' their hands over my red hair for luck.

With the captain gone, Bingham seems to feel the need to prove his power, so he sets about changin' all the routines the captain established and orderin' the men around just to prove he can. The men's attitudes sour even worse, and visits to the stockade become fairly frequent as Bingham takes any question as a personal affront. Of course, his time in charge will likely be short-lived, because come the spring thaw, they'll send an officer of higher rank to replace Tucker—at least I hope so.

March brings the first thaw, and Bingham is quick to start callin' for patrols. He orders me to make the assignments, so I arrange a list, sendin' soldiers out in twos to ride the trail, which he promptly squashes, sayin' one man is adequate and not to waste resources or leave the fort undermanned. I can't figure the man. Is he simply hateful, or is he really that ignorant? He won't hear any of my arguments, so I make a new list of rotatin' patrols and post it for the men.

Bingham also decides to send single replacements to the outposts along the Bozeman Trail. Again, I argue for at least two for each outpost, but he dismisses me. I've come to believe if I argued for one man, he'd send three, so I stop tryin' to get him to do what is sensical and start agreein' with him at every turn. I can't help but chuckle when it works.

At long last, a wagon train arrives from Fort Fletcher, bringin' much-needed supplies and additional men. Along with the train comes our new Captain, William Judd Fetterman, a thin man with slick black hair and hooded eyes. Unlike Tucker and Bingham, Captain Fetterman is an experienced officer, havin' fought with distinction in the war. But like Bingham, Fetterman tends toward arrogance and doesn't seem to understand the minds or abilities of the natives. To him, they are primitives and heathens only.

It's small comfort that Fetterman and Bingham don't seem to hit it off, so Bingham is relegated to administrative duties. That evenin' when Fetterman calls me to his office, I'm surprised to find Bingham is not present.

"Come in, Corporal."

"Yessir." I stand before his desk at attention. Tucker wasn't a stickler for formalities, but that doesn't mean Fetterman isn't.

"I've been going over Captain Tucker's reports from his tenure here. I must say, he was quite impressed with you."

I don't know what to say, so I stand rigid and stare at the wooden slats lining the wall behind his head.

"According to Tucker, you single-handedly fended off an Indian attack. Is that true?"

"Oh, nosir, the men were with me. Everyone fought bravely."

Fetterman twirls the end of his long moustache. "Hmm, I see. Well, Tucker reports you rode right into the midst of the heathens alone."

"The men were behind me all the way, sir, firin' at the natives. That's what scairt 'em off."

"Is that so?"

"Yessir."

"Hmm. You know, Corporal, I've often said if I had eighty men behind me, I could ride through the Sioux nation like you did out on the plains and scatter them like geese."

"Yessir. Although it was hardly the Sioux nation, sir. More like thirty men."

"Perhaps one day, they will provide me the men I require and set me to the task."

"Yessir." I hope not.

"Well, now. So, Lieutenant Bingham has you assigning daily patrols."

"Yessir."

"We will continue those. Add the new men into the rotation as soon as they are squared away."

"Yessir. Sir, may I request we send two men out per patrol?"

"I do not see why, Corporal. The men are simply scouting the enemy, not engaging them."

"Yessir, but what happens if the enemy engages them anyway?"

"They will retreat, return to the fort, and make their report."

So much for Fetterman being an improvement over Bingham.

"The men have become lackadaisical over the winter months, Corporal. It is time for you to get them back into fighting readiness."

"Yessir."

"I want morning drills reinstituted immediately. I want to see uniforms in good condition. And clean. Men perform better when they demonstrate respect for themselves and toward their superiors."

"Yessir." I can't think of a single thing less important than a clean uniform in these parts. Fetterman might be experienced, but not under these conditions. Union officers had the luxury of requirin' their men to look the part from their comfortable Southern homes they commandeered as headquarters. I'm takin' a keen dislike toward this man.

"We will be discussing plans to strike the natives soon. Red Cloud and his Lakota Sioux have clearly violated the 1865 treaties and must be brought to heel. I will expect a full report from you on the preparedness of our troops to engage the Indians by the end of the week."

"Yessir." He can't think to take forty men out against Red Cloud's more'n 4000 men?

"In June, Colonel Carrington will arrive with two battalions. By then, we will need to know Red Cloud's strength and location, as well as ascertain the status of the neighboring tribes—Crow, Cheyenne, and Arapaho—and whether they will join with Red Cloud to fight or stand by their treaties. Your task and the task of your men will be to gather this information prior to the June arrival."

"Yessir."

"Colonel Carrington will be establishing new forts throughout the Powder River country, so it is imperative we have accurate information for him when he arrives. The lives of his men may depend on it."

"Yessir."

"Henceforth, patrols will focus on locating Red Cloud's Lakota, determining his numbers, and observing his interactions with the other tribes. We must know if they are forming alliances. Carrington hopes Red Cloud is a lone dissenter, and the other tribes will have no interest in taking on the United States Army. You'll let me know if he is correct."

"Yessir."

"Very well, Corporal. Dismissed."

I execute a pro forma salute, but my hope and respect for our new commander is gone.

Martin meets me as I exit the building and head back toward the barracks. "Well? What'd ye think?"

All I can offer is a groan. We walk in silence, my steps draggin' heavy against the barren ground. I want to check on Blossom, so Martin and I part ways. I know he is scheduled tomorrow mornin' for patrol, and now that the ground is thawed and the buffalo have returned, the chance of spottin' an Indian huntin' party or runnin' afoul of a couple of Indian braves has gone up significantly. The stubbornness of our two officers rumbles in my gut like meat gone over, but all I can do about it is punch the inside of Blossom's stall. It's a mighty feeble act, but I guess that's better than gettin' myself hung.

Sleep is long in comin' for me, and the bugle call before dawn finds me already starin' at the back wall, dreadin' the day. At breakfast, Martin is his usual, cheerful self. I don't know if his jokin' around is a cover for his fear, or if he is truly fine goin' out alone. I walk with him to get Murphy ready.

"You sure you don't want me to ride along with you a while?"

"Ye would have to face Ramrod."

I snort. "I don't care about him. Right now, Fetterman likes me and doesn't like Bingham, so I'd come out on top in a confrontation."

He turns to face me and takes my hands in his. "Mac. All is well. Dunnae worry yerself none."

"You come back, ya hear?"

"I plan on it." He flashes a bright smile and hoists himself on Murphy, snaps the reins, gives a quick salute, and takes off toward the gate. I'm left standin' in the stable, rubbin' Blossom's nose.

"If something happens to him, girl, I..." I can't finish the thought. I promised myself I wouldn't do this again, get myself attached to someone—and here I am, carin' and vulnerable, on the brink of possible devastation once more. I'm such a fool.

CHAPTER SEVENTEEN

The dinner bell sounds but still no sign of Martin. I've been a nervous kitten all day, pacin' and hissin' at everybody and scurryin' around lookin' for something to occupy me. Now, my throat constricts like fingers are chokin' me, my chest aches like a hammer is poundin' on it, and I can't get enough air to catch my breath. I check one more time with the sentry, to no avail. I can't bear one more second of inaction. So, I hurry to the stable to collect Blossom.

Bingham sees me mountin' up and marches quick-like across the barren dirt of the compound. "Where do you think you're going?"

"One of the men hasn't returned from patrol. I'm gonna go find him."

"Absolutely not. It's a fool's errand. At least he has a chance to make his way back to the fort by following the glow from our fires. What will you follow to look for him? You can't track him. You won't be able to find anything in the darkness."

"I'll look for his fire."

"If he has one." His already pinched mouth is a paper-thin line as he shakes his head. "No, you will not. If he is not back by tomorrow, you may ride out in the morning to search—not before."

Martin is my responsibility. I sent him out. It's my hand that wrote his name on the list—my orders he's followin'. He is also my friend. No. I'm not gonna wait until mornin' and hope he makes it back by the glow from our fires. Bingham can afford the luxury of waitin' twelve more hours, 'cause he didn't sign the order. He doesn't care about Martin because he doesn't even know him. I care. Against my better judgment and my vows to the contrary, I have let myself care. I will not leave my good friend alone in the wilds, at the mercy of the natives and whatever else might be prowlin' out there. Nosir. Without a word, I give Blossom a nudge with my knee, and she takes off toward the gate.

"Corporal, you are disobeying a direct order. Come back here at once."

We barrel through the gates to the sounds of Ramrod screamin' my name.

Once outside the gates, the darkness swallows us like a snake consumin' a field mouse. I slow Blossom to a crawl as we work our way through the snake's throat into the icy blackness of its gullet. I'm afeared Blossom might come to injury, rammin' her legs against something unseen or trippin' and fallin', so I hop down and lead her behind me, draggin' my feet along every step of the way to feel for obstacles and test the ground.

I scan in every direction from beyond the fort but detect no telltale signs of fire—no light source at all except the thumbnail sliver of the moon. Shadow within shadow—that's what the world becomes for me. On rare occasion, I can make out indistinct shapes, a clump of scrubby trees here, a boulder there, but mainly I'm walkin' blind. Lieutenant Bingham is impossibly irritatin', but he's not wrong about the difficulty with trackin' Martin tonight. Queasiness clenches my gut. I can't fail. I mustn't. I've gotta find him, no matter how long it takes.

Every once in a while, I hear some scratchin' or shufflin' sounds, some kinda animal movin' through the brush or rubbin' against bark. In those moments, I stand stock-still and wait. I don't wanna run afoul of a bobcat, or worse, an elk. Them horns'd spear me like a fish in a creek.

Distance and direction and time become phantoms, elusive as mist in the never-endin' black. I could be wanderin' in a circle for all I can tell, but I refuse to go back. Like my Pa always said, "Yer heid be sae solid a horse's kick coudnae wallop sense intae ye." He's right. I'm as stubborn as an ol' mule, but I can't bear the thought of leavin' Martin, a city boy by his reckonin', out on the plains alone all night. A parade of possible tragedies march across my vision—captured by the natives, trampled by buffalo, felled beneath his horse, scalped, skewered...stop it. All I'm a-doin' is makin' myself crazy with such thoughts. So, I squeeze my mind down to single bright focus—scan and hope for some sign of his presence—or a miracle. A little help from the Good Lord would be mighty welcome right about now.

My joints grow stiff as the cold seeps deep into my bones. My fingers have tiny fires burnin' under the skin. Holdin' Blossom's lead becomes a challenge, too, as the leather strap keeps slidin' through my hands without my awareness. I wrap the reins around my wrist and hope she don't get spooked by an animal and take off runnin' with me in tow.

The little bit of light I have disappears as the moon settles below the horizon, and the differin' shadows of sky and land become a solid swath of pitch. "Black as th' earl o' hell's weskit," Pa called it.

Nights on the farm out walkin' the land could be like this, when the moon was new and clouds hid the tiny pinpricks of light from the stars, but Pa and I knew the land and could walk it blindfolded without a hitch. I surely do wish I could still talk to my Pa.

Just when I consider I might need to build my own fire to warm myself for a spell, a barely discernable glow flickers in the distance. I thank the Good Lord for buryin' the moon, 'cause the only reason I can see the glow at all is the blackness all 'round me. Hope warms me some, enough to thaw the stiffness out a bit, now that I finally have something to point me in a direction, so I head with all possible haste for what I pray is Martin.

The closer I get, though, the more I'm afeared it ain't my friend. The light is there, but it seems too spread out for a single campfire. I'm afeared I may have found something else, maybe a native camp. So, I close the distance between me and the hillock that hides the glow. Afore I get too close, I tie down Blossom into a clump of scrub, hopin' against hope I can find my way back to her before the sun comes up—or someone or something else finds her. Then, I slither up the side of the hillock, gettin' as near to the camp as I dare, slidin' on my belly until I can peek over the edge.

It is a native encampment. There must be forty or more tipis standin' across the valley. Bein' that it's so early, there's not a lot of activity in the camp, but I do see a few women millin' about, feedin' the cookfires that made the glow I followed, and a sentry or two walkin' on the edges of camp. I'm lucky I didn't stumble on one of 'em when I approached. I figure if I'm gonna see Martin in the camp—if he's here— it won't be 'til sunup, so I slide back down the hill and burrow down into the brush next to Blossom to wait.

I'm feelin' right sleepy when a sharp prick bites the center of my back. My first thought is it must be something in the brush bit me, but when I jerk my head around to swat it away, I find myself starin' into

217

two unblinkin' ebony eyes. The light from the new cookfires gives the eyes a shimmerin' gleam, like the knife point poised inches from my nose. I freeze, my heart gallopin' in my chest like a pony bein' chased. Then, the Indian towerin' over me does the strangest thing—he leans close to my face, reaches out, and touches my nose, almost like he's checkin' to see if I'm real. His smirk tells me he knows I'm no threat to him, yet he still stands over me, as if he's waitin' on me, wantin' something from me. There's nothin' for it—I don't know what else to do but surrender, so I roll onto my back and lift my hands high, spreadin' my fingers wide to show the young brave I'm not holdin' a weapon.

He grunts in what I read as disgust, then clutches my wrists in one hand—a really large, strong hand—and heaves me to my feet with the ease of a father liftin' a toddlin' child. He pushes me toward Blossom, and with his knife pressin' my ribs, he pulls open my haversack on Blossom's saddle. He pulls out the tin cup and fingers it with interest. He sniffs my meager food supplies and drops them in the dirt. He paws at my blanket and bedroll, snortin' in contempt. Then, he pulls out my Bible. Without thought, my hand shoots out to grab it from his rough hands, but cold metal against my throat paralyzes me. He glares at me, then returns his interest to my most precious possession. He opens the leather cover, fingers the pages, then shakes the book. A single sheet floats lazily into the undergrowth—my makeshift calendar I use to mark off my days of service.

Something about that little piece of paper disappearin' into the darkness blows out the last ember of hope remainin' in my chest. My knees tremble as the brave stuffs my Bible in his satchel. He binds my wrists with a thick, coarse rope, loosens Blossom's reins from the bush, and drags me, with Blossom in tow, into the center of camp, jabberin' nonsensical syllables that sound more like he's hockin' something up out of his throat than a language. He barks at a woman placin' strips of meat across a rock over a fire, and she hustles away toward one of the tipis.

After he ties Blossom near the pen holdin' the other horses, he stands rigidly in place, still as a frozen lake, and holds my bindings tight and close to him. I'm shaky and frail, like a disobedient child in the arms of a furious parent who's makin' me wait to see what my punishment is gonna be. If he's wantin' to intimidate me, it's workin'. While we stand and wait, I'm assumin' for the woman to return, I cast quick, furtive glances at my captor, 'cause despite my perilous predicament, I'm strangely fascinated by him.

He stands almost half a head taller'n me, and his angular face, the color of copper, reminds me of a hawk—broad forehead, long, hooked nose, and hooded eyes atop a thick, corded neck. His abundant hair hangs smooth as satin almost to his elbows, a single section braided and snakin' down beside his left ear. In the semi-darkness, his hair looks almost blue, it's so black. Strength emanates from every part of him, from the stern lines of his mouth and jaw to the broad expanse of his shoulders and chest. But it's his eyes that really captivate me, those same black, glistenin' eyes I spun 'round to find starin' through me, with depths like gazin' into the fathomless night sky beyond the farthest star. They speak of intelligence and bravery, power, intensity, and assurance, perhaps even wisdom. This man is no heathern, no wild, crazed animal.

He doesn't look at me but stands straight as a pine and stares unblinkin' toward the tipi where the woman scurried. We don't have to wait long 'til the woman emerges, and behind her, an elderly native bends through the flap to stand in the entrance, his arms folded. My captor takes his cue from the elderly man, shovin' me forward to stand before the elder who I assume is the chief of the tribe. His face is a mass of wrinkles, his skin leathery, darker than the skin of the brave holdin' my arms. His once-dark hair is streaked with white and gray. He stands almost as tall as the brave but is somewhat hunched over with years. Still, his wiry form, wrapped as it is in buffalo hide, carries its own strength.

The elder says a few words to me which could be a question. At first, I say nothing, but he repeats the same words, more insistent this time. Not knowin' what he's askin, or if he's askin', I decide to introduce myself. "My name is Aidan MacAlister. United States Cavalry. Fort Laramie."

"Laramie. Fort." The young brave seems to recognize these words.

"Yes." I nod vigorously. "Fort Laramie." I point to myself. "Aidan MacAlister." Then I point to the elder. "Your name?"

A string of shn's and ch's and ah's and haw's and kah's flow like a stream over rocks in a seemingly endless babble. The young brave argues with the elder, wavin' his arm toward me, shakin' his head. I don't have a clue what they're sayin' about me, but I can tell it ain't complimentary. The elder's response is harsh and short, and the brave drags me away from the elder as he whirls to reenter his tipi. The brave pulls me along behind him to the part of camp where the women are busily preparin' the early meal. He presses against my shoulders 'til I flop onto the dirt, then binds my wrists and ankles together like a roped calf and ties the rope to a stake I'm sure is used to tie up dogs. Clearly, he doesn't think I'm a threat since he's leavin' me to be watched after by the women. He gestures for me to stay, then stalks back to Blossom. He drags her saddle from her back and carries it to the chief's tipi. I suppose they'll be discussin' what's to become of me.

I inspect my bonds and glance around for means of escape, but with the woman workin' nearby eyein' me, it's hard to even try to loosen the thick rope, if I could figure how to reach the knots, and I'm pretty sure she can take me down if I try it. Plus, leavin' Blossom behind isn't an option. I try to comfort myself with the thought that if the brave's wantin' to kill me, he woulda done it when he stood over me with a knife in my face, but I can't quiet my poundin' heart or my racin' thoughts. There's nothin' else for me but to wait and see.

While I await my fate, I use the opportunity to scan the camp for Martin. I wonder if he came upon the camp like I did and got himself captured, too. Hopefully, he's smarter'n me and is already back at the fort, laughin' at his fool friend goin' out in the dark to hunt him. Gettin' myself captured'll sure make a fine addition to his Mac stories, if I ever make it back.

As the sun's glow tints the horizon with amber, the camp gets quite busy. At first, I figure this level of activity is normal, but the intensifyin' air of agitation feels off to me, and I wonder if something is amiss—beyond my presence, which hardly seems worthy of such nervous energy. They appear to be preparin' for something, by the way women and children are dashin' to and fro, settin' out blankets on the ground, and the men are paintin' themselves up like they're goin' to war. Surely, they wouldn't take my stumblin' upon their camp as a reason to attack the fort? A group of braves, their faces painted, enter the elder's tipi and remain there for quite some time. Whatever is happenin', my agitation now surpasses theirs as I imagine all sorts of scenarios, none of which bode well for me or for the soldiers at the fort.

Mid-mornin' brings new questions for me as the group of braves file from the elder's tipi, mount their horses, and ride out of the camp. The natives left behind remain in a state of frenetic activity, dashin' about like ants on a disturbed mound. I don't believe the Indians would attack the fort with only a handful of braves, but I'm not familiar with their ways so nothin' is certain. For sure, the tension in the camp doesn't help my nerves one bit.

The braves return a short while later with a band of natives from another tribe in tow. The dress of the newcomers looks familiar to me. At first, I can't place where I've seen 'em before, but then I realize they are dressed like the natives we met out on the plains on the way to the fort. Crow. My impression is the Crow and the Lakota are enemies, but this gatherin' doesn't look compelled—yes, both sides are on their guard, but no weapons are out and agreeable enough conversation is goin' on, as best I can tell. The women set out a large spread of food for the Crow, and the elder gestures for their guests to sit alongside the strongest braves in the camp. The rest of the natives sit 'round the outside of the main circle to eat with the visitors.

I can hear pieces of their conversation but can't make sense of any of it. The tone remains pleasant overall until they finish their food, then the mood shifts and what I assume are negotiations begin. Hand gestures from the Crow visitors seem to be forceable, maybe indicatin' some demands. For their part, the Lakota seem at worst adamant in their refusal and at best disinterested. At one point, I hear the word fort used repeatedly in the exchange, so I know our presence at the fort is a concern for both groups.

The conversation drones on, so while my captors are preoccupied, I begin to work against my bonds, but the thick rope is unyieldin' and all I succeed in doin' is rubbin' my wrists and ankles raw. As I consider other possible means of escape, the brave who caught me stands with a shout, points in my direction, pounds his chest, and issues forth a flood of unintelligible words, addin' the word "fort" to the mix of syllables. He startles me so, I almost topple over. I wonder if he's noticed my attempts to free myself and that's why he's in a rage.

The Crow turn to look at me, and to my surprise, their eyes widen, several brows raise, a few mouths drop open for a beat or two, then the Crow braves begin to chatter wildly while gesturin' toward me. I guess my uniform scares 'em, although given my bound state, I don't pose a threat a'tall.

One Crow brave calls out what sounds like, iachu-ha-kae. The words ride through the Crow like a wave—iachu-ha-kae, iachu-ha-kae—over and over.

The Lakota brave questions the Crow. "Sungila sá?"

His words sound shocked or maybe skeptical. In response, a few of the Crow warriors jump to their feet, babblin' and gesturin' toward me while they act out some kinda animated war dance, complete with blood-curdlin' screams. The Lakota watch and listen, glancin' at me occasionally with looks of surprise and awe.

My discomfort at bein' the center of their conversation peaks when one of the Crow approaches me, the brave who captured me on his heels. The Crow kneels before me and gestures back toward the brave behind him. "This one catch you as he say?"

I'm so taken aback by English comin' from his mouth I stutter for a moment before I regain my senses. "Yes, he did."

The Crow stands, turns, and grasps the Lakota brave's forearm. "Iilápaachitche."

The Lakota nods and returns the grasp. "Tahansi."

What just happened? My hands drip with sweat. It's like I'm tryin' to swallow the fat knot in the rope that binds my feet and hands. Beyond the two men, I see the Lakota elder stand and hold his arms wide. He calls the two warriors back to the circle, but I need to know—to understand.

"Wait. Wait a minute. What're they sayin' 'bout me? What means iachu-ha-kae?"

The English-speakin' Crow brave glances over his shoulder. "Means...red fox. Iáxuhke."

"Sungila Sá." The Lakota brave nods once and waves his hand in my direction.

"I don't understand. What's shung-he-la-sa?"

The Crow points to himself, then to the brave. "Iáxuhke. Sungila Sá. Red fox." He turns his back and walks with the Lakota back toward the circle.

"What're you sayin'?" A desperate, crawlin' feelin' as if a swarm of locusts has taken up residence in my gut overcomes my better judgment. "Tell me. What does it mean?" My curious interest in my captors is long gone. Now, I'm overcome with a feverish urge to leave this camp. I start wallowin' in the dirt, tuggin' and wrenchin' the ropes with everything in me. I even try bitin' the one section I can reach. Nothin' works.

The elder, gesturin' at the two braves, makes a long speech. They're all oblivious to my frenzied wrestlin', or they know it don't matter none. He points to the two men, then he waves his arms and walks 'round the circle like a struttin' rooster and repeats the words the brave exchanged with the Crow warrior—ta-han-she.

"Tahansi."

"Iilápaachitche."

"Tahansi."

"Iilápaachitche."

One by one, the warriors clasp hands and share the words. I gather they're exchangin' some kinda greetin' or a promise. In my addled mind, I imagine they're agreein' on how they're gonna torture me—set me in amongst them and perform that strange, screamin' war dance then feed me to foxes? Some distant part of me knows this ain't likely, but I can't make no sense of anything that's happenin'.

After they exchange the words, the men settle back into their circle while the women clear away the remains of the food, and the feeble and young leave to allow the warriors to finish the deal. The elder pulls out a long pipe, holds it above his head, and intones a few words. He pulls a burnin' twig from the fire, lights the pipe, and inhales, blowin' the smoke into the air above him. Then, he passes it 'round to the warriors. Lakota and Crow alike share the pipe, each one blowin' the smoke up into the air. Afterwards, the elder stands and makes another speech, this one somber, almost ominous in tone.

I'm still wrigglin' against the ropes and thrashin' about in the dirt when the meetin' starts to break up. The English-speakin' Crow pauses as he passes by my stake and looks down upon me like one might look upon a beaten dog, with a mixture of disgust and pity. In that moment, I despise him and growl up at him, much like that whipped pup.

He squats down beside me. "You—akdúxxiia—warrior. Sheechilíissee. Not afraid death—not like soldier of fort. Iáxuhke. You—ride among us—no kill—still not afraid. Iilíso—scream—like red fox." His hand moves toward me like a gentle wave across a lake. "Name."

A strange calm settles over me, almost as if his hand has wafted a soothing breeze across my skin that reaches deep into my heart and mind. "It was your people I fought..."

The brave offers a solemn nod.

"You were there."

He nods again and points once, twice, three times to other braves as they pass. "Saw Iáxuhke fight. Baaeétchiichiwee."

"What?"

"Told story many time—all know story of red fox—warrior from fort not like soldier."

"That's me." I'm beginning to understand.

"Much respect."

I'm oddly humbled by his honor toward me.

"Lakota catch. Must respect Lakota."

"I see." So, when the Crow braves saw me and heard the Lakota had captured me, the Lakota earned their respect. "Did you make peace?"

"Now Iilápaachitche. Strong friend."

It's hard to believe that my presence is the reason the Crow and Lakota made peace, but I suppose it's a good thing if it means no more death. "Will you fight against the soldiers at the fort?"

The brave shrugs. "If soldier fight." He reaches out and touches my arm. "Not belong fort. Not like soldier. Belong with the people."

"What?"

But the brave says no more. He touches my arm again, and I'm reminded of how my fellow soldiers rub my hair for good luck. Then, he stands, and with a single nod, turns and strides away. He glides like he's carried by the wind, straight as an oak, the muscles in his legs ripplin' like flutterin' leaves, his long hair flowin' out behind him. My heart tugs in my chest, as if I'm watchin' a friend walk away who I know I'll never see again.

The Lakota brave, my captor, approaches and looms over me like a hawk over its prey, fists at his hips, elbows out like wings. The sun is directly behind him, so he casts his long shadow over me. "Sungila Sá." He sneers, his tone sarcastic. "Hiyá. Canl waka." As he did once before he reaches out and touches my nose. When I don't respond, he chuffs, "Canl waka."

I wrestle internally for a moment, then decide to take a risk and say the word I heard the Lakota repeat to the Crow—the word I think might mean what the Crow termed 'strong friend.' "Ta-han-she."

The brave's face darkens to a thunderous cast. "Hiyá." This time, the word takes on a much more ominous tone. I'm afeared I've stepped in it now. He snatches the rope bindin' me from the stake and yanks me to a semi-standin' position, then drags me by the rope, half-stumblin' and mostly fallin' behind him across the camp to the center where they just met with the Crow.

He loosens the knot and frees my hands and unbinds my feet. While he's messin' with my feet, he unties my brogans, pulls them off, and throws them toward the brush. With a flourish, he rips my coat off me and throws it aside, then tears the buttons from the front of my shirt and pulls it over my shoulders until it drops to the ground.

Within seconds, I'm weak-kneed and shiverin' like a scairt kitten. I fold my arms across my chest, which I'm sure makes me look like a shriveled up ol' man. This prompts another sneer and a chuckle. Other braves are startin' to gather to see what's gonna happen between the red fox and the brave. The brave hurls what I'm sure are insults as he stalks around me like a cat toyin' with a trapped mouse, darin' me to run. I'm acutely aware of my humiliation, and a kernel of anger starts to stir in my chest. But I don't want the demon to take hold, so I choke down my pride and stand there, eyes closed, takin' his ridicule. I ain't that much a fool that I'd start a fight with a whole camp full of braves.

He stops before me and pokes my bare chest. "Kicizapi."

I fix my stare on his and refuse to divert my eyes, hopin' this small gesture might back him down.

"Nakiksi. Kicizapi."

A thin, wiry young native with narrow eyes spread wide on his long face and two black braids trailin' across his shoulders steps toward me. "Mato Waäylo say fight. Defend self."

Without taking my eyes off my opponent, I spit back to the brave. "Tell Mah-do Wah-ay-e-lo I said I don't wanna fight."

"Then coward. Canl waka."

"No chahnl-wah-kahn. Ta-han-she."

"Must earn respect. Not given slave."

Slave? Is that what I am now?

"Tahansi only family."

I think about what the Crow brave said about my place bein' with the people. Perhaps I can convince Mah-do Wah-ay-e-lo I want to be family. He pokes me again, harder this time, and I stumble backward, but now that I understand my adversary's words, I refuse to cower anymore, so I unfold my arms and step back toward him. He lifts his head and curls his lip, so I mimic his expression to gales of laughter from the onlookers. The crowd chants, shung-he-la-sa, shung-he-la-sa, mockin' the name given me by the Crow.

"Must fight. Or coward. Slave." I sense the young brave is tryin' to help, although I don't know why. But with his help, I'm beginnin' to grasp what's expected—even required—if I'm not gonna be a slave to the Lakota for the rest of my probably short life.

I think back to my fight with the Crow. That's what the Lakota want to see. They want to see the red fox, the screamin' wild man they saw acted out by the Crow. If that's what it takes, that's what they'll have. I release my restraint against the ragin' demon within and bellow a deafenin' screech as I pounce on my opponent, clawin' at his eyes. He shoves me off like he's swattin' a mosquito, but I'm up in a flash and wrap my arms around his midsection, pummelin' his lower back and kickin' his legs. It only takes him a moment to pull out of my embrace. He holds me at arms' length, his huge hand encirclin' my throat while my arms flail and my fists pound down on his arms to try to get him to release his grip.

226

My vision is grayin' around the edges when he releases me to tumble in a heap in the dirt. I gasp in some air, then I'm up again, rushin' at him headfirst. This time, I manage to catch him unawares. My head crunches against his ribs, and he collapses beneath me. I sit astride him, a flurry of punches bloodyin' his nose and face. He rolls and tosses me off, and he's up on his haunches like a mountain lion ready to pounce. I scramble back, assumin' my own crouched position, and we eye each other, both of us heavin' for air. The gathered crowd is hollerin' and hootin', and I vaguely wonder which one they're cheerin' for.

With the grace of an eagle takin' flight, he rises to his feet, and in one motion he's at my side, liftin' me in the air as easily as he would hoist a child. He holds me over his head like a prize as I kick and spit and hammer my fists against his head. I can't tell that he even feels my punches.

The brave beats me every time on strength alone. The one thing I have on my side is quickness. I have to stop fightin' him on his terms. I allow my body to sag, relaxed in his arms, and when he loosens his grip, I flip and twist from his hands, grabbin' around his shoulders as I fall. I hang on his back, my arms locked around his neck and legs around his waist. He slaps at me, but I use his bulk against him, duckin' my head beneath his shoulders when he reaches for me. He tries spinnin' 'round to shake me off, but I've broken horses my whole life, so I hold on and ride him.

At long last, the brave is gettin' frustrated. I'm hopin' that means he'll tire of this game. He doubles over and tries to pull me over his head. I keep my grip. Whenever he stops to catch his breath, I tighten my lock on his throat and squeeze as hard as I can until he resumes his thrashin' 'round.

If he was thinkin' clearly, he'd slam me against the ground beneath him, which would knock my air out and incapacitate me, but he hasn't thought of that yet, so I cling tighter and tighter, ready in an instant to somersault off him should he start to throw himself down. Instead, he runs straight toward a clump of scrub trees, and as he nears them, he turns and slams his back into the closest trunk. My teeth rattle like they're gonna shake out of my head. But I manage to hang on. He takes two steps forward and starts to propel himself into the trunk again, but I flip off his back before he hits. He takes the brunt of the strike as I scamper out of his reach.

He shakes his head and rubs his throat. My efforts must be takin' a toll. Unfortunately, he recovers quickly and strides toward me, seethin', his teeth clenched so tight I can see his pulse along his jaw. I guess I'm makin' him look bad in front of his tribe.

I need this fight to end before he kills me, but if I surrender, he and the tribe will view me as a coward, which means I'll be killed anyway. Plus, if I survive, I have to live with myself. At least I can go out with some self-respect. If letting him win doesn't work, perhaps brazen mockery will earn respect from the natives, although I'm not sure where that fine line is between showing courage and gettin' myself killed. Oh, well. My back ramrod straight, I toss my head in challenge, flash him a look of utter disdain, bare my teeth in a sneer, and turn my back on the brave.

The natives whoop and stomp their feet on the packed dirt. I'm insulting him. Amongst the noise of the hollerin' tribe, he rushes me and spins me around to face him. I stand toe to toe with him, keepin' my head raised so I meet his stare as he glares down at me. Then, I do the unthinkable. I reach up with one finger and touch his nose.

Dead silence descends on the observers as they wait to see how the brave responds. His jaw ripples beneath the skin, his brows a thundercloud of fury, his chest heavin' like the tide, and I figure I'm a goner, but I refuse to lower my eyes or back away. We remain in deadlock for what feels like an eternity, until at long last he grabs my arm and drags me back to the stake, shoves me to the ground, and ties my wrists and ankles to leave me under the supervision of the women once more.

CHAPTER EIGHTEEN

The days pass in the monotonous boredom of sittin' and watchin' and waitin' while nothin' happens of note. The natives' days are filled with routine—the men hunt, and the women gather berries and roots, prepare meals, and make clothes, arrows, and other necessaries from buffalo hides, bone, and fur.

When the men return from the hunt, the women skin and prepare the slaughtered buffalo. I'm surprised and impressed by their strength. Nothin' seems beyond these women. Sometimes, they even go out with the men on a hunt, carryin' blankets with them. On those days, I'm left bound and tied to the stake, a wayward dog who can't be trusted to wait for his master's return.

Breakin' camp is a feat in and of itself. I've never in my life observed such efficiency of effort, even within the armies. Everything is portable—no energy is wasted. The natives can break down, move, and reset a camp in one day. At first, I'm relegated to observer in these moves, dragged along by my ropes like one of the horses, but after a time, the women loosen my ropes and allow me to help carry some heavier loads of wood from tipis and mounds of furs for trade durin' the move.

The women provide me with clothin' and mocassins made from buffalo hide, since my uniform was destroyed in the fight with Mah-do Wah-ay-e-lo, whose name I've since learned means "Angry Growling Bear." Appropriate name.

The young brave who speaks some English has sorta befriended me, at least as close to a friend as I can have here, as a slave. His name, he says, means "Silent Grasshopper." To me, it sounds like "Ga-noo-sh-kah Ah-e-ne-lah," but he laughs at me when I try to say it, so I call him Grasshopper.

He comes in the early evenings and talks with me, in part I think to help him learn more English to benefit the tribe, in part to learn more about the ways of the soldiers at the fort, and in part to try to teach me some native words so I can communicate. I admit I am a slow learner.

Summer passes in a series of moves across the plains to follow the buffalo herd. Mah-do Wah-ay-e-lo decides he will allow me to feed and take care of Blossom while I tend to his horse, so I suppose I earned some small measure of regard durin' our fight. However, other than draggin' me away to do chores for him, he doesn't interact with me, so my fascination to learn more about him remains unsatisfied. Whatever I do learn, I glean from Grasshopper, who holds Mah-do Wah-ay-e-lo in high esteem salted with no small measure of fear.

After I've helped a bit with several successful moves, the chief instructs the women to teach me their chores and unbind me durin' the day so I may help them.

Accordin' to Grasshopper, the chief says I must earn my keep if I am to be fed. I don't mind at all. I'm sick of sittin' and watchin' and waitin'. So, I'm relegated to women's work—all except gatherin' berries and roots. They still won't let me wander from the camp, even though I have no idea where I am or how far we've roamed from the fort. I take quite the ribbin' from the braves while I wash and sew and scrape hides, but I don't mind. It's something to do.

As the cold creeps back in the evenin's, the camp begins a flurry of activity in preparation for the winter months. Meat must be dried and stored. Winter provisions and firewood must be collected. Other natives come to the camp, and the Lakota trade buffalo fur and hides and dried meat for corn and potatoes and vegetables farmed by the other tribes. Grasshopper tells me these tribes rely on the Lakota to defend them if attacked by enemies, since they are farmers and poor warriors. He reports this with some contempt. These trades continue until the first snow.

I've lived through one hard winter on the plains while I lived at the fort, but there, I had a barracks and other buildin's against the cold. I don't know how I'll survive the hard winter months in the camp. To my surprise, the chief permits me to sleep inside a tipi with Grasshopper, or I'd for sure freeze to death, but I remain bound even while sleepin'.

The men remain in camp durin' the heaviest snows, but when the weather clears, a few warriors range out for short expeditions in search of buffalo or elk. They rarely bring back any game, so we exist on the stored meat and dried berries from the summer and fall trades. Durin' these months, I spend a lot of time with Grasshopper, tryin' to understand Lakota words and learnin' their ways. To my surprise, the Lakota believe in a Great Spirit and have a deep reverence for life. In fact, their beliefs don't seem terribly different from my own, so I risk sharin' some of my beliefs with Grasshopper on the long, cold nights holed up in his tipi. He's especially interested in the man who died in the place of others, which he says shows great courage.

Accordin' to Grasshopper, Jesus would be considered "Tahansi"—strong, respected friend. Finally, I gather my own courage to tell him Mah-do Wah-ay-e-lo took my book with the stories of Jesus in it. He promises to ask Mah-do Wah-ay-e-lo about it.

As best as I can keep track, it's December when natives from a neighborin' tribe arrive at the camp. All the men of fightin' age leave with them, includin' Grasshopper, which leaves me without anyone to talk to until he returns. The men are gone for more'n three weeks— three weeks of grunts and angry gestures as the only communication I receive. Between the snows, the cold, and the silence, I think I might go mad.

When the men return, there is a huge celebration. A massive fire is built in the center of the camp. The warriors dance around the fire, thrustin' and shakin' their spears in imitation of combat, while the women beat drums and shake rattles in a circle around them.

Everyone sings and whoops and yells until the air vibrates with their cacophony. Mah-do Wah-ay-e-lo, a fierce gleam lightin' his eyes, forces me to remain and watch through the night, almost as if he is makin' a point I don't understand. This display goes on into the wee hours of the morn. The dancers don't seem to mind the cold, whipped into such a fervor as they are, but I'm miserable, even under my buffalo pelt blanket.

When the frenzied dance ends, Grasshopper comes over to me, jubilant with glee. He proclaims the Lakota have won a great victory. He says Arapahoe and Cheyenne fought side-by-side with the Lakota and ambushed men from Fort Laramie in the Peno Valley beyond Lodge Trail Ridge, killin' all of 'em.

Fetterman. Ramrod Bingham. The men I fought beside against the Crow. Perhaps even Martin, if he returned to the fort in my absence—all dead. A sick feelin' grips my stomach, and I have to swallow to keep from retchin'. Grasshopper calls it the battle of the hundred slain. He continues to describe the scene in gruesome detail, but I barely hear him. All I can think of is their bodies, lyin' mutilated out on the cold plains, hacked to pieces by these men I had begun to respect and even admire. Now, hatred and disgust fill my belly. I stare, mute, when Grasshopper finishes his tale, his face expectant, as if he's waitin' for my congratulations.

All I can manage is to croak out, "Why?"

Grasshopper frowns. "Soldier from fort steal Lakota land." He says this real matter-of-fact-like, as if he's surprised I don't already understand this obvious reason.

Truth is, I do understand. I didn't want the Yanks stealin' my land, either, and I was willin' to kill over it. How can I judge the Lakota for doin' the same? But knowin' they killed my fellow soldiers is hard medicine. My chest feels broken, ripped in two as easily as one could tear a thin piece of cloth. A deep shame over my own actions durin' the War returns full force, along with this new shame for abandonin' the men at the fort to their fate. Could I have kept the massacre from happenin' if I'd been there? Would they all still be alive?

I wander away from Grasshopper into the frigid darkness, my heart reflectin' the same state. My beliefs, my values, my reason for bein' a soldier in the first place, my reason for bein' a soldier alongside my enemies—all of it is in question now. How can I make sense of it, in the face of the natives killin' my fellow soldiers for the exact same reason my Pa and I went to war? Is the land as important as Pa claimed? Is it worth livin' and dyin' for? Do the natives have a right to kill for their land like we did for ours? Accordin' to Pa, the Good Lord says to fight for your land, and plenty of heroes in stories in the Old Testament do just that. But it sure feels different when it's your fellers who're bein' kilt. I sleep that night under the stars, wrapped in my buffalo pelt. At least for now, shiverin' is better'n bein' around the natives.

As the weather breaks and the sun warms the plains, life in the camp returns to the normal rhythms I got used to over the summer and fall. Durin' the spring months, the warriors spend long days away from camp. I wonder if they are rangin' to hunt, fightin' against other tribes, or attackin' the fort or outposts along the Bozeman Trail. No one bothers to tell me. But it's one of those long absences now, which means I'm expected to do the tasks usually handled by the braves.

I struggle durin' these times, 'cause when the chief's wife babbles out a list of instructions, I only catch some of her words, and I have no one to ask what she said. Her switch against my back hurts somethin' fierce.

An ear-piercin' shriek causes me to drop the load of wood I'm carryin' for the fire, and I hear shouts of "Pawnee! Pawnee!" echoin' across the camp. Women are herdin' children into tipis while the elderly men are comin' out, carryin' bow and arrow or clubs, and I see one or two rifles.

Another shout rises within a cloud of dust, and I see for the first time the invadin' Indians. They have crests of hair stickin' straight up down the center of their heads, most adorned with feathers, and their faces and chests are painted in bright red swaths. They look like roosters to me, which causes a cackle of hysterical laughter to escape my lips.

One woman runs across my path, carryin' a wee bairn in her arms. I hear a strange thud, and the woman stops in her tracks, an arrow protrudin' from her back. She falls to the ground, her bairn squawlin' beside her. I'm movin' before I realize it, runnin' for Blossom. I unwrap her rope and swing myself up on her bare back. It's then I notice I have a thick piece of firewood in my hand—I suppose I picked it up from the pile I dropped when the first shout sounded. Blossom, already agitated from all the yellin', bolts at my kick. We race across the center of the camp toward the Pawnee, who are pourin' into the camp in a seemingly endless flow, like a creek when a beaver dam breaks. Arrows whiff by my head, one strikin' true but most fallin' to the ground as I barrel into the Pawnee, swingin' my stick of firewood like I'm choppin' down wheat in the fields.

Children throw rocks at the invaders. Women hurl spears and shoot arrows alongside the elderly men. One of the Pawnee grapples a woman into a chokehold and drags her toward his horse. Red-hot rage boils up like bile into my mouth. I turn Blossom with a press of my knee toward the pair, gobblin' up the ground between them and us in her powerful strides. With a banshee shriek, I swing my club at his head, and he collapses like a sack of grain tossed from the barn loft. One of the men calls my name—"Sungila Sá!" When I turn, he lifts his rifle in the air. Is he offerin' it to me?

I continue to pelt the Pawnee with head blows as I urge Blossom closer to the elderly man. As I thought, he tosses me his rifle as soon as I'm near enough. I spin Blossom around, bellow, "Shung-he-la-sa"—because it's the first word that comes to mind—and race back into the middle of the Pawnee, firin' with one hand and swingin' my club with the other. Blossom's fluid motion as she weaves amongst the invaders helps keep me on her back, or I'd fly right off her.

Wounded Pawnee crawl across the ground beneath me. The rest turn to flee from the Ragin' Red Fox. Some of the women rush forward to stab the wounded in the chest, while the men continue to fire arrows into the retreatin' braves. As the last of the Pawnee disappear over the rise, shouts and hoots of victory vibrate the air. But the cost is severe. Some children lie dead, either trampled or pierced by arrows, and several women are dead or wounded. I see one of the council elders spread face down on the ground, blood poolin' beneath him.

I swing off Blossom and a stab of pain reminds me of the arrow stickin' out of my left thigh. But something more pressin' is weighin' on me—the mother and her infant child. I limp back to where the arrow struck her and find the bairn in the arms of another woman, and three women wrappin' the injured mother's body in a robe. For some reason, an image of my mother hangin' in the doorway of our barn, with my sisters kneelin' before her dead body flashes in my mind, and my throat closes. Heat rises up my neck. I turn away before the women see my tears, but one of the women calls to me. "Sungila Sá."

I respond with a grunt.

"Wahin kpe." She points. Arrow.

Noddin', I turn my back on her.

234

"Tankal. Hechena hci."

I'm not sure what these words mean, but when I glance at her with a questionin' look, her gestures tell me it has to come out.

"Wichasa wakhan. Iyaya!"

Go to healer. I bow my head in agreement and limp away from the tragic scene, swallowin' my tears. Not surprisingly, given the numbers of wounded, the healer is not in his lodge. Rather than struggle across the camp to find him, I decide to wait in his lodge for his return, so I lean against a pile of buffalo pelts and make myself comfortable.

I must've fallen asleep, because when I open my eyes, I'm surrounded by the tribe's healer and a herd of chatterin' women, all fussin' over me. I try to sit up, but my vision gets cloudy, and my head feels like it's gonna float through the hole in the roof with the smoke from the fire, so I fall back against the pelts. Their concern seems genuine enough, which in my state feels quite strange to me. I wave their hands away and try to rise again. This time, the healer pushes me down with a stern command to stay.

A searin' pain shocks me out of the fog. The healer is cuttin' my leg open. Images of soldiers stacked like wood as a doctor, his apron smeared with blood, moves from table to table to hack off their limbs, skitter across my vision.

I howl, "No!" and try to scramble away from the healer, but the women press against me on all sides, and I can't move. Terror chokes my breath. His fingers knead inside my leg, and a wave of nausea washes over me.

With a satisfied grunt, he lifts a pointed piece of stone to show me. One of the women strokes my brow while another scurries away and returns with a bowl filled with a foul-smellin' mixture. The healer chants some words, blows some smoke in my face, then scoops the mixture and smears it into the wound. Another woman leans in my face and presses a clay bowl filled with steamin' reddish-colored liquid to my lips. I risk a sip and am surprised the tea is a bit bitter but pleasant smellin' and soothin' at the same time. At her urgin', I finish the bowl.

The women surroundin' me start fussin' over me again, one wrappin' me in a thick blanket, another dabbin' my face and neck with a wet cloth, and another shakin' some kinda rattle over my chest and legs.

"Thank you," I murmur, which I know they don't understand, but I've not yet learned how to say thank you in Lakota. The healer chants a quiet song, which the women join, and I feel myself driftin'.

A yell startles me awake. I'm alone in the healer's lodge. The soft color of the sky through the hole above me tells me it's dusk. More tortured cries rise outside, warblin' and howlin', and I struggle to push myself up off the bed of pelts to see what's happenin'. I manage to hop to the openin', although my leg is painin' me almost beyond bearin'.

The warriors have returned. The women and elders crowd around the group of men, their hands reachin' out to stroke or embrace several of the braves who are wailin' at the darkenin' sky. I try to find Grasshopper, but I can't make him out in the crowd of larger braves.

I notice Mah-do Wah-ay-e-lo standin' in the center, as he towers above the rest. He seems to be a comforter rather than someone bein' comforted. How strange—I find I'm actually holdin' my breath until I see his normally somber expression and know he isn't one of the mourners.

I'm too far away to make out any of the words, not that I could understand many of them anyway, but I glean the women are sharin' the story of the Pawnee attack, and I assume the mourners are the ones who lost loved ones. The woman who gave me the red tea points toward the healer's lodge, and Mah-do Wah-ay-e-lo plows through the crowd, stridin' toward me in long, pressured steps, his hands clenched in tight fists, his brows lowered over narrowed eyes. My chest tightens. Does he blame me for the Pawnee killin' so many of his tribe?

He stops before me, right outside the lodge where I'm leanin' against the entrance. His hands remain closed by his side, his glare piercin' through me like the arrow, but I don't flinch. I've learned with Mah-do Wah-ay-e-lo I must keep my eyes up and on his, or he will perceive weakness. Without a word, he steps toward me and grasps my arms in his massive hands. Is he gonna shake me to death? Crush my bones? Instead, he draws me close and embraces me. My face buries against his chest so I can't speak, but his words come out in a rush, accompanied by tears, much to my surprise. I recognize Shung-he-la-sa and Pawnee and Dah-wee-chue, which is the word for wife, but nothing else. Did his wife die in the raid after all? He isn't actin' like it, but I can't figure him most of the time. Surely, he wouldn't turn to me, his captive and slave, for comfort in a time of loss?

Some of the warriors approach us and herd around Mah-do Wah-ay-e-lo, poundin' my back and rubbin' my hair. When Mah-do Wah-ay-e-lo finally lets me go, I spot Grasshopper wanderin' through the camp, his head down and his feet shufflin' like an old man. When I wave and call for him, he stops in his tracks but doesn't look up or respond. What's wrong with him? I look questioningly at Mah-do Wah-ay-e-lo and gesture toward Grasshopper. Mah-do Wah-ay-e-lo's face softens. He shakes his head and lowers his eyes. "Ina."

"Ee-nah?" I don't know this word. I look back to Grasshopper, who has turned and is now draggin' toward me. He's close enough now for me to see his copper face is blotchy, and his eyes are rimmed with red and sunken within gray-black circles. Did he lose someone in the attack? "What's wrong, Grasshopper?"

Tears brim in his eyes again, and he swallows several times before he speaks. "Ina—mother." He gasps and his mouth hangs open a few seconds, then closes. His jaw ripples. "Dead."

"Oh, Grasshopper, I'm so sorry." Guilt floods through me. Why didn't I save the life of the mother of my one friend in the camp? I shoulda moved quicker, paid more attention to protectin' the women...I shoulda done something.

Tears well in my eyes. "I let you down. I grieve deeply for you." In the Lakota way, I cross my fist across my heart and pound my chest.

"No. Sungila Sá no let down. Save many wives, mothers, children. With only stick, fight arrow. Many say."

"But you are my friend, and I didn't save your mother. I'm truly sorry." It's as if someone has reached through my chest, grasped my heart, and pulled it from its place. I don't even know which woman was his mother, and now I will never know.

"Sungila Sá love the people, fight for the people. Sungila Sá Lakota," he lays his hand across his heart, "here."

Mah-do Wah-ay-e-lo turns to Grasshopper and grunts out a question. Grasshopper responds, and Mah-do Wah-ay-e-lo grips Grasshopper's shoulder. His shoulders heave beneath Mah-do Wah-ay-e-lo's grip. His silent weepin' finally subsides, and he says, "Wee-yealah," which I know means 'ready'. Mah-do Wah-ay-e-lo lifts me with the ease of carryin' a pet dog and totes me to the fire in the center of camp with Grasshopper trailin' behind. At his direction, boys dart from tipi to tipi to bring all to the fire. The elder chief is the last to join the gatherin'. All the while, Mah-do Wah-ay-e-lo cradles me in his arms like a wee bairn.

Once the chief arrives, Mah-do Wah-ay-e-lo calls forth the women one by one to retell the story of the Pawnee raid. Grasshopper translates for me as they weave their tale. The truth is, they paint me in a much better light than I deserve, makin' it seem like I defeated the Pawnee single-handed. I shake my head, but Mah-do Wah-ay-e-lo gives me a stern glance, so I remain silent for the rest. Once they finish, Mah-do Wah-ay-e-lo brings forth the woman who the Pawnee was draggin' away and gestures for her to speak. She shares in exquisite detail how I clubbed the Pawnee and saved her from certain violation and death.

I notice Mah-do Wah-ay-e-lo holds his head high and his eyes are shiny in the firelight. Then, Grasshopper explains. "Hanhepi Wi Nagi tawicu—wife—of Mato Waäylo."

I saved his wife's life.

The elder who threw me his rifle shares his part of the story. Grasshopper says the elder calls me Wicasa Watogla, which means wild man, and says I am no longer wasicu, which means a white man, but Lakota.

Mah-do Wah-ay-e-lo then makes a speech, recountin' how he captured me in the brush and thought me canl waka, a coward, but how I've proven I'm neither a coward nor a slave. He raises my arm and says he now calls me misu, which Grasshopper says translates as younger brother, and he demands every member of the tribe consider me tahansi, a word I recognize. He stares through me for a moment, then makes a solemn pronouncement.

Grasshopper translates again. "Mato Waäylo say Sungila Sá have what he want of Mato Waäylo—owning. Sungila Sá—payment."

"Tell him he doesn't have to repay. I'm glad I was able to help."

Grasshopper shakes his head. "No refuse. Insult."

"Oh."

"Make claim what want."

I know two things to request right away. "May I claim only one thing?"

"Mato Waäylo say all what want. Big trust give Sungila Sá."

I can see how Mah-do Wah-ay-e-lo is indeed offerin' me a huge amount of trust. I can claim anything I want—his tipi, all his possessions, his daughter. But I only want two things. "Tell Mah-do Wah-ay-e-lo I desire two things. My horse. My Bible."

"By Bull?"

"The book he took from me when he captured me. The book about Jesus."

Grasshopper nods and repeats my requests. Mah-do Wah-ay-e-lo's face softens in a way I've never seen before, and he offers a slight smile before he replies to Grasshopper.

"Mato Waäylo say Sungila Sá man of high honor. Respect. Claim only what taken from him, no more."

Mah-do Wah-ay-e-lo clamps his mouth in a tight line, nods, and says a word I know. "Há." Yes.

A tight heaviness I haven't been aware of until that moment rises from me like early mornin' mist from a lake. Blossom is mine again. And I haven't lost my Bible, my most valuable possession. I can return both to Mary—one day.

Mah-do Wah-ay-e-lo issues a single command, and like they did with the Crow, each member of the tribe faces me, clasps my hand, and says, "Tahansi." Grasshopper whispers that I must respond in kind, or it is an insult, so I repeat, "Ta-han-she," each time it's spoken to me.

The crowd around me parts and grows silent as the chief approaches. He stands before me for several seconds, his eyes searchin' into the depths of mine, seekin' something, but I don't know what. Finally, he clasps my hand and says, "Tahansi."

"Ta-han-she." For some reason, I'm deeply moved by his gesture. I glance at Grasshopper. "Does this mean I'm part of the tribe?"

"No. Must—prove."

"Prove?"

But Grasshopper shrugs. He doesn't know an English word to explain.

Once the ceremonial moment is complete, Mah-do Wah-ay-e-lo carries me back to the healer's lodge and deposits me on the bed of pelts with a grunt and a stern point. I'm to stay here tonight to sleep. Hahn-hepee Wee-Nagee kneels beside the pelts, takes my hands in her long, graceful fingers, and lays her forehead against my hands, her thick ebony hair flowin' across my arms. I understand her gesture, but I don't know the appropriate response—and Grasshopper isn't here to help me. I'm afraid I'll offend Mah-do Wah-ay-e-lo if I don't acknowledge her in some way, so I repeat, "Ta-han-she." I have to remember to ask Grasshopper how to say, 'thank you'.

The healer and the two women helpers return to the lodge and begin their ministrations. While he reapplies the stinkin' glop and wraps my wound in hide, one woman feeds me the bitter red tea while the other chants and shakes her rattle down the length of my body. Once again, I struggle to keep my eyes open as they smooth my hair from my forehead. Their quiet hummin' is water dancin' over rocks in a stream.

Sunlight flickerin' through the hole in the lodge roof skips across my lids, and they flutter open. I'm groggy and hot, my tongue swollen and rough as sand. "Water." The word sounds more like my Pa scrapin' bark off of logs than language. "Water." I try to sit up but I'm frail and weak as a kitten and flop back onto the pelts. "Water."

The healer comes into my vision field, his face a mask of concern. He leans down and pours cool water from a leather pouch down my throat. Blessed relief.

Buzzin' in my ears makes it difficult to concentrate. The healer fusses over my leg, which hurts in a strange, distant way, almost like it's happenin' to someone else. The woman returns at some point with more tea, but I sputter and spit when she ladles it in my mouth. It burns. I want to sleep. Why won't they leave me alone? She's insistent, puttin' the cup to my mouth. I turn my head, but she growls and snatches my head around to pour more tea down my throat.

A sharp pain rouses me from my fog. It feels like the healer is diggin' inside my leg. "Stop. Stop it." I try to scream but it comes out a groan. He continues his pokin' and proddin' and scrapin' and I keep right on moanin' and writhin' under his hands.

I open my eyes to find the light has softened again. Have I been asleep the whole day? The healer has piled heavy blankets over me durin' my sleep, and I'm sweatin' like a pig underneath their bulk, but when I try to shrug them off, they're too heavy for me to move.

That's when I notice Mah-do Wah-ay-e-lo standin' in the entrance, his arms folded across his chest, and Hahn-hepee Wee-Nagee kneelin' next to him, rockin' back and forth, her moans and wails vibratin' the walls of the lodge. I try to croak, "Thank you for prayin'," but they wouldn't understand even if they could hear me.

My next awareness finds darkness. The healer pours small sips of water in my mouth, then offers me a few bites of meat, which I'm grateful for. More red tea, and I drift again.

A shake on my shoulder makes me open my eyes. Hahn-hepee Wee-Nagee stands over me, her black eyes bright with the mornin' sun and her smile. Grasshopper stands beside her; but his eyes appear dull and lifeless compared to Hahn-hepee Wee-Nagee's.

"Healer say time Sungila Sá leave." Grasshopper offers his arm to help me up.

I do feel better. My mind is clearer, and I have an appetite. I'm able, with his help, to sit up on the pelts and swing my legs to the ground.

"Hanhepi Wi Nagi say Sungila Sá stay with Hanhepi Wi Nagi and Mato Waäylo. Come. Eat."

"Grasshopper, how do I say, 'thank you'?"

"Pilamayaye."

"Pee-lah-mah-yah-yea?"

"Há."

"What does Hahn-hepee Wee-Nagee's name mean?"

"Mm—Soul of Moon? Moon Shadow?" He shrugs.

"What a beautiful name. It suits her. Hahn-hepee Wee-Nagee, pee-lah-mah-yah-yea."

Grasshopper leans down and throws my arm around his shoulder, then lifts me slowly to standin'. I can't put weight on my injured leg, so Grasshopper acts like a crutch, and I hop the long, slow trek toward Moon Shadow's tipi. But on the way, the elder chief blocks our path and speaks to Grasshopper. His head falls to his chest. "Sungila Sá, time now for Nagi Gluhapi. You come, chief say."

"What is Nagi Gluhapi?"

"For dead. Keeping of soul."

I can tell Grasshopper is pained by my questions, so I decide to hold my tongue and follow. Mah-do Wah-ay-e-lo joins his wife and takes Grasshopper's place beneath my arm.

The chief takes Grasshopper's arm in his and begins a slow, solemn march across the camp. Mah-do Wah-ay-e-lo's, who still supports me, follows, along with Hahn-hepee Wee-Nagee. We move into a stand of scrubby trees on the outskirts of camp. In the limbs of the trees stand several scaffolds, each one holdin' a body wrapped in a brightly colored robe. Next to the bodies, I see bundles of clothes, weapons, pipes and food. At the base of each scaffold, a small buckskin bag rests on a bed of colored stones. One by one, men and women gather under the scaffold where their loved one rests. Grasshopper moves away from me to stand beneath one of the platforms.

At the chief's signal, everyone begins to wail. To my horror, Grasshopper picks up a sharp rock and gouges his arms bloody. Then, he leans down and rips the stone across his legs until blood drips onto his moccasins and wets the dirt. Other children mimic the mutilation. The men tear at their clothes, pull out their hair, and cut themselves with knives.

The women observers begin to sing a mournful chant, which mixes with the cries of grief to form a strange cacophony liftin' up to heaven. I'm moved by the depth of their grief and by their honesty, their openness with their pain. I've never witnessed anything like it. Although I don't know any of the dead, I find my heart is achin' for the magnitude of the loss to the tribe. So many dead, and most of them women and children. A tear trails down my cheek. I want to let them know I share their pain, but I have no words.

The chief smokes the pipe, blowin' smoke until it curls like the tendrils of a spider's web around the scaffolds, then raises his hands in the air, and each mourner picks up the small buckskin bundle and grasps it to their chest.

Others scatter the colored stones around the bodies, while the chief intones what I believe is a prayer. I recognize the words nagi, which means soul, wakan, which means spirit, waka which means holy, and Wakan Tanka, the Great Spirit. He says where the soul now lives is a holy place and instructs mourners to live in a holy way with eyes of spirit and hands of spirit—at least, that's what I can glean from the words I understand.

Families are to live at peace. No bad is to enter the holy place. And something similar to teach others the holy way. To me, it sounds very much like something a pastor might preach over the dead in church.

As soon as Grasshopper's deep mournin' is over, I want to ask him about the chief's speech. Our previous conversations about the natives' beliefs about the Great Spirit left me wantin' to know more. I wonder if by holy place the chief means heaven.

When his prayer is finished, my spirit beckons with a deep longin' to share the hope I have of seein' my family again, but I don't know how to explain it. But the persistent voice in my head won't let me alone, so I know I must try.

"Ga-noo-sh-kah Ah-e-ne-lah." I begin with Grasshopper's true name, because I believe it honors him for me to say it. His tortured face turns toward mine. I can't take my eyes off his bloodied arms and legs and the agony etched in the lines on his brow and around his mouth. More than anything, I want to offer him comfort.

"Wakan Tanka says your...ee-nah has now gone with him to another place, a holy place we call Heaven. Wakan Tanka says your ee-nah is woh-wah-ghwah. Now she is at peace."

To my shock, Grasshopper's face crumples into a mask of fury. He screams, "Hiyá! Hiyá!" followed by a torrent of words, punctuated with a shakin' fist. It seems he misunderstands me. I must've used the wrong words.

Grasshopper holds out the bundle toward me. "Keeping soul. Ina stay with Gnus'ka Ainila. Not gone. Stay. YOU...do not speak of Wakan Tanka or ina. You know nothing." He spins back toward the scaffold. I can hear his anguished weepin' floatin' up into the sky.

What have I done?

243

CHAPTER NINETEEN

The days that follow are torturous. Grasshopper will not speak to me. Even Moon Shadow seems distant and cold. Since no one else in camp speaks English, no one can tell me what I've said or done that is offensive. I can't even do my chores, as my leg is still healin', so I'm left to sit around and wonder at my great sin, no longer a slave but not a tribe member either, just an outcast.

Durin' these days, I consider more than once runnin' away and tryin' to find the fort again, even though I know the futility of my plan. I'd never find it on my own. Besides, everyone is dead, so the fort may still be deserted. More than likely, I'd die wanderin' the plains, or I'd be captured by the Crow, or worse, the Pawnee, who have good reason to torture and kill me.

It's when the braves return after a long huntin' expedition with buffalo sighted, and the chief tells us to break camp that Grasshopper approaches me. "Chief say make peace with Sungila Sá. Sungila Sá is Lakota wicasa, no longer wasicu—white man."

"Tell me what I said that offended you, Grasshopper."

"Sungila Sá say ina gone, that Wakan Tanka take ina away."

"I didn't know those words would hurt you. I would never want to hurt you on purpose."

"On pur-puss?"

"Umm—like I tried to do it."

Grasshopper nods. "Lakota belief nagi—soul—remains with family until soul pure. Soul watch over family. Also, family must live in way honor soul. Always see only good, do only good, or soul not made pure. No fight—this why Sungila Sá no stay Grasshopper. We fight. Must make right."

"So, when I said Wakan Tanka takes ina to heaven, you think I'm sayin' Wakan Tanka stole ina's soul before she is pure."

"Very bad medicine."

"I see. I'm sorry. I didn't mean...Will you let me explain why I spoke this way?"

"Speak."

"Do you remember when we talked about the Great Spirit, who we call the Holy Ghost?"

"Same spirit."

"Yes. And you remember the story about Jesus, who died in the place of others?"

"Há. Jesus of great courage."

I smile. "He is, há. Because Jesus died, we believe our nagi is already pure. So, instead of keeping the nagi, the Holy Ghost takes the soul on to the afterlife, to a place we call Heaven. This is a holy place, a place of only peace. We all look forward to going to Heaven. That's why I thought what I said would bring you comfort."

"Who watch over families?"

"The Holy Ghost does."

Grasshopper scrunches his eyes, then shakes his head. "Wakan Tanka watch over world, not Gnus'ka Ainila."

"We believe, because of Jesus, the Holy Ghost watches over each and everyone."

"Why because Jesus?"

"Well, because Jesus makes us pure. Now the Holy Ghost is with us, not just over the world. He lives in our wakan."

"Jesus makes pure Lakota also? So Wakan Tanka live in Lakota?"

"He can, há. If you ask."

"Why ask?"

I laugh. "You have a lot of questions, don't you? Because it's our choice if we want Him to make us pure or not. We must invite Him to live in our wakan."

Again, Grasshopper's brow furrows. "Jesus man. No live in wakan."

"Jesus was man, now wakan. He died but He came back to life then became wakan, like ina became nagi." I'm surprised Grasshopper has no problem with this idea, but when I think about it, the Lakota already believe in the soul residin' in their home for a spell, so I guess it isn't too far a leap to believe a man could also become a spirit and live in a person.

246

"Jesus give choice—to respect Lakota?"

"That's right. He honors us with the choice because He respects and loves us."

"How Jesus love Gnus'ka Ainila? Never met."

"Oh, I believe you have met Jesus. How else could you know Wakan Tanka?"

Grasshopper's shocked face makes me laugh. "You say only know Wakan Tanka if know Jesus?"

"Há, that's right."

"How Sungila Sá know this?"

"In the story of Jesus, it says this is so. In the Bible."

"Book of Jesus."

"Há."

"Read Gnus'ka Ainila."

My heart feels full to burstin'. "I will. When Mah-do Wah-ay-e-lo returns Bible to Sungila Sá, we will read the story together."

A commotion stirs in the camp. When we turn to see what's causin' it, Grasshopper squeals in delight. "Jed!"

I follow his gaze and spy a large, bearded man—I suppose he's white, but he's so filthy, it's hard to tell—laden with masses of fur, his brown hair matted, his long, bushy beard salted with gray. My Ma woulda tanned his hide for gettin' so dirty.

His face is broad and jovial, what I can see of it, but his teeth are mostly missin'. His brown pants are ragged and torn, his leather moccasins worn to a sheen. Grasshopper seems ecstatic to see the massive man.

"How do you know this Jed?"

Grasshopper almost trembles with glee. "Jed teach English. Gnus'ka Ainila go hunt with Jed. Help make wicasa from hoksila."

"Hoksila?"

"Boy."

I look back to the bear of a man, who helped my friend become a man, and I know I must get to know him. But what if he tells the soldiers that a white man is livin' with the Lakota? Will I put the people at risk by meetin' this man? "Grasshopper, why don't you go to your friend."

"Sungila Sá come."

I hesitate. "I'm worried if Jed tells the soldiers about me, they will come to the camp and kill the Lakota."

Grasshopper scoffs. "Jed no speak. Hates soldier at fort."

"Will he hate me, then?"

"Sungila Sá make strange word. Sungila Sá Lakota. Misu of Mato Waäylo. Come."

Against my better judgment, I accompany Grasshopper to greet Jed. As we approach and Jed spots me for the first time, his eyes narrow, but he offers a toothless smile, nonetheless. "Well, now, what have we here?" He sticks out a pudgy hand, which I take and wince as he squeezes my hand until the bones grind together.

Grasshopper points in my direction. "Sungila Sá—Red Fox."

"Aidan MacAlister." I'm not sure why I offer him my given name. I haven't used it in a long time.

"Jedediah Miller. Most folks call me Jed."

"Well met, Jed."

"Well, now, I have to say I didn't expect to be seein' other white folk when I visited this fine day. How'd you come to be with the Lakota?"

I grimace. "Not by my choice." But Jedediah frowns, as if I'm insultin' his friends, so I add, "At least, not at first. I was a soldier from Fort Laramie when they captured me."

"Fort Laramie, huh? Nasty business near there not too far back."

A clawin' anxiety clenches my chest. "Do you know if anyone—survived? Is there anyone at the fort?"

"I hear there's soldiers there, but they're having a rough go of it. Can't handle the winters hereabouts. They won't be a threat to the Lakota for some time." Jed turns back to Grasshopper and speaks in the Lakota tongue. I wonder if he's sayin' something about me and doesn't want me to know.

Grasshopper responds in Lakota, and some of the other natives chime in. Soon, a whole conversation is swirlin' all 'round me. I'm a lost sheep standin' amongst a pack of wolves.

Grasshopper must notice my discomfort, because he lays his hand on my arm and says, "Talk of buffalo." His eyes gleam. "Jed follow Lakota for hunt."

I'm amazed at how well Jed communicates with the people. He speaks Lakota like a native, quick and easy with a natural flow, unlike my haltin' attempts at the language. If he's accompanyin' us to the buffalo herd, perhaps he can help teach me. Still, I notice him eyein' me ever' so often, and I wonder what he's thinkin' about the interloper white man livin' with his friends. I get the feelin' Jed has no love for the white man, while his respect for the Lakota is obvious, and they embrace him like a welcome friend. He is Ta-han-she.

Grasshopper calls over his shoulder as he and the other natives lead Jed toward the chief's tipi. "Jed trade chief bear pelt for buffalo meat."

I'm not invited to this sit-down, so I return to Mah-do Wah-ay-e-lo's tipi. Moon Shadow is there, gatherin' up their things for the move. Soon, Mah-do Wah-ay-e-lo will tear down the tipi and the whole camp will travel the plains. Moon Shadow glances my way but doesn't acknowledge me. I ache at her disregard, where before she seemed to hold genuine affection for me and made a fuss over me whenever she saw me.

"Ga-noo-sh-kah Ah-e-ne-lah and Shung-he-la-sa make woh-whah-ghwah." I don't know if she'll understand my poor attempt to let her know that Grasshopper and I are friends again, or if it won't matter to her since my sin is so great in her eyes.

"Wowahwa?"

"Peace, há. Who-whah-ghwah. We make peace."

Her eyes soften and a slight smile graces her lips. She is exceptionally beautiful when she smiles. Her whole face glows as if she carries the light of the Great Spirit in her, so filled with it that it overflows from her in a luminous waterfall. I melt in her dazzlin' radiance. I decide then and there that Soul of Moon is the better translation of her name, for she brightens the darkness like the full moon on a clear winter's night.

She gestures for me to collect my things, which I do, then I help her carry the bundles from the tipi. By the time we finish, I suppose the trade with Jed is concluded, because Mah-do Wah-ay-e-lo arrives, and the three of us remove the hide draped over the lodge poles. Then, we untie the thick rope used to bind the poles together and stack the poles on a kind of sled for transport.

As we work, I hear Soul of Moon whisper Grasshopper's name to Mah-do Wah-ay-e-lo. I hope she understands what I was tryin' to tell her, and that Mah-do Wah-ay-e-lo will be pleased. After everything is packed on the sled, Mah-do Wah-ay-e-lo leads their horses and Blossom to the sled.

Two of the horses are harnessed to the sled, leavin' two horses for them to ride, and Blossom. To my relief, Mah-do Wah-ay-e-lo hands Blossom's reins to me with a grim smile and a nod. After this exchange, which I believe means she is officially my horse again, he reaches into his pack, pulls out my Bible, carefully wrapped in a piece of buffalo hide, and holds it out in two hands as if he's offerin' a precious gift to me. He has no idea how precious it is. I lower my head slightly, as I've seen the Lakota do, to let him know I honor his gift—still keepin' my eyes up and on his, of course—and I accept the Bible. He lowers his head in return. With the exchange of honor, we are Ta-han-she and brothers once more.

Grasshopper rides near the front of the line beside Jed, so to avoid long periods of silence, I urge Blossom to move forward next to Grasshopper, which means conversation with Jed, too. I hope I can learn more about him and maybe prove to him I'm not an enemy of the people, but he's engrossed in conversation with Grasshopper—in the native's language, of course—so I might as well have ridden with Soul of Moon and Mah-do Wah-ay-e-lo. At least with them, I'd feel honored in my silence.

I'm about to drop back when Grasshopper turns to me with a smile. "Sungila Sá prove when camp. Chief say. Become one with Lakota."

Now, this is interesting. "How do I prove?"

Grasshopper looks to Jed, whose chuckles sound like the rumblin's of a grouchy ol' bear. "Ever heard of running the gauntlet?"

"Nosir."

"Well, now, the ancients used to use it for punishment and execution, if that tells you anything. Indians used it to torture prisoners back in the day. Not so much now. But many of the Indian tribes have their own form of running the gauntlet they use to test the manhood of young natives, and sometimes to see if prisoners—like you—are worthy to join the tribe."

"What do I have to do?"

"It's pretty much like it sounds. The Indians form two lines with an alley between them. You run through the alley. That's about it."

I doubt that very much. "And what are the Lakota doin' while I run through?"

"Well, now, that depends on the tribe."

I can imagine things they might do, none of them pleasant. "Have you run the gauntlet?"

"Me? Oh, no. I'm not much of a joiner, if you know what I mean. I left all that behind when I came out west."

"Where's your home now?"

"Here and there. I'm not much on settling down in one place."

He has no land, no roots, no attachments. I have to wonder what's happened to Jedediah Miller that turned him into such a loner. "You don't get lonely?"

"Well, now, I have my different tribes I trade with, and I run into miners now and again, so I'm content. How about you? Do you miss your soldier friends?"

Martin's smilin', freckled face rises before me, and without thinkin', I blurt out, "Only one."

"Oh? That so?"

I don't like Jed's raised brows and condescendin' glance. I can't help but imagine he's gatherin' up condemnin' information on me to run to the fort and tell whoever is in command now about the deserter he found. Honestly, I can't figure why I've taken such a dislike to him. I know very little about him. The Lakota seem to trust him. So, why do I wish he'd go back wherever he came from and leave us be?

I can't make him leave, but I can choose who I'm gonna be around, so I mutter something about checkin' on Mah-do Wah-ay-e-lo and Soul of Moon, and I turn Blossom and trot back to their place at

251

the end of the line, where Mah-do Wah-ay-e-lo's task is to guard the rear against attack.

Durin' the silence of the next leg of the journey, I consider how quickly the Lakota forgive and wonder if their belief in the Great Spirit has anything to do with it. In previous conversations, Grasshopper shared the Lakota values of respect, compassion, caring, humility, generosity, honesty, and wisdom, and in turn, I shared how Jesus taught us to value love, truth, faith in God, taking care of the poor, the widows, and the orphans, service to others, sacrifice, humility, and of course, forgiveness.

Although he didn't mention forgiveness on his list, I notice he's a better model of Christ's instruction to forgive than I am. I have no real reason to distrust Jed, but I do. My hatred for those men who killed my Ma and sisters boils just beneath the surface, ready to be unleashed at any provocation, like it was against the Pawnee. My malice toward the Union officers, and even my fellow soldiers, hasn't lessened with distance and time.

I still have a seethin' anger when I recall those Yankee deserters attackin' Mary and her girls. My list is long and continues to grow. If I keep collectin' names, my heart's gonna choke on bitterness. The Good Book warns against this very thing. How much longer before my demons consume me?

Maybe teachin' Grasshopper from the Bible will bring back my peaceful heart and remind me of the truth I once knew so well. What would my Ma say if she could see me now? Wrathful, judgmental, unforgivin'—she'd have a few things to say, and my ears and rear would burn when she was through with me.

What would she say about me soldierin' to get back our land? What would Pa say? I can't help but smirk, thinkin' about the knock-down fight I'd start if I could ask them that question today.

Would Ma condone killin' the Pawnee who were killin' women and children? Would she denounce the Lakota for killin' the soldiers who've come to take their land? Would she condemn Pa for doin' the same thing to the Yankees? Would she see all the killin' as the same sin? More than anything, I wish I could ask them both what they would do. As it stands, I'm lost and confused and utterly alone.

Sunset brings the column to a halt. Fortunately, the weather is warm enough for us to sleep under the stars without discomfort. Mah-do Wah-ay-e-lo takes first watch and gestures for me to join him on his perch overlookin' the sprawlin' tribe. We might not be able to communicate beyond the handful of words I know and some clumsy gestures, but at least our silence has an air of peace and ease I don't have with anyone else, not even Grasshopper.

Our watch passes without incident, and when he's relieved, he motions for me to return with him to Soul of Moon for sleep. I'm grateful for the chance to rest. My thoughts, runnin' here and there and back and forth all the long day, have exhausted me. Sleep's slow to come, however. My mind won't close down, so I tussle around under my blankets. Soul of Moon must hear me tossin' about, 'cause she starts hummin' a slow, sweet tune. I can feel all that worry and anger oozin' out of me like water squeezed from a sponge, and before I know it, the sun is peeking its rim over the edge of the world and everyone is up and movin', ready to leave.

Grasshopper seeks me out to tell me we should reach the buffalo herd and make camp today. He shows me a kindness for certain, to come and find me, and my heart softens once more toward the young brave. When he's not around Jed, he's as friendly as ever. Or maybe he's fulfillin' an obligation. My bitterness grinds down the edges of my recognition of Grasshopper's kindness with suspicion and doubt. I want to ride with Grasshopper today, but without a thought as to why, I slink to the back of the line once more.

Mah-do Wah-ay-e-lo wriggles on his horse's back like someone standin' on a hornet's nest. His eyes gleam in the blazin' sun—I can almost see him salivatin'. I believe, if he could, he'd give his horse its head, chase the wind to the buffalo, and take the whole herd himself. As it is, he's chafin' at his position at the back of the line.

As Grasshopper predicted, the chief calls for the halt on a grassy slope overlookin' a broad valley with a creek snakin' through it. The buffalo are near—they, too, need a water source. The rest of the afternoon is spent reconstructin' the camp, a slower process than the take-down but still amazin' in its efficiency. As the sun sets on our labors, the women build a roarin' fire in the center of camp, and the warriors, dressed in full regalia, perform a ritual dance to prepare for the hunt. Once again, I'm an outsider lookin' on, an observer only and not a true part of the tribe. I wonder if that is to be my lot. No one has mentioned anything about my test.

Once the celebration ends, everyone wanders to their tipis to rest before the big hunt. As we walk in the moonlight, I gather from Grasshopper the tribe expects to kill enough buffalo on this hunt to provide for all through the long winter months—he even laughs that if I could accompany the tribe on the hunt, the most I could hope to kill is a calf. I'm quick to retort that surely a red fox can kill more buffalo than a silent grasshopper, and he should watch out that he isn't trampled underfoot. It's nice to resume our friendly banter, but I remind myself Jed will be on the hunt tomorrow, and a cloud settles over me like the gray smear crossin' in front of the moon.

I settle down beneath my blankets and am soon dead asleep. A stiff shove startles me awake. I turn to find Mah-do Wah-ay-e-lo loomin' over me, his arms folded. He issues a command I recognize as "Come," so I scramble up and follow him through the flap.

Have the buffalo wandered into the valley in the night? I spot many braves standin' near the rekindled fire in the center of camp and wonder if they've decided to include me on the hunt after all.

I catch a glimpse of Grasshopper amongst the braves, his slight frame decidedly out of place next to the broad shoulders of the others, but when I try to catch his eye, he looks away.

Mah-do Wah-ay-e-lo thrusts me in front of him and lifts his hands. I can only recognize a few words—Shung-he-la-sa, people, fight, warrior—but the rest of his speech is lost on me. Grunts and shouts of approval ring out as he becomes more excited, his gestures wilder and more expansive. Soon, the entire group is worked up into a frenzy, hootin' and cawin' like a flock'a birds. Mah-do Wah-ay-e-lo gives a final shout, and the braves file into two lines while Mah-do Wah-ay-e-lo drags me to the end nearest to where I'm standin'.

Grasshopper, his face grave, steps in front of me. "You must reach Gnus'ka Ainila."

"Is this my test?" But Grasshopper doesn't respond. Instead, he turns slowly and strides to the opposite end of the two lines.

The braves begin hollerin' again, stompin' their feet and clappin', and Mah-do Wah-ay-e-lo wallops my back, sendin' me stumblin' between the first two braves. They proceed to pummel me with their fists about my head, shoulders and back. I try to cover my head with my arms and scamper forward into the clutches of the next two men, who punch my gut and ribs, and before I know it, I'm on my knees and six braves set in on me like buzzards on a carcass.

I'm not gonna make it to the end if I keep takin' hits like this, so I push myself to my feet, lower my head, and run as fast as I'm able through flailin' arms, poundin' feet drivin' the air straight outta me, and fists whalin' on me. Blood trickles down the sides of my face and oozes out of one corner of my mouth, and one of my eyes is swolled almost shut, but still, I pitch and roll on like a waterlogged canoe through rapids. My good eye burns with the blood runnin' in it. The end of the line looks to be a mile away, but I keep on staggerin' forward. I will not lose the small measure of respect I've gained from defendin' the women and elders.

One brave lowers his shoulder into my chest, and I go flyin'. The braves near me are flies on a piece of rotten meat until I manage to crawl away from their barrage of kicks and strikes to the next two men. Before they have the chance to start in on me, I scuttle sideways like a spider and scramble around 'em, only to be met with a sharp kick in the face by Mah-do Wah-ay-e-lo, who is walkin' outside the lines, I'm a-guessin' to keep me inside the lines.

My face feels like butchered meat. My head's woozy and spinnin'. Yet, something in me, some deep-seated force beyond my knowin', fixes my eyes on the fuzzy image of Grasshopper in the distance, and by sheer force of will, I numb the feelin' of the punches rainin' down on me and force my legs to drive me forward, ever forward. I fall once, twice, three times, but I refuse to stay down. The whoops of the braves sound like Granda's church bells ringin' on Sunday mornin' away in the distance, echoin' off the river.

Grasshopper's image fades to red-tinted gray, but I won't stop. I can't stop. The firelight tilts crazily to my left, and I reel into the waitin' arms of a brave, who welcomes me with a clout on the side of my head, causin' my ears to ring so loud I can't hear the church bells anymore.

The next brave punches my leg right in the spot the arrow hit, and I hear someone screamin' and I'm a-watchin' him crumple to the ground in agony.

"Get up! Get up!" I'm screamin' at the poor, bloodied creature lyin' in a pile on the dirt. "Get up! You gotta move!" The fool curls up under the beatin's of the surroundin' braves. The braves don't care a whit that he's already down. They aren't gonna hold back, even if it means killin' the poor soul. I try to will him to his feet, but he won't move. "GET UP!"

With the whoosh of a hawk divin' for the kill, I'm back in my body and forcin' my wobblin' legs to stand. My injured leg won't work, so I drag it along behind me as I pull and slog and stumble my way closer and closer to what I pray is the end.

Two braves step directly in my path, lockin' their arms, darin' me to fight my way past 'em, and my demon rage starts to rise up in me. From behind, the other braves continue to thrash my back, squeezin' me closer to the two braves blockin' my way, which makes it a good bit harder to pry them apart. Then, the two in front try to slam my face into the ground, and I've had enough. I yell my fury to the night wind and launch myself onto the two warriors, diggin' my fingernails and heels into their skin as I climb their bodies and throw myself over the top of their heads to tumble to the ground and land on all fours. I scurry forward, hopin' against hope I can out-race them to Grasshopper, 'cause I'm of a mind that one more hit against my head's gonna knock me plumb silly. To my surprise, I find myself face to face with my friend, fallin' into his waitin' arms.

I did it. "I have fought a good fight. I have finished my course. I have kept the faith." I have "run that ye may obtain." I collapse but Grasshopper holds me up as the other braves gather 'round us, cryin', "Sungila Sá! Sungila Sá! Sungila Sá!"

Mah-do Wah-ay-e-lo, who is apparently my sponsor or the Lakota equivalent, makes another rousin' speech, and all the braves cheer. Grasshopper leans close and whispers, "He welcomes you to the people and calls you misu—brother and tahansi—dear friend. Anyone who not accept Sungila Sá as brother must fight Mato Waäylo."

I try to say, "Pilamayaye"—thank you in Lakota, but it comes out soundin' like ffeyayayyaya through my puffy lips, which receives a boisterous round of laughter and several unwelcome claps on the back in response.

Mah-do Wah-ay-e-lo lifts me into the air, to the cheers of his fellow warriors, then he and Grasshopper carry me back to the tipi, where Soul of Moon waits with cool water and healin' balm for the cuts and bruises coverin' my body. I must say, her soothin' ministrations almost make the gauntlet worth it. Almost.

Despite my exhaustion, sleep comes slowly to me. Between the excitement of becoming a part of the people and the full-body aches from the beatings, I find myself tossin' and turnin' in fitful discomfort beneath my blankets. I want to do something. It's as if the demon is awakened and won't give me peace until he has his measure of blood. But given my physical state, I'm not sure I'll be able to participate in tomorrow's hunt, which would probably satisfy his bloodlust, so I'm left with fightin' my covers as a poor substitute.

Mornin' breaks with lowerin' clouds and heavy rain, but the spirits of the hunters aren't dampened. I'm movin' like an eighty-year-old man, bent and bones creakin', as I slog through the mud to breakfast. Mah-do Wah-ay-e-lo and Soul of Moon are already eatin', and Grasshopper is talkin' with Jed, so with no place to settle, I grab some meat and fry bread and make my way back to the tipi.

On the way back, I hear Jed snickerin' behind me. "Well now, boy, what a pitiful sight you are. You look like you were trampled by thirteen horses." Grasshopper's liltin' laugh joins Jed's. I raise one mangled hand to acknowledge him, but my demon doesn't like his comment one bit. I hear his whispered voice suggestin' Jed didn't run the gauntlet 'cause he couldn't do it instead of the reason he gave, that he preferred not to join, and offerin' to provide Jed the opportunity to run his own special gauntlet against me, but I say nothing. Pitiful, am I? I vow to go on the hunt no matter how much it pains me. And I'm goin' as Lakota.

I've watched the braves paint themselves for war countless times since I've been amongst the people, so I grab Mah-do Wah-ay-e-lo's jars of black and red warpaint and try to mimic the smears across his cheeks and brow. Let's see Jed make fun of my bruised and battered face now.

My red curls don't lend themselves to braids, but I'm determined, so I yank Soul of Moon's comb through my locks in an attempt to straighten them some and pull them into two long braids over each shoulder, tied at the ends with thin strips of buffalo hide. All that's left is to find a feather or two to adorn my head. I don't have time to go lookin' for my own feather, and I know not to bother the eagle feathers Soul of Moon has collected, as I've learned they are sacred and used for burials and ceremony, but I believe she won't mind if I take one of the many hawk feathers she has hangin' from a decoration in the center of the tipi. I can always return it once I find my own. I pluck one of the smaller feathers from the hangin' and shove the tip down into my curls so that it stands up at the back of my head.

Mah-do Wah-ay-e-lo has used my tin cup since my capture, fascinated by it in some way, so I pick up the cup from his pile of supplies and use it as a makeshift mirror to see how I look. The face I see starin' back at me looks nothing like the boy who left northern Georgia to defend his land. This man is gaunt—aged beyond his years, his skin reddened, lined, and leathery, his eyes cold and haunted. If they could see me, my Ma and Pa wouldn't recognize me. The warpaint forgotten, I throw down the cup and sink onto the pile of buffalo hides that serve as my pallet. Tears well unbidden.

Mah-do Wah-ay-e-lo and Soul of Moon enter the tipi to find me sittin', head in my hands, my newly applied warpaint runnin' in streaks down my face, to my shame. Soul of Moon rushes to my side and seems to be checkin' my wounds, but Mah-do Wah-ay-e-lo stands over me, arms folded across his chest, his mouth a thin, firm line.

"Ina je." Stand up.

Dashin' a quick scrub across my eyes, I stand before the massive man. Never before have I felt so aware of my frailty. How could I be so blind? Mah-do Wah-ay-e-lo could snap my neck like breakin' a twig between his fingers. Only his honor and grace kept me alive when he held me prisoner. Now, he calls me brother.

A wave of awe tingles my stomach. I want to be worthy of the honor he offers me so freely, so I square my shoulders, hold my head high, and meet his eyes.

He places his hands on my shoulders and juts his chin. "Sungila Sá chanté tinza. Akicita yelo. Tatanka olepi etaha catkuta." He picks up a bowl of red paint and smears thick swipes of it across my cheeks, nose, forehead, and chest.

Then with a single finger, he strikes a line of black paint beneath each eye and a jagged smudge of black across my chest and shoulders. Finally, he retrieves a bowl of white paint and coats his fingers in white, then presses each cheek with the imprint of his fingers. He ends with a cross-shaped dab of white in the center of my forehead.

I point to the white cross. "Cross?"

"Anpo wicapi."

"Ahn-po-wee-chah-pee." I repeat it because I want to remember to ask Grasshopper what it means.

Soul of Moon brings out two more feathers and nestles them in my hair with a gentle smile.

Mah-do Wah-ay-e-lo nods his approval. "Sungila Sá tatanka olepi." He shakes my shoulders before he turns to go.

I recognize the word for buffalo, so I assume Mah-do Wah-ay-e-lo is repeatin' it is time to go kill buffalo. I gather up the bow and arrows they provided for me, and with a newfound sense of belongin' like I've never known, I follow Mah-do Wah-ay-e-lo from the tipi to mount Blossom and participate as Lakota in my very first buffalo hunt.

Thankfully, the rains are slackin' off. Grasshopper meets us on our way to the horses. He's practically bouncin' in place, he's so excited, which makes me laugh. But he pulls me up short, spins me toward him, and stares at my face, mouth agape.

"Mah-do Wah-ay-e-lo did it," I explain.

Grasshopper seems drawn to the white cross on my forehead, which reminds me to ask him what Mah-do Wah-ay-e-lo's words mean. "He called the cross ahn-po-wee-chah-pee. What does that mean?"

"Most sacred. Holy. Mean morning star. Morning star kahyá—symbol—courage, new beginning, guide. Mato Waäylo give great honor Sungila Sá. Morning Star guide Sungila Sá."

I'm struck mute. The verse in the Book of Revelation floods my mind: 'I am the root and the offspring of David, and the bright and morning star.' What does it mean that the Lakota see the morning star as the guide, the symbol of new beginnings and of courage? This can't be a coincidence. When I finally regain my speech, I'm compelled to share this revelation with Grasshopper. "Do you know what the Book of Jesus names Jesus?"

"Jesus Christ, Sungila Sá say."

"Yes, of course, but He is given other names. One of those names is the bright and morning star."

Grasshopper's eyes widen. "Jesus also kahyá."

"Actually, morning star is kahyá for Jesus. Jesus is our guide. Jesus gives us a new beginning—remember, he makes our soul pure? And Jesus has great courage to die on the cross for others."

"What cross?"

I point to the symbol in white on my forehead. "When the bad men killed Jesus, they put nails—um, stakes—okátan—through his hands and put him on a wooden cross that looks like this. Now, for us, the cross—this symbol—means Jesus died for us to make us pure."

Grasshopper points to the sky. "Jesus in sky? Star guide Lakota?"

"He is a light to guide us, but no, He isn't just in the sky. He lives in your heart—chun-tay. But don't you see? The people and those who follow Jesus have the same kahyá. This proves Jesus knows the Lakota."

"Sungila Sá Jesus. Mato Waäylo say."

I'm horrified. "No! No—I'm not Jesus. Jesus is spirit—wakan. He is good. I am not good."

"Sungila Sá Jesus phiyá thunpi."

"What does that mean?"

"Born again. Like Sungila Sá say, Jesus born again."

"No! I follow Jesus. I'm not Jesus. It's very important you know I'm not Jesus. I can't save you. I can't make you pure. Only Jesus can."

"Why then Sungila Sá anpo wicapi?"

"I'm sure Mah-do Wah-ay-e-lo drew the morning star on my head because I follow Jesus—like Lakota follow the morning star as their guide."

Grasshopper nods. "Ah. Same kahyá. Sungila Sá say."

I breathe a deep sigh in relief. "Yes. Kahyá."

We walk a little farther in silence, then I recall another phrase Mah-do Wah-ay-e-lo used, so I ask Grasshopper its meaning. "I know chun-tay is heart. What is te-een-za?"

"Mean brave heart."

"What about akeh-chee-tah yay-lo?"

"True warrior."

My eyes fill again. Mah-do Wah-ay-e-lo called me a brave heart and a true warrior. I can't remember the other phrases he spoke over me, but those are enough. I pray I live up to his words.

We reach our horses, and as if she can sense our excitement, Blossom stomps and paws at the ground restlessly as I untie her and gather her bridle to walk her to the crowd of hunters already mounted and circlin' their horses.

Mah-do Wah-ay-e-lo calls me forward and points to a place on his right before the crowd of riders. Grasshopper trails directly behind us, with Jed ridin' to his left. Mah-do Wah-ay-e-lo lifts his spear, adorned with an array of feathers, over his head and bellows the now familiar Lakota war cry, and we're off, with Mah-do Wah-ay-e-lo and me leadin' the way.

We ride full speed most of the mornin' and stop only to water the horses as we follow the windin' river flowin' through the valley. Over knolls and across open plains we ride, always veerin' back toward the river. I relish the feel of the wind coolin' my face, blowin' short locks of hair free from their bondage in braids, and the smooth rhythms of Blossom's muscles rollin' beneath my legs like Ma kneadin' dough for biscuits.

As we water our horses again at the base of a rise, I catch a rank smell on the wind. "Tatanka?" I ask Mah-do Wah-ay-e-lo.

But he is sittin' forward on his horse, alert, starin' up to the top of the knoll. He barks an order, and the usually cheerful hunters fall into grim silence. Mah-do Wah-ay-e-lo urges his horse forward to begin the slow climb up the rise, gesturin' for me to follow. We pick our way through the wavin' grass, silent as the grave, the shush of the stalks against our horses' legs and the occasional creak of leather the only sounds. Despite Mah-do Wah-ay-e-lo's stern expression, I'm giddy with hope that we've finally found the herd. I want to pull out my bow and ready an arrow, but I dare not risk the noise. Heaven forbid I be the one to startle the buffalo.

Mah-do Wah-ay-e-lo is first to the top of the knoll. He stops his horse in its tracks, and his face melts into a mask of horror. The stench is almost unbearable. A broad expanse of plain lies before us—the entire landscape is scorched. Piles of what from this distance appear to be buffalo carcasses smolder across the grassland. Nothing moves except the tendrils of smoke risin' from the mounds of burnin' flesh.

The remainder of the hunters gather along the top of the ridge. Not a single word is spoken. Their grief-stricken faces speak to the tragedy laid out before us. All the life drains out of me as if someone turned a spigot wide-open and left it runnin' the day through. I can hardly breathe. I slide from Blossom's back and flop to the ground, a boneless sack.

At long last, Mah-do Wah-ay-e-lo swings down from his horse, kneels on the ground, and begins to wail. One by one, the other braves follow his lead until the valley reverberates with the cries and moans of a people mournin' the wasted deaths of these magnificent creatures.

Who would've done such a thing? This is not the work of the native peoples. I know Lakota and most other tribes honor the buffalo and consider the creature sacred, killin' only what they need and wastin' nothing of the animal as a way of honorin' their sacrifice for the survival of the people, so I understand the magnitude of this loss. But my feelings tend more toward terror than grief. What will the people eat come winter? How will they survive? Everything they have they make from the buffalo. They'll run out of meat before winter comes. If they have nothing to trade with the farmin' tribes, they'll have no vegetables to eat, either. What will they do? What will *we* do?

Grasshopper slides next to me and takes my hand. "Soldier from fort," is all he whispers.

Surely not. The soldiers rely on the buffalo almost as much as the natives do when the wagon trains can't make it to the fort through the winter snows. But then I notice that none of the carcasses have arrows in them, and I can spot no arrows dottin' the ground. That leaves only two options—trappers like Jedediah Miller or the U. S. Cavalry. Grasshopper may be right.

"Well, now, I heard whispers of this amongst some of the folk making their way down the Bozeman." Jed shakes his matted hair. "Folks were saying the soldiers at the forts had plans on killing all the buffalo to drive the Indians from their land."

I hear, "Why?" choke from my mouth before I can think who it is I'm askin'.

Jed shrugs. "They're in the way."

Rage boils up in me like the Richmond fires. I race down the side of the hillock to the nearest mound, pawin' through the hides, pullin' them off one another. I must find something usable before it's too late.

Grasshopper is at my side in a heartbeat. "No, Tahansi. Leave tatanka to rest."

"Can we save nothing?" I'm pantin' now.

"No, Sungila Sá. Nothing to save." He tugs my arm to pull me back up the hill to be with the people.

"Maybe some escaped. We need to track them, try to find where they went."

"Follow tatanka another day. Time for achéya. Weep."

I turn and scan the vast plain dotted with blackened burial mounds, standin' arm in arm with Grasshopper. A gasp clutches my throat closed, and hot tears flow.

CHAPTER TWENTY

Mah-do Wah-ay-e-lo instructs two of the braves to return to the camp and bring the rest of the tribe to the site of devastation, as we gather on the hillock to guard the tatanka and achéya, as Grasshopper calls it, over their death.

Scavengers—coyote, wolf, buzzard—hover around the edges of the scene all seekin' to take advantage of the situation and eat their fill, but our wailin' is keepin' 'em at bay for now. I expect they'll get bolder soon. The stench of fresh kill will be hard to resist.

The braves and the remainder of the tribe arrive, with the chief in the lead. The anguished, piercin' cries of the women join with ours, but the chief is stony and mute as he surveys the gruesome scene. A buzzard swoops down from its lazy circle above the carnage, lands atop a pile of carcasses, and begins its feast. Rage sings in my heart, and I move to rush the creature and shoo it away, but Grasshopper restrains my arm. "Is way of things."

"What do you mean, the way of things?"

He gestures toward the buzzard and other marauders. "Death feeds life. Nothing lost, no waste. Tatanka feed bird and ground, grass grow from ground, bird scatter seed for grass, more grass grow, tatanka eat grass. See?"

I do see. For the first time in my life, I catch a real glimpse into the perfect system God created when He made the world, life that sustains itself in intricate harmony and balance, and I understand a little more why the people worship the land and the sky and the creatures. Lookin' through their eyes, death—even a pointless death like this—is beautiful as it plays its part in the eternal song. If only they knew the true Creator of it all.

The wails grow quieter and finally cease, and the elder chief steps forward, hands raised. He chants a song that to my newly opened ears matches the movements and rhythms of the harmony playin' out below us and the grief echoin' in our hearts. Grasshopper leans close

265

and whispers, "Chief yuwákhan makhá—make holy ground. Owíchahe—burial place of Great Tatanka."

The chief pulls out the familiar ceremonial pipe, lights it, puffs a billow of smoke into the air, then lifts the pipe high. His voice firm and resonant with authority, he ushers tatanka to the next life. Each male takes the pipe in turn and blows curlin' tendrils of smoke—and for the first time, Grasshopper passes the pipe to me. I gape at him but make no move to take the offered pipe.

"Sungila Sá now Lakota. Take."

"But..."

Grasshopper pushes the pipe into my hands. "Take. Honor tatanka. Send mahpíya—you say 'hay-vn.'"

"Heaven." I'm not entirely sure buffalo go to heaven, but I do want to honor the great animal and grieve their loss with the people, so I take the pipe and blow a puff of smoke into the sky, followed by a brief fit of coughin'. Mah-do Wah-ay-e-lo takes the pipe from me and after a long draw blows out a large plume of smoke. It swirls with the wind that dances through the burial field to carry the chief's mournful song and the soul of the tatanka into the clouds.

As the chief turns to leave this place, the breeze stills and I hear no sound—no words, no footfalls, no distant scrapin' of teeth against bone. Everything stops, as lifeless as the chief's expression, almost as if the whole world pauses to acknowledge the gravity of the terrible loss. We ride in silence back to our camp, and no one speaks the rest of the evening or through the night, each one inhabitin' their own thoughts—alone.

The mornin' finds the elders and main warriors gathered in the chief's lodge, while the rest of the camp goes about its daily routine—all except me. I find I have to remind myself to breathe as I wander about aimlessly and wait on how they will plan for our survival. I see no way. We don't have enough meat to feed the people for all of autumn, let alone winter, which they were countin' on collectin' from this hunt. Any tribes nearby are in the same fix, so they can't help us. We've traded for vegetables and collected what roots and fruit there are, but those supplies will run out long before the cold sets in. All I can see before me is starvation, a slow, lingerin' death.

By mid-mornin', the elders are still meetin', so I look for Grasshopper, who I find sittin' with Jed, his filthy face creased and somber. I don't wanna talk to Jed, but I feel an urgency to speak with Grasshopper and hear how the people have handled this kind of difficulty in the past, so I swallow my pride and join them, sittin' cross-legged on the ground. Their silence is unnervin'.

"What do you think's goin' on in there?"

Jed snorts. "Well, now, I figure they're considering if they want to kill a scrawny little white boy, so they have meat for their supper."

"Jed!" Grasshopper glares at the trapper and shakes his head. "No joke this day." Jed harrumphs and turns his face toward the wood.

"I can't figure what they can do. Aren't you worried?"

"Hiyá. Always follow tatanka."

"What happens if you can't find the buffalo?"

Grasshopper shrugs. "Still search. Follow."

The voice, more soft touch than sound, which I haven't heard in what seems like so long, whispers inside my head. *This is faith.*

Faith? What does that mean? "I don't understand."

I'm unaware I spoke aloud until Grasshopper says, "Táku?"

"Uh...nothin'. Never mind."

This is faith, the voice said. What is it He wants me to see? Grasshopper believes the hunters will find the buffalo if they search—but it's more than belief. It's absolute trust without question. And still, more than that, it's followin' that belief by travelin' across the plains in search of the herd, as long as it takes and as far as they must go. Grasshopper has unwaverin' certainty. So, he sits and waits without fear, just as the rest of the tribe goes about their daily chores without apparent concern for their future—this is faith.

Jed's twistin' hands and furrowed brow let me know he shares my worries. He's wrigglin' like a worm on a hook, which makes me think he's on the verge of jumpin' up and leavin' us for better huntin' grounds. For my part, I would ration food, maybe even set a meetin' with the white soldiers to make peace at any price and trade what I could for their resources. But as I look at Grasshopper's calm countenance and observe his patient stillness, I'm put to shame. No wonder God wants me to take notice.

Before the sun touches the western horizon, the elder chief strides from his lodge and calls the people to gather around the central fire.

"Well, now, that's my cue to exit." Jed stands and stretches his long arms over his head. "I'll be seein' you in a few moons." He ambles toward the horses and disappears into the gatherin' shadows.

Grasshopper remains by my side and translates. "In wisdom, the elders speak. Hanthéhan—far into night—in one voice, the people hóyeyä—um, send voice away?"

"Pray?"

"Ah—in one voice the people pray for Great Tatanka return to people. Dawn come, the people gather all and walk in way of wóayupte." He looks at me quizzically. "What white word mean hear after pray?"

"Do you mean an answer? Is chief saying to seek the answer from Great Tatanka?"

"Great Tatanka hear our one voice call. All walk in way of an-sir."

"I see. So, we'll break camp and hunt for the herd."

"No hunt. Tatanka come."

Once again, I've not seen such faith since Ma, whose belief in God's promises couldn't be shaken, even by the deaths of her babies. My heart aches to know such faith, to believe and trust so deeply that I don't have a smidge of doubt, that I would walk in the way of wóayupte.

Without a word, the people scatter to gather blankets and prepare for the vigil. Women bring wood to feed the fire through the night and adorn themselves with feathers and beads. Men paint themselves and bring their spears, drums, rattles, flutes, and pipes. As we circle the fire, one of the elder men starts a steady drumbeat—one loud beat followed by one soft and repeat, almost like a beatin' heart—on a large, round tree trunk covered with hide.

The chief sits on a pallet of buffalo hides and intones, "Toka-shay-la-anagopta-awayaye-lo." In one voice, the people join the song, echoin' his words. It reminds me of responsive readin' at church, only sung instead of spoken.

I'm amazed by the simplicity, the movement, and the harmonies of their song. As the verse repeats, I try to join in as best I'm able, although I don't know what I'm singin'. I hope the Good Lord will understand and forgive me if I'm doin' Him wrong, but in my heart, whatever my words are sayin', I'm callin' out to Him for His help for the people.

The braves dance around the fire, poundin' their feet against the packed earth. Some crouch low over their knees and spin in a circle, some leap and twirl their spears around them, while others skip and thrust their spears at the dancin' shadows like they are phantom buffalo.

The men who are not dancin' are beating smaller drums along with the elder's deeper beats. The women shake rattles as they sing, and some join in the dance with the men, while others stand behind the drummers and sing high notes in harmony. A few blow flutes, which adds a mysterious quality to the sound, like the hoots of an owl or the call of a loon.

Grasshopper pulls my arm, gesturin' for me to stand and join the dance. I find I'm embarrassed, which surprises me. I'm more an interloper than a true member of the tribe, but he insists, so I stand beside him and mimic his movements, stiff and awkward as a child learnin' to walk. After a time, the shadows of the dancers playin' over the trees and the lickin' flames before me put me into some kinda trance. Someone tosses me a spear, and I heft it over my head and thrust it into the shadows like the other men. It's not long before I'm in a frenzy, singin' at the top of my lungs and spinnin' wildly around the fire.

When I can't imitate the words of the chief, I cry out to God with "groanings which cannot be uttered" as Scripture says, like a man speakin' in foreign tongues as they did in the Acts of the Apostles. It's a strange feelin' to be so carried away that your spirit soars outside your body into the heavens.

The dance goes on and on. Braves take turns in the dance, but the singin' never stops. All I want to do is lie down and sleep, but my body keeps agitatin' like Ma scrubbin' our clothes in the creek, and my raw throat keeps cryin' out to the Father for aid.

Finally, as a hint of gray blossoms in the distant sky, the chief stops his chant, and the people fall silent. The chief stands, pulls a flamin' twig from the fire to light the ceremonial pipe, and lifts it above his head. On cue, each family lights their pipe from the fire. I don't have a pipe yet, so Soul of Moon pulls me gently beside her to share Mah-do Wah-ay-e-lo's pipe. Each member of the tribe draws deeply and blows the smoke into the darkened sky to join with the swirl of smoke risin' from the fire and carry our song to the Great Tatanka.

A mist covers my eyes as I watch our prayers rise in such a tangible way, to be collected by the Holy Ghost and carried to the Father, who I know will hear them and respond. My throat tightens and, in my bones, I know He will.

Despite their exhaustion, the people begin the laborious process of breakin' down the camp. The women douse the fire, sendin' a new plume of white smoke billowin' into the air. Breakfast this mornin' will be cold, dried meat and flat bread, a meal of haste. I drag myself behind Mah-do Wah-ay-e-lo and Soul of Moon to tear down the tipi, and even though they danced and sang the whole night, they work with the same speed and energy as the last time we broke camp, not that long ago. I, on the other hand, feel almost useless.

By mid-mornin', we are ready to go. The chief declares we are to go north, beyond the holy ground where the buffalo lie slaughtered. I mount Blossom and ride out beside Mah-do Wah-ay-e-lo and Grasshopper, hope repeatin' the chief's song in my heart as I thank the Good Lord for givin' us a beautiful day for our journey and showin' the chief the way to go.

We skirt the sacred buffalo burial ground and head north across the vast expanse of the plains. Scouts ride out often, ahead of the long line of horses and pulled pallets, to look for signs of the herd, circlin' back when they find nothing. We sleep under the stars at night, with a small fire to warm us and for cookin', and we're off at daybreak, each day expectin' to meet tatanka as they return in response to our prayer, and each day findin' no sign. I begin to wonder if the cavalry soldiers slaughtered them all, but I don't voice my fears, as everyone else maintains their certain faith that tatanka will come.

On the seventh day of our journey, a scout gallops into camp, cryin' that he's seen sign of the herd. We turn to follow his direction, turnin' northwest until we reach the place where it's clear the remnant of the herd has been. The grass is trampled into the black soil, which is churned up like the herd was runnin'.

Icy fingers grip my heart as I imagine cavalry soldiers on horseback, chasin' the buffalo, runnin' them down, shootin' them, and leavin' them in burnin' piles of decayin' flesh.

"Please, Lord, not that."

""Táku?" Mah-do Wah-ay-e-lo looks at me, his brows gathered over his hawk-like nose.

Grasshopper leans close to me. "Sungila Sá pray?"

I offer him a sardonic sneer. "Sorta."

"Pray heard. No need pray now."

"Always pray, Grasshopper. You never know what waits for you 'round th' bend."

"Roun t'ben?"

"Things you cannot see."

"What cannot see, Sungila Sá?"

But I shake my head. I refuse to dampen their excitement by voicin' my worst fears aloud.

The hunters press their horses to full speed and pull away from the tribe, so I urge Blossom to a gallop and race across the blackened swath left by the buffalo. The rest of the tribe is soon out of sight behind us, but still no buffalo. Their trail winds across the open plains, over hillocks and down through low areas, around copses of trees juttin' out onto the grasslands. The farther we go, the faster the braves race, probably feelin' the same urgency I do. The tatanka have come, and we can't lose 'em now.

The trampled ground flows over another rise, and when we reach the top, down in the valley we see them—tatanka, grazin' near a stream. My glee surpasses receivin' a present Christmas mornin'. No one races down the hill. No one fires an arrow. It's as if we're afraid to disturb the creatures that remain, out of reverence.

The herd is significantly diminished. Mah-do Wah-ay-e-lo barks an order, and the other hunters move slowly and quietly to encircle the buffalo. Mah-do Wah-ay-e-lo, Grasshopper, and I wait for the chief to arrive to give instruction, for to kill too many is to destroy the future for the tribe, and to not take enough is to relegate us to starvation.

When the chief arrives and surveys the scene below, he waits several moments in silence, then whispers instruction to Mah-do Wah-ay-e-lo. He sends Grasshopper down one side of the hill to pass the word along to the other hunters, and he goes down the other side to complete the circle.

Once they meet on the far side, Grasshopper waves his arms over his head, my signal to barrel down the hill and send the buffalo toward the water. After watchin' the buffalo scatter toward the water, the other braves rush in from the sides and, according to the chief's direction, they kill the old and the weak, but leave the young and strong to thrive to ensure the survival of the herd. I manage to hit one laggin' behind the herd at close range—my first kill with an arrow.

A loud cry sounds from atop the rise. "Wasicu! Wasicu!" I recognize the word, used more than once to refer to me when I was still a slave. White man. All the hunters turn as one and gallop up the rise. At the top, we see a small unit of cavalry soldiers comin' across the plains from the east. Fortunately for us, they are blinded by the sun in their faces and don't see us.

Mah-do Wah-ay-e-lo bellows a battle cry, and the warriors race headlong toward the soldiers. I understand the seriousness of our situation. If we don't run the soldiers off, and they discover the herd, our efforts to protect the buffalo and ensure their survival will be for nothing and all will be lost.

The soldiers see us at the last minute as we approach from their flank, but they barely have time to turn their horses before we are upon them, arrows flyin' and spears diggin' into flesh. The thought of the soldiers slaughterin' the remainin' buffalo rouses my rage, and I screech the cry that earned me my new name as Blossom pounds through the middle of them like a rockslide down a mountain. We outnumber them three to one. I'm not sure the soldiers even get off a shot—none of our warriors are hit. After what seems like seconds, the soldiers turn tail and run back the way they came, away from the herd. We give chase for a spell, firin' arrows toward their fleeing backs to make sure they don't give a thought to comin' back our way anytime soon.

The survivin' buffalo are gone when we finally return to the site of the hunt. The women are spread across the area with wood pallets to carry the meat back to camp. Accordin' to Grasshopper, the chief has instructed the women not to leave the traditional sacrificial meat on the plains, since the tatanka have already given too great a sacrifice. Instead, the women remove the hides, pile them on a pallet, then cut all the meat into slabs and pile them up another pallet, then collect all the usable parts—bone, sinew, guts, hooves, and horns—and stack them on another pallet. Finally, they cut out a liver from one of the animals and bring it to the warriors who killed the buffalo to eat. I don't relish the idea of eatin' raw liver from any animal, but if I am to be Lakota, I must learn their ways.

The hunters follow the women, who are pullin' their pallets behind them up the rise, to the place where they left everything for the new camp. Something in me bristles at watchin' the women heavin' the heavy carts up the hill while the men languish on their horses, but when I ask Grasshopper, he laughs at me and says I insult the women if I do their task, so I join the hunters who claim a kill around the newly built fire and wait for the liver to pass to me.

The bloody, metallic-tastin' bite makes me gag, but I cover it well, and thankfully, I'm able to swallow it down without retchin'. The other men gather behind us, chantin' and dancin' as we eat.

I understand from Grasshopper that usually after a hunt, the hunters are allowed a long rest while the camp celebrates and gives thanks to the buffalo for their sacrifice, but this hunt is different since we must raise the camp. As I watch the women scrapin' and stretchin' the hides and cuttin' and hangin' the strips of meat, I wonder aloud, "Will it be enough?"

"Tatanka came. Wakan Tanka provide." Grasshopper's gentle smile settles my heart.

"Yes, Wakan Tanka provides."

"Also name Jesus."

I return his smile. "Yes. Thank you, Jesus."

Our brief rest and celebration come to a close, and Mah-do Wah-ay-e-lo beckons me to join him in raisin' the tipi. The rest of the men work into the night to set camp, while the women continue their work with the buffalo. My guess is they'll be at it all night and into tomorrow, but as soon as our tipi is raised, I collapse into my pile of furs. I'm asleep before I pull up my blanket.

Despite our shared exhaustion, the relief in the camp in the mornin' is palpable. Spirits are high. Steps are light and quick. Everyone joins together for a good, hot breakfast of newly cooked buffalo strips and fresh bread. The women even throw in some berries to go along with our meal, which is quite a treat.

The day's work of finishin' the camp set-up and doin' our normal chores keeps us busy. I love the sound and feel of our camp when it's bustlin' and energetic. The season of mournin' seems to be over, now that tatanka is found again.

Soul of Moon, with Grasshopper in tow, comes to me as the time for the evenin' meal approaches. Her demure smile takes me off guard as she loops her arm 'round mine. She speaks softly, but with obvious excitement—and I have no idea what she's sayin', so I look at Grasshopper, my brows raised.

"Hanhepi Wi Nagi say she want for Sungila Sá mate."

"What?" I'm aghast. Surely, Soul of Moon wouldn't betray Mah-do Wah-ay-e-lo in such a way.

"Hanhepi Wi Nagi say Sungila Sá too old for no mate. Hanhepi Wi Nagi say mitaka ki—sister from tribe of Hanhepi Wi Nagi ready for mate. Very beautiful. Hanhepi Wi Nagi want Sungila Sá mate sister."

Relief washes over me, followed by a sudden clench in my gut. Mate? How can I mate with a woman I don't know? And to marry a Lakota—would it even be a marriage in God's eyes? I can't live with a woman I'm not married to. A strange mixture of confusion, fear, disgust, and, yes, anticipation swirl through me. Can I even consider such a thing?

I rack my brain for Scriptures that tell me if Soul of Moon's request is possible under God's law. I won't do anything to bring harm to Soul of Moon's sister, because I love Soul of Moon and Mah-do

Wah-ay-e-lo, and to wed her sister outside of God's law would be—well, unthinkable.

"Grasshopper, wouldn't her sister be ashamed to be married to a white man?"

"Sungila Sá Lakota. No wasicu."

"But she'd look at me and see wasicu."

After an exchange with Soul of Moon, Grasshopper shakes his head. "Hanhepi Wi Nagi say sister proud to marry most excellent warrior Sungila Sá, famous among all tribes."

"But what about leavin' her family? Won't she miss 'em?" I'm scramblin' to think of a way to refuse without offendin' Soul of Moon.

"Hanhepi Wi Nagi leave family for Mato Waäylo. Most happy."

"Grasshopper, the...um, Great Spirit..."

"Also name Jesus..."

"Yes, Jesus, Mornin' Star, Wakan Tanka—He has rules for marriage."

"What ru-els?"

"Things you must follow. Like your ceremonies—you have certain things you do for each ceremony. For Jesus, marriage is like that."

"Lakota have ceremony."

"Yes, but—is it a ceremony like Jesus says?"

Grasshopper tosses his head and thrusts out his chin. "Sungila Sá say Jesus not like Lakota ceremony?"

"No, no, I'm not sayin' that. I have to follow His rules."

"Lakota follow Wakan Tanka."

"I know you do."

"So follow ru-els of Jesus. Same same."

I can't think of an argument against his point. Now what?

"Hanhepi Wi Nagi sends brave to bring sister before moon rise. Come soon."

Today? Now? My nervousness turns to sheer panic. "Does Mah-do Wah-ay-e-lo know about this?"

Grasshopper raises one brow.

Of course, he does. Soul of Moon would never act without his approval. I'm at a loss of what to say or do. "What is Soul of Moon's sister's name?"

"Sister name Wiwílamni Kalúsya. Most happy mate Sungila Sá."

"Grasshopper, I can't...I..." The warnin' look on Grasshopper's face pulls me up short. I know this look. I'm about to cause great offense. "I...I would love to meet Wee-wee-lah-mnee Kah-lue-zay-ah."

Grasshopper gives me a self-satisfied nod and a mischievous smile. His eyes sparkle, and prickly heat rises up my neck and colors my face a deeper red. "Meet soon. Ceremony when sun rise."

That soon? I won't know her at all. I won't know anything about her. I don't even know what her name means. "What does her name mean?"

"Flowing Spring. Most beautiful." Grasshopper clasps my hands before his chest, and Soul of Moon squeals with joy.

I try to swallow down the huge ball lodged in my throat, but it won't budge. I imagine I look something like a fish dyin' on the shore of a lake, gaspin' for air, openin' and closin' my mouth, squirmin' but unable to get back to the water. Soul of Moon squeezes my hands in hers and flutters off, I suppose to plan for my wedding. Grasshopper claps me on the back. "Misu of Mato Waäylo mate mitaka ki of Hanhepi Wi Nagi. Good medicine."

There ain't no way out now.

I watch the sky for the moon like I'm waitin' on a death sentence to be carried out. I guess most folk'd be excited, facin' a chance to receive the love of a beautiful woman—and I'm sure Grasshopper is right, she's beautiful, because Soul of Moon is the loveliest woman I've ever seen—but guilt wracks me.

What would my Ma and Pa say if they could see me now? They'll be turnin' in their graves. And will I be offendin' God and corruptin' Flowing Spring if I agree to marry her? And what of the admonition, "Be ye not unequally yoked together with unbelievers"? Despite what Grasshopper says, the Lakota are not really followers of Jesus.

Time creeps forward, and I still see no way out without great offense to people I love—and it's that thought that brings me the first small measure of peace. "Thou shalt love thy neighbor as thyself" is what Jesus calls the second greatest commandment, like the first, which is to love God. To love these people, my neighbors, well, I must honor them and honor their ways. Nothing about marryin' Soul of Moon's sister takes away my ability and desire to love God. In fact, perhaps as her husband, I can teach Flowing Spring to love Jesus, and through her bring Jesus to the whole tribe.

Is it possible this could work? Is this—maybe—a gift from God to bring me some happiness? As these thoughts flit across my mind, the moon rises over the horizon, and two horses arrive at the camp.

I'm still as nervous as a long-tailed cat in a room full of rockin' chairs, but an ember of hope flickers in my chest. I smooth my untamed braids, hopin' Flowing Spring isn't humiliated by my appearance, splash water on my face to wipe off any grime from the day's work, and take a step toward the arrivin' party. At that moment, the realization hits me—she won't understand a single word I'm a-sayin'. My heart drops to my feet, and the ember snuffs out. Unless we bring Grasshopper into our tipi permanently, we'll sit in continuous silence, starin' at each other. What have I done?

I see Soul of Moon approachin' from across the camp, holdin' the arm of another woman—or is she a girl?—and resist boltin', only by an act of will. As she nears, the lump returns to my throat and my eyes fill—Flowing Spring is exquisite. Her skin shines like burnished copper. She is slight and delicate, her movements graceful as a dancer, even more so than Soul of Moon. Her onyx hair, reachin' to her waist, glistens in the moonlight. She wears a simple garment of leather, bound at the waist with a beaded belt, but she wouldn't-a looked any prettier had she been wearin' a ball gown. Her eyes are downcast as she stands before me, but when I touch her chin gently, she lifts her face, and her bright smile and luminous eyes swallow me whole.

She doesn't seem ashamed a'tall—or forced against her will. Her smile beams as she envelopes my rough hand in her warm, soft ones, and we start toward the risin' moon, leavin' the grinnin' Soul of Moon behind.

As we walk together, I discover words don't matter much. She emanates peace and joy, as if her soul is so in tune with God, she walks more in spirit than in flesh. I'm caught in her wake, tumblin' wildly, spinnin' under, unable to breathe, then explodin' into the night air and inhalin' beauty. I join her in the realm of spirits, floatin' above the ground like I'm walkin' on a cloud. The moonbeams dance through the branches of the trees, puttin' on a show—for us.

Then, I realize I'm so flustered I can't remember how to say her name. Mortified, I stumble over a few words I do know, then I point to myself and say, "Red Fox—shung-he-la-sa." Maybe she'll take the hint.

"Sungila Sá. Há."

I spread my hand across my chest. "Red Fox. Aidan MacAlister."

Her smile doesn't falter, but I can tell she has no idea what these strange words mean.

"Chah-zjay." I hope she can understand my poor pronunciation of the Lakota word for name. I point to her chest.

Her smile broadens. "Wiwílamni Kalúsya."

Yes, that's it. "Há. Flowing Spring." I point to her again and speak slowly. "Flowing Spring."

"Fulow-in-spree-na."

"Close. Flow-ing Spring." I move my hand up and down like a wave on water. She throws her head back, laughs, and claps her hands together, so much like a child. I'm reminded of my sisters and Mary's girls, and my eyes mist over again.

She touches my face lightly. "Sungila Sá." She places her delicate fingers against her throat. "Flow-ing-spreen."

I want to tell her that, if we marry, her name will be MacAlister, but I don't know how to explain last names to her. Such a strange experience, to be two people at the same time: Shung-he-la-sa, Lakota warrior, brother to the mighty Mah-do Wah-ay-e-lo, and Aidan MacAlister, Scot-Irish son of a Georgia mountain farmer and a poor preacher's daughter.

I also want to ask her if this marriage is what she wants, but I don't know how to say it, and if I ask Grasshopper to ask her, he'll answer for her. I want to make sure she has a say in her own life, a real choice. But how can I? She's so young and innocent, and I don't have the words.

278

We sit on a fallen log in silence and watch the clouds race across the face of the three-quarter moon. When I reach to take her hand, she lowers her eyes, her thick lashes featherin' her cheeks, but her smile lets me know she doesn't mind. Despite my awkwardness, I decide to try to share how I feel in my clumsy way.

"Chun-tay ee-phee-ya." I think I'm sayin' she makes my heart full, but her titter lets me know I've butchered it.

"Chanté skuyé."

"Chahn-day skue-yea."

"Há." She points to my chest and back to hers. "Ptáyela." She repeats the gesture.

"Pdah-yealah."

"Ptáyela. Oiha ke waníl."

My frustration with feelin' ignorant boils over, so I stand, pull her to her feet with a grunt, and stride back to the center of camp in search of Grasshopper. Ma told me I would always have more to learn, and in my stubborn, childish way, I set out to prove her wrong—shoulda known Ma was right.

At first, I don't see Grasshopper anywhere, so I scurry toward his tipi and see him comin' from behind it carryin' some wood for his night fire.

"Grasshopper, I need your help. What does Chahn-day skue-yea mean?"

He looks up and twitches one side of his mouth. "Sweetheart."

"And pdah-yealah?"

"Together."

I turn to Flowing Spring and take her arms. "What was the other word? I can't remember." She, of course, can't understand me, so I groan and gesture for Grasshopper to translate, which he does.

"Ptáyela oiha ke waníl," she repeats.

Grasshopper gives me a smirk. "Together forever. Sungila Sá romance Wiwílamni Kalúsya."

All the wonderful feelin's of our first walk have turned into one massive humiliation. Not only do I have to bear Grasshopper's teasin', I'm forced to use him as a go-between or we can't communicate at all, and I'm left feelin' like an idiot in the process. "I want to ask her a question, and I don't want you to answer for her. I want to hear her answer. Understand?"

"Understand, há."

"Ask her if she wants to marry me or if she's bein' forced to against her will?"

Grasshopper makes a face. "No understand question."

"Will you just ask her?"

"No word for question."

"Fine, ask her if it is her choice to marry me? Does she really want to?"

"Wiwílamni Kalúsya no understand if I speak question."

My growl causes Flowing Spring to pull away. None of this is goin' like I want it to, and I keep makin' it worse every time I open my mouth. Maybe I should go back to the silence.

"Say this—tomorrow we marry. Is this what you want? Is that a question she understands?"

Grasshopper speaks a few syllables, and Flowing Spring smiles and reaches for my hand. "Há. Tahila it a higato Sungila Sá."

"What'd she say?"

"Wiwílamni Kalúsya say yes, she loves very much to marry Sungila Sá."

The tension drains from my shoulders like bath water washin' off a full day's dirt. The look of relief on my face seems to shock Grasshopper. "Why surprise, Sungila Sá? Wiwílamni Kalúsya most— um, very blessed—mate Sungila Sá."

"I don't know why she feels blessed. I don't even have a tipi for us to live in."

Grasshopper chuckles as if I've made a really good joke. "Plenty want marry Sungila Sá. Chiefs of two tribes taku kicicu for mate Sungila Sá."

The chiefs met and discussed me? "What is dah-cue-kee-cheechue?"

"Um—make trade?"

"Like an exchange?"

"Wiwílamni Kalúsya chief give big price for most famous warrior Sungila Sá. All tribes fear. Wiwílamni Kalúsya have many strong, brave wakayaja."

"So, you're sayin' her chief paid our chief for the right to marry her off to me, so she'd have lots of brave children?"

"Big price, há. Almost price give for Mato Waäylo mate Hanhepi Wi Nagi. Good trade."

I guess it's nice to know I almost live up to my older brother. I start to make a comment to that effect when it dawns on me. "Grasshopper, is Flowing Spring the other chief's daughter?"

"Há, younger daughter after Hanhepi Wi Nagi."

"And is..."—I almost don't want to ask—"Mah-do Wah-ay-e-lo our chief's son?"

"Há. Eldest son."

For the first time, I understand the profound significance of Mah-do Wah-ay-e-lo claimin' me as his brother, and the chief acknowledgin' Mah-do Wah-ay-e-lo's claim by callin' me ta-han-shee. I'm not just a member of the tribe. I'm a son of the chief. "Will one day Mah-do Wah-ay-e-lo become chief?"

Grasshopper smiles. "Possible become chief. Must show wisest all Lakota."

"I see."

"Wiwílamni Kalúsya chosen. Best. Most happy."

Our chief demanded the best for his sons, and received, as Grasshopper put it, a big price for the privilege. I put aside my initial unease at the thought of barterin' over people's love lives when I recall that rich white folk, like Mary, bring a dowry to give to the husband when they marry, so I guess it ain't so strange after all. I still feel some measure of disquiet over the negotiations takin' place behind my back, however. I suppose I shouldn't expect to be included in such things— after all, I was a slave before I became misu.

The idea that Flowing Spring wants to be with me—is excited to feel chosen—makes me want to skip and dance with joy. I pick her up and twirl her 'round and 'round like I used to do with little Maisie. Her laughter, like the tinklin' of a thousand tiny bells, provides the song for our dance. When I set her back on the ground, I take both her hands in mine, gaze deep into the moist, deep pools of her eyes, and repeat her phrase. Together forever.

CHAPTER TWENTY-ONE

The healer enters our tipi at the risin' of the sun and ushers me to the center of camp where all the women of the camp sit in a circle around four drums. I see Flowing Spring seated outside the circle on a large blanket. The healer gestures for me to join her on the blanket, then calls for the ceremony to begin.

Four braves enter the circle as the women stand. As the men pound a syncopated beat, some of the women begin to dance. The rest go to prepare the meal. The rhythm gets faster, louder, and more rhythmic as the women gyrate and chant on opposite beats.

I risk a sideways glance at Flowing Spring, but I don't see any of the nervousness that cuts creases in my stony face. She is beamin' and swayin' along with the dancers, sometimes clappin' along with the drums, havin' the time of her life.

I, on the other hand, sit as stiff as a hickory log with my hands clenched together between my crossed legs. The cooks bring food, first for the two of us, then for the healer, and finally for the dancers while the dance continues. The cooks now take their place, stompin' and twirlin' around the drummers, until the first group of dancers finish their meal. For the rest of the mornin', the dancers take turns, and when the midday meal comes, the women split the tasks of dancin' and meal preparation for the tribe, but the dance never stops.

I'm weary of sittin' when the healer stands again and makes a proclamation. Grasshopper and Mah-do Wah-ay-e-lo take me by the arms, while Soul of Moon and three other women surround Flowing Spring, and the whole group herds us like cattle to the outskirts of camp where stands a new elk skin lodge, its tent flap open.

Grasshopper leans close and whispers, "Hanhepi Wi Nagi make tipi for Sungila Sá and Wiwílamni Kalúsya. Custom bride mother make, but bride mother with Great Spirit many moons, so Hanhepi Wi Nagi make. Go. See."

I can't speak—so this is why Grasshopper thought my comment so funny. Such an extravagant gift, so many hours of labor for Soul of

Moon, and I never noticed her workin' on it. She musta done it during the night when I was sleepin'.

Flowing Spring glides through the flap, then turns and gestures for me to come. Inside, everything we need to begin our married lives is already provided—buffalo pelts for our bed, new blankets, a carved basin for carryin' water and for washin', my Bible, extra clothin' for both of us, even my little tin cup is there. Tears spring unbidden down my cheeks. Flowing Spring, seein' my emotional response, wraps me in her arms. My earlier tension is wiped away, and I'm ready to take her as my wife.

I collect my Bible, determined that some part of our ceremony be Christian, and we walk hand in hand from our new home. The healer makes another speech, which Grasshopper tells me is the announcement of the official marriage ceremony. The four drummers arrive, each holdin' one of the corners of our large blanket to carry it over their heads. In their outer hands, they hold their spears. The healer pushes us under the blanket, and we, the four warriors, and our friends and family, who I suppose are considered our weddin' party, parade around the entire camp, led by the healer, who holds up a green staff like a drum major leadin' a band. He cries out for everyone to come and celebrate.

We keep marchin' 'round and 'round until the sun gets low in the sky. Flowing Spring is bustled off with Soul of Moon and the other women. Grasshopper instructs me to collect wood and build the first fire for my new lodge while he and Mah-do Wah-ay-e-lo stand guard. As the fire kindles, the chief enters my tipi, with Mah-do Wah-ay-e-lo and Grasshopper trailin' behind him. Surprised and awed by his visit, I go to kneel before him, but he raises me up, places his crooked hand on my shoulder, looks to the sky, and speaks, as Grasshopper translates.

"Wakan Tanka, you give life again. Earth cold. Tatanka fled. But now we hear songs. Your two children sing and make lighthearted. Time for your children to make happiness together. Time to build nest. Time for pairing. Time of eagle. Wakan Tanka good. All creatures partner. You make us such way. Each wing needs mate. Each feather needs likeness. You make us such way. In secret, we carry likeness close to heart until meeting and your life starts in us. Your song sings in us. Your happiness comes to us. We praise you. He hechetu."

The chief pulls his pipe from his tunic, lights it from my newly built fire, and holds it in the air. Instead of takin' a draw, he hands the pipe to me. In some way I can't explain, I understand he is honorin' me with this gesture. I take a draw as I've seen Mah-do Wah-ay-e-lo do many times, blow the smoke to the top of the tipi, and give the pipe back to the chief, who smokes, then allows Mah-do Wah-ay-e-lo and Grasshopper to smoke. The pungent aroma swirls in the tipi, up through the hole in the center, christenin' our new home.

The chief leaves, and soon I hear the chatter of female voices outside. When I open the flap to stand next to Grasshopper and Mah-do Wah-ay-e-lo, the women lift their torches in the air and sing a melodious tune as they carry Flowing Spring to my arms.

"Now claim her." Grasshopper gestures toward her head.

"Claim her? What do you mean?"

"Claim her. Touch head. Say 'mitáwa'."

"I don't own her."

"No, say I take her for mate. Say 'mitáwa.'"

"Wait. First, I have to read from the book of Jesus. Will you translate for me?"

Grasshopper gives a solemn bow, so I begin. "He which made them at the beginning made them male and female, and said, 'For this cause shall a man leave father and mother and shall cleave to his wife: and they twain shall be one flesh.' Wherefore they are no more twain, but one flesh. What therefore God hath joined together, let not man put asunder."

Grasshopper frowns. "Hard word."

"Cleave means to join together and make one, whole. Twain means separated into two. Asunder means to tear apart."

"Ah." And Grasshopper spoke the Scripture in Lakota for all present to hear, ending with a firm, "Jesus wico íye." Jesus words. At the end of the recitation, Flowing Spring smiles and strokes my cheek, and my heart is snow in the warmin' midday sun.

So, I touch her head lightly and say, "Mee-tah-wah." The gigglin' women scatter, Grasshopper and Mah-do Wah-ay-e-lo bow to me and leave, and Flowing Spring and I are left alone at the entrance of our new home.

Feelin' suddenly reserved, I offer her an awkward, formal bow. She throws back her head and laughs, as melodious as bird song, reaches for my hand, and pulls me stiff-legged into our tipi. She sits upon our mound of buffalo pelts and pats the space beside her for me to sit.

"Would you like some water? Mnee?"

"Híya." She smiles and pats the fur again. "Iyotaka."

I'm painfully aware how little I know about Flowing Spring. I don't even know how old she is. "Oh-yah-kay about—umm, wah-hay-chal..." and I point to her, hopin' I've not butchered the words too badly and that she'll tell me more about herself. Otherwise, I'm afraid I'll feel like I'm violatin' her instead of lovin' her.

She cocks her head to the side and smooths her hand over her long, luxurious hair. The fleetin' image of buryin' my face in her hair sends a rush of blood up my neck and into my cheeks. "Sungila Sá iyokipia." She shrugs one shoulder with a tentative, perhaps hopeful smile.

I think she said I make her happy, but I want to be sure. "Ee-yue-shkee?"

"Há. Iyuski liglila."

Very much happy. "Shung-he-la-sa ee-yue-shkee lee-glee-lah too."

She beams and pats the pallet once more. "Hí. Híyo wo."

She wants me to come to her, so I swallow hard and slide my feet forward a little at a time until I'm standin' over her. Rather than ask me to sit again, she stands.

Our faces are inches apart. She reaches up with her soft, graceful hand and strokes my cheek. I'm suddenly self-conscious of the rough growth of red beard on my face and vow to find some way to make it smooth for her, smooth like the chins of her kind. She then runs her fingers through my long locks, her eyes captivated by their look and color and feel—I wonder how she feels about me lookin' so different from her people.

Without thought, I run my rough hands through her hair. It feels a lot like the silk of some of the cavalry officers' shirts or Mary's children's sleepin' gowns. I lift it to my nose and inhale the scents of smoke and juniper and sweetgrass.

I want Flowing Spring to feel safe with me—protected, secure, loved—but I don't know what she expects. All I have to go on are my observations of Mah-do Wah-ay-e-lo and Soul of Moon. Certainly, Mah-do Wah-ay-e-lo is fierce in his protection of his beloved mate, and he makes it clear how much he values her in every way. At the same time, their love is passionate, yet sometimes fierce.

I'm much more comfortable with the gentleness of the touch we are sharin' than I am with the frenzied passion I observed when I lived with Mah-do Wah-ay-e-lo and Soul of Moon. But what if Flowing Spring desires something different? What if I disappoint her?

Her hands leave my hair and trail down my shoulders and arms, then she takes my hands from her hair and touches them to her mouth. I lean down, and allow my lips to gently, hesitantly search out her mouth, savorin' the taste of her.

My nervous thoughts, my questionin', my embarrassment and awkwardness, even my deep anger, all dissipate like the chief's smoke through the hole in the tipi, and I envelope her, lower her down into the soft caress of fur, and begin my exquisite exploration of her being.

We lie together the rest of the night, alternatin' between sharin' our newfound love, restin' in each other's arms, and short periods of sleep. Once again, I see how unnecessary words are to communicate how I feel and to understand her feelin's. It's as if the words of Scripture that I spoke over our union have supernaturally come to pass—we are one mind, one body, one soul, one spirit.

As the day breaks, my awareness of how deeply I love her, despite how little I know about her and how little time we've spent together, dawns in me like the sun bringin' the light of a new day.

For this moon and the next, our lives fall into a comfortable routine. We share breakfast together, then we both have chores durin' the morning hours, she with the women and I with the other braves.

The midday meal is shared with the tribe. In the early afternoon rest time, Grasshopper sits with us as we learn each other's language and practice our communication.

Once we know more about each other, the topic shifts to spiritual beliefs. I share about Jesus Christ, the Morning Star, the God who became a man and died for others.

She has no problem believin' the Great Spirit became a man, as many of their myths tell of spirits becomin' animals and people, and people becomin' animals. They believe Wakan Tanka can take many different forms. Like Grasshopper, Flowing Spring finds great honor in Jesus' sacrifice and in His humility in takin' punishment for others. Because of His sacrifice, she accepts readily that Jesus is one of Wakan Tanka's forms and wants to know what it means to follow His ways.

Our conversations shift then to the stories in the Bible. Flowing Spring says the people most highly value respect, honesty, generosity to others, and wisdom, so I find as many verses as I can about these values. I share Jesus' instructions about givin' to the poor and takin' care of widows and orphans, which they approve. Then, I show them the book of Proverbs and explain it is a whole book devoted to wisdom. Flowing Spring asks me to read words from the book of wisdom each day.

The stories of the three Hebrew men who refused to bow before a false gold god out of respect for Wakan Tanka, and Daniel who refused to stop prayin' to Wakan Tanka even when it meant bein' eaten by a lion are their favorites. Flowing Spring is also fascinated by the story of Samson, which she says proves Wakan Tanka speaks in the book. She explains the people's hair is sacred and carries their spirit. I witnessed the ritual after Grasshopper's mother was killed where he kept some of her hair in his tipi so her spirit would remain with him. Flowing Spring tells me that the people also cut their own hair when greatly grieved or in the face of great injustice, because their spirits are wounded by such events, like Samson.

When I share the story of creation, however, Grasshopper and Flowing Spring shake their heads and politely inform me my book is in error. They tell me of White Buffalo Calf Woman who gave the people their rituals and values and taught them how to survive.

They weave an intricate tale of Inyan who creates Maka and Wi, the sun, how Wi marries Hanwi, the moon, and they have a child, Falling Star. Maka creates the dawn, and Skan, the judge, forces Han, the darkness, and Wi to chase each other around Maka forever. Ite, daughter of Old Man and Old Woman, marries Tate, the Wind, and has sons, Tate Tapa, the Four Winds. Ite is sent to earth, and Tate and their children create the heavens. Ite tells Iktomi, a lyin' spirit, to find the people, who are brought up from the underground to great sufferin'. This is when White Buffalo Calf Woman comes to the people to save them.

I'm not sure why their story is more believable to them than God creatin' everything in six days, but they are both insistent. With the exception of Genesis, though, we find more similarities than differences in our stories and beliefs, particularly the teachings of Jesus. Flowing Spring finds the Beatitudes particularly meanin'ful and says they echo many beliefs of the people.

Followin' our afternoon conversations, evenin' chores and meal preparation round out her day, while I'm included in meetin's with the elders about the threat of the white man, the problem of the buffalo, and the fraught relationships with other tribes. Although I'm now privy to the discussions, I'm not yet allowed to offer my input on decisions and directions for the tribe. This chafes me.

At the same time, I'm fascinated by the way these meetin's are handled, so I'm relieved I can at least be a part, albeit a silent one. The chief sits, silent and watchful, as the braves speak their minds. It's quite a contrast to the dictatorial style of leadership of the cavalry officers. Open and sometimes loud disagreements are common, but no one ever speaks ill of another member. Each man makes his case before the chief. No one gets defensive or accusatory, for if that happens, the chief exiles the offender from the meetin'.

Finally, after all arguments are presented, the chief speaks—usually a single phrase—pronouncin' his decision. Occasionally, he adds some words of wisdom, which visibly settles the men into calm acceptance. I wish I had some writin' implements to take down his words, because they are profound and meanin'ful to me. I can see why

Grasshopper says if Mato Waäylo is to be chief, he must show himself to be the wisest of all Lakota.

During the second moon, in the final month of summer, I experience my first Inipi. Grasshopper explains the sweat lodge serves the people by purifyin' the mind, body, and soul, seekin' wisdom and healin' for the people, and givin' thanks to the Great Spirit. I've never felt anything like Inipi. The heat is so intense it feels like everything in you is comin' to a boil—all the ugliness, all the fear, every hatred and malice, all bitterness and regret vomit from you in a cleansin' and outpourin' of your soul. We chant, we pray, we beat drums—at one point, I leave my physical body and travel up into the sky to speak with the moon and the stars. When I return, all heaviness in me is lifted. I can soar like an eagle.

After my strange experience, I share Isaiah 40:31 with my brothers: "They that wait upon the Lord shall renew their strength; they shall mount up with wings as eagles, they shall run and not be weary, and they shall walk and not faint." They agree the words of the Great Spirit I share reflect the purpose of Inipi, and they marvel that wasicu would know of such things. They see the white man as vicious, unfeelin', and filled with hate, havin' no honor or respect or wisdom. I can't argue with 'em.

The buffalo problem becomes the dominant conversation as fall arrives. Mato Waäylo points out the buffalo will be returning from the far north soon, to face possible annihilation at the hands of the wasicu, and our responsibility to protect and care for the buffalo as keepers of the land. No one has any answers.

We sit for long silences, starin' into the chief's fire and listenin' for direction from the Great Spirit, but He is silent. I find myself squirmin', frustrated with the inaction, yet the Lakota seem at peace waitin' for wisdom and vision to come.

After the meetin', still with no answers, I walk hand-in-hand with Flowing Spring along the edges of the wood to the top of the knoll on which we first found the survivin' tatanka after the slaughter. I guess she can sense my unease because she asks, "Is my love distressed in spirit?"

"I am."

"What distresses my love?"

"Tatanka returns, but we have no way to fend off the wasicu. If tatanka die, Lakota die."

"My love speaks true."

"I hear no words from Wakan Tanka."

"Wakan Tanka speaks to others?"

"No, He remains silent."

"My love must wait for words. Unwise to act without guidance."

"Há, we wait. But I feel..." I can't think of the Lakota word for nervous, so I settle for frightened... "nihínciyä."

"My love does not follow words of fear."

"Híya, I do not."

"Must wait for truth."

"Há, Flowing Spring speaks true."

"Tonight, my love prays to Jesus for truth."

"Flowing Spring and Sungila Sá pray as one."

Her face glows. "Há, my love. When Wakan Tanka speaks, my love speaks His word to the people."

Her trust in me and childlike faith in Jesus shatters me. While she believes without question that the Great Spirit will answer our prayers, my doubt gnaws in my gut like rats after the food stores. I don't believe He notices or cares about our plight, and I fully expect silence in response. My Ma must be weepin' at heaven's altar.

Determined to correct my skeptical attitude, when we return to our tipi, I pull out and unwrap my Bible, lean close to the fire, and pour over the words for something—anything—that speaks to the people's predicament. Do we surround the cavalry, beat drums, hold up torches, and holler like wild men, like God instructed Gideon? Do we march 'round the fort until it falls to the ground like God told Joshua? Do we stretch out a staff over the river in the valley below and ask God to bring it crashin' down on the army's horses like Moses and Pharaoh's chariots?

Flowing Spring stands behind me and rubs the creases between my brows. "No more, my love."

I take her hands in mine and guide her to sit beside me. "The words of Jesus do not speak."

She strokes my cheek. "Sungila Sá suffers long like waskuyeca of Wakan Tanka."

"Sweets?"

"Love, joy, peace, suffer long..."

"Ah. Fruit. Fruit of the Spirit." And then it hits me. Peace. The Spirit brings peace. I envelope Flowing Spring in my arms. "You're brilliant!"

Flowing Spring tilts her head. "What brilliant?"

"The fruit of the Spirit. Peace. God would tell us to make peace."

"Peace with wasicu?" Flowing Spring shakes her head. "Híya. Wakan Tanka never speak peace with wasicu who destroy land and kill buffalo without reason. No honor. No respect."

"I know."

"No trust."

"But..."

"The people have sacred wichóh'an to protect land. Land sacred, like land of promise in book. Sungila Sá say Wakan Tanka promise land to His children name of Israel. Also promise Lakota land to the people and give duty to protect and honor sacred land. Wasicu take land from the people like bad man take land from Hebrew children. Wakan Tanka show Hebrew children ways to fight for land. Lakota also fight."

I take her hands in mine. "The people cannot win this fight."

"Chief no make peace with wasicu. Red Cloud tries to speak with wasicu. Soldier makes promise, does not keep. Bad faith, Red Cloud say. Other chiefs say same."

"But what choice do we have?"

"Sungila Sá say Wakan Tanka always defend against enemies of His people."

"Há, I did say."

"Better to allow defense by Great Spirit than make false peace."

I can't argue her point. Deep in my gut, I know the soldiers will never leave the people in peace. The wasicu desire the land. Their desire is a ravenous, gluttonous, insatiable cravin' like men for spirits once they've tasted them and felt their effects. They'll keep pressin' the people north, farther from their sacred land. They'll be forced to leave their loved ones' burial sites and their holy grounds behind.

The wasicu will slaughter tatanka and all the other animals until they are no more, and they'll leave the land barren and lifeless before they move on to take the lands of other tribes.

"Then we fight."

Flowing Spring shakes her head. "My love, how fight enemy with so many soldiers, more than all Lakota, and weapons that fire objects from far away? Best to follow Great Spirit like Israel."

I bite my tongue before the accusation boilin' up against God like acid flows out and singes my love's gentle spirit. After a deep sigh, I acquiesce. "Há, my love, you are right, of course. We will fight like the tribes of Israel."

"We lie together and pray, my love. This is right."

So, I lie down on the soft pelts, and Flowing Spring snuggles down next to me. She sings a soft prayer for the protection of the Great Spirit, but I'm asleep before she completes her song.

Noises in the camp startle me awake—shouts and the sounds of runnin'. As I rise, Flowing Spring stirs, her long lashes flutterin' against her flushed cheeks. "Something's goin' on. I'm gonna find out what it is. You stay here."

I stick my head through the flap and call to a brave runnin' past. "What happens?"

"Soldiers."

It's a long way from the fort and a long distance for the cavalry to range, but here they are. Powerful hands squeeze my heart inside my chest. I step back inside the tipi and gather up my arrows, bow, and spear. "Flowing Spring, I must go. Remain inside."

Her wide eyes give me pause. I rush to her side and kiss her, a long yet gentle kiss, thinkin' I want her to remember me by this kiss instead of by my fear and doubt.

She clutches my hand in hers and pulls it to her chest. "Return to me," is all she says.

"I will." I hurry to where Blossom is tied with the other horses, throw my leg over her, and urge her forward with the other braves. The phrase, "I thought we had more time," keeps repeatin' inside my head like the rhythm of a heartbeat or the poundin' of our war council's drums.

The scout leads the war party southeast, directly toward the risin' sun. This time, the advantage belongs to the cavalry. The sun is in our eyes, blindin' us, so we are forced to rely on the scout's memory of where he saw the riders. But we must ride to them. If we let them come to us, the women and children are in peril. I know personally what the soldiers do to the women and children of their enemies.

The scout rides into a thicket of trees and slows to a walk. We collect at the edge of the thicket to peer out, and right away we spot the cavalry—a larger contingent this time than the last one we faced. Their numbers almost equal ours, so this isn't a scoutin' party. They are out to raid and burn encampments.

I squint against the sun to try to see their weapons. If they have repeatin' rifles, we don't stand a chance. Many will die. But we can't let them get through to our camp and murder our women.

I look to Mato Waäylo, who studies on the soldiers as they ride in the open, his jaw locked and neck pulsin'. As the soldiers reach the lowest point in the valley, he sends half of our braves to the left to circle around behind the troops. "Remain within the trees. Call the ghosts of our ancestors to carry you in silence."

Without a word, the men leave, swift and silent as a snake. Mato Waäylo then turns to me. "Take half of these men and ride to their right flank. When you see us ride into the valley, ride against the soldiers."

I understand his strategy. He sacrifices the frontal assault and right flank braves so that the men attackin' from the rear can take the soldiers by surprise and overpower them. It is a bold and costly attack. My group's only chance of survival is for the soldiers to be so focused on Mato Waäylo's group, they miss seein' us until we are in their midst, too close for their rifle fire to be most effective and close enough for our spears and arrows to strike true.

My group rides out, skirtin' the cavalry position behind a shallow rise until we are directly on their flank. Within minutes, Mato Waäylo leads his men screamin' down the side of the rise, his hair flyin' behind him and dirt from the poundin' hooves billowin' clouds that seem to carry the riders on the wind.

The cavalry fire immediately. They were anticipatin' an attack—so much the worse for us. Mato Waäylo's men loose arrows into the cluster of horses, and I raise my spear to signal our attack. We gallop over the rise and down into the melee, thunderin' into the sides of their horses and skewerin' men with our spears. I jab my spear into the side of one soldier, then another.

Some of the soldiers turn to meet our attack. A brave to my right falls from his horse, blood blossomin' from his shoulder. I hear many cries from Mato Waäylo's men as they tumble to the ground wounded. My spear breaks off in a cavalry horse, so I pull out my bow and fire arrows to my right and left as fast as I can set the arrow and pull back the bowstring. It isn't fast enough.

We are on the verge of bein' overcome, when the braves attack from the rear. Their cries echo 'round us like the songs of angels, mixin' with the screams of the soldiers as they are struck down. My braves push through to the middle, and the rear assault collapses on the cavalrymen like foldin' a blanket.

My arrows gone, I now use my hatchet to strike blows on the soldiers' heads. The sting of a rifle butt slams into my back. When I turn, my hatchet raised, there is Martin, sittin' astride Murphy. My hatchet falls from my hand as I gape at him. And it's him all right, freckled face burned from the sun, his unruly red locks flowin' from beneath his cap.

"Martin?"

He rears back his rifle to take a swing at me, but in mid-arc, his eyes bulge, and he lets his rifle drop to his side. "Mac?" his voice is more a squeak than a question.

"Martin. You're alive."

"What...what in th' name of all that be holy be ye doin' here? And dressed like...that?"

One of the men shouts at Martin to kill the dirty Injun, but Martin continues to stare, his mouth hangin' open.

"I was captured...it's a long story." A nearby soldier raises his rifle to fire at me, so I duck down and press Blossom into a gallop toward the man. Blossom rams his horse, and the soldier falls off, his rifle topplin' end over end into the dirt to be trampled under many hooves. I give a quick glance back over my shoulder, but Martin is exchangin' blows with one of my braves, so I turn to face two more cavalrymen, armed with my fists and my horse.

A trumpet blares the retreat, and the soldiers disengage and gallop off to the southwest, away from our camp. Mato Waäylo signals to let them go. He doesn't want to risk more deaths—so many have fallen. "Gather rifles and powder from dead soldiers. Quickly."

Martin slows and turns in his saddle. I lift my hand high in the air, an odd combination of relief, remorse, and grief stirrin' within me. He raises his cap high in response and calls, "So long, Mac!"

I mutter a quick prayer under my breath. "Please don't tell anyone about me."

CHAPTER TWENTY-TWO

Since we repelled the cavalry, we haven't seen hide nor hair of the soldiers. With winter snows fast approachin', Mato Waäylo figures we won't see them again until spring. I hope he's right.

The buffalo, as predicted, return to the valley below us, drawn to the river. The herd is terribly depleted. Many express concerns tatanka may soon be gone and question if we should hunt at all, but the need for food outweighs their concerns. We're careful to take only what we need for winter, and only the ones not likely to survive the hard months anyway. After the hunt, our chief performs a blessin' over the herd. To my surprise, at Grasshopper's insistence, Mato Waäylo asks the chief if I may also bless tatanka, and the chief says I may.

I ask Flowing Spring to stand beside me and to pray with me for the herd. She first sings a prayer of blessin', then I raise my hands as I've seen the chief do. "Jesus, Bright and Morning Star, our Até in Heaven, hallowed be Thy name. Please protect the Great Tatanka durin' the hard months of winter. Feed them as You feed the sparrows. Protect them as You protect the land. Shield them from the arrows of their enemies. Bless them, Até, and bless the land we share. Amen."

"He hechetu," the chief intones. He glances at me, his old eyes twinklin', and offers me a single nod. I can't describe how pleased I am by his approval. It almost feels like havin' Pa say, "Weel dane, son."

As we return to the camp, Flowing Spring wraps her arm 'round mine, almost hangin' on me as we walk. I'm a-thinkin' she's proud of me for my prayer, until she stands on tiptoe, leans into my ear, and whispers, "I carry my love's child."

I stop short, grab her shoulders, and gawk like she's some kinda mythical creature—a leprechaun, a unicorn, or a magical fairy. "A bairn?"

"I carry son of Sungila Sá."

My wits return, and I wrap her in a tight embrace. "I can't believe it! How? It's...I'm..."

"My love knows how."

297

Laughter bubbles up from my chest, the greatest joy I've ever felt in my life. "A son? How do you know that?"

"Ask most gracious Jesus for boy. Believe for boy."

"Son, daughter…I'm thrilled either way."

"Happy, my love?"

"So happy. Ecstatic. Now, you gotta be careful. Don't go carryin' heavy loads of wood or pelts or anything."

Flowing Spring scoffs. "My love believes I am fragile flower, not strong like Jesus say."

"Oh, I know you're strong, my love. You are the strongest, most beautiful, most amazin' woman in the whole world. But the little bairn growin' in there isn't strong yet."

"Jesus protects."

I think of the infants lyin' buried in the ground behind the barn and shake my head. "Sometimes, babies aren't strong enough."

"Son of Sungila Sá most strong of all. Brave warrior and leader of men. One day chief."

My chest puffs out like a brown thrasher doin' his matin' dance. Imagine my son, chief of the tribe. Like a bolt of lightnin', I'm struck by a blast of fear washin' over me. "When will he be born? Durin' the winter?"

Flowing Spring chuckles. "When flowers come and rain makes fresh grasses, child born soon."

A rush of air blows from my mouth. I didn't realize I was holdin' it in. The swirl of feelin's from intense joy to utter terror makes me realize the next few moons are gonna be quite a challenge. Hopefully, I won't drive Flowing Spring from the tipi with my hoverin' and worry. She seems completely at peace, unlike her jittery husband. "You must eat well over the winter. You eat my food, too."

Her sideways glance lets me know she thinks me ridiculous. "My love must eat. I have plenty."

"You're eatin' for two."

"My love worries not necessary. All is well. Healer say."

So, I swallow my concerns, hold her close, and kiss her precious, sacred hair. "My love makes Sungila Sá most happy of all men."

Her belly grows through the winter months, and I spend hours lyin' with my head on it, feelin' the kicks of my boy against my cheek and listenin' to her heart beat for two.

We sing to the bairn, and I read from the Scripture about God's love for children. The winter is relatively mild compared to the two winters before, which I thank the Good Lord for providin', and the tribe doesn't have to move south, which is a great blessin'. During breaks between the heavy snows, we are able to take some walks together. Wrapped in our buffalo pelt coats and fur-covered boots, I'm sure we look like strange, two-legged animals crossin' the plains—maybe bears, if they didn't hibernate during the winters.

Jed returns durin' the winter with news of sickness at the forts along the Bozeman Trail. He urges the chief to avoid the area because the sickness spreads quickly, and many are dyin' from it. He and Grasshopper spend a lot of time together, which takes him away from our language lessons. But in a way, it's nice to share that time with Flowing Spring alone. We talk at length about our plans for our child, our fears about childbirth (mine more than hers), and our desires for the future.

The question of our child's name comes up frequently. I'm insistent on him having the MacAlister name and express my desire to name him after my Pa, Liam. But Flowing Spring argues we must wait until the child is born and see what name the Great Spirit bestows based on his disposition. I laugh and point out that Silent Grasshopper talks more than anyone in the whole tribe, and perhaps naming a child based on their infant disposition isn't such a great idea. I can see my flippant response upsets her, and though I try to take it back, she remains somber and distant for the rest of the afternoon.

That night after the tribal meeting, I find her already curled up under the blankets, turned away from me. Is this our first fight? Over our bairn's name? If it is, it looks very different from the open, raucous, and contentious fights my Ma and Pa used to have. I can't bear the silence, so I sit beside her and touch her shoulder as gently as I can.

"My love is angry. I'm sorry. I did not mean to cause offense."

299

She looks over her shoulder, and her eyes are smolderin' coals. "Sungila Sá act like wasicu. Make fun of the people's ways." She turns back over and buries herself under the piles of blankets.

"No, I didn't mean to make fun of you. I'm so sorry. Names are important for the people. They are important for me, too. I desire my child to have a strong name that will take him forward very far in life. Where my family comes from, MacAlister is a powerful and important name. I know it means nothing here, but it means everything to my family."

After a long silence, she turns onto her back and looks at me. Her face has softened, and her eyes appear wet. "Most difficult the differences between us." Her voice catches. Tears trail down her cheeks.

"I know. I don't mean to make it harder. Let us talk more about this without anger. I promise my love I will listen."

"Sungila Sá..." Her words choke in her throat. "Believe Flowing Spring family now. Not true?"

"Yes, yes of course it's true."

"And child in belly?"

"Yes, Flowing Spring and my child are my family now."

"And the people?"

I hesitate, although I don't know why. Perhaps it's because of the strange mix of feelin's I had when I saw Martin. Perhaps it's rememberin' my Ma and Pa's arguments. Whatever it is, I recognize the Lakota have treated me as a brother, so I swallow down those other stray thoughts. "Há, the people, too."

Flowing Spring reaches up and touches my cheek in the way she always does. I'm so close, so one with her when she does that, I'm happy to agree to whatever name she chooses. But she doesn't take advantage of that power she has over me.

"Will my love wait until birth, feel child's spirit? Whatever my love feels, whether Liam or MacAlister or Lakota name, it will be so."

"My love is wise and good. It will be so." She opens her arms to my embrace, her anger forgotten.

The next morning after the meal, Jed takes me aside. "Well, now, seems some folk at the fort are throwing around questions about some soldier dressed up as Lakota and fighting for the wrong side. They're calling him a deserter, a traitor, and a murderer. Any chance they're talking about you?"

I close my eyes against the news. Martin betrayed me to the officers. "I s'pose they are."

"Well, now, this is quite a pretty pickle. Yes, indeed. Them soldiers is madder than wet hens and out for blood, boy."

I don't know what to say to Jed, since I don't see how it affects him, one way or 'nother.

"Why do you care?" I know I sound rude, and Ma would whip me for my rotten attitude when he's tellin' me something I need to know, but I still don't like the man.

Jed takes my tone in stride. "You do see the danger, don't you?"

His question brings me up short. Danger? I know if they found me, they'd hang me for a deserter, but I don't know of any other danger, certainly not to Jed. "I know they could capture me durin' a raid. I've known that all along."

His bushy brows lower over his eyes until he resembles a riled black bear more than a man. "You haven't thought this through, boy."

"What d'ya mean?"

"Well, now, you put a target on the back of this tribe just as sure as the man in the moon. Them soldiers are on the hunt. They want to find you, and they want to hang you. Who do you think gets wiped out in the process?"

He's right, I hadn't thought this through. Martin seein' me is more of a problem than I realize. Why did my friend betray me? I can't make sense of it. My anger and hurt spills out toward Jed. "What can I do about it? Turn myself in? Is that what you want?"

"You got to leave."

What? What is he sayin'? "Leave? I can't leave. I won't."

"Then you sign their death sentence."

"No, there has to be another way. I'm not leavin' my wife and child. The Lakota are my family now. I'm not leavin' 'em, no matter what you say."

Jed shrugs. "Well, now, you tell me how you're planning on keeping them soldiers away."

It's like I've been dunked in a freezin' stream. Silence settles heavy between us, hard and cold and immovable. After a long wait, Jed shrugs again. "I guess I could help you out."

I'll take anything at this point, even help from a man I despise. "What're you thinkin'?"

"Them rumors—well, now, I could squelch them proper. Tell them I heard the white soldier got hisself killed. I could even say I killed him my own self."

"Would they believe you?"

"More likely to believe it if I say you got killed in a fight with another tribe. I don't know that they'd believe I would kill my own kind."

For some reason, I have no trouble believin' Jed has killed many a man of his own kind, but I keep my thoughts to myself. "Why would you do this for me?"

"Not for you, buck. I'd do it in a heartbeat for Gnus'ka Ainila. I'm quite fond of the lad, and I don't want to see him dead over some fool thing, like you letting yourself be seen by the soldiers."

"It was an accident. I didn't expect to run into any soldiers I knew. All of them who knew me were supposedly killed with Fetterman. But the one who saw me, he and I were friends. He's the one I left to find the night I was captured."

"Not much of a friend, you ask me."

I can't argue with him at this point. "I guess he found his way back to the fort after the Fetterman massacre. Now he's recognized me."

"Wish he'd killed you."

"Thank you for that."

"Well, now, that's where we are. I'll mosey on to the fort and lie for you. Hopefully, they'll buy it. I'll make it sound like an oh, by the way, so they won't suspect I have another motive. They don't know I prefer the natives over their company any day and twice on Sunday."

I hate bein' beholden to Jed, but I can't see another way out of the mess. "I do appreciate you takin' care of Grasshopper, even if you don't want to help me out. It means a lot. You're a good friend to him."

"You know now you can't take part in any more fights against the soldiers. 'Cause if they see you again, they'll never believe me a second time."

I haven't considered that point, either. How can I benefit the tribe if I'm not allowed to fight? I'll be considered canl waka—a coward. He must notice the color drain from my face, because he sighs and leans close to me, his rancid smell wormin' into my nostrils and mouth until I wanna spit.

"Listen, truth be told, the army isn't going to let the natives stay here much longer anyway. I hear tell they're going to sell the Lakota nation a treaty to give them lands farther north in exchange for a promise to leave them alone, which of course they have no intention of keeping."

"Should I try to convince Chief to leave now, before the treaty forces him to go?"

"You'll never convince him to leave. Heck, I don't know if he'll leave when he is forced. You know, the whole 'land is sacred' thing. Chief is a stubborn ol' nut."

"I believe the land is sacred. I believe we should fight for our land."

Jed chuckles. "I'm sure you do, Johnny Reb. How'd that work out?"

My anger overcomes my common sense, and I storm away with an unintelligible growl.

He calls out to my retreatin' back. "Never you mind, young buck. I'll take care of your problem for you."

I spit back a grumbled, "Thank you so much."

Grasshopper tells me at the evenin' meal that Jed left for the fort, and I breathe a sigh of relief. I don't wanna have to tell anyone—not the chief, not Mato Waäylo, not Grasshopper, not even Flowing Spring—of the danger I've brought to their door. There's nothin' for it. All I have left is to put my hopes in the hands of the gruff codger and pray the problem goes away and my family stays safe.

When the weather warms, Flowing Spring's belly is as round as if she's swallowed a watermelon whole. She amazes me, though, how she continues to do her chores and the work of the tribe. I believe if I were holdin' such a weight, I might sleep all day, but she carries the same workload as before.

In sharp contrast to Flowing Spring's lightheartedness, I'm as nervous as a squirrel in the shadow of a hawk. Spring means the soldier's raids resume, and I'll have to tell Mato Waäylo I can't be a part of the fight. The chief will want to know why, and my secret will be out. But at least there's plenty of work I can do now.

The buffalo return from the south with new spring calves—a hopeful sign. Flowing Spring wishes for a white calf to be born, sayin' the sign of a white calf birth in the same season as her child's birth would mark him as special before the tribe. Even though I can't fight, I can still hunt, and Mato Waäylo offers me the honor of leadin' the first hunt of the spring.

Once again, we're careful to take the older and weaker members of the herd, stayin' away from females as well, and we only take what we need. The chief asks me to bless the herd again, so after the hunt, he and I stand side-by-side on the hillock overlookin' the herd and say our prayers of blessin'. Everyone seems confident the prayers will work again.

We don't see any sign of the soldiers from the fort durin' the rainy season, and I begin to relax a bit. Perhaps the illness Jed mentioned took its toll, and the soldiers have no interest in fightin' the Lakota. I certainly hope that's the case.

As Flowing Spring predicted, new grass and flowers dot the hillside when she wakes me in the night, sayin', "He comes."

I race to find the healer, who comes with Soul of Moon and several of the women. Soul of Moon kicks me out immediately. I can't say I'm upset about it, because I can hear Flowing Spring's cries of pain. I don't think I could stand to see her sufferin' right in front of me and do nothing, so it's better I sit cross-legged by the fire with Mato Waäylo and Grasshopper to wait.

To my surprise, as Flowing Spring's cries seem at their worst, the healer and all the women leave the tipi. They remain nearby, talkin' together, but show no concern as Flowing Spring continues to holler. "What're they doin'? Why aren't they in with her?" I push myself up but Mato Waäylo grabs my arm.

"Childbirth sacred," Grasshopper explains. "All women birth alone. Special time for mother and child to share."

"What if she needs help, though?"

"Women will know. Healer will come."

"I'd better go to her." I start to stand again, but Mato Waäylo pulls me down, more forcefully this time.

"Stay. Wait. Baby comes. Most sacred."

Finally, Flowing Spring's cries fade, and I hear the tiny, shrill squeal of my newborn child. I look to Mato Waäylo to see if I may go now, and he smiles and gestures for me to go to her.

When I reach the tipi, I stop at the entrance to listen. The squallin' has stopped. If I listen closely, I can barely hear little grunts and smacks and suckin' sounds, which I know means Flowing Spring is feedin'.

"May I enter?" My voice is barely a whisper.

"Come, my love."

I push through the flap into the most beatific scene I've ever witnessed in my entire life. Flowing Spring's lovely hair is mussed, her face red and wet with sweat. Blood darkens the twisted, rumpled pelt beneath her bare legs. Across her chest lies my child, wrinkled and red with a shock of black hair, suckin' milk with surprisin' vigor. Flowing Spring's glowin' smile would put an angel to shame.

"Come, my love. See son of Sungila Sá."

"A son." I breathe in deep and long, tryin' to hold back tears, but as soon as I see his little face, the dam bursts. "He's so small."

"Strong. Like father."

"Strong like mother. You're amazin', my love." Words fail me. I want to sing and shout and dance and scream. Mostly, I want to hold her and my son so tight that I squeeze them inside of me until we merge into one bein'.

"Give hand." I offer her my hand, which she places on my son's slimy back. "Feel son."

"I feel him."

"Feel wakan of son."

I wait. I'm not exactly sure what I'm tryin' to find, but I trust Flowing Spring, and she is confident I will feel his spirit and know his name. I murmur a prayer. "Father, help me know who he is. Give me his name." Before I am aware, the words spill from me. "Súnkawakan Sápä." And I know why this name comes. His wakan reminds me of Blossom—strong, spirited, filled with devotion and love, never failin', carryin' those weaker than himself, determined, patient, loyal, and true. He will be Spirit of Black Horse—Súnkawakan Sápä—for this is who the Great Spirit created him to be.

"Súnkawakan Sápä." Flowing Spring repeats his name. It dances on her tongue like gentle water over smooth rocks in a streambed. The bairn stirs, and I know in my heart he approves.

When the bairn stops sucklin', Flowing Spring hands him to me. The depth of my awe surprises me. He is perfect. His tiny fingers grasp and pull my hair when I hold him to my chest. His little toes curl as I rub his feet. Chunky little arms and legs flail about when I hold him up in the air. His tuft of hair feels like cotton, and his eyes are deep pools in which I can see the light of heaven. Everything about him is fascinatin', every inch of him magical.

Flowing Spring rises from the pallet, pulls on her shift, and gathers up the bloody pelt.

I don't know what I expected, but I didn't expect her to get right up after her ordeal. "Let me take care of that."

She looks shocked. "My right."

"What?"

"Part of me. My right to bury."

"Bury?" It's my turn to be shocked. "Why? I figure you'd burn it."

Her mouth twists in disgust. "Sungila Sá knows nothing of Lakota ways."

"What did I do now? I don't understand."

But she carries the bundled pelt from the tipi and leaves me standin' there holdin' the bairn, who immediately starts to wail, as if he can feel his mother leave. I try everything I know to soothe him, but he refuses to be comforted, so I carry him out of the tipi in search of his mother, more than a little annoyed that she left me in such a predicament.

Flowing Spring is nowhere to be seen. By the judgmental looks I receive, I gather I'm doin' something wrong, so I duck back into the tipi, pacin' and rockin' and singin' and cooin', to no avail. As an ultimate insult, he pees down the front of my tunic.

At long last, Flowing Spring returns, her hands caked with dirt. She glowers at me, dips her hands in the washin' bowl, then takes our son—snatches him from me, really—and he accommodates her by quietin' right away. I'm a wilted flower, all crumpled and flat and turned in on itself.

Flowing Spring wraps the bairn to the front of her body and strides to the entrance.

"Wait. Please...I...I didn't know. I'm sorry."

She whips toward me, her witherin' glare like fire burnin' my skin. "Nothing sacred for Sungila Sá. Wasicu destroy, waste, strip life from land—no goodness in heart, only hatred."

My chest rips apart as if she's cleaved me with an axe. "Flowing Spring knows me. This is not me."

"Not know you." Her words explode from her as if they've been waitin' for just the right amount of heat to boil over. Tears spring in her eyes. "Not understand you."

"I don't understand you either. But I'm tryin'. Help me to understand."

"No eyes to see."

"What do you mean?"

"Lakota say all life sacred. Sungila Sá say burn part of Flowing Spring. Part of Súnkawakan Sápä."

"Why is buryin' it better than burnin' it? You're right, I don't understand."

"Return to earth. Become part of all things. Not destroy."

I stare, numb, as the weight of her words crushes me. She thinks I want to destroy part of her and part of my own son. No wonder she's filled with rage and hurt. I struggle to calm myself, to swallow my own anger at what I believe are false accusations against me, so I may understand her feelin's. I can't speak at first, finally knowin' what she thinks of me. When I do, I can barely muster a whisper. "Flowing Spring feels...this way about Sungila Sá?"

Her tears flow freely. The pain and anguish are etched on her face like a sculptor carves a stone.

I inhale a shudderin' breath, close my eyes, and allow my sigh to carry my own agony out of my body and up through the hole at the top of the tipi into the open arms of the Great Spirit. When I reopen my eyes, I am calm.

"My love, I see now my great offense, and I beg for your forgiveness." I want to say more, to tell her I love her, that I would never allow anything to harm her or our son, that I will protect them for the rest of my life. I want to ask how she could ever believe I would intend her harm, but the small voice whispers for me to wait, to be silent, to listen.

Her shoulders heave, but she makes no sound. So, I wait as the voice commands. Our shared silence echoes in our lodge louder than the warriors' battle cries.

It's Súnkawakan Sápä who breaks the silence, rousin' to protest his hunger. Flowing Spring unwraps him and allows him to suckle, her eyes closed and her tears still wettin' her cheeks. Smackin' noises and contented grunts soften the heavy air. She shifts her gaze to the bairn, enfoldin' him in love. I'm reminded of drawin's I've seen of Mary holdin' the infant Jesus, with Joseph lookin' down on them, and I want to rush to her side and embrace them both, but the voice continues to urge patience.

After what seems to me like eternity and a day, she looks up at me. Her eyes still glisten with tears, but the hard edges have left her face.

"Flowing Spring also ask forgiveness Sungila Sá. Expect Sungila Sá know without teaching." She shakes her head and looks down at our son. "Wrong to expect infant know words without first teaching how speak."

"I promise, I will take great care to honor all life as sacred."

"Flowing Spring promise teach Sungila Sá."

"Thank you, my love. Do you forgive me?"

"Há, my love, forgive like Jesus say. Does my love forgive?"

"There's nothing to forgive. My pain is great for my offense toward Flowing Spring and Súnkawakan Sápä. Sungila Sá will listen to Flowing Spring's teachin' and will make right."

She lifts her hand, curvin' her fingers to beckon me to her side. As I move beside her, she takes my hand, as she does so often, and places it against her chest. "Chanté kstó chanté yeló." My heart your heart.

"Há, chanté wanzí, wakan wanzí." One heart, one spirit. I press my mouth over hers under the watchful eye of Spirit of Black Horse, our wakanyaja—little sacred one.

CHAPTER TWENTY-THREE

Time changes when you have a child. Each day seems endlessly long and impossibly short, each new moon comes before you realize any time has passed, and the child transforms with each returnin' sun while in futility you will the sky to stop turnin' so you can spend more time experiencin' him as he is.

The summer months overflow with joy for me. After arguin' with me that only women carry infants around with them, Flowing Spring relents and shows me how to wrap Súnkawakan Sápä in a cradleboard so I can carry him comfortably on my back. I hear the snickers of the braves, but I don't mind. Truth be told, I want to spend as much time with him as possible. Most afternoons, Flowing Spring and I lie on a blanket with him in the sun, playin' with him and talkin' to him for hours at a time. At night, he sleeps cuddled between us. Flowing Spring explains this is the way of the Lakota, that children are never left to cry because of a need, and that it is our job to anticipate his needs and meet them before he cries. Cryin', she says, is bad for a child's spirit. She gets no argument from me—although my Ma and Pa would be rantin' about him gettin' spoiled rotten. I can't bear it when he cries.

She also teaches me why infants are called wakanyaja. She shows me the soft spot beneath his thick black hair and explains that Wakan Tanka speaks to him through this spot, and his spirit speaks back, until it closes. She says if we listen as we cradle him, we may hear the voice, too. Many nights I spend with my head lyin' close to his, listenin' for the Great Spirit's voice, but the Great Spirit speaks only to Súnkawakan Sápä. I'm content to be near him as they talk.

Súnkawakan Sápä is strong and crawls by the turnin' of the leaves. He's walkin' before the last snows leave the plains and speaks his first words soon after. Every movement, every step, every word, I'm bustin' open with pride. His dark eyes sparkle with understandin' greater than he can express, and I know he's gonna be too smart for his own good.

Once he starts talkin' and can understand, Flowing Spring begins teachin' him Lakota ways. The first lesson is how to care for his belongin's. After listenin' to my sisters complain about their chores, I'm amazed at how happy Súnkawakan Sápä is as he folds up his blanket of a mornin' and puts away his toy at the end of the day.

As Flowing Spring shows him skills, she often peppers her instruction with Lakota beliefs and values, even though he doesn't comprehend their full meanin' yet.

"The people have only what they need. No more." "Always give to others who have need." "Honor all life in all your ways." "Speak only truth. To speak falsely is to break honor with yourself and others."

I love listenin' to her speak the Lakota words. It reminds me of the countless nights I spent by the fire at my Ma's feet, listenin' to her read Scripture, repeatin' what she read until I memorized it, and talkin' about what each verse meant.

One day, I will sit with Súnkawakan Sápä by the fire and read the words of Scripture to him. Still, in my heart, I rejoice that Súnkawakan Sápä is learnin' Lakota ways and not the ways of wasicu. It seems to me wasicu have left behind the teachin's of Christ, while the Lakota, who may not yet know His name, follow His ways.

When the moon of his birth comes, I strap Súnkawakan Sápä onto Blossom, pull myself up behind him, and teach him how to ride. His laughter rings across the plains when I give Blossom her head, and she runs fast enough for his hair to catch the wind, but not fast enough to jostle him from my arms. "This horse is your namesake. You share her spirit." He giggles and nuzzles her mane. After that, we ride together almost every day.

Although we've not seen the cavalry soldiers in quite some time, the problem of wasicu still comes up occasionally in council meetin's. The chief is convinced their proposed peace treaty is filled with lies.

The Cheyenne and Arapahoe have agreed with the terms, but the Lakota have not signed, still havin' fresh memory of the wasicu violation of their first treaty with Red Cloud. The treaty offers land to the north, promisin' the land will forever be native land, its borders to never be crossed by wasicu. It also promises to close the outposts along the Bozeman Trail, and to shut down the trail itself to white travelers, givin' the Powder River lands to the Lakota. But chief says, "White man gobbles land like ravenous wolf pack who is ever hungry."

Mato Waäylo grunts his agreement. "They have no honor."

Chief nods. "When they use up this land and leave it like bones in the desert sun, they come for more. Sungila Sá, you say?"

It's so rare I'm asked for my opinion, I have to stop and formulate my thoughts into Lakota words. "I say wasicu believes the land is theirs to give to the people. If they believe such, they will also believe the land is theirs to take away from the people."

Murmurs and nods show approval of my response. "Sungila Sá speaks wisdom." Chief stands to signal the meetin' is comin' to an end. "We speak more about this tomorrow."

The pall over me from the council lifts as soon as I enter our tipi, and Súnkawakan Sápä runs into my arms. "Let's go for a walk, whadya say, young man?"

"Does mother come also?" Flowing Spring cuts her eyes and gives me a half-smile.

"Whadya say? Does mother come?"

Súnkawakan Sápä grins. "Há. Há."

"Very well, then. Come along, mother."

The moon is almost full, and the new grass shimmers in its light. Holdin' Súnkawakan Sápä's hand, and with my arm wrapped around Flowing Spring, we walk slowly to the top of the rise. In the distance, I hear the howls of wolves bayin' at the moon, maybe on the hunt after an elk or deer. Flowing Spring shivers once beside me. "What is it, my love?"

She doesn't answer right away, so I turn her face to mine. "What?"

"Nothing. All is well. Cool air of night."

"Let's go back, then." Súnkawakan Sápä lifts his arms to be picked up, which I do, and we make our way back to the camp and the warmth of our home.

The next evening at war council, the buffalo herd is the first topic of discussion. Mato Waäylo reports our scouts have followed the herd, now farther south, which indicates a harsh winter. "We must move south with herd."

I blurt out, "But that brings us close to the fort," earnin' me a harsh rebuke from Mato Waäylo. "Forgive my disrespect, Chief. I speak without permission."

I know I should tell them the soldiers are lookin' for me, but I don't want the chief to know I've brought such danger to the people. I'm afeared he'll make me leave, for the safety of the rest of the tribe.

Mato Waäylo sneers. "Sungila Sá suggests we remain here and starve in fear of soldier fort."

Chief does not look to me for response, so I keep my information to myself. One of the elders expresses concern that our presence near the fort will be seen as a challenge and bring war, and a few of the elders agree. The argument wages back and forth for some time, many braves and some elders agreein' with Mato Waäylo. Finally, the chief raises his hand.

"The people must have meat for winter." He looks to Mato Waäylo. "Camp moves with herd."

My breath catches in my throat. Now, I have to figure out how to stay out of sight of the soldiers durin' the hunt or disguise my white skin and cover my red hair so if seen the soldiers do not suspect I am the deserter. The people—and my family—will be in even more danger. If the soldiers recognize me...no, I can't let that happen.

The proposed treaty is the next topic of discussion. Mato Waäylo and several other braves suggest joinin' with other Lakota tribes to attack the fort as one nation. The elders, however, oppose this move, sayin' all the tribes will not agree, and our tribe will be left to the slaughter. I must say, I agree with the elders, but not for the same reason they give.

"Great Chief, forgive my interruption. May I speak about wasicu?"

"Speak, Sungila Sá."

"I hear the wisdom of the elders, and I agree. I fear, even with all Lakota nation as one, wasicu cannot be defeated with bow and arrow. Their weapons bring death upon death, and we have only a few. Their numbers are larger than the count of the stars, so even if Lakota win battle, they lose war. More wasicu will come, and more still, and the hungry wolves will still consume the land."

Many of the elders murmur in agreement, but Mato Waäylo stands in anger. "Does Sungila Sá say Lakota are weak?"

"Hiyá. I say Lakota are stronger than wasicu, but even with great strength, their numbers overpower ours. We could kill ten to their one, and they would outlast us."

"Lakota would kill ten to their one and have done so."

"Há, I have seen."

"Sungila Sá kill twenty without one wound."

"And still wasicu come. Red Cloud kills 100 and still wasicu come."

Chief lifts his hand. "Treaty is tasty-looking apple concealing rotten, worm-filled core. But Sungila Sá speaks true. Wasicu will swarm sacred land like locusts and Lakota will be no more."

Mato Waäylo, true to his name, growls. "What then is answer?"

Chief hangs his head. "Treaty may purchase us some time, but we must look ahead, beyond the coming swarm of locusts, and seek new lands far away from reach of wasicu. Lands they can neither give nor take away."

"So we sign?" Mato Waäylo is incredulous.

"First, we seek. If land can be found with plenty buffalo, we go. If not, we sign and continue seeking." Chief breathes a deep and raspy sigh. "But either way, we leave our sacred lands."

Cries and groans and the slaps of fists against chests fill the chief's lodge.

"The people will gather to ask Wakan Tanka for light to show way to new lands." Chief stands, and we leave to call everyone to the fire for prayer.

Flowing Spring sees my downcast expression as soon as I enter our tipi. "My love is filled with sorrow. What happens?"

"Chief decides we must leave this land to escape wasicu."

"Hiyá."

"But first we move camp to buffalo herd—near soldier fort."

"My love worries."

"Há." I can't bear the guilt gnawin' at my gut because of my terrible secret, so I take Flowing Spring's hand. "I must tell you something, something bad for us."

315

"Speak, my love."

"One of the soldiers from the fort recognized me. Now the soldiers look everywhere in anger for Sungila Sá for fightin' against soldiers and killin' soldiers."

"Sungila Sá Lakota now."

"They don't see it that way."

"What say Chief?"

I swallow hard. "I haven't told Chief."

I look away from her reprovin' stare. "Must tell Chief, Sungila Sá."

"I know. It's just...I'm frightened Chief will force me to leave, and I can't leave you and Súnkawakan Sápä."

"Why Chief make Sungila Sá leave?"

"Because I'm wasicu and a danger to the people."

"Chief no make Sungila Sá go away. Sungila Sá Lakota. Family."

"Very well, if Flowing Spring say. I will warn Chief as soon as prayer is over."

She nods, picks up a sleepy Súnkawakan Sápä, and walks with me to the fire in the center of camp. The people are already gatherin', their faces solemn. Apparently, word of the decision has spread through the camp.

Flowing Spring walks straight to Soul of Moon, and the two sisters embrace and share words of comfort. Mato Waäylo stands behind his mate, starin' far in the distance at nothing, his arms crossed over his chest. I take my place by his side, mimickin' his stance.

As the chief strides to his place before the fire, an elder drums a steady rhythm and some of the women begin to chant. Chief calls on the Great Tatanka to bring us to a land filled with buffalo, and to Wakan Tanka to bring us to a land of peace, free of wasicu and free of war, where the people can thrive and Wakan Tanka can bless the people. He then asks Wi to warm the earth and hold back the worst of the winter, and to light our way to our new land. Some of the braves dance 'round the fire while the women chant, but Mato Waäylo and I remain still and stiff as oaks.

The prayer ends, and Chief dismisses the people. Flowing Spring catches my eye and gives a quick gesture, so I hurry to the chief before he enters his lodge. "Great Chief, may I speak with you?"

The old brave stops and turns slowly to face me, but his eyes are far away, perhaps listenin' for the voice of Wakan Tanka to guide him.

"Chief, I received news from the old trapper. News that affects the tribe. He hears rumors of the wasicu at the solider fort searchin' for Sungila Sá, having learned he is a white man and a former soldier who fights for the Lakota and kills many soldiers. The old trapper says they search in anger. I fear for the people if they discover I am here."

The chief's face doesn't change a lick. His eyes remain fixed on a distant point. I'm about to ask him if he heard me when he speaks. "This is your concern about following tatanka."

"Há, Great Chief."

"What say Sungila Sá?"

I don't know what to say, but I know he's askin' me for my solution to the problem I presented him. To offer the solution when you bring a problem is the Lakota way. I work up my nerve and offer what little I have in the way of an answer. "I thought I would paint my skin and cover my hair for the hunt. As long as soldiers only see from a distance, perhaps they will not recognize me as wasicu."

"Sungila Sá not wasicu. Sungila Sá Lakota."

"I am most honored to be Lakota, Great Chief. Wasicu will only see white skin, not Lakota."

"Sungila Sá speaks true." Silence sits uncomfortably between us, although I get the feelin' I'm the only one who is uncomfortable. "Follow as you say. Keep greatest distance from eyes of the fort. If soldier approaches hunters, ride swift and sure a great distance to trees."

"I will, Great Chief."

"Return to camp when danger is no more." Without a word or glance, the chief shuffles to his lodge, his bent back the only indication of the weight of responsibility he carries.

The mornin' brings a flurry of activity as a few hunters leave in one direction to find the herd, a scoutin' party heads in the other direction in search of new land, and the rest of the people start the process of breakin' camp. I'm naked and vulnerable with so many of the men away from the camp, acutely aware of the responsibility for protectin' the families of those who are gone. Still, I'm clear why the chief assigned me to remain behind.

By midday, we are packed, and the camp is movin' south in the general direction where the buffalo were last spotted. It's more difficult with so many men away, but we manage, everyone carryin' more than their weight and workin' well together. I'm always impressed with the efficiency and simplicity of the people. Even Súnkawakan Sápä does his part, carryin' his little blanket and toy as he rides in front of me on Blossom. With Mato Waäylo away with the hunters, Flowing Spring and I help Soul of Moon tear down and carry their lodge. Blossom seems to have no difficulty with the extra weight.

The train spreads across the open plain between the river and the fort. We are in no hurry. We must hear from the hunters about the herd's location before we go too far and walk ourselves away from our destination.

Soon, we see a horse approachin'. But wait, it isn't one rider returnin' to guide us—it's all the hunters, and they're racin' toward us at full gallop. I think I hear a distant call, but I can't make out the words. Then, someone at the front of the train calls back to us at the rear. "Akhíthi! Akhíthi!"

Something has happened. The hunters are yellin' for us to return to camp. I scan behind the riders for the cavalry, but I don't see clouds of dust or any signs of movement. I turn Blossom in a wide arc, and our family becomes the lead horse on the train. Now, we have a reason to hurry, but such a long train of heavy pallets can only go so fast. Soon, the hunters have caught up with us.

Mato Waäylo races up beside us. "Buffalo all dead. Soldiers slaughter, as before, and leave on plains beyond fort. Hawk Feather see soldiers in fort mounting horse as if to come out, so we hurry to warn the people. Must hasten beyond reach of soldiers."

"I didn't see the cavalry followin'."

"May have wanted chase us away. Once gone, they stop."

"I hope so." I crank my neck around to see if I can spot any cavalry in the distance, but it's difficult to make out anything because of the length of the train stretchin' back across the plains. "Mato Waäylo, should you and I go back and cover the rear of the train? If cavalry does come, the rear is vulnerable."

"I go. Sungila Sá call on the people to move quickly. Lead them home."

"I will." I ride up and down the front section of the line, urgin' the people forward. "Ináhni. Waínahni." Make haste.

Thank the Good Lord, the cavalry doesn't come after the riders, and we're able to make it back to the camp by nightfall. The women build a fire in the center of camp, and by its meager light, we set the camp again near the hillock overlookin' the river. The set up takes most of the night.

Now that the danger is passed, I have time to consider the implications of the news that our buffalo herd is decimated. Winter is fast approachin'. What are we gonna eat? How will we survive? Difficult circumstances have now become life-threatenin', and I can't see a way forward.

We're all operatin' on no sleep, but the chief calls an urgent meetin' of the council anyway, emphasizin' for me our desperate situation. The meetin' is tense and more contentious than usual from the start.

"We should have attacked the fort while we had the chance."

"No, we should have gone with those sent to seek a new land and settled wherever we found buffalo. Now we have no food."

"Chief has led us to our doom."

"Why didn't we protect the buffalo? It is our responsibility to care for them. We allowed wasicu to slaughter, their lives waste."

"This stain on our tribe has sealed our fate. We deserve whatever comes."

"We should have diverted them away from the fort, at least. Instead, we did nothing."

"Age has dulled Chief's senses."

"We knew wasicu could not be trusted. Why did we remain here?"

The words fold one on the other until I can't make out what anyone is sayin'. Yet, the chief sits in silence and allows the babblin' rants to escalate until I have to cover my ears against the din. Only then does the chief speak. "I hear many shoulds but no answers. Who is able to see the way forward by looking behind them?" His question is met with chastened silence. "One who turns head backwards stumbles and falls into the pit. Who among you can change the past? Let us seek answers for the way forward."

"What way forward? Without tatanka, we starve." Many elders and braves murmur their agreement with the elder's argument.

Mato Waäylo, silent and thoughtful beside me, stands to command the group's attention. His words crack like a whip. "The Lakota way is the way of honor, respect, courage, truth, wisdom. Since when do Lakota speak defeat? Since when do Lakota speak fear?" He pauses and stares, his eyes searchin' the eyes of each member of the council. I marvel at his ability to sway others, his natural leadership, and his wisdom. He is surely the one to be the next chief. "Since when do Lakota show disrespect toward most wise chief?"

Another pause, another glare around the circle. "Chief speaks true. The path forward is one of change and growth and perseverance, not one of blame and hopelessness. Yes, the herd is gone. Yet, still Wakan Tanka provides. Do we not have elk, deer, and antelope? Do we not have fish in the river? Has reliance on buffalo made Lakota weak? Lazy? Incompetent? Is this what you say?"

A chorus of no's reverberate in the lodge.

"The path forward is difficult, like steep and narrow path up mountainside. We have walked the way of buffalo, running the plains and grazing at our pleasure. Now, we must walk the way of bighorn sheep, a treacherous daily vertical climb for small tufts of grass. Do you claim Lakota are not strong enough or skilled enough to walk this path?"

More no's, louder this time. He's gettin' them riled up—smart, since we'll need stirred spirits to sustain us over the long road ahead.

"The Lakota way will sustain us as it always has. Let us not stray from its guidance." With those final words, Mato Waäylo sits to murmurs of assent.

One of the elders who criticized the chief takes up Mato Waäylo's call. "Mato Waäylo speaks true. Wakan Tanka provides, Lakota hunt. The people must hunt now before snows of waniyetu, fish and deer, elk and antelope, all birds and animals of the plains. No longer may we ride in wild freedom for one big hunt. Now we must walk in silence and wait with patience. It will take much time."

"Each must hunt according to his best skill," another elder adds. "We have no time for mistakes."

I know a thing or two about huntin' deer, and I imagine elk and antelope are similar, so I open my big mouth. "The wise elder speaks true. To hunt deer, you seek sign of deer passage, then wait in a hide in silence and stillness for deer to return. This is a skill I have. I will share my skill with the people." The glassy stares I elicit let me know I would've been better off keepin' quiet. I guess my words are an offense to the brave warriors, as if some young wasicu can teach them anything about huntin'.

But Chief is gracious. "Sungila Sá will hunt deer." He clears his throat. "Indeed, all must contribute fully and equally."

My afternoons of play in the sun with my wife and son are gone now. I hear the chief's quiet admonishment, carefully spoken. It will take every single member of the tribe workin' all day every day until the first snow to hunt the same amount of meat we'd get from one good buffalo hunt. Our work is cut out for us.

The braves divide the hunting grounds and work in pairs. I'm glad Grasshopper is my partner. I enjoy his company. We hunt from sunrise to sunset, and if we don't kill anything, we sleep out on the plains and start again the next mornin'. When we run up on an antelope or elk herd, we may take down one, or two if we're lucky, before the herd bolts. Even on horseback—which spooks the animals anyway—we can't catch them once they start runnin', not like buffalo. So, we take to creepin' near the herd on foot and takin' what we can. Then we cart the animals back to camp to be prepared by the women, and head back out to hunt again. Deer take even longer to find and are almost always single kills.

The women who aren't preparin' game and the elders span the length of the river through our lands to fish. One or two of the women walk up and down the river to collect any fish caught, take them to camp, and prepare them for storage, then return to the river to collect the next batch. For what it is, our system is as efficient as it can be, but the work is slow and tedious, and the hours are long. Ten days into this routine and we still don't have enough food for a half-moon, much less for the long months of winter.

The people are amazingly resilient, though, and they don't lose heart. If anything, they work harder and longer as the time wanes. As for me, I'm not so hopeful. My heart aches for Flowing Spring and Súnkawakan Sápä, and my days in silence are consumed with imaginings of my little boy wailin' because of hunger, or my sweet Flowing Spring wastin' away to bones before my eyes.

Instead of strengthenin' me, these thoughts wear me down until I'm dismal company for Grasshopper. He, however, remains energetic and positive. During the night, when we can talk in more than brief whispers, he is full of questions about Jesus and the Bible. Some nights I read, and some nights I try my best to answer his stream of questions, but my attempts are half-hearted at best. I'm too consumed with worry to sustain these conversations and quickly become irritable and short with him.

One particularly miserable night, rain pelts us as we huddle beneath a clump of trees under sodden blankets to wait out the worst of the storm before me make camp. As usual, Grasshopper wants to talk about Bible stories, but instead, I go on and on about my worries—we're not killin' enough game, we're gonna starve to death, we're gonna freeze to death, the cavalry is gonna attack us at our weakest and kill us all. I end my diatribe with the declaration, "This is pointless. It's too late to make a difference."

"Sungila Sá, do you not believe words of Jesus?"

I sigh, knowin' the truth, deep down, that I don't have the kinda faith I should. "Which words are those?"

"Jesus say, Take no thought of life, what eat, what drink or what put on body. Jesus say life more than these things, and Jesus say Great Father feed bird of air who do no planting like Lakota, so if feed bird will feed Lakota. Sungila Sá read such."

"Yes, He did say something like that."

"Jesus also say, Take no thought for next day, for next day has own thoughts."

"Yes, He did."

322

"Sungila Sá no trust words?"

"I do trust words, Grasshopper. I miss Flowing Spring. And I worry for my son."

"All father want good for son, like Great Father. No reason lose hope."

His words grind against my skin like a thorny bush, and before I know it, I snap. "What do you know? You can't understand. You don't have a son."

"Was son to father."

"It's not the same. Besides, you don't have anything to lose."

Grasshopper is silent for some time, long enough for my regret to ooze over me like slime over a stagnant pool. I'm about to apologize when he whispers, "Think Sungila Sá worry more for Sungila Sá than for mate and son."

My irritation flares again. "What do you mean by that?"

But Grasshopper just looks at me.

Why would he say such a thing? Of course, I'm worried about Flowing Spring and Súnkawakan Sápä. Of course, I don't want them to suffer.

But listen to your own words. The whispered voice presses against my head like a vise.

What did I say? *You don't have anything to lose.* A knife twists in my gut. What a horrible thing to say. But, worse than that, Grasshopper is right. My own words expose my selfish motives. I don't want to lose them or watch them suffer for my own sake. Shame coats me with thick, sticky sludge. "I'm sorry, my friend. My words were hateful. Will you forgive me?"

"Sungila Sá forgiven. Must forgive, Jesus say, because Grasshopper has done wrong and Jesus forgives. Not right to see wrong in other and not see wrong in self. Jesus say."

"You're right. And you're right about my selfishness, too." My groan reminds me of a cow givin' birth. "I'm such a poor example of someone who follows Jesus. I must make it harder for you to learn about Him."

"Bible say all do wrong thing. No man different."

323

Grasshopper shows more of God's grace than I've seen from anyone in my life. "Thank you for being my friend."

"Sungila Sá tahansi. Good friend." He claps my back with a toothy smile. "Now Sungila Sá must forgive self."

Grasshopper turns and walks on ahead to make our camp, but my feet stick in place like I'm ankle-deep in quicksand. Memories flood me, the horrible things I've done and said, all the men I've killed, every failure on parade before me until I can't hold back the gut-wrenchin' cry of my soul, and I begin to weep.

I'm afeared, now that I've started, I'll never stop—so much pain I've caused, so much agony I've felt, so much hatred I've carried—all exposed before me in a steamin' pile. My chest heaves. My shoulders tremble.

Forgive as I forgive you whispers through me. A coverin' over my heart begins to crack open—it aches and stings as it peels off, piece by tiny, jagged piece.

Before I realize it, I'm on my knees, my face planted in the mud. Every muscle in me is frozen in place. A second whisper weaves its way through the first like tendrils of smoke curlin' in and around each other until they merge and become one. *I love you.*

If someone were shovin' their hand through my chest to grab my heart and rip it out, it wouldn't pain me as bad as those whispers. My throat locks closed, and I can't get air. I'm pressed to the ground, paralyzed, as if a giant is standin' on top of me. If I had to lift my little finger to save my life, I couldn't do it. My thoughts are black as night. I know I deserve death for all I've done—for what I've become. "Just go ahead and kill me, Lord." My mutterin's soak into the mire.

Another whisper swirls 'round me, a gentle caress with a light and airy sweetness in stark contrast to the solemnity of the first two. *I have never left you.*

My mind screams, but I don't know if the shriek is the protest of my demon or the bellow of my own self-hatred. "Why? I don't deserve Your love."

You are my child.

Images of Súnkawakan Sápä consume me—astride Blossom, his hair catchin' the wind and the trill of his laughter ringin' in the air—

toddlin' through the grass up to his eyes to fall into Flowing Spring's arms—carefully foldin' his blanket to lay it neatly on his pallet—ridin' on my shoulders as we watch the golden sunset over the distant hills—and I remember the kinda indescribable love that brings tears to my eyes and makes my chest feel like it's about to burst.

In that moment, I taste a little of what the Good Lord feels for me. Something in me breaks, not a shatterin' like a broken heart but a breakin' open like a butterfly pushin' its way through its cocoon or a cicada crackin' open its shell to fly free. The rest of the hard coatin' on my heart sloughs off. I'm raw, vulnerable. Every inch of me hurts. It's like I've come through surgery, and the army doc has cut off a gangrenous limb—it's horrible and a relief at the same time.

The terrible giant lifts his weight from my back. I gasp in a long breath and push myself to my knees. My face is awash with tears. I swipe my cheeks with muddy fingers, which leave a gruesome imitation of war paint. His whispered words are seared into my brain and etched on my heart. Forgive as I forgive you. I love you. I have never left you. You are my child. I repeat them over and over like an incantation. My fists open and close, as if I'm graspin' to keep a-hold of what I just experienced.

I must tell Grasshopper. I have to thank him. He must be wonderin' what I'm doin', grovelin' in the mud. When I stand, a wave of dizziness washes gray fog over my eyes. I'm as weak-kneed as a bairn tryin' to walk for the first time. My vision clears, the clouds part, and the white moon lights my way, stumblin' and sloggin', to Grasshopper's new campsite.

"Fire slow to catch. Wood wet."

I can't help myself, the tears flow again as I grapple Grasshopper from behind and engulf him in my embrace.

"Sungila Sá..." He can barely get my name out through my squeezin' arms. "Wha..."

"I will never be able to thank you...you don't know...your words...thank you, my dear friend. Thank you. A thousand times, thank you."

He wrenches from my hold, turns to face me, and grasps my arms. "Not understand Sungila Sá." He searches my face, his eyes wide and an uncharacteristic crease between his brows.

"Your grace—your words, tellin' me to forgive myself—your generous kindness—you helped me more than you can ever know."

"How help?"

"I can't explain it. I just know Jesus spoke to me, and all the anguish and regret and pain and anger lifted from me."

"Jesus speak Sungila Sá?"

I smile, and I wonder if my cheeks are gonna break wide open at the edges of my lips from the stretchin'. "He did."

"Sungila Sá write word like Paul."

I throw my head back and laugh with a lightness and joy I haven't felt since I was a youth on my farm playin' with my sisters. "Trust me, I'm nothin' like Paul. But Jesus spoke to me, and His words healed my wounds. He freed me."

"What wound?"

I point to my chest. "Heart wounds. Deep pain from war and and killin' and grief."

"Truth make free Sungila Sá?"

"Yes, He did. Like He said."

Grasshopper claps me on the back again with a beam. "Like Jesus say."

CHAPTER TWENTY-FOUR

The first snows find our food stores less than half of our usual winter supplies. Chief designates Hawk Feather as distributor of rations, a job he clearly doesn't relish. I think it's wise of the chief to choose a warrior for the position—the people are more likely to comply without argument than they would with a woman. When we are deep into winter and bellies are empty, a brave standin' guard over the food is a good deterrent.

The first snows also bring a messenger from Red Cloud. The largest Lakota tribe plans to sign a peace treaty with the wasicu, and Red Cloud invites our chief to attend the signin'. Mato Waäylo argues vehemently against Chief goin', but Chief sends Red Cloud's messenger back with his promise to come. "All Lakota face hard winter. Cannot face wasicu soldiers at same time." So, the chief, two elders, and three braves journey to the fort with plans to sign the treaty.

While Chief is away, Jed makes his last visit of the season to our camp. Aware of the fate of the buffalo herd, he brings bear pelts and deer meat to trade for two of our wasicu rifles. If we weren't so desperate for meat, I'd argue against the trade, but I understand Mato Waäylo's decision to accept Jed's offer. Thankfully, Jed doesn't stay long. Hospitality is a Lakota value, so as long as he's here, we have to feed him—and he's a big man.

Mato Waäylo was right when he said the buffalo goin' farther south means a harsh winter. The snow falls thick and deep, and we don't get the usual respites of brief thaws where we can fish the river or hunt in the woods, so our stores dwindle even more quickly than in years of plenty.

The one savin' grace for me is I get to spend the entire winter holed up in our lodge with Flowing Spring and Súnkawakan Sápä. After bein' away so long on the hunt, it's pure joy for me to fill my days playin' with him, readin' to him like Ma used to read to me, and holdin' him close to me at night to keep him warm. His little spirit is showin' more and more.

I watch him imitate me—my actions, my words, and even my expressions—and I remember the whisper, *You are my child.* The love I feel from Jesus flows freely toward Súnkawakan Sápä. His smile is as bright as the moon glistenin' on the snow. Yes, we're terribly hungry, but our hearts and our lives are full.

In the worst of the winter, we must bring Blossom into our lodge, so she won't freeze to death. Súnkawakan Sápä loves it, but Flowing Spring is less than thrilled, as is Blossom. I use the opportunity to teach Súnkawakan Sápä how to care for Blossom, and we spend hours brushin' her and cleanin' her hooves.

Over the winter, I share some about my experience out on the plains with Flowing Spring. At first, she seems concerned about me, as if my experience means I'm unwell, but I relate it to the sweat lodge, which she understands. "But Sungila Sá and Gnus'ka Ainila not in sweat lodge."

"No."

"How hear spirit world?"

It seemed so much easier to explain it all to Grasshopper. "Jesus is spirit, yes, but also flesh like man."

"Like White Buffalo Calf Woman."

"Well, no, not really. See, Jesus was born to a woman, but His Father was Wakan Tanka."

"You say Jesus is Wakan Tanka."

"He is."

"How Jesus Wakan Tanka and son of Wakan Tanka?"

At moments like these, I realize the magnitude of the change Jesus has made in me. In the past, I would've been frustrated, and I might've given up tryin' to explain, but He's given me a patience beyond my understandin'. "Let me start at the beginnin'. Hmm—Wakan Tanka decides He must come to the world."

"Why come to world?"

"We'll get to that, hold on. So, Wakan Tanka sends a messenger to a woman named Mary."

"Ma-ree."

"Yes. The messenger tells Mary the Great Spirit will visit her and she will be with child. And when the child is born, she is to name Him Jesus."

"Jesus born to Ma-ree and Wakan Tanka."

"Jesus carries the spirit of Wakan Tanka inside Him. That way, Wakan Tanka can come to the world. So, Jesus is a man, flesh and bone and blood, but He carries the spirit of Wakan Tanka."

"Ah."

"Here's the part about why He comes to the world. Many bad men feared the power of Jesus because He carries Wakan Tanka's spirit, so they set out to kill Him by hangin' Him on two crossed logs stuck in the ground. But you see, Jesus wanted to die all along. He wanted to die to take our place."

Flowing Spring frowns. "All die."

"Their flesh does...but that's a story for another day. So, when they kill Jesus, He sacrifices Himself to die in our place."

"How man kill Great Spirit? Not possible."

"You're right, they could only kill Jesus' flesh. Then, three days later, He comes back to life again, this time as flesh and spirit. Those who follow Him can touch Him and feel His flesh, but He rises into the air as Wakan Tanka reborn. So, Jesus is both flesh and spirit. He is son of Great Spirit and Great Spirit reborn. That's how He can come to me and speak to me. I don't have to go into sweat lodge to enter spirit world. Jesus comes to me in this world."

Her eyes gleam. "Sungila Sá chosen one of Wakan Tanka."

"No...well, yes, but so are you and so is Súnkawakan Sápä and so is Gnus'ka Ainila and so is Mato Waäylo and Hanhepi Wi Nagi. All the people are chosen by Jesus."

"Wasicu are chosen?"

"Yes."

Flowing Spring spits. "Jesus not Wakan Tanka."

"Yes, He is. He made all people, even wasicu. But many wasicu reject Him like the bad men who hung Him on the crossed logs."

"Then not chosen."

"Jesus chooses them, but they do not accept Him. They walk away from Him and His ways."

Her eyes narrow. "So now not chosen."

"He would still accept them if they returned. One day, I'll read you the story of the Prodigal Son, and you'll see how Jesus loves everyone, even those who walk away from Him. One of the whispers I heard from the Great Spirit on the plains is that He loves me. He told me He loves me despite all the bad things I've done."

Flowing Spring gives a satisfied grunt. "Sungila Sá chosen one. Jesus say to Sungila Sá on plains."

I decide to try another approach. "Gnus'ka Ainila says Jesus is man of great honor to sacrifice Himself for others."

Flowing Spring gives a thoughtful nod. "Há," is all she says. Later, she looks up from her sewin', her mouth pressed in a thin line. "Make decision."

"What decision?"

"Will accept Jesus who chooses Sungila Sá." She cocks her head to the right. "But prefer Samson."

I can't help but laugh out loud.

Chief remains away for many moons. Mato Waäylo says he would be concerned if not for the deep snows, which he believes keeps the chief stuck at the fort. But he also says we must make decisions soon, without Chief if necessary. We are already on one-third rations, and the food supplies are gettin' dangerously low. "If snows stop and sun melts so less deep snow on ground, we must go find more food."

"Go where?"

"Go north, cross river and beyond wasicu Bozeman Trail to tribe of Hanhepi Wi Nagi and Wiwílamni Kalúsya. Family will welcome family."

"We're already starvin'. To take down the camp and travel so far—I don't know if we can make it. And the horses...they're terribly weak."

"Must try or all die."

"How will Chief and the elders find us when they return?"

"Chief will know to wait for scout to come for him."

So, we wait for the snows to dwindle and the temperatures to rise enough to start a melt. Tensions run high as our hunger worsens and weakness sets in. Poor little Súnkawakan Sápä lies on his pelts most of the time now, moanin', starin' at nothing, or sleepin'. I try to give him more of my food, but it's like he has a hard time eatin' at all and barely keeps anything down. Flowing Spring's milk is dried up, so he doesn't even have that to sustain him.

Like Súnkawakan Sápä, Flowing Spring spends more and more of her time sleepin', yet her eyes remain sunken deep in black-smudged hollows like someone who hasn't slept in weeks. During her sleep, she cries out and strikes the air, and when I wake her, she screams something about wolves comin' for her in the night. I can't convince her she's safe, no matter what I say or do.

Prayer has become my sustenance. I repeat Jesus' words of love over my precious son several times a day as I ask Jesus to please hold Súnkawakan Sápä in His arms and keep him safe. I pray for His soothin' peace to fill my Flowing Spring, even if she has no food to fill her belly. I recall Grasshopper's description of the verses in the Book of Matthew. "Jesus feeds the birds of the air who do not plant like Lakota; He will feed Lakota, too." And I believe.

The mornin' dawns clear and bright, and soon water begins to drip from the stakes of our tipi. Mato Waäylo stands at my entrance, his gaunt face chiseled with lines that weren't there before the winter. "Sungila Sá correct when say the people too weak to break down camp. Worse now. I will go to the family of Hanhepi Wi Nagi and beg for help."

"Mato Waäylo, you are chief. You can't leave the people. Let me go, as husband of Wiwílamni Kalúsya, and plead for help."

"They see wasicu and kill with arrow before you enter camp."

"They know of Sungila Sá. I will approach and call out my name. They will welcome me. I will bring food and help."

"Then make haste, Sungila Sá. Go now before snows return. If you are caught in snows and don't return to us soon, know that you will find us dead when you come."

"I know." I gaze at my precious family, love poundin' in my heart like a hammer on an anvil. I loathe leavin' them, but I know it is the best choice—perhaps the only choice—we have left.

After Mato Waäylo exits, I sit beside Flowing Spring. "My love, I must leave you. I must go to your family for help."

She clutches my hand, her fingers claw-like, her grip as weak as a bairn. "Híya."

"I must, or you and the bairn will die. I will come back. I promise."

Flowing Spring turns her tear-streaked face away with a guttural groan.

I lean close and breathe, "I love you."

I can barely hear her whispered reply. "Chanté él yúzä."

"And I hold you in my heart, my love."

I lift Súnkawakan Sápä and place him in her arms, set out all our food and ample water within arm's reach by her pallet, then collect my rifle, knife, and hatchet, blankets for warmth, my cup, a small clay jar of black warpaint, my Bible, and a small ration of meat, and with a final, "I'll come back," I leave my family and trudge through the meltin' snow for Blossom.

Blossom is terribly thin, but her eyes are undimmed. I smear her head and neck with warpaint and pray. "My Father in heaven, strengthen this animal for your purposes. Help her to not waver or stumble. Deliver us to my family across the river and protect us both on the journey." As I spread the rest of the warpaint on my face and neck, I continue my prayer. "And Father, give my body endurance and my heart the strength I need to persevere. Carry me if I falter. Please, dear Lord, bring me back to my family in time. Amen."

I wrap my bony frame in a large buffalo wrap and two blankets, slide a rope halter over Blossom's head, pull myself on her back, and begin the journey to cross the river and the Bozeman Trail, to the tribe of my beloved.

Under different circumstances, the journey to my wife's tribe takes a full day on horseback, but in slushy snow with a weakened horse and rider, I'm afeared it may take longer. I can't afford for it to take longer, though, so I whisper in Blossom's ear. "We gotta go fast, girl. You gotta get me there today. Run, girl. Fly. For Spirit of Black Horse, fly like the wind."

Blossom plows through the snow, her neck strainin' under my clutched hands. I can feel her muscles pulsin' beneath my legs. Up the rise and down again, and across the open plain to the edge of the river she carries me, her feet swift and sure. I murmur a quick thank you to God as I jump off to inspect the ice on the river.

Sure enough, the ice appears intact, but I'm not sure it'll hold both her weight and mine. The only way to know is to try it, so I climb back on Blossom, and we begin the slippery trek across the ice. We near the middle of the river without incident, but on the next step I hear what sounds like an elder poundin' a drum, then a creak. I look down and see spider webs of cracks beneath Blossom's hooves. She steps forward—another boom, a thump, a loud crack, and ice heaves up before us, and with a loud cry, Blossom slides into rushin' water up to her chest.

I try to keep my feet out of the water, but it's too late. The water rushes into my moccasins and wets the bottom of my leather leggin's. I urge Blossom forward, but she's too deep in the water to get her legs up on the ice, and even if she could, she'd slide right back off. There's nothin' for it, I have to get off and see if I can pull her forward, but I gotta be careful lest I fall in and get swept downriver under the ice.

I slide down Blossom's side and push off, tryin' to land as gently as I can beyond the broken ice. Blossom's panicked eyes let me know I have very little time to get her out before she freezes to death. I grab her lead and try pullin' her forward, but the ice won't break against her chest, so I lie on my belly and use my hatchet to break up the ice before her.

Inch by torturous inch, we push forward. My hands feel frozen to the handle, and I'm shiverin' so hard I can barely swing the hatchet. Blossom screeches in terror, shakin' her head, pullin' against me, but I keep pushin' us forward.

Just when I think my body is gonna quit on me, we reach the shallows. Blossom scrambles up onto the ice and dashes the rest of the way to the shore. I slip and slide my way to her and leap onto her back. Normally, I'd make a fire to warm and dry us, but I can't afford to take the extra time, so we're off again, poundin' as hard as we can through drifts, over hillocks, and across valleys. My shoes are caked in ice and I can't feel my feet or my fingers, but still I press on. If I'm gonna find the other tribe, I have to do so before it gets too dark to see.

The sun disappears behind the distant mountains, and the sky turns to gold and rose as my heart races faster than Blossom's gallop, still without any sign of the tribe. Then, in the distance, I see an abandoned outpost, so I know I've reached the ol' Bozeman trail—which means I'm not gonna make it to the tribe before nightfall. Despondent but resigned, I push Blossom toward the outpost. One section of the roof of the only buildin' still standin' is collapsed under the weight of the snow. Still, they might have firewood, and some cover is better than none, so I push against the door, which opens a crack before buttin' up against piled snow. I'm able to squeeze through the crack—one advantage of starvin', I guess—and climb across the snow drift, to find a second room with the roof mostly intact and a firepit with some stacked logs left behind by the soldiers. Breathin' another prayer of thanks, I build a fire and get it goin', then I use a piece of wood to shovel the snow away from the door, so I can bring Blossom inside. She snorts her appreciation.

The room fills with smoke, but I don't care. Soon, my fingers feel like someone is pokin' 'em with a thousand needles. I peel off my now-wet moccasins and lay them next to the fire, then I spread my blankets and buffalo coat out to dry. Blossom stamps her hooves, likely feelin' some version of the same needle pricks I do. I melt some snow in my cup and drink, then melt some more and offer it to Blossom who slurps it up gratefully.

Once all my things are dry, I pull out my piece of meat and sit on a blanket to eat. I munch slowly, savorin' each morsel. I feel sorta bad since Blossom doesn't have anything, but I hope in the mornin' the snows will melt enough for her to dig up some tufts of grass.

Sleep falls on me before I know it. My next awareness is Blossom nuzzlin' me and the weak streams of light snakin' in through the gaps between the logs and under the crooked door. The sun is bright again, so at least no snow for now. Blossom and I share water again, then I put on my moccasins and buffalo coat, wrap myself in blankets, and lead Blossom outside for our final leg of the journey.

My prayer this mornin' is brief. I gage north from the sun's position and head out, followin' the trail at first. Ever' so often, Blossom scrapes the ground along the edge of the trail until she finds some weeds and dead grass to eat, but other than that, we push ahead as fast as she's able. When the trail turns northwest, we venture due north off the trail, and the goin' gets tougher through the thick snowdrift.

A thin column of smoke over a ridge in the distance catches my eye against the backdrop of blue mountains, so Blossom and I slow and climb the ridge with caution. Down in the valley, praise be, sprawl the tipis of Flowing Spring's family. I hop down from Blossom and lead her carefully down the steep ridge face. All I can do is hope I won't be seen 'til I'm close enough to call out my name.

Rememberin' my first encounter with Mato Waäylo, I do my best to keep behind rocks or clumps of brush until I can hear the noise of the camp, then I step out into the open, holdin' Blossom's lead, and walk boldly toward the camp.

"Greetings! I am Sungila Sá, husband to Wiwílamni Kalúsya, daughter of your great chief." Silence falls over the camp like a curtain, as every eye turns to stare at the scrawny wasicu, painted like a brave and pullin' his emaciated horse behind him. "My name is Sungila Sá. My wife is Wiwílamni Kalúsya, whom you know. I have come to speak to your great chief. May I enter?"

A brave, his eyes narrowed and cut sideways, approaches me like he's stalkin' a deer. "You say you are Sungila Sá."

"I am."

"You lie. Sungila Sá strong warrior, shoulders blot out sun, fiercest warrior of all."

"I promise I am he. Brother to Mato Waäylo. Now son of your chief. I have come for aid."

"Why Sungila Sá beg for aid?" His suspicion turns into a sneer.

I muster the memory of the demon who once raged within me and scream like the red fox who is my namesake. The echoes of my scream ring against the distant rocks. "You may sneer at me if you will, but I will speak with your chief. Now." The brave scampers away as the onlookers lower their eyes and huddle over their fire.

It isn't long before the brave returns with an impressive man, whose stiff, straight back reminds me of ol' Ramrod, and whose stern countenance speaks of unquestioned authority. He appears older than

Mato Waäylo but not as old as our chief, and I see the glimmer of Soul of Moon's eyes in his.

"Father of Hanhepi Wi Nagi and Wiwílamni Kalúsya, I am Sungila Sá, husband to your second daughter." The chief stands before me, his legs spread wide and his arms folded across his chest, but he says nothing. "Mato Waäylo sends greetings. I have come to ask for your hospitality and generosity. The wasicu slaughtered the remainder of our buffalo herd before the season's change, and with the winter harsh with deep snow, we do not have enough food to feed our tribe. Your daughters and your grandson are starving. I have come to request your aid."

"What do you request, Sungila Sá?" His voice is deep and resonant. I can't tell if he believes who I say I am or not.

"Mato Waäylo and I request, on behalf of our chief, that you allow us to join our tribe with yours, and that as a gesture of your generosity and hospitality, you send many braves with food to help us break down our camp and move it to join with yours here."

"This joining—it is to be for the winter only?"

"No, Great Chief. We request to join with your camp and become one family. Our need for food is desperate. Your buffalo are plentiful. We will work hard, hunt by your side, and provide protection should wasicu attack, as members of the tribe."

"Who shall be your chief?"

Mato Waäylo and I didn't discuss this question. Honestly, I hadn't even considered it. But the way I see it, we have no choice. "You, Great Chief, will become our chief."

"Your chief allows this?" He shakes his mighty head. "What proof do I have of your story? How do I know this is not a trick to divide our braves and lure us in for slaughter?"

"Great Chief, I love your daughter with all my heart and soul. Do you know she and I have a son? His name is Súnkawakan Sápä. He lives twenty-two moons, but he will not live twenty-three unless you help us." I figure it can't hurt, so I add, "He has your fierceness and his mother's eyes. Your grandchild. He lies dying in his mother's arms as we waste time with talk."

The chief bristles and raises to an even greater height over me, but I've learned Lakota ways now, so I curl my lip and raise my eyes to meet his with a stare that I hope bellows I will not back down. "Do you follow the ways of Lakota, or do you not follow our ways?" My brain is skitterin' through possible plans for stealin' what we need if my ploy doesn't work.

We remain this way, our eyes locked, until he breaks the standoff and calls for several of his braves. "Prepare to leave for camp of Hanhepi Wi Nagi." He marches to the women, currently workin' over the fires, and I follow behind. "Wrap three days food for camp in sacks for carrying on horseback." He turns to me. "I will come with my braves. If you lie, know that your camp will be destroyed."

"I do not lie."

"Very well. Come. Eat."

"I do not wish to take the time to eat, Great Chief. I desire to return to my beloved and my son with food for them to eat before I do."

For the first time, the chief's face softens. "Honorable." He gestures to the scurryin' women. "We go! Make haste."

The braves gallop up on horseback—armed with bow, arrow, spear, and rifle—bringin' extra horses with them, and the women sling roped sacks of food over the riderless horses' backs. The chief mounts one of the horses, so I run back to Blossom and pull myself up on her back. Quick as greased lightnin', we're off.

The race back to our camp is a blur. I'm numb from head to toe, holdin' onto to Blossom by sheer force of will. We struggle to keep up with the braves—sometimes, they are well beyond my sight—but I know the way, and I trust Blossom to get me home.

The chief rides on into the night, for which I'm grateful beyond words. However, crossin' the river in darkness proves more difficult than they expect. Fortunately, another day of sun has weakened the ice coatin' more, so they take the horses in a line across, and when one breaks through, the next horse moves past them to break the ice, and so on, until they make a chain of horses wadin' across the river.

We barrel over the final rise and ride into a muddy, desolate encampment to find its fires cold. From what we can see, the camp appears deserted, inhabited only by ghosts. I point the chief toward Mato Waäylo's lodge and dash straight to our tipi. To my great relief, Flowing Spring raises her head as I enter. "My love." Her words sound like a ragged croak.

"Súnkawakan Sápä?" I hear the desperate plea in my voice. In my mind, "Please, God," repeats like the babblin' of a lunatic.

"He lives."

I collapse beside her pallet and throw myself across them both. "Oh, thank God. Thank you, God. Thank you." I weep over them.

"Does father come?"

"He's here. He brings food and braves to carry you back to his camp."

She strokes my matted hair. "Sungila Sá saves tribe."

"Your father saves us all."

The next three days, life returns slowly to the camp. Everyone is weakened, but the food provided by Flowing Spring's father rejuvenates us, and soon we're working together with his braves to break down the camp. Snow doesn't return, and the temperatures rise enough to thaw the ice on the river, so when we're ready to leave, one of the braves finds a narrow point shallow enough for us to cross with our pallets, and we're able to ford the river without incident.

Unlike my initial arrival, when the chief leads our tribe into camp, we're greeted with cheers and warm welcomes. The women take us all under their wing, feedin' us more than our share and offerin' us their lodges until ours are rebuilt.

That night, they plan a huge celebration. They dance and drum and sing until late into the night. For the first time in so long, I can breathe.

I sleep until late mornin' like a bairn, with Flowing Spring wrapped in my arms, and Súnkawakan Sápä lyin' on my chest. I swear I'll never let them out of my sight again.

Winter passes into spring, and spring into summer. The two tribes flow together as easily as herbs and honey in hot water. Flowing Spring's father is thrilled to have his daughters back under his care. I've come to like the man, even though he is more unyieldin' and severe than our chief, but I know his sternness hides a soft heart. I get to see it every time he's around Súnkawakan Sápä.

Our chief joins us in the early spring, but his time at the white man fort has aged him. As he speaks of the long, difficult peace negotiations and the promise from the wasicu of all the lands north of the Powder River and the ol' Bozeman Trail for the Lakota people, his eyes are hooded, his face haunted—in fact, his whole manner reveals he has no trust in wasicu promises. He speaks bitterly of livin' among wasicu through the harsh winter, describin' their stink and their filth, their complete lack of honor or respect, and their disregard for the earth and for all life, even of their own kind. His eye is always on me as he tells his tales.

He relinquishes bein' our chief with gratitude, sayin' he's too old to carry such weight on his stooped shoulders. The long winter with wasicu has taken its toll. The great chief spends long hours alone in his lodge. Some nights I hear him chantin' prayers and songs of mournin'. Most days he spends in silence, refusin' to eat. It isn't long before he takes ill. The healer works over him for several days, but the chief dies before summer begins.

The women of our tribe clean, prepare, clothe, and wrap his body as the men build a scaffold and decorate it befittin' the greatness of the man. I'm pleased when our new tribe joins us beneath the platform to honor his life as if he were their own chief. His hair is given to Mato Waäylo as his eldest son.

Soon after, we move the camp with the buffalo herd as it migrates farther north for the summer months. Food is plentiful. The treaty is holdin', so we have no more fear of the soldiers down at the fort. Our lives take on an uncustomary ease. The people have taken to callin' it blokétu wóablakela—the summer of peace. My life has made me wary of such times, and I remember the great chief's anguished eyes as he spoke of wasicu, but even I find myself relaxin' and enjoyin' the time I get to spend with my son.

Súnkawakan Sápä has passed two years now and has his own little personality—as strong-willed as his mother, but with a sweet tenderness that melts my heart. He loves Blossom and helps me care for her each day, never tirin' of the brushin' or cleanin' she needs. And I swear he'd ride her all day long if I let him.

We also read Bible stories by the fire every night, continuin' my family tradition. Sometimes he acts out a part of the story, like Gideon's men lappin' up water or Joshua marchin' around Jericho. His antics send Flowing Spring into spasms of laughter.

In mid-summer, she sits the two of us down with a flourish and announces she has been given a great gift from Wakan Tanka. "Guess gift."

"Horse for me?" I burst out laughin' at Súnkawakan Sápä's innocence.

"No, no horse for Súnkawakan Sápä, not yet. One day. Guess once more."

My chest puffs up. "Are you with child?"

"I am with child—a second child. Súnkawakan Sápä, you will have a brother or sister."

His eyes widen. "All mine?"

Flowing Spring chuckles. "The gift is for us all."

I stand and enfold her in my arms. "My joy overflows beyond all measure." I lean and whisper in her ear. "Is it a boy or a girl?" Secretly, I hope for a girl this time. One of each would be perfect.

She cocks her head. "I am unsure."

"Really? You were so certain last time Súnkawakan Sápä was a boy."

"Yes...but this time...?"

"Is something wrong?" I knew things were too good to last.

She scrunches her face. "No, of course not. Why would you say this?"

"I'm sorry. I can't believe how blessed we are."

"Wakan Tanka is good, like Sungila Sá read in great book."

"He is indeed."

"No worry, Sungila Sá. All is well."

Late in the summer, we hear rumors of wasicu travelers crossin' Lakota lands to the west of us. A Cheyenne delegation comes to our chief the next moon and reports the wasicu have discovered gold in the lands to the north and are crossin' native lands to mine the gold.

"Red Cloud say treaty forbids crossing Lakota land or settling here." The chief's anger is palpable and intimidatin'. "Must seek permission from Lakota."

The Cheyenne brave shrugs. "Still, they come."

Mato Waäylo lifts his hand to speak. "Our chief once described wasicu as locusts coming to consume our land. They devour and destroy everything they touch and always hunger for more."

The Cheyenne brave nods. "Red Cloud decides to no longer fight with soldiers. Say now we must fight with government for our land."

The chief balks. "How can Lakota fight government? Cannot see to strike with arrow or spear."

I heave a sigh. "I try once to fight against government when they take my land."

"Did you reclaim land?"

"No, they still have my land. I do not know how to win against government."

The chief stands and paces the lodge. "Red Cloud has become canl waka. We will not fight against phantom government. We will fight against soldiers and the locusts who come to consume our land. War parties will ride across our land. We will kill all wasicu we see where they stand."

A warnin' sings in my chest, the ol' chief's haunted stare ever before my eyes. "You may stir soldiers sleeping at fort to rise from their nest."

"Let soldiers rise. We fight soldiers. On our land. Our way."

"More will always come."

"We kill all who come."

"Cheyenne stand with Lakota. Arapahoe also fight with Cheyenne and Lakota." The chief and the two men clasp arms and beat their chests.

I don't know how to explain to the chief the idea of a war of attrition. The South faced these same problems and believed the same lies, that the righteousness of their cause would produce certain victory. In the end, the North had more men and more resources, so they won, and righteousness had nothin' to do with it.

Blokétu wóablakela is over.

CHAPTER TWENTY-FIVE

The chief organizes small raidin' parties and sends them out to crisscross our lands in search of wasicu travelers. I can't stomach the slaughter of innocent men, women, and children, so I ask to serve as a scout to watch the movements of the soldiers at the fort.

I know it's a big risk. If I'm seen, the soldiers will hunt me down, and if I'm captured, I'll be executed as a traitor. But it seems a better option to me than killin' folk who don't even know they're violatin' sacred ground. The chief refuses at first, sayin' Sungila Sá's infamy will frighten the interlopers away, but he relents when I argue the soldiers are a greater danger to the people than the miners, and I would serve the people better by makin' the soldiers think twice before they attack such a warrior. Of course, I have no intention of bein' seen by the soldiers, but at least I can keep an eye on them and warn the chief should they come our way.

Bein' a scout is lonely work. I hate leavin' Flowing Spring and Súnkawakan Sápä for days at a time, but at least I ain't killin' innocents. Before long, I sense a change at the fort—more activity, more soldiers arrivin'. The chief's raids have gotten their attention.

The miners are travelin' in groups now, and the cavalry starts sendin' out a detail to guard every wagon train filled with miners and settlers. When I return to camp and make my report to the chief, instead of backin' down, he sends out larger raidin' parties. War's comin' just as sure as the sun's gonna rise, and I imagine the ol' chief recognized war was inevitable, too. But there's nothin' I can do to stop it any more than he could.

It isn't long before a whole cavalry platoon rides out. I don't know what they're up to, so I follow them from a distance, careful to leave no sign of my presence. To my surprise, they aren't headin' for our camp, but instead turn west. What I don't know until it's too late is the buffalo herd has moved southwest since I was last in camp, and the soldiers are goin' for the herd, like before. When I see the herd trapped in a wide valley with a narrow passage at one end, revulsion and panic clog my throat, makin' it hard for me to breathe. I swallow back my retch. These canl waka soldiers are willin' to destroy these noble, majestic animals to drive off the people—the people who first lived on this land, who cherish their land and care for its creature inhabitants, who are one with the earth and sky and who honor its Creator, even if they don't know His true name. The canl waka do so without honor, refusin' to face the people or risk their own lives. Instead, they use the buffalo to do their dirty work for 'em, and they don't even give the buffalo a fightin' chance, trapped as they are with only one way out of the valley.

The soldiers divide into two units. The first spreads out to form a wide semicircle 'round the grazin' herd. The second unit creeps to the passage at the end of the valley and takes positions on the high ground. I see their plan right away—drive the herd toward the passage, then slaughter them as they try to run through the narrows, like shootin' fish in a barrel. I can't let that happen.

The only hope I have is to drive the herd away from the passage, toward the circlin' soldiers. That means comin' out in the open and revealin' my presence—more than that, it means ridin' straight toward the soldiers myself. I have to sneak past the soldiers entrenched on the high ground, then hope they don't shoot me in the back before I can rile the buffalo into a stampede.

I'm used to sneakin' places, seein' as how I used to be a sharpshooter, but how can I sneak Blossom through right under their noses? I decide to rain fire down on 'em from above and see how many I can kill before they target me, then hope if they start shootin' up at me, it'll spook the buffalo away from the noise. If I'm still alive, I can race Blossom down the hill, shootin' above their heads, and chase 'em hard and fast through the soldiers' positions. They'll get some of 'em, sure, and they'll likely get me, too, but it's the only plan I can think of with a whisker's chance to work.

So, I tie Blossom in a clump of bushes behind the rise and steal over the hill. These soldiers are clumsy and lazy. They're not even tryin' to hide themselves on the hillside, I guess 'cause they ain't expectin' anything but buffalo, and they think the buffalo are stupid. But seein' as how I can get real close to 'em without them noticin', I decide to pull out my knife and take down as many as I can that way.

344

The first two go down without a sound, and they're far enough from the others so as to appear they are still in position. My Ma's voice chimes a distant bell, "Thou shalt not kill," but I squelch the sound with the argument that God placed man in dominion over the animals, to care for them, and these men intend to destroy God's creatures for no good purpose—at least, not the purpose God intended for them.

The third man cries out when I attack, so I duck behind the brush and scamper away from him. I can hear the other soldiers callin' to one another, tryin' to find out what's goin' on. I run low to the ground until I reach a high point on the hill behind a thick clump of bushes, where I set up my nest. I scan the remainin' soldiers and reckon I can shoot two or maybe three of 'em before they start firin' on my position. Before I shoot, I scout out my next position, one that gives me a line of sight to the opposite hillside, then I take aim at the farthest soldier and fire.

By the time the shot echoes from the facing hill, I'm reloaded and fire on the next man. Someone from down the hill shoots wildly in my direction, but not seein' where I'm set up, he doesn't come close. I risk one more shot, at the soldier who fired at me, then I bolt to my next position. Soldiers below me on the hill are firin' at my last position while I take aim and pick off two of the soldiers on the facin' ridge. Now, fire is comin' at me from both sides of the pass. Keepin' low, darting from bush to bush, I run up the hill in Blossom's direction, and stoppin' near the top, I risk one more round of fire, once toward a soldier runnin' up the hill from below me and once toward a soldier standin' in the open across the way. Then, I dash for Blossom.

As I mount her, I notice the buffalo are already stirrin' below. The ping of the shots and the shouts of the soldiers have them movin' back away from the narrow pass—good, all the better.

"Here we go, girl." I wrap an arm around her neck, then lie low on her back, my face behind her large head, and shout, "Yaw!" She takes off over the rise and races down the side of the hill into the valley. Shots ring out around us. I hear the thuds as they bury in the ground.

I don't waste time tryin' to turn and fire on the soldiers, an impossible shot from the back of a gallopin' horse, but instead keep low and murmur a quick prayer. "Protect her, Lord. Don't let her fall."

As we enter the valley, I sit up on Blossom and start shoutin' while I fire my rifle in the air above the buffalo's heads.

"Get'on outta here! Run! Hee-yaw!" I holler with the scream that earned me my Lakota name and fire again. As I hoped, the buffalo turn and take off runnin', straight toward the soldiers to their rear.

Shots rain down on me from all sides, now. I keep screamin', and I fire each time I manage to reload, but the soldiers firin' at me from all sides is what has the herd in a frantic state. I hear a familiar voice cry out, "Cease Fire! Hold yer fire!" Martin. And he's smart enough to figure that shootin' at me is causin' the buffalo to keep runnin'.

I'm thankful when the soldiers stop shootin' at us, but the buffalo then try to swing left, and I can't let them turn back toward the pass. So, I fire once and plow Blossom right in amongst them, to make my voice and shots all the louder. Somehow—I truly believe God is helpin' me, 'cause it seems impossible what's happenin'—the buffalo turn back and stampede down through the valley, runnin' straight through the soldiers.

Some of the soldiers who aren't on their horses are trampled, and the stampede causes the horses of those mounted to buck and run away. It's a miracle, plain and simple.

Blossom runs with the herd straight through the lines of soldiers, and there before us, astride Murphy, sits Martin. His face is a red mask of rage. I can see the sweat standin' on his brow as he raises his rifle and aims it straight at my chest.

I don't flinch. I don't stop or turn Blossom away. I plow straight for him, darin' him to shoot. When I get within shoutin' distance, I see the pain in his eyes. It's a familiar pain, the kind that comes from bein' torn between duty and love, responsibility and righteousness.

I want to stop and embrace him, to tell him I understand, I've felt what he's feelin', and that I'm sorry we ended up on opposite sides of things, but instead I stare into his sorrowful eyes as I ride past him and say, "Thank you, friend." His head drops to his chest as he lowers his weapon.

Blossom and I urge the herd to keep goin', but no longer sensin' the danger that had 'em so spooked, they seem to be slowin' down. I hear Martin shoutin' orders behind me for the men to ride forward and corral the herd for the slaughter, so I know I have to keep 'em runnin', and even then, if the soldiers can catch up to us, their numbers will mean most of the herd will be lost. So, I circle Blossom through the herd and come back around behind them, shoutin' and firin' again.

Hooves poundin' the dirt some distance behind me sends my stomach into my throat. I don't know if the herd has enough of a head start to outdistance the soldiers' horses. Desperate to make them run like they're runnin' for their lives, I push Blossom into the middle of the herd and use my rifle to whack some of the bigger males on the backside, then fire again toward the lead runners. I know I'm sacrificin' some of the slower animals, perhaps the young and old ones, as they straggle behind the main herd, but better a few die than the whole herd is lost.

Still, the solders keep comin', and they're gainin' on us. Behind me, some of the herd splits off and runs left toward the hills. There's nothin' for it, I have to let 'em go. The only blessin' in it is the soldiers chasin' us veer off to kill those buffalo, leavin' them farther behind the main body of the herd. But it means the loss of as much as a third of the animals.

I decide splittin' the herd offers the best chance that some of the herd will be spared, so I plow Blossom forward through the middle of the buffalo, yellin' and firin' my rifle once—twice—until part of the herd veers off toward the right across the valley. I believe the soldiers will most likely follow where I'm a-goin', since I'm makin' such a racket, so, gagin' the largest group went right, I follow the rest of the herd straight across the plains and continue shoutin' and shootin' behind 'em to keep 'em runnin'.

Ever' so often, I risk a glance to the right to watch the main body of the herd, hopin' and prayin' they'll make it over the hills out of sight before the soldiers finish their slaughter and come after us again.

Sure enough, I hear shouts in the distance and know my reprieve is over. I whoop and holler to attract the soldiers' attention while I keep an eye on the herd chargin' up the hill to my right. If the soldiers catch sight of 'em before they make it over the hill, they'll follow the larger group, but if not, I hope they'll believe the buffalo I'm spurnin' on are the whole herd. Plus, I figure they'll covet the additional prize of the infamous Sungila Sá, the white deserter turned native.

The lead buffalo reach the top of the first rise and disappear over it. It's as if the angels lifted twenty sheaves of wheat off my shoulders. There's hope. I turn and fire back toward the distant cloud of dust, so the soldiers hear my shot. Blossom pounds next to the herd, steerin' 'em away from the main body slowly vanishin' behind the hill.

"Please, God, please hide 'em from sight. Please lead 'em to safety."

Another quick glance back tells me the soldiers are still followin' me—and they're gainin' ground. I've gotta get the buffalo runnin' faster, so I turn Blossom in an arc around behind the herd and, usin' the last of my ammunition, I fire over their heads one last time. In a final act of desperation, I turn Blossom and gallop headlong toward the soldiers. If they want me badly enough, maybe they'll let the buffalo go.

At first, the soldiers are obscured by the dust, but as Blossom and I close the distance between us, I can make out flashes of the dark blue of their uniforms and the various shades of brown and tan of their horses through the cloud. It isn't long before I hear some cracks of rifle fire, but I keep on a-comin'. At the last possible moment, I turn Blossom toward the hills to my right, where I fear I'm gonna find the first group of buffalo, butchered. I bellow my demon yell to help motivate the soldiers to follow me and wave my hands over my head in challenge. But they don't turn to follow me. In a panic, I pull Blossom's head toward 'em again. If I have to ride right in amongst 'em, so be it.

I lean low over Blossom's back as she gobbles up the ground beneath her hooves. Shots ring out again. We swerve left, then back right again, dodgin' the unseen bullets more by faith and instinct than anything. I can hear the soldiers' yells—they want me dead.

My brazen challenge tests their sense of superiority and questions their bravery, and their great offense fuels their anger toward me, so at long last, the column turns and runs straight toward me. The only thing left for me is to close my eyes and accept my fate.

A distant, ululating cry echoes behind me. I risk liftin' my head to give a quick glance back, and there, ridin' over the top of the hills behind me, are several Lakota braves, one of the raidin' parties sent out by our chief. I urge Blossom into a wide turn, and soon we are racin' toward our friends, the soldiers on our heels. The whistle of arrows tears the air above my head. I can hear the occasional thud of one hittin' home. When I near the Lakota, I recognize Hawk Feather, the leader of the party—and Grasshopper is one of the riders. The braves are in a frenzy. Apparently, they've seen the slaughtered buffalo beyond the ridge and are out for vengeance.

Blossom and I fall in beside the warriors and ride straight toward the cavalry. I have no ammunition or arrows, so I'm pretty useless, but I'll make do with the butt of my rifle and my knife.

The poundin' rhythm of hoofbeats mirrors the thump of my heartbeat in my ears. A familiar feelin' consumes me, like when I used to dive underwater in the lake, and water filled my ears and made everything sound hollow, and I would float there, suspended in time in my own little world.

I see the approachin' soldiers through a thick fog. Their yells sound like dull, flat hums. Glints of sunlight shimmer off their weapons like little stars in the night sky. Muzzle fire explodes in a dizzyin', slow motion kaleidoscope of orange and yellow and blue-white. Even the war whoops of the braves are dim echoes. None of it seems real.

We collide with the soldiers with a thud, and everything is utter chaos. My eyes water from the sting of churnin' dirt, so I swing blindly to the right with my rifle and to the left with my knife, hittin' something occasionally, but generally strikin' the air. Blossom is more effective. She butts her shoulder into horse's chests and soldier's legs, causin' more than one to topple to the ground. I'm vaguely aware of Grasshopper next to me, his arrows strikin' true.

As if a spectre risin' from the mist, Martin materializes before me, and all movement around us seems to suspend. I can't—I won't—strike him, not even to pull him off of Murphy or to protect my tribe. His stare rips through me cleaner than the piercin' of a sword. "Tell me why."

"I went lookin' for you and they captured me. I was their slave, but they welcomed me as part of them. They...all they want is to remain on their land and be left alone—just like me."

"Ye've taken their side?"

349

"I believe they're in the right."

"They've killed yer own people."

"You gave' em no choice."

The moment passes, and the fury of the battle ragin' all 'round invades us. Nothing else is spoken between us. Martin turns to swing his sword toward the head of a brave—it's Grasshopper!

"Stop!" My scream reverberates in the air as I push Blossom past Murphy to position me between my two dearest friends. Martin's sword whooshes past my shoulder, and I s'pose he diverted his strike at the last minute, or he'd have taken my head clean off. Grasshopper bellows his rage and lifts his hatchet to throw at Martin. I raise my arms in the air and shriek, "No!" But I'm too late.

The hatchet tumbles through the air and lands square in Martin's chest. A spurt of his blood lands with a sickenin' splat on my thigh.

I watch Martin's face transform into my Pa's when he was shot—his eyes vacant, round holes, his mouth an "O" of shock. And like Pa, he slides slowly from Murphy onto the ground and lands face-down in the dust.

This can't be happenin'. Not again. I leap from Blossom and turn Martin onto his back, but his glazed eyes show no recognition, and his scored chest doesn't move.

"Oh, Martin...oh God, please...I didn't mean for this. . .I didn't want any of this to happen." I hold my friend against my chest. "It shoulda been me. It shoulda been me." I look to the sky above me, glarin' white in the noon sun. "Why didn't You take me instead?" My tears burn like scaldin' salt water on an open wound.

The fight has moved past where Martin lies. The Lakota continue to press the cavalry back until someone calls out for the retreat. I think they lost heart when they saw their officer fall. The Lakota celebrate their great victory—all except Grasshopper, who rides up, jumps from his horse, and squats at my side.

"Friend of Sungila Sá?"

"He was. A good friend."

Grasshopper claps me on the back. "Good death for wasicu of courage." He leans close to Martin and cuts a lock of his hair with his knife. "Take, Sungila Sá. Keep. Wakan of friend stays with you."

"I would like to bury him with honor."

"How bury wasicu with honor?"

"We return him to the earth and mark his grave with the symbol of Jesus, the crossed logs."

Grasshopper nods. "Put friend on back of horse. Carry to camp for bury with crossed logs."

I can hardly breathe out a "thank you." Grasshopper pulls his hatchet from Martin's chest, and I lift Martin carefully across Murphy's back, wrap Murphy's lead around my wrist, and mount Blossom. Two of our braves have also died, so once the victory celebration is over, the men gather the horses of the fallen, wrap them in blankets, and strap them to their horses. We make a sorrowful processional back to our camp.

I know better than to carry a cavalry officer into the Lakota camp, so while the braves go on to inform the chief and loved ones of the two fallen warriors, I stop outside camp and begin the slow, difficult process of diggin' Martin's grave. Grasshopper soon joins me, so we should be able to make it deep enough to prevent animals from diggin' him up. It takes us well into the night, so as darkness shrouds us, Grasshopper takes a few minutes to build us a fire.

"Could you find two stout branches to use to make the cross?"

"Há, Sungila Sá, will find best branch for most special Jesus crossed log."

"Thank you." I appreciate his kindness, especially since he must feel mixed emotions, bein' he's the one who killed my friend and his sworn enemy—still, he doesn't show me anything but grace.

I wrap Martin in his saddle blanket and place him gently in the grave, then cover him with dirt. When Grasshopper returns with two logs, I take the strip of hide tyin' back my hair to bind the two logs together as a cross and anchor the cross in the ground at his head. I glance at Grasshopper, then look back at the cross. "Would you stay with me as I speak some words?"

"Há."

"Martin Murphy is a good friend, a brave soldier, and a great man." My voice quits on me, catchin' in my throat. I shake the tears away and with a hoarse rasp, I begin again. "Sown in corruption; it is raised in incorruption...Sown in dishonour; it is raised in glory...Sown in weakness; it is raised in power...Sown a natural body; it is raised a spiritual body. As we have borne the image of the earthly, we shall also bear the image of the heavenly. O death, where is thy sting? O grave, where is thy victory. Thanks be to God which giveth us victory through our Lord Jesus Christ. Amen. Martin, I..."

Again, I can't speak past my tears. Silence blankets the hallowed field which is his final restin' place, as if the angels themselves mourn. "I will miss you, brother." My whisper can't be heard beyond my own ears. "I will see you again."

I kneel beside the grave and place two hands on the packed earth. Grasshopper wanders away, another kindness, so that I may weep openly without shame. Every death I've suffered or caused, all the losses, and all of the agonies pile on top of me as I lie on Martin's grave. I rail against the demon death until my rage is spent, and I'm left with only empty, hollow, searin' pain and a heaviness weighin' down my soul. I lie in the dirt with my friend until mornin'.

Grasshopper returns for me the next day. "Chief calls meetin' of braves and elders to make plan. Many tatanka die. Must plan for winter."

I wish I had the time to bathe and change out of my clothing, but Grasshopper insists the chief demands we come right away. When we enter the chief's lodge, everyone else is already gathered.

Mato Waäylo paces beyond the seated group. "You do not understand. We have gone through this before. With most of tatanka dead, we cannot survive the winter. We must leave."

Most of the herd? What does he mean? I whisper my question to Grasshopper, who informs me the fleeing soldiers, on their way back to the fort, came upon the larger half of the herd I sent runnin' over the hill into hidin' and slaughtered them in revenge for the death of their commander. "Only small portion of herd lives."

About one-sixth of the animals are left. I failed in my mission, and now the entire tribe will suffer the consequences of my failure.

Amongst the grumblin' from the elders, one of 'em barks, "And where would Mato Waäylo go?"

"North. North to reservation."

"Abandon our land?" The brave who speaks stands as if to challenge Mato Waäylo.

"Há, as we were forced to abandon ours."

The brave spits at Mato Waäylo's feet. "Canl waka."

Mato Waäylo growls and steps toward the brave, fists clenched. I move forward to stand with him when the chief raises his hand and barks a rebuke. After a brief standoff, the brave lowers his eyes, and Mato Waäylo and I sit. "Our Lakota brothers join us in unity. We will not behave as wasicu and fight amongst ourselves. We fight beside one another for the good of all."

I clear my throat. "Great Chief, may I offer my deepest, heartfelt apology for my failure to save tatanka from wasicu?"

Mato Waäylo stands again. "Because of most brave acts of Sungila Sá, some tatanka remain. Who here would stand alone against entire cavalry raiding party?"

Murmurs of approval ripple through the tipi.

"Sungila Sá begs apology, but I say Sungila Sá great Lakota warrior deserving of many thanks."

"As say I," Grasshopper chimes in. "I was with Hawk Feather and saw Sungila Sá's great bravery against wasicu."

I turn my head away from the group. "It matters not. I did not save tatanka for tribe."

Another of the elders speaks, one from our tribe. "I say your situation is not the same as ours. You have many tatanka still. With trade with other tribes, perhaps we can survive the winter."

"Then what do we do?" Mato Waäylo starts pacin' again. "If we kill remaining tatanka, how are we better than wasicu? We must not destroy entire herd. Would it not be better to leave and go to reservation where food is plentiful, and allow this herd the chance to grow in number again?"

"We do not have to kill all tatanka. With trade..."

One of the braves interrupts the elder. "Who will trade with us? Cheyenne? Arapahoe? Crow? They suffer worse than Lakota."

Mato Waäylo grunts with satisfaction. "Prowling Mountain Lion speaks truly."

The elder raises his voice over the murmurs of the crowd. "Mato Waäylo suggests we run away like frightened children. Are you frightened children?"

"Wisdom is not the same as fear." Mato Waäylo stops his incessant pacin' and stands behind the chief at the head of the circle. "Wisdom is based in truth. Fear comes from falsehood."

"What truth?" the elder retorts.

"Truth. Tatanka lie rotting on the plains. Truth. To hunt what is left of herd to destruction is reckless and foolish. To do so ensures our death. Truth. We cannot store enough food to survive this winter with tatanka that remain, even if we kill them all. Wisdom. We must go from this place if we are to survive."

"You would give our lands to wasicu?"

My groan must be louder than I thought, 'cause every eye turns to me. I don't want to say the words I know are true. I don't want to shatter the dreams that remain for the people. But I know I must. "Dear friends, wasicu have already taken our lands. More will come, and more after that. Wasicu outnumber Lakota beyond measure. They crave what your land holds in its heart. Their desire and their greed have no bounds. So, they lay claim to your lands, and they will take your lands— as they took ours. It is the way of it. If you want to live, you must find new lands."

"How will the people survive in new land? How will we live? Better to die with courage than to wither away like canl waka."

"Better to live than to die." Mato Waäylo pounds his fist in his hand. "Who is canl waka? He who fights for life, or he who gives in to pointless death?"

The discontented mutterin's of the crowd are silenced by the raised hand of the chief. "I hear the words of the mighty Mato Waäylo, but I do not believe they are mighty words. I hear the words of Sungila Sá, but in them I hear weakness, not strength." Many of the braves and elders grumble against us in agreement with the chief. "Who has come to join our tribe? Weak and helpless children who refuse to fight for what is rightfully ours?"

Mato Waäylo's face looks like a pot of boilin' water, red hot and churnin' with steam risin' from it. He looks on the verge of leavin', so I risk speakin' again. "Great Chief, I fought a war against a greater force to keep my rightful land, and lost everything—my mother, my father, my sisters, and my land. This fate I would spare my friends, if only they would listen."

The chief bristles at my challenge. "You speak of wasicu wars, fought in wasicu ways. Lakota braves outmatch wasicu soldiers four to one, as you witnessed on the plains."

"What you say is true, Great Chief, but wasicu outnumber Lakota a thousand to one or more. No one can win against such numbers. Not even Lakota."

"Sungila Sá speaks truly. Are you willing to lose all, even life of children, to fight for land?" Mato Waäylo peers from face to face, his hawklike countenance and piercin' eyes callin' for an answer from each man present. One by one, I see men drop their eyes or lower their heads under his penetratin' gaze.

After several moments of tense silence, the chief stands. "What worth is life of children if they live as slaves on wasicu land? We will not go. We will stay and fight."

Cheers erupt from the majority of the crowd. I look to Mato Waäylo, whose slumped shoulders and tortured grimace reveal his agony. He catches my eye and motions for me to leave with him, so I stand and march from the meetin' with my brother. Prowling Mountain Lion, Hawk Feather, and Grasshopper leave with us. The rest remain behind to discuss plans for huntin' tatanka and war.

"We must take our families and go." The impassive and taciturn Mato Waäylo practically spits his words. I've never seen him so undone.

"Where will we go?" Grasshopper asks.

"We take wasicu offer and go north to reservation."

Hawk Feather stops in his tracks. "Mato Waäylo suggests we defy chief? Go alone?"

"Há."

Prowling Mountain Lion and Hawk Feather exchange nervous glances, then Hawk Feather shakes his head. "We cannot go alone. Five warriors with women and children traveling through disputed territory? If wasicu does not kill us, the Apache or Cheyenne will."

Prowling Mountain Lion places his hand on Mato Waäylo's shoulder. "I agree with you. The chief's plan is foolhardy. But we need another choice besides putting our families out for slaughter. Perhaps after winter, when tatanka are no more, chief will change his mind and whole tribe will go to reservation."

"We have shown Chief we do not agree," Hawk Feather adds. "He will listen to us when the snows come, and we run out of food."

I step up to stand beside Mato Waäylo. "Mato Waäylo and I have seen what happens when the snows come, and you run out of food. Had your chief not come to our rescue, we would all be dead. Who will come to our rescue now? As you said, Prowling Mountain Lion, what tribe is in better shape than we are? No one will come. And all will die."

"Winter fast approaches. We must go, before the snows, and take our families to a land where tatanka are plentiful so we may hunt before cold and hunger take us." Mato Waäylo turns toward his tipi, and Grasshopper and I follow, but Hawk Feather and Prowling Mountain Lion remain behind.

"Mato Waäylo. Sungila Sá." The three of us turn to see an elder standin' in the chief's lodge entrance. "The elders have chosen you to seek trade with wasicu hunters and neighboring tribes. Return to hear your task."

I stare up at Mato Waäylo. "Can we refuse?" I'm not sure of Lakota rules about such things, as I've never seen anyone refuse a chief's command, and our chief's decisions always included everyone's feedback, unlike this chief.

"He sends us as sons, husbands to his daughters. It would be a terrible insult to refuse. Most dishonorable."

My heart sinks down to my toes. I know Mato Waäylo will never do something he considers dishonorable. "What do we do? You know the fate of their choice. Do we accept the fate they create for us?"

"We must." Mato Waäylo sighs. "Perhaps when we return with nothing from trade, Chief will reconsider."

"By then, it will be too late to go to the reservation. We will have to wait out the snows."

Mato Waäylo says nothing, but his eyes speak of a resignation and despondency I can't accept. "What will Chief do to me if I refuse?"

"You will die, and your wife and child will be sent away from the tribe to starve and die alone."

"He would not do that to his own daughter."

"To suffer such an insult in silence, he would lose his position as chief. He would, and he will."

Grasshopper's eyes plead with me to listen to Mato Waäylo. If someone grabbed each of my shoulders and ripped my body in two, it wouldn't hurt as much as this torment. Because of the pride of a single man, my wife and child and unborn bairn will suffer and perhaps die, and there's nothing I can do about it. I can't decide whether to explode with rage or dissolve into tears. All I can manage is an animalistic scream, my fists clenched at my sides so tight I get the blood in my palms.

The elder's face darkens, the furrows on his face runnin' so deep they look like the bloody gashes in my hands. "Come. Now." He waves us back to the chief's lodge.

Mato Waäylo turns to Grasshopper. "Go, gather as much food and supplies as you can carry, and divide the supplies between you, Soul of Moon, and Flowing Spring. Run quickly, before Chief sends a guard to protect the food." Grasshopper sprints away without a word. Hawk Feather and Prowling Mountain Lion follow him, while Mato Waäylo and I drag ourselves back to the elder's meeting.

As we enter the chief brightens. "Há. Mato Waäylo and Sungila Sá. We have chosen you for the great honor of making trade with all nearby tribes and with the wasicu trappers and hunters you know. You will leave right away and return at the first snows. Go now and collect what you need for the journey. Take furs, woven blankets, rifles, and knives for trade. Be ready to leave before the midday meal. You may take food with you for the journey."

I must admit, it is a brilliant move to send away his two strongest adversaries, and to require they remain away until the first snows. Once he begins rationin', he might get unseated, and Mato Waäylo made chief, if the two of us are around when things get rough. Without a word, Mato Waäylo bows ever so slightly and exits. I don't mask my anger or bother to bow but turn on my heels and stomp from the lodge.

"He's gonna trade away the rifles? I don't understand."

"Chief believes bow and arrow better weapon against wasicu."

I can't believe someone this ignorant is chosen as chief. Our chief had true wisdom and humility, as is the way of Lakota. How an arrogant fool ever appeared to be a good choice to the people is beyond me.

"I must go to Flowing Spring. I have not spoken with her since I returned. I fear she will be most unhappy with the news."

"As will Hanhepi Wi Nagi."

"Do you think they could speak to their father and change his mind on this course of action?"

"They would not attempt."

"Then I must go and try to soothe her worry."

"Come to lodge when ready to leave."

We stand for several seconds, starin', unblinkin', at each other, our eyes filled with the knowledge we're headin' out on a fool's errand, but both of us powerless to stop it.

Flowing Spring leaps like an antelope into my arms when I enter our tipi. After burrowin' into my chest and shoulder for a while, she caresses my scruffy cheek. "Sungila Sá needs bathing and shave face."

"I do. I missed you so much."

"We miss Sungila Sá." Out of nowhere, she slaps me.

"Ouch! What?"

"You no return with others. Worry Flowing Spring sideways."

My chuckle fans the flames of her irritation. "I think you mean 'beside yourself'. I'm sorry, truly. I...had to bury a friend."

"Who friend?"

"Someone from before I was Lakota. Soldier friend."

She frowns. "How Sungila Sá have friend wasicu soldier?"

"Like I said, a friend from before. He died in the battle, so I buried him. It was the least I could do."

She huffs and tosses her hair, pouting like a bairn that she was forced to wait and worry because of a wasicu soldier.

"I have more news. Your father is sendin' me away to trade with other tribes. Mato Waäylo goes with me."

"When leave?" Her piercin' whine makes me shudder.

"Right away."

"Sungila Sá only now return."

"I know. I don't want to go."

"Father punish Sungila Sá for burial of wasicu soldier." The 'I told you so' flip of her head vexes me.

"No, he doesn't know about that. I buried Martin...um, the soldier, outside of camp."

"Punish Sungila Sá for not saving tatanka."

"Maybe. But I think he's punishin' me for standin' against his plan."

Her mouth drops open, her eyes wide. "Sungila Sá argue against chief?"

"As did Mato Waäylo."

She shakes her head. "Father no like."

"I can see that. Our chief would always listen to other ideas and take feedback. I've seen Mato Waäylo go toe-to-toe with him many times. I guess I'm not used to your father's ways."

"How long away?"

"Until the first snow."

Her face crumples and tears brim in her eyes. "Do not go."

"You're suggestin' I refuse your father? You just said he won't tolerate argument."

Flowing Spring stomps her foot, her fists clenched at her sides. "Apologize to father."

"I would if I thought it would change anything. But your father won't back down now. He has to save face."

"What mean, 'save face'?"

"Protect his pride in front of the tribe."

Flowing Spring's head drops to her chest. "Sungila Sá speaks truly. Father save face all times." She pats her belly. "Bear-n grows while away."

I walk to her slowly and wrap her in my arms. "I know. I don't want to miss talkin' to the wee bairn and singin' to him..."

"Her—may be."

"Singin' to her and feelin' her kick and move."

"Sungila Sá must hurry to return. Pray to Jesus for snow."

I squeeze her a little tighter. "I don't want the snows to come before we have enough food. I won't have you go through that again."

As if on cue, Grasshopper sticks his head through the flap. "I bring food."

"Come." He brings in a basket filled to overflowin' with food from the storage. "This is all for Flowing Spring?"

"Há. Already take basket to Hanhepi Wi Nagi. Basket for me outside lodge."

"Hurry and take it to your tipi, before someone sees. Thank you, tahansi."

Grasshopper grins and fires off a fair imitation of a salute, and with that, he bolts from the tipi, leavin' us to our goodbyes.

"Spirit of Black Horse will wake soon. Sungila Sá no leave without goodbye for son."

"I won't."

We sit together on the pallet beside Spirit of Black Horse. My heart aches with longin' as I stroke his back and his thick mane of hair. If I could think of any way to defy the chief, I'd do it in a heartbeat, but the consequences...well, I don't know what the prideful man would do. So, I hold my beautiful bride in my arms, rub Súnkawakan Sápä's back, and wait in silence for him to waken from his nap.

When at last he opens his eyes with a yawn, I scoop him up and press him against me so tight, he starts to squirm. "Tehila it a."

"Tehila it a, ahte."

"I must leave again with Leksi Mato Waäylo to trade for food." Súnkawakan Sápä rubs his eyes. "Go away, ahte?"

"Há, but I will be back at the first snow."

"Ohán." He wriggles in my arms for me to put him down, and as soon as I do, he's off to play with his toy drum.

"Ohán, my son. I will see you soon."

Flowing Spring wraps her arms around my waist and buries her face against my chest. "How Flowing Spring ohán without my love?"

"Everything will be well. I will return soon with more food for the tribe. In the meantime, you keep the food from Grasshopper hidden and safe."

"Keep secret?"

"Há, secret."

We kiss, our embrace deep and long and fierce, before I prepare for the journey. I wash the grime from my face and arms and change my filthy clothes, but I don't shave, promisin' Flowing Spring that I'd shave as soon as I return. "The fur'll help keep me warm at night while I'm away from you." I gather a bundle of the things I need, then with one final kiss on top of Súnkawakan Sápä's head and a brush of Flowing Spring's lips, I leave to find Mato Waäylo.

CHAPTER TWENTY-SIX

Mato Waäylo and I ride in silence, keepin' to cover where we can and only givin' the horses their head when we're on the open plains. We decide to try the more permanent settlements first, the plains natives who build their lodges from earth or thatch—the Pawnee, the Santee, and the Yankton Dakota tribes. Given that the Pawnee attacked our land and almost killed Mato Waäylo's wife, we choose the Yankton for our first attempt at trade. The long, silent days and sleepless nights on the trail weigh on me, as if a stone has tumbled from the hillside and landed square on my chest. I ache for my family, Flowing Spring's touch, and the sweet smell of Súnkawakan Sápä's hair.

The Yankton chief is pleasant enough, welcomin' us and offerin' us a meal, but as we feared, his tribe is no better off than we are, havin' the buffalo herds on their lands decimated by the wasicu as well. So, after a restful evenin', we ride on to the Santee. More wordless days— more empty nights.

The Santee are farther east and north and seem to have fared a little better than the Yankton. They, too, welcome us as Sioux brothers, feed us, and provide us lodgin' for the night. Their chief is only interested in our rifles and makes a good trade of buffalo meat for five of our wasicu weapons. They also offer us two bottles of brown liquor, wasicu alcohol, but I warn Mato Waäylo against the drink, explainin' how I've seen it make wasicu lose control and do horrible things they wouldn't normally do. Mato Waäylo wisely heeds my warnin' and refuses the liquor. Instead, he says he prefers more meat, which the chief provides.

Buoyed somewhat by our first success, we make our way south to the Pawnee settlement. We must be wary and vigilant on this leg of our journey, takin' turns on watch at night—so, even less sleep and greater loneliness. Two warriors meet us on the outskirts of camp, their faces stonelike, and their eyes narrow with suspicion. Mato Waäylo shows the braves our wares and requests audience with their chief. One of the braves rides back into camp, and when he returns, he ushers us into the settlement, but we can tell he's not pleased about it.

The Pawnee chief, a fierce man with a broad, flat face and piercin' eyes, meets us in the center of camp. So, unlike the other Sioux tribes, he is unwillin' to invite us into his lodge, which bodes poorly for the trade. He paws briefly through our wares, showin' particular interest in our two remainin' rifles, but at the end of it, he flips his hand in the air. "Nothing worth trade." He turns his back as a way to dismiss us, and the two braves escort us out of camp the way we came.

As we turn our horses east, Mato Waäylo sighs. "Must go to Crow, Cheyenne, Blackfoot, Cree, Arapahoe."

"Do you think we'll have any better luck with 'em?"

Mato Waäylo shakes his head. "All suffer as Lakota. No buffalo."

"Maybe the Cree will have some meat from rangin' north."

Again, he shakes his head. "Then they have no need of our furs."

"Then I guess our best bet is to look for Jed and the other hunters to the west."

"Trade with hunters last." Mato Waäylo's distaste for the white hunters crinkles his long nose. I share his dislike, but I wonder if we'll be wastin' time goin' to the other plains tribes who hunt buffalo for their livelihood like we do. Still, I follow Mato Waäylo's lead as my elder.

The Crow seem glad to see the infamous Iáxuhke, the screamin' red fox. The English-speakin' brave comes to me and grasps my arm. "Iilápaachitche."

"Tahansi."

"Ah, Iáxuhke has learned Lakota words."

"I have, yes. I wed a Lakota woman and have one child and one on the way."

"Iáxuhke has been busy." He chuckles and claps my back. "No more a slave."

"No, I am one with the people."

"Very well. Welcome, Iáxuhke. Welcome, Great Warrior Mato Waäylo." He grasps Mato Waäylo's arm in greeting. "Why come to visit Crow neighbor?"

"We come to make trade." I lift the blanket that covers our items for trade.

The Crow brave glances at the items, but I can tell by his crestfallen expression he was hopin' for some items they need, for they, too, are hungry.

"We have two rifles," I interject, hopin' to spur on more conversation.

But the warrior shrugs. "We have rifles from trade with white man."

"Knives?"

"With sorrow I say we have no need for more knives. Perhaps chief would trade for some of the pelts?"

"Do you have need of pelts?"

"I fear we will when winter comes with no buffalo."

"Then, we make trade for pelts."

The Crow warrior escorts us to his chief's tipi and introduces us, addin' a good deal of embellishment to his description of my escapades. The chief is warm and open. The Lakota and Crow have good relations since the meetin' I witnessed when still a Lakota slave. But, to our disappointment, the chief believes his tribe's need for meat outweighs their need for warmth. Like with the Sioux tribes, we receive a warm meal and a pallet for sleep, but we ride out the next day empty-handed.

Mato Waäylo's somber expression heightens my nervousness. "It was good to see the Crow tahansi." Anything to lighten the mood.

But Mato Waäylo only grunts in reply, and we ride in oppressive silence throughout the day.

My spirits are lower than the blue-gray clouds blanketin' the tops of the distant mountains. Images of Flowing Spring lyin' on her pallet of furs, barely able to move, her eyes hooded, and little Súnkawakan Sápä sleepin' on top of her frail body—not the sleep of a peaceful child but the sleep of death—haunt my nights on the trail. Behind my visions runs the continuous drone of a hopeless chant—'We shoulda gone to the reservation. We shoulda gone to the reservation.' Once the snows come, it will be too late.

Finally, I can't hold it in any longer. "Mato Waäylo, we need to return home and convince the chief to let us travel north to the reservation, before it is too late."

"Chief say no."

"We must change his mind. Don't you see? This is pointless, a waste of time. No one is going to help us. No one *can* help us."

"Still many tribes to try."

"All in the same boat."

Mato Waäylo stares at me with one brow raised, perplexed by my strange expression.

"I mean we all suffer in the same way."

"Hunters able to help."

"Maybe, but why would they? We have nothing of value to them for trade."

"Hunters trade fur to wasicu for silver coin."

"Then if that is our best chance, let us find the hunters' camp and make trade now." Mato Waäylo seems to waver, so I press my advantage. "Mato Waäylo, think of Hanhepi Wi Nagi. You know I speak truly. You knew it before we left camp on this fool's errand."

After a heavy pause, Mato Waäylo closes his eyes and blows out a breath. "I do know."

"Let us ride with haste to the hunters' camp."

Mato Waäylo stares into the sky, and I'm afeared he's gonna reject my plea. But with a jerk on the rope halter, he turns his painted stallion west, and our horses' hooves rip up the ground as we race across the plains in a cloud of dust.

We ride into the night, usin' the stars to keep our direction. When we stop, we rest for only a couple of hours. Both of us are ready for this trek to be over. Another day's ridin', and we know that after we sleep, we'll be comin' into the hunters' camp by mid-day next. Pressured frenzy replaces the somber silence that coated our journey like tree sap. Just one more day and night.

Mato Waäylo wakes before the birds, rekindles our small fire, and cooks up come chokeberries into mush for our breakfast. Before light touches the sky, we're off again, and we ride into the hunters' camp before the sun reaches the top of the sky.

Jed sees us comin' and raises his arms in the air to greet us. "Well, now, looky at what we have here."

I lift my hand in return. "Jed." As much as I distrust this man, I must try to be nice. He's our last hope for any help. The other hunters, those that are in camp at the present, will follow his lead.

Mato Waäylo wastes no time. "We bring items for trade. Furs, tools, weapons."

"Well, now, that's nice. But before we talk trade, come, sit down a spell, let's have a chat."

"No time. Must return Lakota camp." Mato Waäylo has no intention of spendin' any more time than necessary with these wasicu.

"Very well, then. Let's see what you got."

I jump down from Blossom and uncover our supplies. As he strokes the furs and examines the knives, Jed drawls, "Having trouble again with the buffalo, are you now?"

Something in my spirit warns me not to give him too much information. I glance at Mato Waäylo who gives a barely perceptible shake of his head. "We're wantin' to see if you have anything for us. Tradin' with the other tribes has been scarce." All true, but not revealin' our true plight.

Jed picks up a rifle. "Understand you had to join your father-in-law's tribe..."

"Safety in numbers."

"Uh-huh." He picks up a knife and flicks its edge. "I might be able to take a few of these items off your hands. The rifles, for sure. You have some nice knives. And I guess I can take these furs to the fort and sell them." He looks to Mato Waäylo. "What're you looking for in trade."

"Meat. Other food."

"We have a good amount of deer and elk meat. How about you and I wander over to the stores and see what we can do?"

Since I'm not invited to the trade talks, I wander over to a fire to speak to some of the hunters sittin' there, but as I approach, they eye me like I'm bringin' the plague. "Have you'ns found any good huntin' grounds nearby?" My question is met with stony silence. "Mind if I join ya 'round the fire?"

"Move along, Injun."

They can tell I'm white-skinned, same as them, but their glares pull me up short. "There's no call bein' rude."

One of the men, a burly, hairy beast with a wild, black beard down onto his chest stands and confronts me, his fat fingers clutchin' and openin' at his sides as if he's tryin' to decide whether he's gonna deck me or not. "Look here, don't you come 'round sayin' we're rude when your kind is out slaughterin' women and children on the trail. You're lucky I don't kill you where you stand."

"I haven't killed any women or children."

"Maybe you has, maybe you ain't. But your kind is murderin' heatherns, plain and simple." He sits back down. "G'on with you, then."

Rather than make a scene, I walk back to the edge of camp where I left Blossom tied and wait for Mato Waäylo and Jed to return. As I feared, the chief's rage is already stirrin' hatred against the people, makin' things worse for us instead of better. Why can't he see what he's doin'?

How long before the soldiers ride out in force and slaughter us like they slaughtered the buffalo? The only thing keepin' 'em at bay is the tenuous treaty signed by Red Cloud and the Lakota chiefs—and that treaty is already bein' violated by the wasicu. I'm afeared it won't be long before the reservation will be forced upon us. Better to make the choice while we still can, and maybe get a better situation than if they send us there at the end of a gun.

I see Mato Waäylo stride across the camp toward me, but Jed is nowhere to be seen. Mato Waäylo's face is reddened, his eyes sunken deep within furrows and hooded by his brows, his mouth a thin, hard line. He barks, "Come," and leaps onto his stallion.

"What happened?"

"No make good trade."

"Jed said..."

"Liar. Insults the people."

This doesn't surprise me. Jed's insulted me many times before. But Mato Waäylo's reaction to it does surprise me. "So, we have nothing?"

"No make good trade." He kicks his horse, who bolts from camp like he's leavin' a bramble. Mato Waäylo's long hair flows behind him in a contemptuous wave, his final and absolute rejection of all things wasicu. Blossom and I follow along behind him, but my heart sags into my stomach like a rock in water, and my soul, even my body, aches with the prospect of another winter like the one we barely endured.

When I catch up to Mato Waäylo, I want to question him, to press him for answers, but the look on his face urges me to wait. I know him—he'll speak when he has something to say worth hearin'. Rats are gnawin' my insides, though, 'cause we appear to be ridin' to our doom, so it's hard to be patient.

The sun brushes the horizon when he finally speaks. "Sungila Sá speaks truly. We must convince chief to leave for reservation."

"Are we too late? The nights have grown cold, and the air feels quiet and like ice in my breath."

"We must ride through. No sleep. No stop except for horses' water and eat. No fire."

"The horses..."

"They must be strong, as we must be strong."

"Are we too late?" I press him for an answer because my fear has become a vise 'round my chest and chokin' fingers on my throat. But Mato Waäylo doesn't answer.

As we ride north, cold descends on us, seepin' into our bones and usherin' in our fate, to die a slow, lingerin' death from starvation. I'm plagued by the memories of Súnkawakan Sápä wanderin' so close to the shadowlands, and Flowing Spring lyin' weak and motionless, despairin' and in pain—and there was nothing I could do about any of it.

The burden of responsibility for their lives crushes me beneath its weight, so much so I can barely lift my arms to pull Blossom's reins. My head bobs on my chest. My neck feels broken by the heaviness of the load. When Blossom gallops, I flop around on her back like one of Maisie's ragdolls.

We ride through the night, stoppin' only once to water the horses and allow them to feed on the grass around the stream. "Ice is formin' along the edges." I point to the skim of ice where the water's flow is slowest.

Mato Waäylo juts his chin to gesture toward thick clouds building over the distant mountains, lit up by the three-quarters moon. "Snow cloud."

"Let's go." I jump on Blossom, my desperation freezin' me more than the bitter cold.

The dawn rises bright, and the snow clouds remain over the mountains, so my hope rises a little with the sun. Poor Blossom is coated with lather, despite the cold. I'm afeared we're pushin' 'em past their limits, but Mato Waäylo is relentless. He seems determined to get to the camp by the next day—which means another night without sleep or rest and even more pressure on our horses.

We stop midday for a brief rest and water, sharin' some strips of dried meat while the horses munch grass. Both of us are too tired to talk. Inside my head, I'm imaginin' things too painful to speak aloud. I don't know where Mato Waäylo is, but I know he isn't present with me.

To my horror, late in the afternoon, the snow clouds leave their perch over the mountains and start to roll across the plains. The temperature drops as the afternoon wears on, and when night arrives, the first flakes of snow begin to fall. Still, Mato Waäylo refuses to stop.

"It's too late."

Mato Waäylo turns on me with a fury I've rarely seen. "Silence. I refuse your belief. Never will I give up."

"I'm not giving up."

"Then stop speaking death."

We ride in cold silence the rest of the night. I'm alone with my miserable thoughts, unable to adopt Mato Waäylo's hope as my own, while he rides ahead of me, his stiff back a reminder I have caused great offense to my friend. Deep in my heart, I want to apologize—hunger for it, even—but I can't make my mouth form the words. I can't seem to find even a sprinkle of hope to seed something good inside me. So, I'm smothered in silence and despair.

When the sky lightens behind the thick clouds, we pull up to rest and take water. The snow falls in soft, lazy flakes, coatin' the ground but not enough to hinder our final leg of the journey. Still, the horses are exhausted, as are we, and I'm startin' to wonder if we're gonna make it to camp today as Mato Waäylo planned. Mato Waäylo allows a longer rest this time. We both check our mounts carefully, feelin' their legs and lookin' at their hooves, because if one of them come up lame, we're done for.

Once we've finished eatin' what little we have, Mato Waäylo suggests we walk the horses for a bit instead of ridin' them. I don't complain, even though I'm asleep on my feet, because I know Blossom needs a break from carryin' my weight. We walk at least an hour. Neither of us is dressed for this weather, so my feet are soon numb inside my moccasins, and the blanket over my shoulders is heavy with snow and crusted over with ice.

Finally, Mato Waäylo indicates we can ride again, so I shake off my blanket and mount Blossom. Mato Waäylo breaks into a full gallop, and Blossom and I follow, gobblin' up the snow-covered distance between our loves and us. He refuses to slow again, pushin' us all to the edge of collapse, until we run into a large patch of trees I recognize. Our camp isn't too far from here. We're gonna make it!

We're forced to walk through the trees, for the safety of our horses, and Mato Waäylo's impatience emanates off him in waves, but I feel a great sense of relief. Before nightfall, I'll hold Flowing Spring and Súnkawakan Sápä in my arms again, and if the snows remain light, we can leave tomorrow for the reservation. I'm determined that even if the chief refuses to see reason and the rest of the tribe remains, I'm takin' my family to safety—and food.

Mato Waäylo suddenly pulls up short. I ride up beside him. "What is it?"

He points to smoke risin' in the distance. "Near camp."

"It's the fires. They built more because of the cold. Besides, we can't see the camp from here. Too many trees."

"See smoke."

"Yes, but it's their fires."

Mato Waäylo's jaw bulges and works like someone chewin' tough meat. "We ride." He kicks his stallion, heedless of the undergrowth, and races through the trees. I have no choice but to follow, hopin' against hope I don't hurt Blossom any more than I already have.

We emerge from the trees unscathed, beyond some scratches from limbs and brambles, and race across the open ground to the trees borderin' the entrance to our camp. Mato Waäylo has gotten far ahead of me, so I try to hurry Blossom along, but I can't blame her for bein' slower than usual after our arduous journey. I'm quite sluggish myself.

Mato Waäylo dips out of sight, so I know he's reached the edge of the trees and started his descent into the valley where our camp is set up. A few seconds later, a hollow cry echoes back to me, like a howl—an animal of some kind? It must be—if it's a human cry, I don't recognize the voice. I urge Blossom faster, and she tries her best, I can tell, but it takes what seems like forever to get to the edge of the trees.

When we break out of the trees and start the trail down into the valley, I can barely see the camp beneath what appears to be a cloud of fog—or is it smoke?

"Hurry, girl." I lean over her back and push her with the force of my will and the newfound energy from my risin' panic down the hill into camp.

I find Mato Waäylo kneelin' on the ground beside his stallion. What is he doin'? Another howl splits the air around me, and I realize it's Mato Waäylo. My brain feels wrapped in the dense, harsh-smellin' fog. What's happenin'?

Mato Waäylo leans back and bellows a third time, then drags his fingers down his face, leavin' tears in his flesh. Blood wells up in the ripped skin and drips off his chin. His eyes remain fixed on the sky, almost like he's blind and starin' at nothing—but when I follow his gaze, all breath rushes from me like I'm hit by a ball from a Union cannon.

Hanhepi Wi Nagi hangs from a limb. Her face is bloated, distorted almost beyond recognition, but it is her. Soul of Moon—her soul gone from this world.

Flowing Spring. No no no. I won't believe it. I can't.

I leap off Blossom and run like a man chased by a herd of stampedin' buffalo into the center of camp. Fires smolder everywhere. Every lodge in heaps of ash and smolderin' wood. Bodies strewn on the ground, dusted with snow. Blotches of red tintin' the snow like a sunrise before a storm.

I run to the place where my lodge once stood to find a burned-out pile of rubble and remnants of a clay bowl here, a broken pot there. Strangely, I find the feather Flowing Spring hung from the center of the lodge lyin' beside the rubble. I pick it up. Something about holdin' her feather wakes me from my strange torpor. I tear through the rubble, lookin' for bones or a body—nothing. Did she escape? Frantic, I scramble from the ashes and run left, right, back—I start turnin' over bodies in camp—I'm vaguely aware of some faces I recognize—I see women, children, chests ripped open by gunfire—I wander through the sea of blue and red bodies. One thought keeps me movin'—they escaped. They must've escaped.

Near the far side of camp, I find Grasshopper's body. I leave him in the pool of soaked-in blood and snow and ash and move to the next body, and the next. They escaped. They must've.

"Flowing Spring! Flowing Spring!" Surely, she's in hiding. Surely, she'll come to my call. "Flowing Spring!" My son. My unborn child. My gut clenches and I lean over and vomit up hot, burnin' bile. "Flowing Spring!" Please, I beg you.

The tranquility of the scene before me, so incongruous with the violence wrought here, does something to me. I crack open—transform—molt like a snake. I become someone else. I watch myself run from body to body, from lodge to lodge, but I'm aloof, outside, a motionless observer from afar, quiet as a winter lake.

As I watch, the hysterical, blubberin' man turns and looks beyond the outskirts of the camp. I whisper, "Don't do it," but the man dashes through the tall grass anyway, kickin' up white clouds—is it snow or ash? Pawin' the ground, racin' to and fro, until he makes his way to the open space beyond his former lodge.

"Don't look," I whisper again. Heedless of my warning, he lopes across the field, continuin' his strange ballet, so much like a war dance. But the war is over, can't he see?

Then, he stops and falls to his face, and I'm caught in the swirl of unbridled pain and sucked back into his body. Súnkawakan Sápä. He could be sleepin' if not for the bloody clothin'. His mother would never allow him to go to bed in such a filthy state. He lies on his back, his long, black hair in a cloud around his head, his arms folded across his

373

little chest, his face flecked with snow. A roarin' fills my ears—a rush of wind or throbbin' of thunder, I can't tell which, but suddenly it breaks free and pours from me in a flood of torrential agony. The storm rumbles and crashes, and rain streams from my eyes. The gale is relentless, pressin' me against the tiny body—willin' him to come back to me.

I don't know how long I lay there. I've become a hole, a deep, black pit, and I've fallen into it. The crushin' ache in the center of me sucks me down, down, deeper and deeper...I can't breathe. A reflexive survival instinct forces me to sit bolt upright, and my breath returns in heavin' gasps. And beyond the body of my son, I see her tiny, delicate feet, bare as an infant's. She lies on her stomach. Her dress is hitched up to her neck. As if one of the cavalry soldiers has come upon me and sucker punched me in the gut, I double over and retch again and again until all my insides pool on the ground.

My throat burns. My heart pounds in my ears. I have to see her, touch her—I have to tell her I'm sorry I failed her in every way. But I can't move. There's nothing left of me. I'm the void, the emptiness of a night sky, the hollowness of a dry well. My Flowing Spring.

My hand grazes Súnkawakan Sápä's cold skin, and the reality of my loss crashes over me in another wave of wailin' anguish. I scramble to her side, gently turn her over, and brush the dirt from her beautiful face. She ran. She picked up our son and ran away—and almost made it. My strength and my anchor—she almost made it.

"My love." The words croak from my raw throat. "My dearest love. My heart. I'm..." My voice catches as I struggle to breathe. "I'm...so...sorry."

A preternatural calm slows my heart and breath as I stand. I lift Súnkawakan Sápä in my arms, holdin' him against my chest for a final moment, then lay him carefully on his mother and fold her arms over his little body. Then I lift her—she's so dainty, it's like liftin' a feather—and carry her and Súnkawakan Sápä back to the trees where I left Mato Waäylo.

He is still kneelin' beneath his bride, his skin pale and taunt, pulled tight over his cheekbones like a death shroud. I say nothing—there's nothing more to say. I place Flowing Spring, holdin' our son, on a bed of straw, then climb the tree holdin' Soul of Moon and shimmy out onto the limb. "Help me get her down."

Mato Waäylo doesn't move, doesn't change his expression, doesn't even move his eyes. It's as if he's become a statue, frozen in time and space forever at the moment of the end of all things.

"Mato Waäylo. Help me. I don't want her to fall." No response. So, I lie on the branch, hold up the rope with one hand, and cut it where it's looped over the limb. As the rope frays and breaks, I do my best to lower her closer to the ground before I'm forced to let her go, and she crumples to the ground in a heap.

Mato Waäylo rouses from his stupor and crawls to her side. He stretches her out, smooths her dress, caresses her face, and begins to chant—a mournful, achin' moan more than a song. I climb down and kneel beside Flowing Spring and Súnkawakan Sápä. Mato Waäylo pulls his knife from its sheath, grabs his braid, and slices it off near the nape of his neck. He places the braid tenderly on Soul of Moon's chest. Then, Mato Waäylo draws the edge of the knife across his throat.

I scream and leap to his side. Blood gushes from the slit, bathing Soul of Moon in his blood. I try to stanch the blood, but it throbs under my fingers and flows down my arm. Mato Waäylo teeters for a few moments, then he collapses on top of his beloved.

"No! No! Why? Why did you do it?" Without thinkin', I pummel his back, all of my rage and pain explodin' from my poundin' fists and pourin' out against my dear friend. But I wear myself out quicker this time, and before long, I pick up Mato Waäylo's knife and drift back to Flowing Spring's side. I lift my braids, one by one, and hack them off, placin' one on Flowing Spring and one atop Súnkawakan Sápä. I fondle Súnkawakan Sápä's thick hair for a few moments, savorin' the silky feel and recallin' how his hair flowed in the wind as Blossom carried us across the plains. I cut a clump of strands and wind them in a loop, then I cut some strands from Flowing Spring and loop her strands around my fingers.

Standin', I place the locks of hair in my Bible in my saddle pack. When I turn, I see the tableau of death before me, and I know what I must do. Most of the wood in the camp is burned beyond use, but a few of the thickest pieces survived, blackened but still useable. I wander through the camp, collectin' what I can find. As I scour the camp, I find Grasshopper's body again, so I carry him back to my little burial site, to lay him to rest with my family. Usin' my hatchet, I trudge through the woods and cut trunks and stout limbs, carryin' them back to where Flowing Spring, Súnkawakan Sápä, Mato Waäylo, Soul of Moon, and Grasshopper lie waitin' for me to send them on their way.

It takes me the better part of two days to build the scaffolds for my loved ones. Rememberin' Grasshopper's ceremony, I search the ruined lodges for any colored stones I can find—I manage a few, not nearly as many as were used for Grasshopper's Ina, but it will have to do. I also have no other clothes to send with them, no robes to wrap them in. So, instead, I use the blankets Mato Waäylo and I took to trade to wrap around their bodies. I place Flowing Spring and Súnkawakan Sápä together, with him lyin' in her arms—I don't know if this is the Lakota way, but it feels right to me. The rest, I lay on their own scaffold and place a few stones next to each one. As Grasshopper had done, I put my saddle bag beneath Flowing Spring's scaffold for the ceremony.

Now, I have the problem of what to use for a pipe. The chief's pipe was burned with the rest of his belongin's, and I don't know how to make a new one, nor do I know what to put in it, so I decide to create the smoke the only way I know how—I build a small fire beside the scaffolds.

As I wait for the fire to catch up, I slide Flowing Spring's single survivin' feather in her hair. The smoke begins to curl and rise, so I stand behind the fire and blow the smoke toward the scaffolds until the tendrils curl amongst the bodies. I try my best to imitate the chants I heard from Grasshopper and Mato Waäylo, but I add my own words, words from hymns I recall singin' a thousand years ago in my Granda's church.

"Just as I am, without one plea, But that Thy blood was shed for me, And that Thou bid'st me come to Thee, O Lamb of God, I come, I come."

"Amazin' grace, how sweet the sound, That saved a wretch like me. I once was lost, but now am found, Was blind but now I see."

"Hey-ya-ah-yah-yeh-yah-hey-yah." I sing and chant and rock and pray, holdin' myself like a mother holds a bairn and weepin' like a little girl.

As the fire dies out, I take a rock and cut my arms and legs, as I witnessed Grasshopper doing. It hurts, but strangely, the physical pain gives me a sense of release. For the final act of the ceremony, I pick up my saddle bag and hold it to my chest.

"I release your wakan, my dearest love. I will keep your hair always with me and hold it close to my heart—always and forever—but I release you. Go and be with your Jesus, whom you love. Spirit of Black Horse, ride on the wind to the Lord Jesus in heaven, where you may ride forever. Ride with Him on your black stallion, finally a horse of your own, and live free, dearest one. I hold you in my heart, but I set your wakan free to be with Jesus. And my little bairn." I can't continue. The bairn has no name. Flowing Spring and I never spoke of names, because the Lakota name children based on their wakan at birth. How can I offer the bairn a name? I don't know if it was a boy or a girl.

"Father God. You know all things. You've known my bairn from the dawn of creation. Please give a name to the little thing for me. And please tell the bairn that he—or she—is loved beyond measure. Amen."

I douse the fire and blow the last billow of smoke across the bodies of my loved ones. "Godspeed, my loves." I wipe my cheeks and blow a final kiss. But when I turn to walk away, I realize—I have nowhere to go. I stop, stock still, and stare into the bleak nothingness. What in the world am I supposed to do now?

PART THREE

It Is for Us, the Living

CHAPTER TWENTY-SEVEN

I'm a ship lost in a fog far from shore—no compass, no landmarks, only gray in all directions. The Lakota way of life has ended. My family and friends are all gone. The only clothes I have are soaked with blood. All I have to my name are some buffalo furs, the contents of my saddle bag, my Bible with its precious contents, my hatchet, two rifles, a knife, Blossom, and Mato Waäylo's horse.

While I was workin' on the scaffolds, I slept in a little lean-to I built from one of the buffalo hides and a couple of charred poles from one of the tipis, but this won't sustain me when the deep snows arrive. I know I have to move—but I can't bear to leave, nor can I bear to stay. I'm an untethered soul wanderin' the earth, hauntin' my former land—a spectre, a shadow of who I once was.

As I wander the camp, I notice fresh tracks in the snow—wolves or coyotes—and a pang of responsibility stings me. I can't leave these noble people out in the snow to be consumed by hungry animals over the winter. But the ground is too hard already to dig graves, and I don't have the tools to dig anyway. To build scaffolds for every member of the tribe would take a month or longer, I don't have enough wood, and even if I did, I have nothing to wrap them in and no way to honor them properly.

With no good options, I do the only thing I know. I carry them, one by one, to the little burial site I created for my family. Then, climbin' the hill outside of camp to the woods on top, I cut down several trees and hack off all the stout limbs I can find, roll them down the hill, and with the help of Blossom and Mato Waäylo's horse, I drag them to the burial site. There, I'll build a makeshift platform and stack the bodies on it. It may not stand through the snows, but it's the best I can do for them.

Several times each day as I labor, I break down. My sobs and wails echo back to me across the plains, as if the land weeps with me in mournin' for the people. I realize if I remain here, I'll die from grief before I die from starvation and the cold, so the mornin' after my task is finally complete, I say a prayer before the mass grave, whisper goodbye to Flowing Spring and Súnkawakan Sápä, pile the buffalo hides and other supplies on Mato Waäylo's horse, tie my meager belongin's on Blossom, and climb on her back. Now I have to figure which way I'm a-goin'.

I have to steer clear of the fort, but I need to go south as quickly as I can. In fact, I need to stay away from all civilized areas until I can find some clothes. I opt for southeast. That way, I can avoid the fort but still make my way south—unless I run into a patrol along the way.

I have nothing in which to carry water, but I do have the meat Mato Waäylo and I received in trade for the rifles. Decidin' it's wise to stay near water, I head out in search of a stream or river to follow that's flowin' in my general direction.

Except for the risk of heavy snows, there's no reason to hurry. I have nowhere to be. So, Blossom and I take our time, meanderin' along and takin' frequent rests. After a spell, we run up on the ol' Bozeman Trail, overgrown from disuse. But I recall there were a handful of outposts that the soldiers built along the trail, most of 'em burned out by the people in retaliation against the wasicu.

"What do you think, Blossom? Should we try lookin' for an outpost or two to see if we can find some more supplies?" Blossom is mute, but I s'pose she's in agreement. "What about you?" I realize I don't know what to call Mato Waäylo's horse. "What's your name? Let's see. You're a painted stallion, so how 'bout I call you Itowa? Paint? Is Itowa a good name?"

The horse seems fine with his new name and doesn't object to lookin' for an outpost, so we stay on the trail, keepin' a wary eye out for stray travelers or soldiers from the fort. As the sun is lowerin' in the sky, I see what remains of an outpost around a bend in the trail. It appears the roof would afford some protection from the cold, so we stop and decide to spend the night there.

Part of a back wall is collapsed, so I'm able to walk Blossom and Itowa into the main part of the cabin. I use some of the wood from the back wall to build a small fire, then I search the rest of the cabin for supplies. Sure enough, in what used to be a storage area, I find some cans of beans and one can of peaches—worth more'n gold to me at this point. I stuff them in my saddle bag and make my way to what served as bunk rooms for the men mannin' the outpost in its day. No clothes, but I'm thankful for what I found.

I decide to save the peaches, but I cut the lid off one of the cans of beans and heat it over the fire. Beans and dried meat—a fine meal, better than I've had in many a day. I offer a prayer of gratitude before I dig in. Who would've thought such a meal would taste so delicious?

Full and contented, I use one of the buffalo furs to wrap myself in and sleep by the fire, the best sleep I've had since Mato Waäylo and I left the camp in search of food. But when I wake, the realization crashes down on me like the beams in Mary's burnin' house that I just enjoyed a meal while my child lies molderin' in his dead mother's arms. Seethin' self-loathin' and disgust forces what's left of my supper to heave up. What sort of perverse, appalling, worthless excuse for a human being does such a thing?

I was actually contented. Contented! A heaviness settles over me so hard I can't get myself out from under the fur, so I lie next to a pool of my vomit while a parade of my worst sins—ones that had once been released through Christ's love and forgiveness—accuse me again. A thousand stains—a thousand deaths at my hands—a thousand reasons I shoulda been the one to die.

"You know they died in proper retribution for your sins. Skin for skin. An eye for an eye. Your child for someone's child. Your true love for someone's true love. It's only fair. You know what it says: God visits the iniquity of the fathers upon the children. That's what you brought to your family—suffering and death."

The voice is right. The multitude of my sins left God no choice. Like David, He took my son. But my sins were so great, He had to take my wife and unborn child as well. It's all my fault. They might as well have died by my hand.

The snow starts again and drifts in through several holes in the roof, and the fire has gone cold, but I still can't make myself move. The tonnage of my horrendous failures as a father and husband flattens me to the dirt. Every muscle and bone in my body aches with the weight of it.

How could I be contented when they'll never feel again? How could I be grateful when they'll never receive another gift or experience another pleasure? They didn't even cross my mind as I sat there eatin' like a pig over slop. What kinda man am I? I'm not a man. I'm an animal. No—I'm not as worthy as an animal. I am my demon.

I spend an unknown number of days and nights huddled under the buffalo fur, alternatin' between dozin' and starin' off into space, with no thought of anything beyond my shame. I don't care about the snow. I don't notice the deepenin' cold. I'm like a corpse who hasn't figured yet that it's time to move on.

Each day brings another round of accusations. "You promised them you'd protect them. You said you'd always be there for them. Their last moments were filled with terror and pain—and where were you? They called out for you, but you never came. If you'd been there, you would've saved them—but no. You didn't listen to the warning in your heart. You went on a fool's errand and left them to die."

More days and nights lyin' in the dirt, starin' at nothing. The voice drones its relentless allegations against me. I stand guilty as charged.

Sometime durin' one of those endless days, a different voice whispers in my head. I can't make it out beneath the inexorable drumbeat of the other voice, but I recognize the tones as familiar. It's then I notice Blossom and Itowa have gone outside, I assume to find some grass and water. It's a wretched thirst that finally moves me. I drag myself to pull in some wood pieces for a fire and fill my little cup with snow, then set the cup near the fire until the snow melts. I repeat this process several times, then walk outside to find the horses.

You must eat. But the thought of food brings a new wave of nausea and a fresh round of accusations. I crawl back under the furs and disappear again into a deep, pitch-black hole—my self-designed prison. Restitution must be made.

Heavy snow falls that night, and the whispered suggestion that we could get stuck here through the whole winter pushes me out of my hole.

You must eat. I force myself to chew and swallow a piece of meat, even though I gag with each swallow. I don't want to eat. I don't want to breathe. I don't want to live. The buffalo fur calls me back under its cover, a hiding place from the reality of this world, where I can sleep the sleep of the dead—but the whisper insists we must leave before it's too late.

Blossom nuzzles me the next mornin' to wake me, and I find the warmth of her touch is enough to get me movin'.

"Let's head out, girl. The snow has stopped, so maybe we can make good time and get ahead of it."

Back out on the ol' trail, the goin' is slow. Thankfully, no one is in sight in either direction. Late in the day, after sloggin' through thick slush, we find another burned outpost. This one has no roof, but we do find some more supplies—a handful of canned goods and an ol' cavalry cotton blouse. The shirt has a hole in it and is two sizes too big for me, but I figure if I roll up the sleeves and keep a pelt around my shoulders, I can pass for a trapper. My beard is long enough, and my hair is filthy and ragged enough. I tell you what, my Ma would box my ears if she could see me lookin' like this. But she can't, 'cause she's gone—gone like everyone else.

"I know there ain't no roof, but let's stay here anyways. Some shelter is better'n nothin'." Blossom agrees.

That night, the louder voice starts in again. "What are you doing? You keep on living your life while everyone you love lies dead, you cold, heartless, loveless beast." There'll be no sleep for me this night.

The snows are heavy the next day, which I use as an excuse to remain at the outpost, although in the secret places deep inside, I know the real reason is I don't want to move forward. I fear another round of accusations, and I don't want to face the certainty that I'm to blame for everything that's happened. But my hidin' place beneath the furs provides no relief, so when the sun rises to a clear sky, I pull myself to my feet, force a piece of meat down my throat, chase it with melted snow, and set out again.

The blessed fog which I once saw as a misery has returned, but numbness is preferable to torment, so I relish the reprieve from pain. Both Blossom and Itowa walk with their heads down, almost scrapin' the ground. Mine rests on my chest. Either the horses sense my despair, or they're gettin' weaker from the lack of food like I am—or both. For their sakes, I hope the sun melts the coverin' of snow, and they can find some patches of grass to eat. If the horses can't continue, none of us will survive the winter.

This passin' thought brings a momentary realization that I'd prefer it if I didn't survive, but I push the awareness away and hide the thought in some closet inside—if I don't, I'll end up like Mato Waäylo.

"You should've stopped him."

"I couldn't. He moved too fast. I didn't know..."

"You never convinced him to believe in Jesus. You just shared silly stories of Samson and Daniel. Perhaps if he'd known Jesus, it would've been enough to save him."

I have no argument I can make. The voice is right. I didn't do enough for him, or for any of 'em. Now, it's too late. I know what Jesus meant when He said His soul was exceeding sorrowful, even unto death. My whole being, heart and soul and mind, groans with regrets.

The end of the day finds us comin' near the fort—too near for my likin', so we turn off the trail and head east for a ways before turnin' back southeast again. The improved weather continues, which is a relief since we're sleepin' under the stars. Blossom and Itowa are even able to dig out some grass with their hooves, and later in the day, we find a stream runnin' south-southeast. Our compass, at last.

But the weather doesn't hold for long. Thick, billowin' clouds build to the west, and an icy wind drives the temperature below freezin' again, sure signs we're in for a blizzard.

"It looks bad." Blossom snorts in agreement. "We've gotta find a place to hole up." My friend, the Crow brave comes to mind. "It's outta the way, girl, but maybe they'd give the Screamin' Red Fox a temporary place to stay durin' the winter. Whaddaya think?" Itowa nickers, urgin' me to decide in a hurry 'cause the clouds are rollin' in above us.

From where we are, I think the Crow are due east or maybe a little northeast, so I turn Blossom away from the settin' sun, and we pick up the pace. It doesn't take long for me to realize how much we've deteriorated since we left our home. None of us have any stamina left. I only hope the Crow settlement isn't too far.

386

Night falls early 'cause of the heavy cloud cover, so I decide to risk ridin' into the night, even though we don't have any stars to follow. We ride as long as I think I can safely push the horses, then hunker down for a few hours in a gully to await the sunrise so we can get our bearin's. Our fire is small and provides little warmth.

The snows begin in earnest overnight. My bundle of furs I use for cover is weighted down with snow and ice when the light finally turns the sky to gray. "We gotta hurry," I urge the horses. "We can't survive out in this another night, and if we get snowed under..."

Snow blinds us as the wind swirls it in our faces and pummels it into our backs. I'm afeared I'm gonna fall off Blossom from the force of the wind, if not from my shiverin'. Each step is a treacherous, laborious slog. I'm also afeared I'll ride right past the Crow camp, not seein' it 'cause of the whiteout. The worst of it is we're hardly movin' forward, and we've gotta ways to go.

The day presses on us like a drainin' hourglass. We're gettin' buried in it. Desperate, I call out in hopes of bein' heard, but the howl of the wind forces my yell into the back of my throat. A surge of hopelessness rises from my gut into my chest, pushin' tears toward my eyes, but they won't leak out in the freezin', whippin' wind.

Itowa stumbles behind me and almost falls, snatchin' on the rope attached to Blossom, but he manages to right himself before we all go down in a heap. The day drags on as the snow continues to worsen. The horses pick their way along, step by tentative step, not knowin' if they're gonna find themselves suddenly on a hillside or slidin' down into a valley.

Blossom lifts her head and looks toward the left. I don't see anything, but I trust my horse, so I let her turn us at an angle and I give her her head. Soon, I catch a faint whiff of smoke—wood burnin', smells like—and my heart starts racin'.

"Good girl." I pat Blossom's neck and urge her forward. A grove of trees pops up to our right out of the blindin' white. I think I recognize where we are from when Mato Waäylo and I rode this way recently. The camp should be beyond the trees, down in a valley near a windin' river. I can't see past the trees, but I push the horses forward on faith that I'm right, that we're almost there, that we're gonna make it.

Once we're past the trees, the smell of smoke becomes more pronounced—still, we can't see a thing, so we have to slow down lest we tumble down the hill as our grand entrance into camp. I try callin' out again, hopin' they have a sentry on post, but I know that's unlikely, and unnecessary, in this weather. Before too long, we find the slope of the hill leadin' us into the valley below, and we make our way down. With each step, the horses' hooves break through several inches of accumulation, so each step sounds like a scrunch, a creak, a thunk, and an icy scrape as with great effort they drag themselves through the piles of snow. At long last, the outline of the first lodge comes into view. We made it.

As we stumble into the desolate camp, I call out the name used by my Crow friend to describe me. "Iáxuhke. Iáxuhke." After a few moments, a few heads pop from their tipis. With great relief, I see the face of my English-speakin' Crow friend. "Iáxuhke," I call and wave my arm, hopin' he can see me through the drivin' snow.

"Iáxuhke?"

"Tahansi!" The word comes out like a long sigh, such is the depth of my relief.

"Why do you come here? Like this?" He ducks from his lodge, grabs Blossom's rope halter, and pulls my little caravan back toward his home. "Come inside. Warm hands. I take care of animals."

"Thank you." Once again, I can barely speak, my words floatin' on the snow like a breath of wind.

"Iáxuhke most crazy man to travel this time. Where Mato Waäylo?"

My reply almost chokes in my throat. "He's dead."

"Most sorrowful. Who defeats the great warrior Mato Waäylo?"

"Mato Waäylo himself."

"Not understanding Iáxuhke."

"Mato Waäylo died by his own hand. Our village was destroyed by the white soldiers while he and I were seekin' to make trade with Crow and others. Mato Waäylo found his wife murdered—hung on a tree. The whole tribe is dead by their hand."

"Iáxuhke say he also has wife and child and soon another."

"They were all killed."

The Crow brave stands, erect and solemn, beside me, not utterin' a word. For some reason, this gesture moves me more strongly than if someone embraced me and told me they were sorry for my loss, and a dam inside me bursts, lettin' forth wave after wave of screamin' wails and gaspin' sobs.

My awareness returns to find me crumpled in a heap on the ground with my Crow friend kneelin' beside me, waitin' with preternatural patience, still and silent as a stone.

"I'm—s—s—sorry." My breath comes in great gulps.

"Come, Iáxuhke. Rest." The Crow helps me to my feet and guides, or mostly carries, me to a pallet of blankets. "Sleep here. Talk later."

The woman I suppose is the Crow's wife sits, wide-eyed, in the corner of the tipi, surrounded by a bevy of squirmin' children. Before he leaves, the Crow brave utters a few words to the woman, who gets up and busies herself preparin' food, her eyes continually trailin' back over to the white man lyin' on her blankets.

I don't know how long I've been asleep when the Crow jostles me. "Food, Iáxuhke. Eat."

The food his wife has prepared includes fry bread, beans, and deer meat with mashed berries. The aroma of it fills the tipi. I'm dizzy with it. But I have to eat slowly, 'cause each bite threatens to come back up. I'm full to explodin' before I finish half of what's before me. My eyes start closin' while I'm still sittin' straight up, but the Crow don't seem offended. The wife gently lowers me back onto the blankets and covers me as I fall into the black hole of dead sleep.

I must've slept through the night, because light filters through the hole in the tipi when I wake. The Crow woman offers me the cold meat, mashed berries, and fry bread left over from last night, which I gobble down like a ravenous wolf. I try to thank her with gestures and the Lakota words, but she stares at me wide-eyed and blinkin', so I simply smile and bow like I've seen the Crow do when meetin' the Lakota.

Soon, the Crow brave returns and gestures to me. "Chief wishes iiwatdío—meet with Iáxuhke. Must clean." He hands me a pair of buckskin breeches and a shirt and points to a basin of water. "Wash. Here."

I cut my eyes to his wife. I s'pose the brave senses my discomfort, because he speaks a few words to her, and with a disgruntled glance at me, she steps from the tipi, with her children and the brave followin' behind her.

I dip my head in the basin and rub tallow in my hair, then rub the tallow on my body. It's quite a relief to wash off the layers of filth. After splashin' myself down and rinsin' my hair, I don my new clothes. I'm fresh, made new, like washin' off the grime has released me from some strange bondage. I'm almost human again.

I pull one of my buffalo pelts around my shoulders and exit the tipi, to find the Crow brave standin' nearby, waitin' for me. He bows slightly and gestures for me to follow. As we walk, my newly restored humanity thinks to ask my companion's name.

"Déaxkaashe."

"Which means what, in white man tongue?"

"Golden Eagle."

I can see that. His skin has a golden bronze sheen to it, like the eagle. "And your wife?"

"Bilápe Daásbahtaache."

"What does her name mean?"

His eyes sparkle. "Um—frown—no, grumpy. Grumpy Beaver."

I can't help but laugh. The sensation of laughter bubblin' up from my chest is foreign to me, and a crushin' wave of guilt washes the feelin' away as fast as it arose. We walk in silence the rest of the way to the chief's tipi.

When we arrive, the chief bids us enter. Golden Eagle introduces me, then translates the chief's words. "Chief say, great sorrow over loss of strong Lakota allies. Loss for all."

"Tell the great chief my deep gratitude. All Lakota respect Crow tahansi."

The two men converse for a few moments, then Golden Eagle glances at me warily. "Chief asks how long Iáxuhke remains with Crow neighbors?"

I sense this question is loaded with unspoken meanin', so I consider my response before speakin'. "Great Chief, your hospitality is unmatched. I would never presume to impose on your kindness and generosity. Due to our shared circumstances, I know the Crow nation suffers as the Lakota from the loss of the buffalo. You also have low food supplies and must provide for your people first. Great Chief, I humbly ask if you would be willing to allow me to hunt, fish, and fight with your great people. On any day I do not bring more than I take, I will not eat. In exchange, I ask only for a place to stay where I am not an imposition. The great chief knows the fame of Iáxuhke as a warrior. I will give my life to protect your great people while I remain, and I promise you, I will leave at the first thaw."

After Golden Eagle translates, he and the chief confer. From their tone and gestures, I can tell Golden Eagle is makin' my case, but the chief seems unconvinced. I understand—one more mouth to feed would've seemed insurmountable for the Lakota durin' our last winter.

"I tell Chief I trust Iáxuhke to keep his word. Iáxuhke man of honor, Mato Waäylo say. Chief sees white man. White man have no honor. Chief does not know Iáxuhke. Does not take word of Lakota brave. But Chief say Iáxuhke dies if goes away from Crow. Bad position for Chief."

"How can I convince the great chief of the strength of my word?"

After a brief exchange with the chief, Golden Eagle raises one brow and looks at me askance. "Chief say Iáxuhke can do nothing to convince chief. Chief say Golden Eagle akíkaawassaakaashe—uh—stand for Iáxuhke, then Golden Eagle responsible for all actions of Iáxuhke and takes punishment for Iáxuhke."

"I will not allow Golden Eagle to take my blame. If I fail, Chief sends me away."

"Chief say it will be as he say, or Iáxuhke leaves now and dies quickly."

The chief doesn't leave me much choice. "I promise you, Golden Eagle, I will be true to my word. Tell the great chief I make him the same promise."

Golden Eagle conveys my words and the chief bows his head slightly. I know enough to bow my head lower than his. The chief turns away, and I recognize I'm bein' dismissed.

Golden Eagle escorts me from the lodge. "Iáxuhke stays with Golden Eagle."

"I appreciate your kindness and hospitality, but Grumpy Beaver will not be pleased. You have many children and no room for Iáxuhke."

"Grumpy Beaver will make room."

I lay my hand gently on Golden Eagle's arm. "Tahansi, if I remain in the home of Golden Eagle, my heart will be broken. Your children remind me of all I have lost. I do not believe I can bear the pain."

Liftin' his brows, Golden Eagle nods and grabs my arm in return. "Then I will find someone without children or wife to offer hospitality to Iáxuhke. Wait in home of Golden Eagle."

"Please do not put anyone out."

Golden Eagle frowns. "Put out? No put someone out of home."

"No, that's a sayin' that means to inconvenience someone."

He smiles. "Ah. No put out." He walks toward a group of tipis and disappears into the first one in the row.

The snow drives me back to the lodge, where I find Grumpy Beaver surrounded by her herd of children, playin' a game together. One of the young bairns grabs my hand to pull me into the game, but my tears well up unbidden, and I shake my head, jerk back my hand, and leave the tipi. I'd rather brave the freezin' cold than face those children. Fortunately, Golden Eagle returns soon.

"Shikáake Káaxte—Boy Who Laughs All the Time—is pleased and proud to have the famous Iáxuhke stay in his tipi. I will show Iáxuhke."

"Let me grab my things." I duck back in the tipi, and under the watchful eye of Grumpy Beaver, who now sees me as a grumpy white man, I'm sure, I gather my meager belongin's.

"Thank you." I pat my belly, then bow low and smile, but I know she doesn't understand.

Golden Eagle leads me to a nearby tipi, where I meet Laughing Boy. I'm interested to know what earned him his name, and it isn't long before I find out. The young brave, probably about the age Grasshopper was when I first met him, is a spirited, exuberant, and according to Golden Eagle, mischievous Crow. I don't know that livin' with Laughing Boy is gonna be any less painful than bein' around Golden Eagle's bairns. Everything here brings up memories of my Lakota home. Since there's nothin' for it, I don't mention my concern to Golden Eagle. He's gone out of his way enough for me.

Laughing Boy knows a few English words, which is helpful, but I know I'm gonna rely heavily on Golden Eagle to let me know what's expected of me. I don't want to do anything wrong, for his sake.

Winter in the Crow camp is a lot like winter for the Lakota—long, dull, monotonous days spent holed up inside the lodge, not seein' anyone but your family—and since I have no family, my days are also lonely. When the snows let up, I join the braves on huntin' expeditions, and thankfully, I'm able to carry my weight. My two rifles come in handy. I promise to leave one of them with the Crow when I move on, as a gift in appreciation for their hospitality.

Despite my best effort to remain aloof, Laughing Boy, Golden Eagle, and I gradually become friends, and the camaraderie between us reminds me of the years with Mato Waäylo and Grasshopper—painfully so. Often, I have to wander off alone while huntin', so agonizin' is our threesome for me. But I can't get away from Laughing Boy when we're together in the tipi, so the empty ache in my heart becomes my constant companion. Occasionally, Golden Eagle will bring one of his bairns by to cheer me up, and sometimes it does—for a while. Then, the weight of my loss bears down on me, and I take to hidin' under my furs for hours on end. Laughing Boy knows to leave me alone on those days.

Most nights, I wake in the dead hours and sit bolt upright—sometimes, I cry out—afeared someone is comin' to attack the camp. The panic runs so deep and is so certain, I have to get up and walk the outskirts of camp, or there'll be no more sleep for me that night. Some of the Crow who've spied me on my late-night treks take to callin' me Alachkapé Ahpaláaxe—Stealthy Walking Spirit. I think I unnerve them.

Other nights, I awaken to find Laughing Boy sittin' beside me on the pallet. To my surprise, I discover tears wettin' my face and blankets. Laughing Boy doesn't joke on those nights, to his credit, choosin' instead to remain quietly by my side and let me weep.

As winter deepens, so does the snowpack, makin' my midnight sojourns more difficult, but I can't make myself stop. I even have to dig my way out of the tipi a time or two, because the snows pile so high it buries us underneath—and still, I'm compelled to go.

Our huntin' trips become more frustratin', too. Game is scarce as hen's teeth, so ice fishin' becomes our focus. What a cold, miserable experience. I'd rather walk a hundred miles in the snow than sit on top of ice and wait for a fish to bite. More times than not, I choose to perch in the trees and watch for any game I can shoot rather than sit on the river and fish. It sure is a blessin' I'm a good shot.

Before I know it, the snows abate, the sun raises the temperatures, and the melt off begins. As I promised, I go to the chief, thank him for his hospitality, offer him one of my rifles, and tell him I'm leavin'. The chief is generous with supplies for the journey—ample food, a change of clothes, and even ammunition for the rifle.

According to Golden Eagle, the chief believes I brought good fortune to the camp, since they fared better than the winter before, largely, he says, because of my skill as a hunter. After I leave the chief with my gratitude, with no small measure of sadness, I bid Golden Eagle and Laughing Boy farewell. Laughing Boy embraces me so hard it squeezes my breath outta my lungs. Golden Eagle is less effusive, but the sadness on his face is unmistakable.

"Will Iáxuhke not consider staying with the people?"

"No, tahansi. I brought grave danger to my tribe. I will not risk bringing the same danger to the Crow, my friends." I place my belongin's on Itowa's back, tie him to Blossom, and with a final wave, we head out toward the south/southeast, followin' the river at Golden Eagle's suggestion.

Our days become a monotony of nothin' but walkin' and sleepin', and I quickly lose count of how long we've been on the trail. Our river eventually dumps into the Missouri, or so I'm told by some settlers I meet on their way to the Montana Territory to look for gold. The Missouri will take us into Nebraska, and then on into Missouri, which is a lot more populated than the Montana Territory or the

Powder River country, so I'll need to stay away from settlements lest someone ask questions I don't wanna answer. Followin' the Missouri, I can cross the Mississippi and head south to Tennessee.

The long-term problem of food blares a worrisome note in the back of my mind. I don't want to use up all my ammunition huntin'—I might need it for more dangerous 'animals' like the white man. I can trap rabbit and catch fish, but those prospects are poor and won't sustain me. Avoidin' settlements might not work after all. At some point, I need to buy some more supplies, and I need money to do it. All I have is my furs to sell or trade, and right now I can't afford to part with 'em, bein' that I'm sleepin' outside. The best I can hope is the weather gets warmer quickly, and as I move farther south, I'll find more game.

'Til I get into the southern states, I still gotta be on my guard against Union soldiers. They might have heard tales of the soldier gone native who abandoned his post, betrayed his unit, and killed his fellow soldiers, and I can't risk them findin' out that's me.

The thought of crossin' the Mississippi brings Mary and her little family to mind, and I remember my promise. Blossom is her horse—Ruth's, actually—and I swore I'd come back with her horse and with Mary's family Bible. It'd be easy to cross Tennessee to North Carolina before headin' home to Georgia. Thinkin' of Mary and the girls brings the tiniest glimmer of hope. Their bright faces. Their laughter like music dancin' on the wind. I have a task—a purpose. I must return Blossom to her owner and give Mary her Bible. To be a man of honor, I must fulfill my oath. After that...well, I don't know after that. But for now, I have a reason to keep on a-goin'.

CHAPTER TWENTY-EIGHT

I reach the Missouri River in a little over three weeks, without seeing another human soul. The trek through Nebraska, parallelin' the Missouri, promises not to be so desolate, which is good for me since I'm gettin' low on food, but also potentially dangerous. I've got to get me a bath and some white man's clothes before I go into any of the towns along the river, where I might be able to trade furs for some food. Otherwise, I'm like as not to be shot as an "Injun"—or a deserter.

The first stream I come to, pourin' its waters into the Missouri, I wander up the stream and out of sight. I build a quick fire before I strip and jump in the stream. The water chills me something fierce, but I bear it long enough to scrub the dirt from my body and hair, then wrap myself in one of my blankets to dry and warm myself by the fire. Blossom and Itowa find some patches of grass beneath the meltin' snow, so I take the opportunity to warm the last of the Crow's beans and a hunk of meat. From now on, it's a steady diet of meat and fish, until I find an outpost or town where I can trade.

The fire soon dies, but I'm a thousand miles away, inside a warm tipi, my arms wrapped around my beautiful wife, watchin' my son play a pretend game of ridin' his stick horse in big circles around the tipi and yellin' at the top of his lungs. It's a day like many others, but it feels as precious to me as if it were a once in a lifetime experience. I don't realize I've dozed off until a shout from around the bend toward the Missouri startles me awake. Blossom snorts a warnin' and paws the ground.

I rise slowly, grab Blossom's rope, and creep deeper into the woods to watch from behind a large tree. The horses stand patiently behind me, perhaps sensin' my tension. The voices from the trail fade in the distance, headin' northwest, away from my direction, so once I can't hear them anymore, I pack up my things, stomp down the ashes, and swing onto Blossom.

"It's time I got presentable, girl—before something bad happens." But once my nervousness returns to the background, I'm left with a renewed melancholy from my dream of home.

It's three days before I run up on a tradin' post near the river. A flat-topped buildin' made of logs and stone, the tradin' post appears empty at the present, so I wrap myself in a buffalo pelt and carry another pelt inside. A solitary man, probably the owner, sits hunkered down by a wood stove in the back. "I want to make a trade." My own voice sounds foreign to me.

"Be right with ya." The old man shuffles up to the front to stand behind the counter. I notice him eyein' my buckskin clothes as he approaches me, so I pull the buffalo hide close around my shoulders. "Whatcha wantin' to trade?"

"I have this fine buffalo pelt. How much will you give me for it?"

"Now, hold on there, son, let me take a look at it first." He runs his fingers through the fur and examines every square inch of the pelt before he speaks again. "Yep, that's buffalo alright. How'd you come by this here fine pelt? You a hunter?"

"Yes, a hunter. How much?"

"Impatient sort, ain't ya. Let's see, now. Ain't much call for buffalo hides round these parts."

"How much?"

He eyes the pelt I have wrapped tightly around my shoulders. "Interested in partin' with that one, too? I'll make ya a good deal."

"No, just the one."

The old man huffs and examines the pelt again. "I dunno. One pelt might be hard to sell."

"Not if they're scarce." I know they're scarce, and I know why. "What's the price?"

"Hmmm." He makes a show of frownin' and fussin' over the pelt as if he's findin' flaws in it. I offer him my best imitation of the stern face Mato Waäylo always made when tradin' with someone, and when the old man glances at me, he shakes his head and sighs. "I'll give ya $3 for it and not a penny more."

"I'll take $5."

"Not a penny more."

So, I shrug my shoulders and turn to walk out the door. He waits until I'm at the door before he calls out to me. "Wait, mister. Fine. $3.50."

"I'll take $5."

"You won't get $5 for it anywheres, not even in Council Bluffs."

"I'll take my chances."

With an angry wave of his hand, the old man turns his back on me, so I walk out the door and start to mount Blossom. As I expected, the old man hobbles out the door. "Mister, you drive a hard bargain, and that's a fact. I'll give ya $4 and that's my final offer. I gotta make a little money on the deal, you know, and you're already pinchin' me out of my profit."

"$4.50."

"That leaves me with no profit. No deal."

"Fine." I grab Blossom's reins.

"Now, wait just a doggone minute. Let me figure." The old man scratches his head as if he's addin' numbers in his head. I doubt he even knows how to add. He heaves a loud, disgruntled sigh. "Fine. $4.50."

We walk back in the post, with him grumblin' the whole way to the back. "Here's your money. Gimme the hide." I hand him the pelt, then walk straight to the stack of clothes along the wall. I pull out a dark red wool shirt, a pair of woolen breeches, and brown suspenders. Then, I pull out the cowboy boots until I find my size. "How much for these items?"

The trader glances at my pile. "$2.75 for the clothes. Them boots'll cost ya $18." I don't have $18, and I need food more than I need nice clothes, so I return the whole pile to the shelves. "Got any used clothes or boots taken in trade?"

"In the back." I follow the old man into the back room, where he has boxes of old used clothes and shoes of all types. "If you can find something that fits ya, I'll make you a good deal."

So, I set out to find me something used that's still in fair shape. I don't need nothin' fancy, but I can't travel into towns lookin' like a native.

After diggin' through all the boxes, I settle on a plain white shirt, a little worn at the collar and elbows but without holes in it, and a pair of dark gray wool pants. I decide to keep my buckskin pants for a spare, knowin' others besides natives wear 'em. And, I find a pair of brown work boots the perfect size—not as nice as the cowboy boots, but functional. I carry my findin's to the counter. "How much for these?"

"I'll sell you the lot for $3."

"You can do better than that. The shirt is worn, and the bottoms of the pants are frayed."

"But them boots is in good shape."

I turn the boots over and point to the worn places on the soles. "They won't last me a whole season."

"Fine, $2.50."

"How much you give me for this authentic Indian top?" I loosen the pelt from my shoulders. "Settlers might give a pretty penny for something like this. Or maybe you could sell it to some natives?"

"Naw. No interest in Indian goods here."

"Couldn't you use this fine buckskin for something?"

The old man slams his hand on the counter, and I can tell I've pressed him as far as he's willin' to go. "Do you want the clothes or don't ya?"

"Yessir, I do." I count out $2.50 from my newly acquired funds and plop it on the counter. "I need some supplies, too. How far to Council Bluffs?"

"On horseback it'll take you about ten- or eleven-days steady travel."

I know I can count on weather slowin' me some, so I plan on two weeks of food to add to the meat I already have. After lookin' over the choices, I settle on canned beans and dried fruit to supplement my diet. It costs me another $1.50. "Thank you, sir."

He grunts in reply as he shuffles back to his place by the stove. I take my packages, add the food to the pack on Itowa's back, then duck behind the buildin' to change into my new—well, used—clothes. I shove my buckskins in the pack and head on my way, feelin' much more at ease on the trail now that I look less like a native and more like a trapper returnin' from the hunt.

As I figured, the clear weather doesn't hold, and we're forced to wait out a spring snowstorm for three days under a lean-to of pelts against a saplin'. But, when we get goin' again, we make good time, and we ride into Council Bluffs less than two weeks after we left the tradin' post.

With fifty cents to my name and needin' supplies for a long stretch on the road, I figure I need to find me some kinda work to earn some money, so I inquire 'round, and the shop keep sends me to the blacksmith. "Hello, sir. I wonder, do you need anyone to help you for a spell? I'm passin' through and lookin' for work."

"You ever smithed before?"

"Nosir."

"It'd take me longer to teach you than to do it myself. But Bart over at the stables needs a hand."

I thank the man for his time and move on to the stables. "Hello. The blacksmith sent me over, said you might need a hand for a spell."

"We got lots of folk passin' through, with springtime upon us. Lots of folk headin' for gold in Montana."

An unexpected flood of seethin' rage bubbles in my belly. These 'folk' are the reason my people...don't go there. I can't think about that. Nothin' I can do about it anyway. "Yessir."

"I sure can use a hand. How long you here for?"

"I'm goin' back to my home, but I need supplies before I set out on the long journey. And I need money to get supplies. So, however long it takes me to save enough money to get the supplies I need?"

"You look like a strong buck, so if you'll muck out the stables and rub down and feed the horses, I'll pay you $1.75 a day for your labor."

"Thank you, sir."

"Where are you staying?"

"Oh, I'll sleep outside. I'm used to it, bein' on the trail."

"Nonsense! You can sleep in the stables. At least it's a roof over your head."

"You're sure it isn't an inconvenience?"

"Of course not. In fact, it helps, you being here to keep an eye on things and make sure the horses are taken care of overnight."

"Thank you, sir. That's most kind."

He sticks out his hand. "Bartholomew Stone, at your service. Most folks around here call me Bart."

I grasp his hand, but my words stick in my throat. What name do I give him? Certainly not Sungila Sá or Iáxuhke, and not Aidan MacAlister, either—what if a U. S. cavalry unit came through and someone mentioned my name? Mr. Stone raises his brows. Before I realize it, I'm speaking. "Murphy. Martin Murphy."

"Nice to meet you, Martin Murphy."

"Well met, Mr. Stone."

He claps my back. "Now, none of that Mr. Stone. You call me Bart."

"Very well, Bart. Thank you again for your kindness."

Bart smiles and hands me a shovel. "Might as well get started."

Through the spring months, I settle into a routine, mannin' the stables for Bart all day and sleepin' in the stable with the horses at night. I relish the solitude. Bart handles the customers when someone comes in to stable their horse. My entire interaction involves takin' their horse's reins. They don't have any desire to talk to a stable hand, and I have no desire to get to know them. The same holds true for most of the townfolk.

All I see when they walk past me is the reason my beloved wife and son are dead. If my tribe had been left in peace and allowed to live their lives on their own land as they saw fit, their slaughter would never have happened. That's all they wanted, to be left in peace. How is that wrong? Why does the white man believe he has the right to take what isn't his? Isn't that what's wrong? Doesn't the Good Book specifically command, "Thou shalt not steal"? I vow I'll never forgive the wasicu for what they've done, and the bubble of outrage coalesces into stone encasin' my heart. May they all rot in the deepest hole in hell.

I enjoy the company of the horses more than people anyway. The horses are content to leave me alone with my thoughts.

On Sundays, however, Mrs. Stone insists I come to their church and eat Sunday dinner with their family. I must admit, it's nice to have a good, home-cooked meal. It reminds me of Ma. But I'm right uncomfortable comin' into their home and sittin' down to eat with the white folk and their children, all six of 'em, little steppin' stones that they are. The young'uns want me to play with 'em, but I can't make myself do it. It hurts too much. Mrs. Stone asks me sometimes why someone so young is so serious and glum. I don't have an answer I'm willin' to give.

Church, on the other hand, is a torture for me. My rage and shame pound in my ears like a beatin' heart. The faces of my tribe float before me in an endless parade of failures, regrets, and blame. And when the pastor preaches on forgiveness or suffer the little children, I slip out the door as quickly and quietly as I can, so I don't break down in front of the whole town. On those days, I make my apologies to Mrs. Stone and return to my comfortable aloneness to start dreadin' the next Sunday.

By the comin' of May, I have saved $57—a small fortune. I'm able to buy another set of clothes, new this time, ammunition for my rifle, a wide-brimmed hat, and enough food to pack on Itowa to last the five or six months left on my journey to return Blossom to Mary and her girls, and I still have some money to spare. So, I thank Mr. and Mrs. Stone and take my leave of Council Bluffs. It's not lost on me that I feel nothing at all as I ride away.

I follow the Missouri all the way to Kansas, Missouri, and from there, I pick up the trail to St. Louis. Where my journey has been solitary before, now the trail is fair teemin' with wasicu headin' west. Dark clouds build in my chest, and storms brew and erupt in thunderous fury. The peltin' rains water the coverin' over my heart, and it grows into a prickly vine, twisted and constrictin', infiltratin' every inch of me until I'm squeezed down into a pit and chokin' on the darkness. And the next day, the squalls return, fiercer and angrier than the day before.

Fortunately, something about me repels the settlers, and I don't have to deal with them approachin' me for conversation or help. It's a good thing for them, too, for I'm capable of murder, given half a chance. Bitter hatred becomes my travelin' companion and my bedfellow. By the time I reach the Mississippi, I'm a blackened shell, and all that was human in me is consumed.

At the crowded shore, most ferry boats arrivin' are filled to capacity. I've no interest in standin' elbow to elbow with a bunch of chatterin' wasicu, but I'm forced to negotiate passage for myself and my horses with the white man captainin' the largest ferry on the river. At least he's as sullen and noncommunicative as I am. I stand in silence as he steams across through thick fog and lowerin' clouds that match my mood. The swoosh and slap of the water against the bottom of the ferry lull me into a daze. Before I know it, we've reached the eastern shore.

Over the next few weeks, I cross through southern Illinois farmland into Kentucky and on into Tennessee. I stop at a handful of farms along the way and work as a hand for a few days to replenish my meager funds, which slows my progress some, but I still think I can make North Carolina before autumn turns to winter. I take some solace from returnin' to the south, even though it isn't the south I left behind anymore. Most places I stop can't afford to pay me anything, so I move on. I can tell they're starvin', and it stirs my memories of the terrible winter watchin' Flowing Spring and Spirit of Black Horse wither away. The hollow ache in my heart becomes a continuous throbbin', piercin' pain.

The journey across Tennessee into North Carolina carries the bitter-sweetness of remindin' me of home—the rollin' hills, the distant blue range, the fog flowin' through the valleys on cool mornin's, the start of the turnin' of the leaves. It reminds me of a Scripture about beauty for ashes—but for me it isn't an exchange of one for the other. I can taste both in my mouth.

All the pain. All the loss. What possible good could come from the shreddin' of a man's soul, the gougin' of everything out of a man's life? I know the words—the oil of joy for mourning, the garment of praise for the spirit of heaviness. I know the promise—all things work together for good to them that love God. Not for me, I guess. Not for me.

Late October finds me near the Tennessee-North Carolina border. If I make my way due east to Asheville, Hendersonville isn't far away. A few days more, and my task will be complete. But a growin' shadow in my mind echoes like a distant bell, ringin' nearer the closer I get to Hendersonville. It foretells an end. In its wake, I see the vast, gray nothingness beyond the day I deliver the horse and Bible to Mary's door. They are church bells announcin' a funeral procession. Blossom seems to slow her pace as we leave Asheville for the final leg of the journey, almost as if she senses these few days are our last.

Ridin' into Hendersonville brings yet another reminder of the poverty throughout the south since the war. Burned buildings still aren't rebuilt. Businesses are boarded up. Women wear dresses ragged along the bottoms and cuffs of the sleeves, children are in clothes at least a size too small for them, and menfolk appear to be few and far between.

I remember how to get to Mary's cousin's house—Marcus, was it? And Aunt Caroline, I think. I take the windin' trail up the hill to the house atop the ridge. It looks a good bit more run-down than when last I saw it. Still, it's in better shape than most of the houses around these parts, those that are still occupied.

With much urgin' on my part, Blossom drags me up to the front steps. The shadow spreads like ink poured in water until my whole soul is black with it. A rap on the door. A long wait. A harsh voice in the distance.

"Who's there?"

I realize I don't know the answer to the man's barked question. Who stands at his door? A stranger to the occupants, certainly—they won't recognize me. Mac is long dead. So, I say the only thing I can think of in the moment. "I'm here to see Mary Monroe."

"She isn't here."

"When will she be back?"

"She isn't coming back. She doesn't live here anymore. Go away."

I don't know why it never crossed my mind once that Mary might've left her cousin's house, but it didn't. Now what? "Where did she go? I have something of hers."

"She moved to Wilmington, and she took everything she had with her. Now get on out of here. We don't have anything for you." I think I hear the distinctive click of a handgun's hammer, so I walk back down the steps, mount Blossom, and wind back down the trail. Blossom's footfalls are lighter, like she senses a reprieve. I, too, feel a strange sense of momentary light in the growin' pitch darkness. My purpose is not yet complete. I have one more stop to make. Wilmington. Where in the world is that?

I figure someone in town will know the direction I need to go, so I head back to the general store and ask the man behind the counter for directions. He pulls out a piece of scrap paper and etches a black line almost due east from Hendersonville.

"Head east to Charlotte then southeast along the border to get to Wilmington."

"Is there a roadway?"

The man sneers. "There's a trail of sorts. It'll take you probably three weeks or so to make the trip. You need supplies?"

I do, but I have very little money left. So, I thank the man, take his scrap of paper, and head out of town on the road due east. Hopefully, I can find some temporary work along the trail.

The shop keep wasn't jokin' when he called it a trail of sorts. Ill-used and poorly maintained, if at all, the trail ain't much different than walkin' through the woods, but Blossom, Itowa, and I make our way along at a fair pace. The good news is there's plenty of grass on the trail and water all along it, so at least the horses are well-fed and watered. Work is scarce, though. Folks is real nervous about strangers in these parts, and I don't much blame 'em.

I make it to Charlotte in a week's time. It's a decent sized town, seemin' to fare better than Hendersonville after the war. Needin' money for food, I try the stables, but they don't need any help. Same for the blacksmith. I check at a warehouse to see if I could load goods, but they turn me away. The man at the dry goods store doesn't need someone to stock, and he eyes me suspiciously when I ask if I can help man the register, so I move on. Finally, I ask the grocer if I can sweep up and stock shelves in exchange for some food, but he declines, although he seems more sympathetic than the others.

There's nothin' for it. I spend my last few coins to get as much food as I can, which will have to last me all the way to Wilmington—at least two more weeks. It won't be enough.

"Here you go, boy. That's the lot of it." I pack Itowa with the meager supplies, and we follow the road the grocer says leads to Wilmington.

After several days on the rough trail, I camp a while to hunt for game, but out of the blue, I become a clumsy flatlander, crashin' through the brush with no sense of what I'm doin', so I have no success. The weather's gettin' colder, especially at night. Since I didn't plan on these extra weeks, I have no gloves or other cold weather gear, only the buffalo hides I use for my lean-to. It seems every which way I turn, I run into another obstacle I can't overcome, another barrier I can't climb. My mind is as frozen as my fingers—solutions for the simplest problems evade me. Hunger gnaws at me like a hive of hornets has taken up residence in my belly, and when I check my pack, I realize as if out of a fog that somewhere along the way, I ate up my whole supply of food without thought to the rest of the journey. What's wrong with me? But the fog descends on me again before I can think of an answer.

I usually wake with the sun, but these days, I find the sun is climbin' toward its peak when I finally crawl outta my makeshift tent, and I'm exhausted before the sun touches the horizon, asleep before I hit the ground. On the days that follow, when I try to get up, my head spins so much I gotta lie back down before I fall faint. Is this dizziness from hunger? I can't tell anymore. The hornets have left my belly and covered my limbs, mouth, and ears.

"Are you well, son?" A distant, hollow voice, as if spoken through a speakin' trumpet, rouses me from my stupor. I'm vaguely aware that I'm half-in and half-out of my lean-to. How long have I been lyin' here? I feel a hand on my back, then one touchin' my head, ice-cold yet soft to the touch.

"He's burning up."

"Help me carry him to the wagon. Johnny, collect his horses and tie them to the wagon."

"Yessir."

"What if he's dangerous?"

"He's not going to hurt anyone in this condition. The man is barely alive."

"But, John..."

"We can't leave him here to die. It wouldn't be Christian."

I try to speak, but nothin' comes out but a croak. I can feel myself liftin' off the packed dirt, a jostled, awkward carry, then I plop onto boards...and darkness consumes me.

A round-faced woman with light brown curls as a halo shoves water in my mouth. I choke and cough and spit, but she pours more in me. Then, she spoons in some foul-tastin' bitter concoction and covers my mouth with her hand to keep me from spittin' it out. Darkness descends again.

My next awareness is a boy's voice.

"He's awake."

"See if you can get from him where he's headed."

"Mister, where are you going?"

I feel around with blind fingers for my pack, but it isn't where it should be—then I remember. They took me from my campsite and put me in their wagon. A well of panic rises in my chest. Mary's Bible. "Pack?"

"We have it, don't worry. And your other supplies. They're all here."

I breathe a sigh of relief, which ends in a coughin' fit.

"You need to rest. You're very ill."

"Thank...you." My words sound like gravel under a wagon wheel.

"Can you tell us where you are going?"

"Wil...ming...ton." My breath won't go deep into my chest. Strange feelin'.

"We're going there. We will take you the rest of the way. You need doctoring, but we don't know where to find a doctor until we get to town. We'll keep you warm, at least."

"No...trouble."

"Don't worry. It's not out of our way at all."

A voice calls from the front of the wagon. "Margaret, ask him if he can eat."

I don't know how to answer their question. Half of me is ravenous, but half of me sickens at the thought of food. I decide to reach for a middle ground. "Broth?"

"John, he's asking for broth. That's a good idea, I think."

"When we stop for the night, then."

I want to reach into my throat and pull the guck cloggin' it out with my fingers, but in some still-rational part of my brain, I know it won't work. It's like I'm breathin' through water thick with mud. The strange buzzin' returns, and the now-familiar darkness creeps in on the edges of my eyes.

The next thing I know, she's ladlin' in more of that bitter, foul liquid. It burns my throat, which in a strange way is sorta soothin'. I become aware of other people in the wagon besides—what was her name? Mary? No, I'm goin' to see Mary. "What...your name?"

"Margaret Willoughby. My husband is John Willoughby. This is our boy, Johnny, and our daughter, Emily Ann. And you?"

"Martin. Murphy."

"Nice to meet you, Martin."

"Horses?"

"They're followin' behind the wagon. Don't you worry. We took care of everything."

"Thank you."

"We'll be stopping soon for the night. I will fix you some nice, warm broth. How does that sound?"

"Good, ma'am."

Another coughin' fit seizes me, and she pats my hand until it passes. "There, now, you have to rest. Don't try to talk. Really, now. No wonder you got sick, sleeping out in the cold like that. Tsk tsk."

The broth does seem to help. I can even feel my stomach grumblin' for some real food, but to be cautious, I don't mention anything to Margaret. She wraps me in my furs and lets me share their wagon for the night. It's a tight fit, with all of us inside it, but we manage.

When I wake up, I feel a swell of gratitude for these kind people who are goin' out of their way to help a stranger. The unfamiliar feelin' washes away some of the bitterness and loosens the prickly tendrils snakin' through my heart, for the first time in a long while.

Hope peeks up like the first rays of a new sunrise, and I fight the urge to shove it back down lest it be dashed again on the rocks. I'd all but forgotten that kindness still exists in this world—yet, here it is, in the shape of Margaret and John Willoughby.

Emily Ann looks to be about ten or eleven, and the thought comes to me that she may know Mary's youngest daughter, if they happen to go to school together. That would be almost beyond coincidence, if the Willoughby's know Mary and her children—but my fear of disappointment smothers my tentative grasp on hope and silences my tongue.

More bitter medicine, and more broth, with a biscuit to sop it up is my breakfast. I keep the biscuit down, but my fever remains, so Margaret won't let me walk around outside the wagon, even though I do feel better. "You don't fan around with a fever," she admonishes.

"Yes, ma'am."

Later in the day, a fit of sweats comes over me, and I waver in and out of consciousness. Each time awareness returns to me, I find Margaret bathin' me down with cold water and little Emily Ann sittin' beside me, strokin' my hand, but I can't feel their touch. Instead, I'm watchin' the scene from above the wagon, like I'm an angel on a cloud with magical eyes to see through the wagon bonnet and observe their lovin' care.

My eyes open to daylight. I'm alone in the wagon, but I hear the rustle of the family outside, preparin' for the day's journey. Margaret sticks her head in and smiles. "Your fever broke last night. You're on the mend."

I struggle to sit up, but her stern look and waggin' finger stops me. "Don't you start fanning around. You still need your rest. I'm fixing a good breakfast for us. Do you feel like eating?"

"Yes, ma'am."

"Eggs and bacon and biscuits. Does that sound good?"

"It does, ma'am."

"Now, you sit tight. I'll bring your meal to you."

"I don't want to be any more bother, ma'am. I can collect my things and..."

"We won't hear of it. John Willoughby won't allow it. You're riding with us to Wilmington, and that's final."

Under Margaret's watchful eye and care, I recover nicely. Within a week, I'm almost myself again, and I'm able to start helpin' John and Johnny with hitchin' up the horses, collectin' the wood, and buildin' the fires. They tell me stories of their journey together to Pennsylvania to visit John's family, and the sites they've seen along the way, and how much they miss their home.

Durin' one of those evenin' story times, I build up my courage enough to ask Emily Ann the question burnin' in my heart. "By any chance, do you know a young woman, about your age, name of Elizabeth Monroe? She lives in Wilmington."

Exclamations hit me from all sides. "Mary Monroe is one of my dearest friends!"

"I know Elizabeth! We play together all the time!"

"Mary lives down the way from us, near the water. Johnny and I look in on her from time to time, to help her with heavy chores around the house."

"How do you know Mary?"

Talkin' about Mary is harder than I thought it'd be. "Mary cared for me when I was wounded durin' the war, when she lived in Richmond. I helped her escape the Richmond fire and brought her to Hendersonville to her cousin and aunt."

"That was you? We've heard the tale. Mac, she called you. Is that a nickname?"

I'm oddly embarrassed, now that they know my real—former—name, like I've lied to them, and they caught me out. "Yes, ma'am. That's what the girls called me. Mac."

John shakes his head. "What an amazing coincidence. What are the odds we'd run up on the person who saved Mary's life, and that we'd turn around and save his life? I see the hand of God at work in this!"

Margaret beams. "You are so right, John Willoughby. Amen."

I mutter a quick, "Amen" under my breath, but I can't meet their eyes. If they knew some of the thoughts I've had toward God, or some of the things I've done against His commandments, they'd spurn me like everyone else. I decide then and there, I can't taint these good people with my filth. But now that I know they know Mary, how can I get away from them? Even if I were to leave them and ride on ahead, they'd come see Mary once they get home—and there I'd be.

Until that moment, it hasn't crossed my mind that in comin' to Mary, I'll bring my evil with me. I couldn't bear to see her touched by such darkness, her beauty and kindness stained by my presence. Death follows me wherever I go. I don't want to bring my demon to her home. Perhaps the Willoughbys would be willin' to take Mary's Bible and Blossom to her for me?

411

At this thought, the shadow creeps back in on me, and my chest clutches, as if the congestion is comin' back full force. I can't speak. I can barely breathe.

"What's wrong, Martin?" When I look up, Margaret's eyes probe me, her brows pinched over her nose.

My head swirls. Too many feelings. I must push them back down, before. . . I try to stand, but a wave of dizziness makes me wobble and sends me to my hands and knees next to the fire.

"Now, see there. You aren't fully recovered. John Willoughby, you worked the boy too hard too soon. Here, help him back to the wagon."

"No. I'm—well. Really, I am. I'm fine." My own voice sounds a million miles away.

"You need your rest."

"Yes, ma'am." I'm thankful I have the excuse of my recent illness to explain away my strange behavior. Johnny helps me to my feet, and I weave my way back to the wagon, where I can collect myself and once again hide from their discernin' eyes.

A long sleep helps me feel oriented again. I rise before the dawn to prepare the fire and begin the breakfast meal preparation. Mrs. Willoughby bustles out of the wagon soon after, tskin' me for workin' too hard and quickly takin' over the cookin' duties. I find I'm able to joke around with her, which seems to put her mind at ease.

We make an early start, and John tells me he thinks we'll make Wilmington around dusk. A strange combination of excited anticipation, terror, and deep heaviness of spirit roil in my gut. Today is the day I will know if I'm beyond redemption, or if hope can be found once again in the form of a widow from Richmond.

CHAPTER TWENTY-NINE

The Willoughbys drive their wagon directly to Mary's home, a beautiful whitewashed two-story near the water, with clapboard siding and a large porch wrappin' around it. The similarity to her former home in Richmond isn't lost on me—only the scale is smaller.

I turn to thank the Willoughbys for their generosity and help, but John is hoppin' down to tie up his horses and Margaret is directin' her children to jump down and come up the front walk with me. In my mind, I picture greeting Mary and her girls alone—seein' their faces, watchin' their reactions, sensin' their feelin's—just in case they don't want me there, as I half-expect. With the Willoughbys in tow, Mary will be forced to welcome me with open arms, no matter how she feels. This isn't the scene I hoped for. But what can I say? I owe the Willoughbys my life.

Margaret, Johnny, and Emily Ann beat me to the front door and knock heartily. Margaret doesn't wait for Mary to answer the door, callin' out to her. "Mary. It's Margaret. Margaret Willoughby."

Within seconds, the door flings open. "Margaret Willoughby!" Her eyes scan the little group gathered on her doorstep. "How nice to..." When her eyes brush past the thin, ragged young man standin' behind Emily Ann, one eyebrow quirks down.

"Look who we found." Margaret's eyes sparkle, relishin' her surprise, as she shoves me in Mary's face.

Mary takes a step back and stares at me. I count my racin' heartbeats, as seconds tick by. Then, her eyes widen, her mouth falls open with a whispered, "Oh," and her hands flutter like butterfly wings until they find her lips.

"He was lying beside the trail, almost dead, mind you. John and I nursed him back to life and brought him to you. Can you imagine the coincidence?"

John ambles up the walk behind us. "Not a coincidence. The hand of God at work, I tell you. Divine providence."

Mary finally chokes out, "Mac?"

413

I don't have words, so I nod and try to smile, but my chin drops to my chest against my will.

Before Mary can speak again, Margaret links arms with her and drags her into the foyer, still chatterin' away. "He was fevered and out of his mind. John said we can't leave him, it wouldn't be Christian, so we took him into our wagon, gave him what medicine we had, and hoped for the best. And here he is! He told us he was coming to find you."

Mary tries to crank her head around toward me as Margaret whisks her away, her mouth still hangin' slack as she disappears around the corner. She doesn't look a day older than when I left them in Hendersonville, standin' on the stoop of her aunt's home, wavin', still as elegant as ever.

As I follow the two women into the foyer, I catch a glimpse of myself in the gilded mirror hangin' on the wall, and it brings me up short. No wonder she didn't recognize me at first. I don't know the hooded eyes starin' back at me from the man with the gaunt, bearded face and skeletal body. What type of grotesque creature have I brought into her lovely home? The walls of the foyer curve and fold toward me— the ceilin' bends and lowers. I close my eyes against the oppression of the room and the horror of my own visage and make my way in the direction Margaret whisked Mary away.

My steps are as wooden as the broad-planked floor when I enter the sittin' room. I hear Margaret still regalin' Mary with tales from the trail from Pennsylvania to North Carolina. Mary bids me sit with them while Margaret's rapid speech doesn't miss a beat. The clackin' noise sends me reelin'.

As a strange pressure builds behind my eyes, the shadow creeps back over my vision, taking on form and substance, with hollow, empty eyes of its own starin' at me. The shadow screeches, "you shouldn't be here," and panic swallows me under, as if I'm drownin' in a lake of fear. I sense the two children walk in behind me, trappin' me in the doorway. Without thought, I turn and shove my way past them, and run headlong into John.

"Whoa, there, what's this?" John grabs my shoulders. "Martin?"

I can't bear it—he's holdin' me under. Doesn't he know I can't breathe? "Let me go," hisses from my lips, but it's the shadow speakin'.

John releases me like he's lettin' go of a hot coal, and I bolt out of the room and through the front door, down the steps and walkway to Blossom's side. I want to climb on her, to race as far away from here as I can, but she's no longer my horse, so instead, I bury my face in her mane and wrap my arms around her neck.

Light, slow steps pad up behind me. "Mac. It's Mary." Her gentle touch brushes against my back. "I'm here."

Tears spring in my eyes. All I can think to say is, "I'm sorry."

"You have no reason to apologize to me. I am just glad you are home."

Home. I try to breathe in that word. It's air to help pull me to the surface.

John Willoughby's voice slices through the moment. "Margaret dear, let's allow these old friends to get reacquainted. A pleasure to see you, Mary." Obviously, the whole lot of them are standin' on the walk, starin' at me, oglin' me as I fall apart. I shrink back down into the abyss and burrow deeper into Blossom's mane.

Mary's sigh sounds like relief, but she protests weakly. "You don't have to go so soon?"

"We need to get home before it gets dark, or we'll never get everything put away. Come along, Margaret."

Flustered, Margaret huffs at her husband. "Mary, we'll talk soon," she croons, then practically stomps her feet as she walks toward their wagon.

"Good evening, Miss Mary. Martin."

"Good evening, Johnny. Emily Ann, will you come back soon so you and the girls can spend some time at the beach?"

"Yes, ma'am. I'd love that." Emily Ann's bright voice sends tendrils of warmth into the depths, beckonin' me back into the light.

John leans near my ear. "I'll tie your horses to the hitching post for you."

That means I have to relinquish my death grip on Blossom. Mary takes my arm, and with her other hand still on my back, she pulls me gently back from the horse. John makes quick work on untyin' Blossom and Itowa from his wagon and retyin' them to the post.

Almost too late, I find my voice. "John. Thank you. For everything." I reach for his hand, with my eyes still glued to the ground.

He grasps my offered hand. "You are most welcome. Have a nice visit." As he leaves, I hear him mutter, "Amazing. Just amazing." And with that, I'm alone with Mary, at last.

When I finally manage to raise my eyes, I'm startled to see she's weepin'.

"Oh, my goodness gracious. Mac? We never thought we'd see you again. It's been—how long? Oh, my." She enfolds me in her arms. "My dear, dear boy." After a spell, she holds me out at arm's length and looks me up and down. "Tell me what happened."

"It's a long story." I sound like a croakin' frog.

"Well, come in and sit and tell me everything. I am so glad you are here! You have no idea. The girls are going to be beside themselves."

"Where are they?"

"They spent the afternoon walking on the beach. They should be home anytime now."

"I brought Blossom back. She's safe. And your Bible."

"I see you did, but Mac, you didn't have to do that. I told you, those were gifts."

Tears well in my eyes. "I wouldn't've made it without them."

Mary gathers my hands in hers, sensitive enough not to press me for an explanation as we walk back into her home.

After I choke the tears back down, I continue. "Blossom and your Bible kept me alive, in more ways than I can say."

We sit in silence for a spell, the kind of quiet that calms a man and gives him peace. Finally, I stand. "Let me go get your Bible from my saddlebag. That's why I came here, to return it to you—and to give Blossom back to Ruth."

"Ruth isn't here, Mac."

"Not here?"

"She married, over a year ago. They moved back to Virginia."

Suddenly, my legs won't seem to hold me anymore. Before I think, I murmur, "So far," and plop back down into the chair.

"If you are thinking of returning Blossom to her, I won't hear of it. Ruth wanted you to have her."

"I made a promise."

"And you have more than kept it. You're here! That is what they—we—all wanted, for you to come back to us."

"But..."

"Enough said. Now, I think long stories can wait for a while. You could use a nice, warm bath and a good, long rest. I will send one of the girls to get you when supper is on the table."

I squirm uncomfortably in my seat. "I really don't want to impose."

"Nonsense, young man. You are not an imposition. I am thrilled to see you, and the girls will be as well. Into the kitchen with you. I'll show you where it is. Do you have a change of clothes?"

I do, but they're filthier than the ones I have on, so I shake my head.

"Very well. We will make arrangements. Do not concern yourself." She claps her hands like an excited child. "Oh, what a wonderful surprise for the girls when they get home."

I follow her like a dutiful dog into the kitchen. She pulls a towel from a shelf and hands it to me. "Take off those clothes and wrap this around you. We will get you some hot water."

"Cold water's fine. I've been bathin' in streams."

"All the more reason for a nice, hot bath." She opens the pantry and slides the tub out into the kitchen. "I will be back shortly."

"Yes'm."

I'm mortified she's gonna see me half-naked like this, lookin' more the scarecrow than a man. For something to do, I fold my nasty, ragged clothes and lay them in a pile on the floor. Then, I stand there wrapped in the towel, awkward and miserable, waitin' for her to return and draw the water.

But when the door opens, it's a round, dark-skinned woman with a massive bosom and frizzy, gray hair who waddles in with a large bucket.

"Miss Mary'll be back soon." She fills her bucket with water at the pump and dumps the bucket into the tub.

This is even worse than Mary seein' me. The old woman eyes my bony ribs and shakes her head. "Whose been feedin' ye, boy?"

"No one."

"'Pears so." She chuckles, a deep, resonant rumble in her chest, and I can't help but smile. She pumps another bucketful and adds it to the tub. Then, she fills a large pot and sets it on the stove. When the pot is boilin', she pours it into the tub. "Get in quick 'fore the warmth gets away from ye." She ducks out of the room.

I drop the towel and step into the tub. The heat makes me tingle all over as I slip down until the water covers my head. Mary left soap sittin' on the edge of the tub in a little porcelain dish, but I try to scrub most of the dirt off me before I use it, lest I taint the soap.

I must admit, Mary's right. It feels quite good—relaxin'. My eyes are saggin' and blinkin' a lot, so before I fall dead asleep and drown myself, I scrub the soap from head to toe, rinse off, and towel down. When I step out, the water is a dull brown. I'm not sure what to do then, so I wrap the towel back around my waist and call through the door, "I'm done."

The old woman reenters and plants her meaty hands on her broad hips. "Lawdy, boy, you's a mess." I don't disagree. "Miss Mary'll be back shortly, went to get ye some clothes from a neighbor."

I groan. "I don't want to be any trouble. I can wear my own clothes."

"Lawdy, naw. Ye just got clean." She gathers up my filthy clothes with distaste. "I'll be a-washin' these right now. Miss Mary'll bring ye yer clothes."

Mary returns soon after. She eyes my pronounced ribs and concave belly, concern etched on her brow, but her grace won't let her mention my state. "I see you've met Willie. She's a freed slave who came to us looking for work. She's a treasure. She loves the girls, and they love her." She hands me a fresh pressed white shirt, a pair of black trousers, long johns, socks, and suspenders. "Here, put these on."

"Ma'am, I can't take…"

"Since when do you call me 'ma'am'? Mary will do nicely. And I don't want to hear another word. My friend was happy to lend you something until we can go to town and buy you some proper clothing.

Put them on, now." She pats my hand. "The girls will be back very soon, and they will want to see you. In the meantime, you can rest upstairs." She turns her back and walks out, leavin' me standin' there with another man's clothes, feelin' like a poor beggar. My shame is complete.

The clothes swallow me, but they provide good coverage, and the suspenders hold up the pants. Once I'm dressed, I pad my way in stockin' feet up the stairs.

Mary calls to me from the sittin' room. "Ruth's old bedroom is the last one on the right. You may lie down in there. One of the girls will get you for dinner."

I peel back the frilly coverlet with care and slide onto the cool, silky white sheets. It reminds me of slidin' on a stream of water flowin' over a slick rock, except the rock feels like a billowin' cloud. I've never felt anything quite like it. I set my mind to thinkin' what I'm gonna tell Mary and the girls about the last five years, but the next thing I know, I hear a tap on the door, and Ester sticks her head in.

Except it isn't Ester, it's little Elizabeth, all growed up. Her long, golden curls bounce as she squeals with delight and bounds into the room. "Mac!" She hops on the bed.

"Elizabeth?"

She feigns a frown. "Where have you been? You were supposed to come back to us before now. And now, Ruth is gone. She's going to be so upset."

"It couldn't be helped. I came as soon as I could."

A beamin' smile brightens her face. "Well, the main thing is you're here, and this time, you'll stay with us forever and ever."

"Uh, I..."

"You will. Mother said so." She giggles and pulls my hand. "Come on. Dinner is ready, and Mother says you need to eat."

Elizabeth drags me down the stairs and into the dining room. The table is overfilled, laden with every kind of dish I've ever said I liked, includin' three pies. Elizabeth leans close to me and points to the pies. "Cherry, Blackberry, and Apple Streusel, your favorite. And we even have ice cream to go on top of it."

"Uh—what—what's ice cream?"

"You'll see."

I stand in the doorway, gawkin' at the table, and I can't seem to make my legs move. Elizabeth skips around to her seat. It's then I notice Ester.

She stands at the china cabinet, her back to me. She's not quite as tall as Ruth was when I left. Her blonde hair falls almost to her waist. When she turns and sees me, her blue eyes light up, shimmerin' like reflections from the sun. Always the quiet one of the lot, Ester doesn't speak a greeting, but she gazes at me as if I'm a messenger of the Lord come to bring good news. Her face is fair aglow with rapture. After we stare at each other a good while, I find my voice. "Hello, Ester."

"Hello, Mac." Her voice is a whispered wind.

"It's mighty fine to see you."

"And you." No questions, no frownin' examinations of my wasted body, no superficial chatter, just pure, unadulterated joy. She's not as stately as Ruth, or as elegant, but she has a simplicity and peace to her, and a pure radiance that reminds me of Flowing Spring. A fierce pang of guilt slices through me at the thought, and I lower my eyes.

Mary clears her throat. "Won't you join us?" She gestures to a chair to her left, across from Ester. So, I'm gonna have to sit across from her, a constant reminder of my Flowing Spring. How can I bear it? I study the wide planks of the wood floor the whole way to my seat.

At first, Mary graciously makes small talk and steers the conversation away from the questions I'm sure are burnin' in the three of 'em about what happened to me for the last five years. I stare into my plate, eatin' slowly lest the food come back up. Mary keeps heapin' more on my plate each time I make a dent in the piles. "Willie will be offended if you don't finish it all."

Elizabeth prattles on about their walk on the beach, the shells they found, the people they spoke to, the horses they saw. "Mac brought Blossom back. We saw her outside when we came home. And he has another horse, a beauty. I've never seen one like him. He's chestnut and white in big splotches all over his body."

"I think Blossom remembers us." I glance up as Ester speaks, to find her intense eyes still on me.

Elizabeth clucks. "I know she remembers me. She nuzzled me as soon as I rubbed her nose."

"Blossom is an amazin' horse, the smartest horse I've ever seen." After my mumbled contribution to the conversation, I bury myself again in my still-full plate.

Mary reaches over and touches my arm. "You said she saved your life."

"More times than I can count." I guess Mary's done waitin' on me to decide to share, so I heave a deep sigh and brace myself for the onslaught of questions.

"Mac, are you ready to tell us what happened after you left us in Hendersonville?"

I studiously avoid lookin' up as I relay in brief summary the events that transpired from findin' my mother and sisters were killed to losin' my land to joinin' the cavalry to my capture and slavery to the Lakota to my inclusion in the tribe to my marriage and child to their slaughter, and my journey to return Blossom and the Bible. The silence in the room when I finish is weighty—and deafenin'.

With a sudden flurry and swoosh of skirts, Ester rises and flees from the room.

Now, I've gone and done it. I shoulda kept my big mouth shut and told 'em a light tale, appropriate for dinner conversation, without all the pain and death. I peek sideways at Mary, who sits in stunned silence.

As I expect, her face is creased with concern, her eyes fixed on the door leadin' to the stairs where Ester escaped. I want to apologize, to say something, anything, but my tongue fails me.

It's Elizabeth who breaks the tense silence. "Oh, Mac. How ever did you bear it?"

I hear her achin' concern, reachin' into my heart like a balm. Comin' from someone who has known her own loss, I know her feelin's are genuine—I know she's been there. "I don't know that I have, really. Borne it, I mean."

Mary grasps my hands in hers. "You are here with us. That is what matters now. We will help you carry the pain of your loss, as best we can. Oh, dear boy, I am so sorry. So terribly sorry."

I know the truth—there is no carryin' this pain. There's nothin' they can do to help me bear it. I'm consumed by it, swallowed whole. The shadow surges over me like a ragin' river, drownin' me again, and darkness clouds my eyes to what sits before me. All I can see is Mato Waäylo kneelin' over Soul of Moon. I see his knife slice across his throat. I see him collapse on top of his beloved in blessed relief. They walk the Shadowlands together, free from the anguish and ache and emptiness, and I long for his journey. I crave it like a starvin' man is consumed with thoughts of his next meal.

"Mac?" Mary's tentative call breaks through the darkness for a split second, only to be pushed back. The relentless shadow pursues me and would have me for its own. It's time to leave.

I pull my hands away and fumble with my napkin, tryin' to put it on the table, but it falls to the floor in a crumpled heap. My chair scrapes the wooden floor as I shove it back. I can't lift my head, can't look in their eyes, or I'll collapse like the napkin, boneless and unmovin'. I have to go. Now. "Thank you for...I..."

"Where are you going?" Mary clutches after my hand but I snatch it away.

"I...I gotta go." That's all I can manage.

"Absolutely not. You will not leave this house in the darkness of night. I won't have it."

I look down at the stranger's clothes I wear. I can't take them where I'm goin'. They'll be ruined. "I'll get my clothes."

"Mac, wait." Mary turns to Elizabeth. "Run upstairs and get your sister. Tell her I need her."

I scramble toward the door but run headlong into Elizabeth, who is obeyin' her mother's directive and runnin' to collect her sister. We tumble to the floor in a pile. Elizabeth starts to giggle, then breaks out in gales of laughter, rollin' back and forth with her arms folded across her stomach. I can't help myself. A strange chuckle, its sensation somewhere between desperation and hysteria, bubbles up in me until it erupts in a kind of frenzied cackle.

Mary rushes to our sides. "Are you hurt?"

Suddenly, the pent-up tears of months of grief burst forth like flood water over a beaver dam, and I'm writhin' on the floor and wailin' like an abandoned bairn. Elizabeth and Mary embrace me on either side as frantic sobs wrack my body.

I don't know how long I weep, but when I come back to myself, Mary is rockin' me like a bairn, Elizabeth has her head on my shoulder and her arms around me, and Ester kneels beside me, her face wet with tears and her hands restin' gently on mine. Humiliation tears through me, and I want to crawl into a hole.

"I'm sorry." My voice sounds gritty and hoarse from screamin', and my body is a shattered, empty husk.

"You have been through so much." Mary caresses my tangled hair. "It is perfectly understandable."

"I didn't mean to upset anybody." I glance at Ester and find her eyes borin' holes into me, but not in hostility. In fact, she exudes gentleness, as if she is willin' her eyes to reach deep into my heart and restore me or comfort me.

Mary gives me a light squeeze. "We are well. Please let us be here for you. You know we all care about you very much."

Elizabeth, her voice muffled against my shoulder, adds, "We really do. You mean the world to us. Don't leave."

I'm warmed by their affection, yet it's Ester's words that still my heart and convince me to remain. "We love you, Mac."

After another, briefer, bout of weeping, I'm able to respond. "I love you, too."

Elizabeth's head pops up. "Then, you'll stay?"

Why do I hesitate? The raw expression of my grief has pushed back the shadow, but I sense its presence along the periphery of my vision, ready to flood back in and overwhelm me at the least provocation. I don't want to reveal my terrible weakness to the people who are the closest thing to a family I have left, nor do I want to subject them to the horror of what I experienced when Mato Waäylo cut his own throat. I realize, if I stay, I'm committin' to live. I'm not sure I'm ready to make that choice. "For now."

Elizabeth burrows against me again. "Good."

"We will take it slowly. We will not press you on your story and ask questions about what happened, right girls? But when you are ready, you can come to us at any time and talk. Any time." Mary tilts my face toward hers. "Is that acceptable?"

"Thank you."

"Do you hear that, girls? Mac will come to us when he is ready to talk."

"Yes, mother," the girls reply.

"Very well, then. It is late, so why don't we say goodnight to Mac and let him go up to bed. Then, we'll clear supper and head up ourselves."

"Let me help you clear the table." I struggle to rise from beneath the enfoldin' arms.

"I won't hear of it. You are a guest, at least for tonight. Tomorrow, we will start fresh, and we will treat you as a regular member of the family, as you were before when you were with us in Virginia."

I recognize, from my feeble effort to stand, that I don't have the strength or will to argue with her, so I nod. Mary stands and offers her hand to help me rise. Ester hooks my arm and stands with me, while Elizabeth hangs on my leg like she did when she was a little girl. It's almost like I'm back in Richmond with 'em—except Ruth isn't here.

"Upstairs with you, then. If you get hungry in the night, there will be leftovers stored in the kitchen. Someone will call you for breakfast."

"Yes'm."

I leave to a chorus of goodnights and wander up the stairs to Ruth's old room. Rememberin' the luxurious feel of the sheets, I strip to my borrowed long johns and slide under the covers and straight into oblivion.

Light beams paint the ceilin' through the window when my crusted eyes open a crack. No one has knocked on my door, so I assume it isn't time for breakfast yet, so I stretch and lay back on the pillows, enjoyin' the momentary peace before my mind begins its swirlin' torment.

I must've drifted off again, because the light has changed, bathin' the far wall this time. I slip out of bed, shrug on the clothes, and pad into the hall. Downstairs, I hear shufflin' footfalls, so I know I'm not the first one awake. I tiptoe down the stairs and stick my head into the sittin' room, but it stands empty. In the dinin' room I find full settin's out on the table and Willie bustlin' in and out of the kitchen carryin' platters of food.

"Is it breakfast time?"

The old woman chuckles at me. "Almost time for luncheon. Here, you come on in the kitchen and help ol' Willie carry out some of the dishes."

"I missed breakfast, then. I'm sorry."

"Don't ye worry yourself none, Mister Mac. Ye needed the rest. But now, ye need to eat, so I fixed ye up a hearty meal. I wanna see a clean plate, now, ye hear?"

"Yes'm."

Willie shoves two bowls of different vegetables in my hands and waves me away. When I enter the dinin' room, Ester is comin' in the other door. "Good morning."

"More like good afternoon, I think." I offer up a wry smile.

She smiles. "Well, almost afternoon. Did you sleep well?"

"I did, thank you."

"Very well. Let me take those." She reaches for the bowls and sets them out on the table, then pulls two servin' spoons from the drawer of the china cabinet and sticks them in the bowls. "Willie made a big meal for luncheon today."

"Yes, she said she wants me to eat a lot to make up for missin' breakfast."

"Willie is a dear."

I stand quietly and watch while Ester moves gracefully around the dinin' room, lightin' the candles and adjustin' the flowers.

Elizabeth bounds in a few moments later. "What's for luncheon? Ooo, it looks delicious. I love fried chicken. It's my favorite. Hello, Mac. I'm glad you're going to join us. You missed breakfast, sleepy head. And it was biscuits and gravy and ham—you love those, don't you? Maybe Willie has some saved for you. Ester, would you want to go with me to the beach this afternoon? I'd like to look for some more shells. I'm going to make something beautiful from them for Mother."

I swear, that girl would tire out a hummingbird.

Ester glances over her shoulder at me. "Mac, would you enjoy a walk on the beach?"

I don't know what to say. Would I? I don't know. I've never seen a beach or the ocean. What would Mary say? Would she wanna come? What would we talk about? Is Ester askin' to be polite? Would I be intrudin' on sister time? Would Elizabeth be disappointed if I came along? I'm sure Ester and Elizabeth are wonderin' why I'm standin' here starin' at nothin' with my mouth hangin' open like a fish outta water, so I gulp and stammer around for a second. "Uh—let me ask Mary."

"You don't have to ask permission, silly." Elizabeth giggles at the thought.

"No, no. Not for permission. I just—um—I thought she might've made plans for me today."

Ester nods, but Elizabeth presses. "Mother's plans can wait. It's a beautiful day. Let's go for a walk, and you can spend the day with Mother doing her plans when next it rains. There, it's settled." She giggles and grabs my hand. "You can help me find shells. It'll be such fun."

I can feel my breath shorten as Elizabeth prattles on, something about a necklace and Christmas presents, but I can't focus on her words. The trapped feelin' returns in full force—there's too much noise, too much activity, too many demands. A walk on the beach suddenly sounds like torture to me.

Mary sweeps into the room. "Mac, you're up. I hope you slept well. My, my Willie has outdone herself, hasn't she?"

Willie waddles in with a cobbler. "We gotta put some meat on that boy's bones, Miss Mary."

Mary chuckles. "Yes, we do. Thank you, Willie. It looks wonderful."

"Fried chicken is my favorite," Elizabeth pipes up.

"I know that be the case, Miss Elizabeth." Willie plops the cobbler on the table. "Enjoy, now."

"May we say grace?" Mary takes my hand and Ester's. I hold Elizabeth's, who reaches across the table to hold Ester's other hand. "Heavenly Father, You have given us so much."

My jaw clenches.

"Your blessings make our lives rich and full in every way. Thank You, Father, for all You have done for us. Thank You for bringing Mac back to us. Thank You for bringing him through his trials."

My gut starts to boil.

"Thank You for keeping us all safe and under Your watchful care."

My chest pounds. Acid burns the back of my throat.

"Bless this food to the nourishment of our bodies, and us to Thy service. In the precious, holy name of Jesus, Amen."

"Excuse me." I slide back my chair and walk from the room. I can feel their eyes borin' into my back as I go. I make my way to the front porch and breathe in the cool air. Ugly thoughts plague me, questions about God's so-called watchful eye and His blessings—"the Lord gave, and the Lord hath taken away," it says. Well, He sure has taken away from me. I swallow the bile in my throat and try to squelch my mind's fury, to no avail.

"Come back inside, Mac." Mary sidles up next to me and takes my hand. "You need to eat."

"Yes'm." I come dutifully, but the shadow edges ever closer to the center of my vision.

The food is delicious, and I'm even able to enjoy a bowl of Willie's cobbler. A sense of normalcy returns durin' the meal, but I realize I can't keep this back-and-forth—whatever it is—up for much longer before something in me breaks, never to be restored. I just don't know what to do about it.

"Mother, Ester and Mac and I want to go to the beach. May we, please?" Elizabeth leans toward Mary and bats her lashes.

"Have you done your homework from school?"

Elizabeth groans. "Mo—ther. I can do it when we get home."

"Work and then play. That's what your father always said. Homework first. Then you may go to the beach."

"Mother, may Mac and I go and let Elizabeth catch up with us?" I jerk my head up at Ester's unexpected request.

"I don't see why not." Mary smiles. "Mac, do you feel like going for a walk on the beach?"

I don't feel like livin', is what I wanna say. I won't be able to stand it, I wanna say. But I'm tongue-tied. "Uh—you said—um I thought—somethin' about—um—lookin' for clothes?"

"There is no rush about returning Mr. Garrison's clothes. Shopping can wait until tomorrow—if you'd like to go?"

Without a good excuse, I drop my eyes and nod.

"It's not fair!" Elizabeth huffs and rises from the table with a flourish.

"Then, I guess you had better hurry and finish that homework." Mary smiles sweetly at her youngest child, whose face is red with her keen sense of injustice. Elizabeth storms upstairs, and the room descends into a peaceful silence.

"Would you enjoy a walk, Mother?"

"I believe I'd better remain behind with Elizabeth, but you two go ahead and enjoy your walk. Elizabeth will join you soon, I'm sure."

Ester stands and picks up her plate. I follow her lead and carry my plate to Willie in the kitchen.

"Thank you, Willie. It was a wonderful luncheon." Ester hugs her neck after she places the plate and silverware on the counter.

"Yes, thank you."

"I'm glad ye liked it. Mister Mac, looks like ye ate good."

"Yes'm."

"You'll be right as rain afore ye know it."

"Yes'm." Actually, I'm deathly ill. I'm not sure my food is gonna stay down much longer. Maybe the fresh air will help.

I walk behind Ester to the foyer. She glances at my socks. "You'll need shoes until we get to the sand."

"Oh." I drag upstairs, swallowin' the saliva that keeps buildin' up in my mouth, and slide on my boots, then run back down to find Ester standin' in the open doorway. "What a lovely day." She graces me with a glorious smile. I almost can't help but smile in return.

She leads me down the walkway, across the road, and down a path through tall reeds. When we break through, it takes my breath away.

Mounds of sand covered with more reeds and green undergrowth stand to each side of our path. Before us stretches a flat, pale tan-colored expanse of packed sand, edged by sparklin' blue water that seems to reach all the way to the horizon. White-covered rolls of water pound against the sand at the shoreline. Even the sky seems bigger out here, puffy white clouds reachin' up into blue depths that mirror the color of the water. I've never seen the like. I want to soak it into me and let it push the shadow away.

After I absorb everything for a while, I glance at Ester. Once again, her intense eyes are starin' right through me into my soul. She smiles. "I thought you'd like it."

"It's glorious." I breathe in the tang of salt in the air. The breeze whips my loose clothes around me like a flag on a pole.

"Come." She kicks off her shoes, hoists her skirts, and glides down the beach. I follow after rollin' up the legs of my pants and pullin' off my boots. I'm sure I look ridiculous, but I don't care.

We walk side-by-side, blessedly wordless. Heaviness sheds off me like feathers from a moltin' bird. Each breath seems to catch some black ugliness inside me in its wake, and when I exhale, it carries the darkness away.

She angles toward the edge of the water and boldly splashes into the waves, wettin' the hem of her skirts. Her laughter sings across the water like high notes on the ol' piano in Granda's church. I wade in with a gasp—the water is unexpectedly cold. Broken shells crunch beneath my feet as the waves ripple up my legs, then rush back out like God Himself is suckin' it up through a rye grass straw. My feet sink down into the sand to be covered again as another wave flows in.

"Come out," Ester calls. She's bouncin' up and down as the waves roll in, her skirts billowin' around her like a huge parasol.

"I don't want to get these clothes wet."

"They will dry."

Such a simple truth. I can't argue with her, so I plunge deeper into the water. A particularly large wave hits me in the chest full-force, and I topple over on my back, inhalin' a nose-full of salty water. When I sit up again, I'm coughin' and spittin', only to be hit in the face and flattened by the next wave. Ester's gales of laughter echo in my ears, muffled by the water, but instead of feelin' bothered, I feel a buoyant sense of joy.

I manage to stand and make my way out to where Ester bobs in the waves. My feet can still touch the sand, but the water is almost to my neck. "How are you floatin' like that?" In the lake back home, you'd sink, so I can't figure it.

"The salt. It changes the water and makes it easier to float."

"Huh." I lift my feet and sink 'til the water is over my shoulders, then magically, I'm floatin' alongside her. "It's like I'm my own boat."

Ester's laughter rings out again, liftin' my heart to new heights. I can almost feel its hard cover erodin' under the force of her joy. Then, I notice her normally rosy lips are losin' color, and she's shiverin'. "You're cold. Let's get you out of the water. Mary'll skin me alive if you get sick."

"I won't." But she takes my hand, and we pull against the force of the tide to make it back to the sand, where she collapses in a heap, her face turned toward the sun. I sit beside her, oblivious to the sand coatin' my black pants. And there we remain, eyes closed and face up, soakin' in the warmth of the sun, until Elizabeth walks up and startles us.

"You got in the water? Ester, Mother is going to punish you for ruining your dress."

A gnawin' fear nibbles my heart. What will Mary say about ruinin' her neighbor's clothes? I should never have gotten in the water.

"Mother will understand." I don't know if Ester is answerin' Elizabeth, or if she's readin' my mind and allayin' my concerns.

"If you say so. Let's go look for shells. Mac, you can help me." Elizabeth grabs my hand and starts gallopin' up the beach at the water's edge, draggin' me behind her. I look back over my shoulder at Ester, who continues to luxuriate in the sun, and long to join her, but Elizabeth is most insistent.

We spend the remainder of the afternoon scannin' the shore, diggin' shallow pits, and collectin' pink, tan, purple, and white shells for Elizabeth's collection. By the time the sun is approachin' the horizon, my pockets and their hands are full, and our clothes are dry.

"I hope Mary will not be angry." I look down at my sand-covered pants and sigh.

"Willie can wash them. It will be fine. Besides, she would wash them anyway before she returns them, if you are going to buy new clothes tomorrow. Oh, I hope Mother will take me shopping with you. I love to get new clothes."

Ester cuts her eyes at her sister. "You have more than enough clothes."

"But new ones are so much more fun." Elizabeth titters. She races on ahead, sayin' she must hide her shells from Mary. "Bring yours to my room, and don't let Mother see you."

I'm relieved Elizabeth ran ahead. Fatigue is bearin' down on me, and I'm havin' a hard time keepin' up with her. Ester, however, seems to enjoy a slower pace, in all aspects of her life. She holds out her palm and brushes the tops of the reeds. "Aren't they beautiful?"

"What are they called?"

"Sea oats."

"Mmm."

We walk the rest of the way in comfortable silence. We remove our shoes before we enter the house, knockin' the loose sand from them onto the grass. Then, we tiptoe through the foyer and up the stairs, deposit our shells in Elizabeth's room, and go to our rooms to wash up and change for dinner.

Fortunately, Willie has washed my clothes and left them folded on the bed, and although they are ragged, they look a good bit better now that they are clean, appropriate enough to wear to supper. I decide to sneak my borrowed clothes down to Willie and swear her to secrecy. She's a good sport about it, chucklin' at my nervousness.

"Lawdy, Mister Mac, Miss Mary don't care none. I can make 'em good as new."

"I can't thank you enough, ma'am."

Her eyes sparkle as she shakes her head and winks at me. "I guess you're one of my young'uns now, Mister Mac."

"I'm honored, ma'am."

At supper, we talk about the day—Mary is surprisingly good-natured when Elizabeth lets slip that Ester and I swam in the ocean—and I learn about Elizabeth's school and her friends, and Ruth's husband

and her home in Virginia. Sleep comes easily to me this night. The shadow is at bay.

The next weeks unfold in much the same way. I help around the house with mornin' chores, takin' care of their horses, chickens, and goats, and doin' minor repairs when needed. Mary often has engagements with friends durin' the day, so on those days I take to helpin' Willie with luncheon preparation, not that I'm much help, but she seems to enjoy my company.

Almost every afternoon, when it isn't rainin', Ester and I, and sometimes Elizabeth if she isn't with her friends, walk the beach. I never tire of the feelin' it brings, the vast space, the crisp air, and the way it chases the darkness within me.

Most of the time we walk in silence, soakin' in every detail as we explore up and down the broad expanse, but when she speaks, it's often to offer a simple truth or profound insight that challenges me to go deeper and share more.

Eventually, I talk about Flowing Spring—how we met and how our lives were together—and about Súnkawakan Sápä and my unborn bairn with a name known only by God. I describe how our son rode Blossom like the wind. She asks very few questions, allowin' me to share as I'm able. I find each day I'm stronger and able to share more.

I explain the Lakota burial rites, which leads to a discussion of Wakan Tanka, the Great Spirit, and the many similarities between Lakota beliefs and the teachin's of Jesus. Then, I tell her about Mato Waäylo and Soul of Moon, and their story. Ester doesn't speak for the rest of the day.

I also talk at great length on the grave injustice perpetrated against the Lakota people and all the native tribes by the wasicu. I often find her in tears as I describe the loss of their way of life as they're forced onto reservations, and about the mass murder of whole tribes, includin' my own.

Finally, I share with her my true name, Sungila Sá. I've not spoken it or heard it spoken since I found the ravaged camp. It feels foreign on my tongue, and for the first time in a while, I sense the shadow creepin' along the edges, so I change the subject. Ester, always in tune, doesn't miss a beat.

I tell her about Grasshopper, which makes her laugh, and about Martin, which makes her weep. I'm amazed at how deeply she engages with my stories, as if she's walkin' inside 'em with me, more observer than listener. I've grown to understand how sensitive Ester is, so different from flighty Elizabeth and aloof and regal Ruth. She might not have the classic beauty her sisters share, but her stunnin' eyes hold untold depths, and her compassion seems to flow from a deep well, along with her patience and gentleness. When I ask her how she manages to remain so peaceful in the midst of everything goin' on around her, she only smiles. "One day, I may tell you."

"When?"

"When you allow me to call you by your name."

I stop dead in my footprints. The thought of her speakin' the native tongue, sayin' my true name, rips a tear in my heart. Part of me relishes the thought of hearin' the name, Sungila Sá, dance from her lips, but most of my heart recoils, desirin' to hold that life and that world for my own, in my memory alone.

No, Sungila Sá died with Flowing Spring and Súnkawakan Sápä and the bairn with a God-name, as Aidan MacAlister died at the hands of wasicu on the field of battle. Martin Murphy is my name now.

As if sensin' my inner battle, Ester lifts the hem of her skirts and begins to scamper down the beach. I'm reminded of an antelope runnin' on the plains. It's like she's floatin' on the air, her long hair flowin' behind her like an ocean wave. She moves with such grace. Flowing Spring moved with the same kind of quiet grace, like she flowed on the clouds—as her name suggested.

My heart jolts as if pinched between giant fingers. How can I compare Ester to Flowing Spring? Such a betrayal cannot be borne. Besides, Ester is too precious a vessel and too young to enter the thoughts of someone like me, aged prematurely from physical and emotional wounds, battered, damaged, used up, a fallen believer unworthy even to call her friend. It's time for me to move on.

CHAPTER THIRTY

When we return to Mary's house, I go directly upstairs to pack my belongin's in my saddle bag. I haven't sorted out where I'm gonna go and how I'm gonna live, but my stay with Mary and the girls—especially Ester—has given me a reason to keep breathin', at least for now. I consider renewin' my desire to reclaim my family land, but with no resources to my name, that hope seems impossible.

Mary will insist I stay the night, but my resolve may waver if I do, so I commit to sayin' goodbye as soon as everyone is together and leavin' right away. A new ache stirs in my chest, yet another loss to add to my list. I've grown accustomed to havin' a family of sorts, even though they aren't my real family, and I've grown quite fond of Ester, to my shame. I'll also miss Mary's calmin' hand in my life, and I'll even miss Elizabeth's frenetic energy. But I cannot stay.

My steps are slower as I take the stairs down to the kitchen to offer Willie my help one last time. Forever wise, Willie senses my downcast mood. "What's stuck in your craw, Mister Mac?"

"Nothin', ma'am." The upturned corner of her mouth and single raised brow tells me she remains unconvinced.

"Then take this bowl of biscuits out to the supper table for Miss Mary."

"Yes'm."

Mary is in the dinin' room when I bring in the biscuits. "Thank you, Mac. You know, I think it's cold enough outside for us to have a fire this evening. Would you be willing to bring in some firewood and build us a fire?"

"Yes'm."

"I have something I would like to discuss with you this evening after supper. Could you stay down with me for a while after the girls go upstairs to bed?"

What do I say? I can't tell her I won't be here, not without both of the girls here. But I don't want to lie. I stare at the floor for several moments, long enough for her to add, "It won't take too long, I promise. But I believe it is important, and I do not want to wait any longer."

I'm stuck now. No matter what I do, it'll be wrong, so I opt for a white lie. "Yes'm."

"Very well." She rubs my arm. "You have made all of us very happy, I hope you know that."

Now, I feel like dirt underfoot. The tear in my soul, begun when Ester asked to call me by my true name, cleaves my heart in two. One part wants to believe Mary, and desires to remain with this family and to explore the potential of lovin' again. The other part, the larger part, seeks to close off, to never risk hurtin' others or bein' hurt again, to refuse to expose the ugliness in my soul and the dark shadow that consumes me. I can imagine what a little lamb feels as it's led to the slaughter—cold, alone, and shattered.

Rather than risk a response, I scurry back to the warmth of the kitchen and Willie's knowin' gaze. "Mary asked me to bring in some firewood."

"Mm-hmm. Better get to it." She hands me a leather sling and points to the stack behind the house.

I pile enough wood for the evenin' in the sling and tote it into the dinin' room, where I lay in the fire. Mary hums as she sets the table, oblivious to the tornadic whirl goin' on inside me.

Ester enters, which only escalates my agitation. The tick-tick of the mantle clock above the fireplace pounds my head like a hammer, countin' down the seconds to facin' them with my plans for departure. If I thought I could get away with it, I'd sneak out the back and be gone before anyone was the wiser. But my Ma raised me to treat people like I would want to be treated, and I wouldn't want someone to do me like that, particularly someone I'd helped as much as they've helped me.

I've arranged and rearranged the logs as much as I can without drawin' notice, so I light the kindlin' and take the sling back to Willie. In exchange, she gives me a platter of meatloaf and a bowl of potatoes to carry to the table. As I leave, she calls after me. "When you're ready, come on and talk to ol' Willie, ye hear?"

I stop in the doorway. I do feel I can talk with Willie. Should I share my plan with her? Should I seek her advice? Instead, I murmur, "Yes'm," and go on my way.

Everywhere I turn, every question I ask, I'm faced with a twelve-foot wall of fear blockin' me. Seems no matter which way I go, someone is gonna get hurt.

Elizabeth has joined Mary and Ester when I arrive with the two main dishes. Willie waddles in behind me with a bowl of snap peas and a lovely, still-warm apple pie.

"Wonderful meal, as always, Willie. Thank you."

"You girls eat them peas, ye hear now?"

"Yes, Willie." The girls beam at her, and she beams back.

Do I really want to leave this wonderful family?

Do I really want to risk destroyin' them by stayin'?

"We can thank Mac for the nice fire." Mary stands at the head of the table and gestures for us to sit in our places. "Mac, why don't you say grace for us tonight?"

I know the common words for the blessin', but my mouth won't form them. So, I simply open my mouth and wait for whatever comes out. "Lord, I want to thank you for givin' me this time with this wonderful family. They've blessed me so much, more than they can ever understand." I pause, but nothing else will come, so I add a mumbled, "Amen."

Elizabeth snickers a bit. "You didn't bless the food, Mac."

It's then I notice Ester's eyes on me—once more piercin' right through me into the deep and hidden places. She suspects something, I can see it on her face.

"I thought it a lovely blessin'," Mary replies. "Please pass the biscuits."

The supper conversation is light and superficial, in stark, disturbin' contrast to my turmoil. Ester and I say very little, leavin' Mary and Elizabeth to carry the conversation, which they do with ease. The mantle clock is so loud at times, I can't hear what they're sayin', but I manage to feign interest in the nonsensical jabber while on the inside, my heart is poundin' down the seconds to my revelation.

Mary is slicin' the pie when I finally work up my nerve, and I stand before them like I'm facin' a firin' squad.

"I have something to tell ya." My words sound pressured and awkward to my ears. Judgin' from the looks I receive from Mary and Elizabeth, they feel the same way, but Ester's eyes are downcast, as if she already knows what I'm gonna say.

I heave a deep breath in and let the exhale carry my words out in a rush and tumble mass. "I've overstayed my welcome, and it's time for me to move on. You've been most kind and welcomin', but I can't keep livin' off you. It's time I move on and find my way. I'll miss you all sorely…" The reality of what I'm sayin' hits me full-force, as if the poundin' of the clock has leapt from the mantle and slammed into my forehead. Tears pour unbidden and unwanted down my face. No more words will come.

Stony silence greets my words. As usual, Elizabeth is the one to break the silence. "Mac, what are you saying?"

"I'm leavin', I have to go."

Mary and Elizabeth speak over each other with a cascade of objections. Only Ester remains silent. She still won't meet my eyes.

"Mac, please sit down. Let us talk about this."

"I really need to go."

"But why?" Elizabeth's pleadin' tone grates on me like penny nails scrapin' metal.

"It's for the best."

"I do not see why it would be for the best. You are one of us, a part of our family."

"We don't want you to go."

"I'm not one of you." I sigh and close my eyes. "I don't mean to hurt you. In fact, that's why I'm leavin', before somethin' bad happens and I hurt you. I just…I have to—before it's too late."

Mary presses her palms against the table. "I don't understand. What have we done to make you believe…?"

"Nothin'. It isn't you. It's me."

"How? How is it you?"

"I'm poison, don't you see that? I destroy everything I touch." My vehemence crashes over the room and restores the silence.

It's in that silence that Ester finally raises her eyes. The crystalline blue is awash with tears, and my heart shatters like pieces of glass and scatters on the floor. "We love you."

"You've been so kind to me, treatin' me like a member of the family and all, but I have to face reality. I'm not. I need to find my own way and forge my own life and stop livin' off your lives."

"But Mac, we want you in our lives. That's what I wanted to speak with you about later tonight. I want to make you a part of the family. I'm not sure if that means a formal adoption or inclusion in my will or what exactly, but I mean to do whatever it takes for you to become one of us."

"That's so—very kind—I just—"

Ester rises, her jaw set, her eyes commandin'. "Come outside with me."

"Wha...?"

Before I can object, she sweeps from the room, her skirts flutterin' behind her, her long hair swishing against her back. I look to Mary, who raises one brow, as if to say, "Well, what will it be?"

So, I follow. She's sittin' at the end of the porch in the swing when I come through the door, so I walk slowly until I stand before her. She pats the bench beside her. When I don't move, she glares. "Please sit with me."

I plop next to her and squeeze as far down to the end of the wooden swing as I can muster. We sit and swing in silence for several minutes before she speaks. "You are running away."

She's right, but I'm not about to admit it. "No, I'm not. I'm sayin'..."

"You are. And it is wrong. It is wrong for you, and it is wrong for me." She reaches across the void between us and takes my hand. "Aidan MacAlister, I have loved you since the first day you stood on our porch in Richmond."

A lump rises in my throat, and I swallow hard.

"I have waited for you, holding onto your promise that you would come back to us." She lowers her eyes. "I was so jealous of Ruth. I thought you wanted her. I despaired of ever knowing true love. But then she fell in love with someone else." She grasps my other hand and

439

closes the distance between us. "I've known since I first met you—you are my soul mate, the one God has chosen for me. You asked me recently how I can be at such peace. The answer is, I am certain. I know. And in that certain knowledge of my own heart—who I love, what I desire, what the rest of my life holds—I have no fear. God has given me this gift. I treasure it and hold it close. I honor it and the One who gave it to me. In this truth is my peace."

The war rages between the broken pieces of my soul, and the shadow, ever seekin' advantage, creeps closer. "Ester, you don't know me—not anymore. I'm..."

"I do know you. You are Sungila Sá, fierce warrior of the Lakota, protector and defender of the people. You are the devoted and loving father to Súnkawakan Sápä and the child with only a God-name. You are adoring husband to Flowing Spring, the man who taught her about Jesus and saved her soul for eternity. You are dear friend to Grasshopper and Mato Waäylo and Soul of Moon and Martin Murphy, whose name you now bear to honor his memory and mourn your role in his loss, even if you are not aware that's why you took his name. You are Aidan MacAlister, son of Liam MacAlister and Mary Connolly, fighter for the land and heritage of his family. And you are Mac, who saved our lives at great risk to his own, who protected our purity, who loves us as his own kin..."

"But I'm..."

"Let me finish...who is broken in spirit from battle and grief, who wrestles with God, yet continues to come back to Him time and again, despite the horrors of this life. I know you. I *see* you. Through God's eyes, I see who you truly are, and with all the pain and brokenness and wounding and anguish, I love you more this second than I have ever loved you. I will love you until the day I die. I have never and will never love another. There is no one else on this world for me but you."

I'm struck dumb. These are not the thoughtless words of a child with a crush, or a girl swoonin' over an older man. These are spoken truths, wrenched from her heart and laid bare before me. I can almost touch her certainty, so genuine and impassioned is her speech, so tangible is her devotion. My heart swells until I think it might burst from my chest and break the dam in me that holds back my deep love for her.

The shadow whispers, "But what of Flowing Spring? Will you betray her memory? Is your love for her so shallow, you would forget her and love another?"

I withdraw my hands from Ester's and drop my head to my chest. "I cannot love you like you deserve."

"Why? I see the love in your eyes when you look at me—when you think I'm not looking. Is it because of Flowing Spring?"

I peer into her eyes and take up her hands again. "I can't betray her."

"Is there so little love in the heart of Sungila Sá? Does your love not grow in the giving?"

"I..."

"What would Flowing Spring say?"

My tension flares as irritation. "That's a bold question to ask, since you never met her. What if she's the type who'd want to keep me all to herself?"

Ester smiles in her knowin' way. "You wouldn't love that type of woman, one who would be selfish or desire to cause you pain."

She's right. Flowing Spring didn't have a selfish bone in her body. Like Ester, she gave her love freely, without expectation or restraint, from the first time we met. Once more, I have no reply.

"The love you share with Flowing Spring is beautiful and wonderful and will last for all eternity. That doesn't mean that our love is any less. Love is always a beautiful expression of God's heart—and His heart is infinite in capacity."

She waits patiently as I absorb her words—and the truth contained in them. Flowing Spring would bid me love her well—I know she would. I can almost hear her say, "Sungila Sá may scream like fox in battle but has heart of bear."

"I imagine Flowing Spring thought herself one of the most blessed women in the tribe, to be loved so deeply by such a wonderful man."

I groan inwardly as flashes of my many sins pummel me with shame. "I'm anything but wonderful."

441

"You are warm and giving and sacrificial and protective and passionate and caring—should I go on?"

I squirm like a worm in hot ashes under her praise, and the shadow is quick with his retort. "My turn. I wonder sometimes if I am quite mad. I hold deep darkness inside me. I'm a murderer, a betrayer, a deserter, a coward. I'm—evil."

Love and compassion flow from Ester's eyes and caress me like a warm bath. "Mac, what you've had to do to survive does not define who you are."

"I feel the darkness in me now, accusin' me."

"Of course, it does. But that isn't your heart. I *see* you. Remember?"

Tears well again. I cover my face.

"Don't hide yourself anymore, Mac. I love you. All of you."

My shoulders heave and shake as my pain gushes from me like the water when Moses struck the rock. Ester wraps her arms around me, her tears wettin' my shirt. We sit together and cry together for what seems like hours. It seems the dam, having burst, now has a never-endin' supply of pain, enough to fill an ocean, but eventually, my tears cease, and we swing quietly, holdin' each other close.

The quiet voice, which I haven't heard in so long, drowned out by the demon and the shadow, whispers. *You are my precious son. Accept my love, and the love now beside you, and let it bring healing to your wounded heart.* Peace settles over me, a peace I haven't known since before the war.

After a long silence, I'm compelled to ask the question I've felt sure would stop everything in its tracks. "What is your mother gonna say about this?"

"Oh, she knows. She's known for quite some time."

"But I'm so old and you're so young."

"I'll have you know, I'm 17 and a half. Most of my friends have already married, and Ruth married when she was even younger. And stop saying you're old!"

"But she—she wouldn't mind her daughter bein' with a poor farm boy with not a penny to his name and a price on his head?"

"She's been desperately trying to find a way to make you part of our family."

"I guess marriage is one way..."

"Are you asking me to marry you?"

Am I? I search my heart, and in the deepest, secret places, I ask God. A vision of Flowing Spring, a little bairn in her arms with a swirl of black hair on her head, surrounded by Súnkawakan Sápä and Mato Waäylo and Soul of Moon and Grasshopper, holds up her hand in blessin'. Ma stands beside them with Pa, his arm around her, smilin' and noddin'. Martin, standin' next to Pa, throws back his head and laughs, then shakes his fist in a kind of cheer. When I open my eyes, I'm flooded with love for the vision sittin' beside me—perfection in every aspect of her bein'. "I am. Ester, will you marry me?"

Her smile speaks of contentment and the fulfillment of a promise long in comin' to pass. "I will."

CHAPTER THIRTY-ONE

Ester and I remain for some time cuddled on the porch swing, with her head restin' on my shoulder and my arms wrapped around her. Rather than affection, I'm more holdin' on for dear life for fear of losin' her, now that I've admitted my love.

When she lifts her head at last, her glowin' smile warms my heart. "Let's go tell Mother."

"Very well."

Despite her assurances that Mary will be pleased, I'm a little shaky when we enter the house. The dinin' room is empty, so Ester guides me to the sittin' room where we find Mary workin' on some needlework.

"Mother?"

Mary lowers the cloth and raises her brows. I decide I should be the one to ask her for her blessin', since Ester's father isn't here to grant it. "Mary, I—uh—I would like to ask your blessin' to..." I swallow hard. "Um—to marry Ester."

Mary's eyes widen, and my heart sinks into my stomach. She looks more shocked than pleased. Beside me, Ester is fair quiverin' with excitement, but my knees are tremblin' for a different reason altogether.

Mary rises slowly and strides across the floor to stand before me. Just when I think I might faint from holdin' my breath, her face breaks into a beamin' smile, and she grabs me around the neck and squeezes so hard I can't breathe. "Of course, you have my blessing. What wonderful news!"

"I'm so happy, Mother."

Mary releases me and embraces her daughter. "And I'm so happy for you. What a glorious Christmas surprise!"

Christmas? Already? I blanch and glance at Ester. I knew it was comin', because Elizabeth made such a production of gatherin' seashells for a necklace for Mary, but I haven't paid attention to the days. I don't recall the last time I celebrated Christmas—before the war, I guess. And now I have no gifts for anyone, and no money to purchase any. I'm sure this family is used to a Christmas Day filled with presents and parties and banquets.

For us, Christmas was wakin' early to receive a hard candy and the girls a handmade doll, and for me new socks, or that one big Christmas, when I was thirteen, a new shotgun. Then, we'd go do our chores like any other day. The reality of our vast differences punches me in the gut, and I wonder if I'll ever be able to make Ester truly happy.

Mary's laughter rings like tiny bells. "In a few days, it will be Christmas Eve, and we will cut our tree and decorate the house. It will be a special celebration this year. We have so much to be grateful for." She embraces me again. "Now, you cannot say again that you are not a member of this family."

"Yes'm." Yet, I don't belong.

Mary kisses Ester on the cheek, then shoos us up to bed. "We have wedding plans to make tomorrow, so get some sleep, dear. If you can."

I'm a stew of gratitude and trepidation and doubt, so no words will come. As we head for the stairs, I manage to throw, "Thank you, ma'am," over my shoulder. The melodies of Mary's laughter follow us all the way up the stairs.

Ester grabs my hands and pulls them to her chest. "See, I told you she would be pleased." I study my boots until she finally asks, "What is it? What's wrong?"

I look deep into her eyes before I reply. "I'm not sure I can make you happy."

"You've already made me the happiest woman in the world."

"But I have nothin' to my name—and no way to provide for you."

"Is that what you're worried about?" She grabs my chin. "Listen to me. All I want is you. I don't want 'things.' I'm happy with very little. In fact, I love simplicity, and the peace that comes with it."

"But you're used to..." I sweep my arm around the hallway. "All this."

"All this means nothing to me. I will be happy, as long as we're together."

She puts a hand on each cheek, stands on tiptoe, and kisses me—a brief butterfly-brush of a kiss. Our first kiss. A surge of love overtakes my doubts. I enfold her in my arms, cradle her head, and kiss her gently, long, and deep.

When we part, her eyes are glued to mine, moist and hooded. She whispers, "Good night," and retreats quickly into her room.

Before I take a step down the hall, the doubt assails me again. How can I prove worthy of such a special, amazin' woman? It's impossible, but I vow every day of my life from this point forward to try to love her in the ways she deserves.

Christmas. What can I give her that would express my love? I have nothin' of value and no way to acquire anything. What do I have of meaning? I lie awake half the night before my mind alights on an idea. I'll need Elizabeth's help, though.

When I make my way downstairs the next mornin', Ester, Elizabeth, and Mary are fully immersed in weddin' plans. Elizabeth bolts up from the table and practically jumps into my arms. "Brother!" I can't help but laugh at her glee. "I'm going to be her maid of honor, and Mother is going to buy me a special dress for the occasion. Isn't it wonderful?"

"It surely is." I pull her aside and whisper, "I need your help with something."

She rubs her hands together conspiratorially. "What do you need?"

"I need a pretty box and a pretty ribbon—thin-like, you know, like you wear in your hair."

"Done. I will bring them to you later."

"Perfect. Thank you."

She pecks my cheek. "Anything for my big brother."

"Mac?" Ester waves me over to the table. "Come help us. It's your wedding, too."

As aligns with her nature, Ester desires a simple weddin' with a few close friends, led by the pastor of their church. We decide to hold it on the front porch in the springtime, when the bloomin' flowers fill the air with sweet fragrances and splashes of color. Mary wants to invite the Willoughby family, a few of her closest friends, and Ester's two best

447

friends and their husbands. I have no one to add to the list, although I'm glad the Willoughbys will be in attendance, as they are the only people I know in town.

Against Mary's wishes, Ester squelches the idea of a fancy feast and big reception. "I want it to be sacred, Mother—special, just for us. Mac and I are coming before God and asking Him to cleave us as one flesh. It is a holy act, not a party."

I'm astounded by her maturity and wisdom. Surely, someone who sees through these eyes will appreciate my Christmas gift, no matter how simple it may be.

Weddin' plans made, Mary and the girls turn to the Christmas celebration. I'm tasked with findin' and cuttin' the tree. "Make sure it's a big, fat one," Elizabeth instructs.

"If it's as tall as Elizabeth wants, you'll have to place the Christmas star." Mary's face glows with delight. "This Christmas will be like we used to have when your father was with us."

I ride out with Blossom in search of a proper tree. The woods outside of town are filled with hardwoods, but it takes me a spell to find an appropriate Christmas tree. The loblolly pines are too tall, and not so full as would please Elizabeth, but when I run up on a young red cedar, I know I've found the perfect tree.

I use my hatchet to cut the narrow trunk, wrap the tree in an ol' sheet to protect its branches, and tie it behind Blossom, then we make the trek back to the Monroe house. All three squeal with delight when I unveil the tree, and I earn a quick peck from Elizabeth and a hug and kiss from Ester for my troubles.

As Mary explained, decoratin' must wait until Christmas Eve. In the meantime, Elizabeth brings me a small, velvet-covered box and an ivory ribbon. "It's perfect. Where did you find such a box?"

"It's from a piece of jewelry Mother gave me."

"Oh, then you need it." I hand it back to her, but she pushes my hand away.

"No, I don't need it. I only saved it because it's pretty. So, really, I was saving it for you. I just didn't know it."

"It's perfect for her present. Thank you."

"Well, are you going to tell me what it is?"

"You'll have to wait for Christmas mornin', just like Ester."

Elizabeth bunches her face in a pout. "But I gave you the box."

"I know, and it will make it extra special for her."

"Oh, very well." Her bright mood isn't dampened, though, as she skips down the stairs, leavin' me to consider now what I can give her as a present—and Mary.

I decide to enlist Willie as my secret helper. When I whisper my ideas to her, she grins. "Lawdy, Mister Mac, you sure have some interestin' ideas."

"Will you help me?"

"Ye know I will."

"Thank you, Willie. I'll bring the materials if you can find me the pins."

"I know just what to do, Mister Mac. Don't ye worry yer head none."

So, the next day, while Elizabeth is at school and Mary is at her friend's house, I head for the beach and collect several brightly colored shells, ones I know Elizabeth will like from watchin' her hunt for 'em for her mother, and a handful of white feathers. Back in the kitchen, Willie hands me five hair pins and some sewin' thread. "Thank you, Willie. These will do nicely. Where did you find 'em?"

"Ol' Willie has her ways, never you mind."

"How 'bout the other gift?"

"Miss Mary's gonna love it, Mister Mac. I'll fix it right up special."

"You're a gem. What do you want for Christmas, Willie?"

She rears her head back and guffaws. "Lawdy mercy, Mister Mac. I tell ye what. Ye give ol' Willie a peck on the cheek, and I'll be just fine."

"Well, here it is, then." I kiss her cheek lightly, and she giggles like a schoolgirl, then shakes her head and walks away to finish my present for Mary.

Christmas Eve is as joyous as Mary predicted. We raise and decorate the tree, then light the candles and sing Christmas hymns together. Ester reads the story of Christ's birth from Luke. We spend the rest of the evenin' sittin' before the fire and the tree, drinkin' hot apple cider as Mary and the girls share stories of their early Christmases with Alex. It's truly a spectacular night.

Upstairs in Ruth's ol' room, I put the finishin' touches on my gifts. I want everything to be perfect, so I check and double-check each detail, fiddlin' with the ribbon on Ester's gift, adjustin' the feathers on Elizabeth's, and smoothin' Mary's gift. I offer a quick prayer for the Good Lord to help them like their gifts, then for my sake I pray they won't be offended or dismiss them as trivial. Sleep stays away, and in the wee hours of the mornin', I creep downstairs to lay in the fire.

It isn't long afore I hear Willie bangin' around in the kitchen. "Good mornin', Willie. Merry Christmas to you."

"Merry Christmas, Mister Mac." She leans in and whispers, "Did everythin' turn out like ye wanted?"

"I hope so. I did my best. Now, I have to wait and see if they like 'em."

She winks at me. "I have a feelin' they're gonna shed some tears this day."

"Tears?" I must look stricken because she pats my arm.

"That's how women say they love it. Don't ye fret none."

"If you say so."

"Now, get along and let me cook the Christmas breakfast. We're havin' pancakes with real maple syrup, a real treat."

I'm sittin' by the tree, watchin' over the candles, when Ester and Elizabeth rush in.

"Do you see any of my presents?" Elizabeth pulls on a couple of branches to search for boxes perched in the tree.

"Wait for Mother." Ester takes a seat on the floor beside me. "Isn't it magical?"

"It's beautiful," but my eyes are on Ester.

Mary comes in a few minutes later and claps her hands. "Let's begin with a prayer of praise and thanksgiving for the coming of the Christ child." Everyone bows their head. "Heavenly Father, we praise Your holy name and thank You for sending Your Son, Jesus, to us. May we celebrate this day the wonder of His birth and may our hearts sing as the angels to Your glory. Amen."

"May I go first?" Elizabeth is practically shakin' with anticipation.

"I'm content to wait and enjoy watching others open their gifts. Elizabeth can go ahead." Ester hooks her arm through mine and lays her head on my shoulder.

Elizabeth reaches into the branches of the tree and pulls out a box. "Is this for me, Mother?"

"It is, dearest. Open it."

She places the box on the floor and opens it carefully with a gasp. Inside is a beautiful, jeweled necklace. "Emerald. My favorite. Mother, it's lovely."

"Open yours from me, Mother. Right there." Ester sits forward as Mary pulls a flat box from the branches.

She opens it and pulls out some delicate, white kerchiefs embroidered with her initials and a spray of pink flowers. "Such beautiful handiwork. When did you have the time?"

"I've been working on them all along. I know you'll need them come the spring—and our wedding."

Mary's hands flutter over the kerchiefs. "They are exquisite. Yes, I will need them. In fact, I need one now." She swipes a tear from the corner of her eye.

I lean close and whisper. "What a thoughtful gift."

"I believe she likes them."

Ester gives Elizabeth a pair of pearl earrings, then Mary opens her gift from Elizabeth. "A shell necklace! However did you make it?"

"Mac and Ester helped me collect the shells."

Ester raises her hand. "You did all the work."

"I love it, darling." Mary ties the necklace on and preens, to Elizabeth's delight. "Here, Ester. Open your gift from me."

Ester stands, searches the tree briefly, then finds a small box. In it is a brooch, decorated with sapphires. "Mother, it's beautiful! And too much."

"Nonsense. You need something blue to wear on your wedding day."

"I love it. Thank you." She dashes to Mary's side and kisses her cheek.

Elizabeth pulls a small present off the tree and hands it to Ester. "This is from me."

Ester's eyes mist over as she opens the gift and finds a dainty silver cross danglin' from a delicate silver chain. "Oh, Elizabeth. It takes my breath away." She holds the cross to her neck and has me clasp it in the back. "I don't think I will ever take it off." Elizabeth's smile would light the whole Christmas tree.

Mary looks at me. "Mac's turn."

"I didn't know I was supposed to put the presents on the tree, so I will have to go get mine from my room."

"Oh!" Mary's look of surprise pulls me up short. "I didn't expect you...I meant your turn to open gifts."

"I'd like to give mine first, if you don't mind."

"Of course. But you didn't have to..."

I raise my hand to stop her protest. "I don't have much but—I hope you know they're from the heart."

Ester's gentle smile puts me back at ease. "We'll wait for you."

I carry the gifts to the bottom of the stairs and leave them on the table in the foyer, so it won't ruin the surprise. I hold Elizabeth's gift behind my back and reenter the sittin' room. "Close your eyes. I didn't have a box it would fit in."

She closes her eyes and holds out her hands, and I lay the decorative hair pins on her palms. Her eyes pop open, and she gasps. "Look, Mother. He's made me special pins for my hair. They're beautiful!"

"The native people always wore feathers in their hair to honor the Great Spirit, so I thought feathers to represent my old life and shells to represent my new life with you as my sister."

"That's so sweet. I love them. My friends don't have anything like this. Wait until I tell them what they mean."

My first gift seems a success, so I return to the foyer and bring Mary's gift, again hidden behind my back. "You'll have to close your eyes, too."

So, Mary closes her eyes, and I lay a cleaned and edged buffalo hide across her lap. "What is this? Oh, my!"

"This is one of the hides I brought from my tribe. It will keep you warm, no matter how cold nights get." I bow before her. "I seek to honor you with the gift of the sacred tatanka, given to the people and shared with you. I hope it will remind you of your importance to our tribe."

Mary pulls out her kerchief and dabs her eyes. "Thank you, Mac." The words catch in her throat.

Now, for the final, most important gift. I say another quick prayer and kneel before Ester with her gift. "For you, my love."

Her mouth forms a little 'O' as she cradles the velvet box in her hands. She opens it and stares for several seconds before speakin'. Then, she looks at me, her eyes huge spheres, and back at the contents of the box. She strokes the ivory ribbon, bindin' two little bundles of black hair.

"I share with you Nagi Gluhapi, the keeping of the soul. Now, you are bound to Flowing Spring and Súnkawakan Sápä, as I am bound to them. We all share one heart, one wakan together. Now, they watch over you as they watch over me."

Ester's mouth remains open as tears flow freely down her cheeks. She lifts the bundles of hair as if they are fragile, priceless works of art and touches the hair to her lips. "This is a great honor you offer. I don't know what to say." A sob escapes her open mouth. She clutches the bundles to her heart and gasps out, "I will treasure them. Always."

How can one heart feel so full and so empty at the same time? I watch Ester finger the hair of my beloved, and I remember when my hands stroked her hair, soft as silk, long and flowin' like her name. I remember scrubbin' my fist on Súnkawakan Sápä's black tufts, to his delight. Never again. Ester's deep emotion stirs mine, and I don't want her to find me saddened, so I turn away, to see Willie, her head peekin' through the kitchen door, tears in her eyes. Nothin' will hold my tears back now. Yet, I don't believe I have ever felt more loved than I do in this moment.

After several minutes, our tears begin to subside. Mary stands and walks to the Christmas tree. "Well, Mac, now that you've reduced us all to tears, it's your turn. We have a gift for you." She reaches into the heart of the tree and brings forth a small square-shaped box covered in velvet, like the one I used for Ester's gift. "This is actually a gift for you and Ester, so open it together."

I take the box and kneel once again before my bride-to-be. Together, we lift the lid to discover a ring—a round diamond surrounded on two sides by smaller diamonds. When I look up at Mary, I imagine my face looks much like Ester's a few moments ago.

"Alex gave me this ring when he asked me to marry him. It belonged to his mother, and her mother before her. It is now yours."

"Mother, we can't take your ring. Father gave it to you. How could you bear to part with it?"

"Father would want you to have it, my dear one. Read what is inscribed on the inside of it."

I hold the ring up to the candlelight and peer inside the silver ring. "It says, 'Forever.'"

"And that is what I pray for the two of you. If you share even a portion of the love your Father and I shared, you will..." Mary dissolves in tears. Ester jumps up and wraps her arms around her mother, while Elizabeth lays her head on her lap.

When their weepin' subsides, I stand behind Ester with my hands on her shoulders. "Nothing could be more special than Ester wearin' your ring. I can't thank you enough."

"Well then, put it on her!"

I take Ester's delicate hand and slide the ring gently on her finger. The diamonds sparkle and glisten in the flickerin' light of the Christmas tree, but their beauty doesn't hold a candle to the radiance of Ester's face at that moment. My love for her swells like the ocean at high tide, and I'm moved to tears right along with the women.

It hits me then, with the force of a wave hidin' a terrible undertow. This is real. It's actually happenin'. Ester and I are to be man and wife. I'm swept into the spinnin', whirlin' abyss of fear and hope, doubt and resolve, betrayal and love.

I reach for the healin' vision of Flowing Spring givin' her blessin', but my unworthiness vomits up and wars with the peace offered by the vision. Why would Ester want someone like me? She could have Johnny Willoughby, a nice, upstandin' young man who I happen to know has his eye on her, or any of a number of other young men in town. Why in heaven's name would she wait for the likes of me? The pull of the tide batters me and draws me farther into the depths.

"Isn't it beautiful?" I strain to see through the murky morass surroundin' me to find Elizabeth admirin' Ester's new ring. They exist in another world, a world I've never shared, a world of light and beauty, of Christmases filled with joy—and I know my darkness isn't welcome here.

I have said you are my precious son. Have you known Me to be a liar? The whispered voice shocks me out of the deep waters, and I suck in a gasp of air as if I've burst to the surface just in time. *Why do you doubt My words?*

"Mac, what's wrong?" Ester, ever sensitive, reaches for my hand.

"I—I can't believe how incredibly lucky I am." I want to ask her why she would have someone like me, but the insistent voice presses on me to trust both Him and her, to accept His love and to believe in hers. "I love you more than I can express in words."

"I love you, too." The depth of feelin' in her eyes belies my doubts and fears.

The storm within me is stilled, and peace returns with a gentling of the waters until I'm floatin' on my love for Ester and a newfound certainty in God's love for me.

Willie sweeps in, hands on her hips. "Time to eat 'fore the food gits cold."

"But Willie, you've not opened your present!" Elizabeth pulls a large, ribboned box from the lowest limbs of the tree and rushes it to Willie's hands.

"My, my, look at this." Willie pats her chest. "You's gonna give ol' Willie a heart attack."

"Open it!" Elizabeth claps her hands and jumps up and down like a little girl.

Willie opens the box and pulls out a lovely dress, made of fine, flower-print fabric. "Lawdy, Miss Mary. Oh, my. I don't know what to say."

"It's for Sunday church. I know how much you enjoy dressing up in your Sunday best, so the girls and I wanted to get you something new to wear."

"It's mighty fine. Mighty fine." Willie brushes a stray tear from the corner of her eye. "Now, 'nuff of this foolishness. G'on and enjoy your luncheon."

Ester embraces the ol' woman. "Happy Christmas to you."

"Sweet child." Willie pecks her on the cheek.

"Thank you, Willie." Mary rises and gestures for us to come along to the dining room. The table is covered with lace, candles, and greenery, and with platters laden with turkey and ham, cornbread dressin', sweet potatoes, beans, and corn, and pies and cake.

"It looks glorious, Mother."

"Let us stand together and give thanks to the Lord for this wonderful meal and for the glory of what we celebrate this day."

"May I lead the prayer?" I'm as surprised as they are at the words that fell out of my mouth unbidden, but my heart feels full to burstin', and I'm compelled to honor Him for what He's done for me.

"Certainly, Mac. Let us take hands."

"Heavenly Father…" I realize these words, so commonly spoken, have new and profound meanin' to me. I'm His precious son—beloved of the one true Father. It's a staggerin' thought. "Heavenly Father," I repeat, "All I can say is—I love You. You've loved me as a son." My words catch in my throat, and I take a shudderin' breath before I can continue. "You've restored me to a family, one filled with joy and love. You've given my heart the strength to love again. You've given me back my faith and my hope. You rescued me in every way. How can I ever thank You for all You've done? But I guess I'll give it a try. Thank You for this wonderful family. Thank You for the love in this room. Thank You for the incredible joy of this day. Most of all, thank You for bein' born on this earth to save us. My words can't express how much Your love means to me. Thank You, Lord. Amen."

"Amen." Ester squeezes my hand and graces me with a smile so luminous, I swear we don't need candles.

We relish the food and the company, and everyone crows about their presents, until we are so stuffed full, we can't hardly move from the table.

Mary groans. "Girls, we'll clean away the dishes later. I want to sit by the fire and the Christmas tree for a while."

I stoke the fire in the sittin' room and spread the buffalo blanket across Mary's lap. She snuggles under it and is asleep in minutes. Ester and I cuddle together on the divan, while Elizabeth curls up in a chair beside her mother. Everything is perfect.

CHAPTER THIRTY-TWO

The day after Christmas, I head to town to meet with John Willoughby about a job. Mary assures me he often has work for strong men at his shippin' company, and that he'll be glad to hire someone he knows and trusts, but I'm still nervous. I only have until April to save enough money to afford a house for Ester and me.

"Martin!" John greets me with a smile and hearty handshake when I enter his offices. "What a pleasure to see you. You are looking quite well."

"Thank you, sir. I've been well fed and cared for."

"That's fine, fine. What can I do for you?"

"I wondered if you had any work I could do? I don't know if you heard, but Ester and I—well, we're gonna be married..."

"Well, how about that? That's wonderful! Congratulations."

"Yessir, and I need a job so I can support her."

"Of course. It just so happens I have a position loading and unloading the ships at port. Would this interest you?"

"Yessir. I'd be most happy with that."

"Excellent."

After I sign a few papers, he walks me down to the docks behind his business and introduces me to Charlie, his foreman. "Charlie, this is Martin. He'll be working for you loading and unloading cargo."

Charlie is a broad-shouldered man with brown curly hair, rough hands, and a firm grip. "Nice to meet ya, Martin."

"He's a good worker, Charlie. You won't have any trouble out of him." John shakes my hand again. "I'll leave you in good hands."

"Thank you, Mr. Willoughby." I turn to Charlie. "Where do I start?"

"See the boys down there carrying boxes onto the pier? You can start by helping them unload that ship."

"Yessir."

"When you're done, come see me and we'll talk about the work you'll be doing regular."

"Yessir."

I'm a little like a fish outta water, jumpin' in with the men who've obviously been workin' on the docks a while, but they're welcomin' enough and seem to appreciate an extra set of hands for the labor. The work isn't difficult, and I enjoy bein' outside in the salt air and doin' physical work. It's gratifyin' to be doin' something productive again, and when we're finished unloadin', I find I'm contented.

Charlie explains my job—loadin' cargo onto outgoin' ships and unloadin' cargo from ships comin' in and takin' the cargo to the warehouse for storage, then loadin' cargo onto trains for shipment across the country. It's a huge undertakin'. The port at Wilmington is quite busy, and there's plenty of work, so I tell Charlie I'm glad to work day and night, all except Sunday mornin'.

The next months are a blur of long hours of hard physical labor with brief respites for sleep. The deep tan color I had on the plains returns to my skin, along with larger arm and leg muscles and a thicker chest. Ester quips it'll look like she's marryin' an explorer fresh back from the seas when the time comes. She and Mary enjoy sewin' dresses for the weddin' and preparin' decorations for the house. As the time draws closer, Ester's excitement, mixed with some nervousness she denies but I see clearly, is barely contained.

I still haven't saved enough money to buy a house for us, but Mary says she'd rather us stay with her a while longer anyway. She says she isn't lookin' forward to the house bein' emptier once we leave, to which Elizabeth pretends to take great offense. I'm a little embarrassed that I can't provide a home for my soon-to-be wife, despite Ester's reassurances.

The day before the weddin', I'm told I must go and stay at the Willoughby home down the street, so I won't see Ester on the day of the weddin'. Apparently, it's bad luck for the groom to see the bride before the ceremony. All the strange rituals and traditions seem odd to me, but I guess the weddin' ritual of the Lakota would seem odd to Ester, so I go along with 'em all. I want her to be happy.

The mornin' of the weddin', Mrs. Willoughby fusses over me like I'm her own son, even tryin' to comb my wild hair and make it manageable. I've bought a new suit for the occasion, but Mrs. Willoughby isn't satisfied until she presses it and adds a sprig of green to the lapel. Johnny agrees to stand beside me, which I'm told is another tradition. Everyone dresses in their finest, and at long last, we make our way up the street to the Monroe house.

Several people are already gathered on the lawn as we arrive, most of whom I don't know. I see Willie, gussied up in her Christmas dress, wearin' a large hat topped with flowers. "You look mighty fine, Willie."

She giggles like a schoolgirl. "Ooo, Mister Mac, don't ye give ol' Willie the big head, now. My ol' hat won't fit me no more. You's lookin' mighty fine yo'sef."

"Thank you, ma'am."

A sudden squeal, a flurry of swishin' skirts, and cool arms graspin' my neck from behind catch me off guard. When I pull back, I find Ruth—older and lookin' more like Mary than ever, but it is her. And she's with child.

"Ruth! I didn't know you were comin'."

"You know I wouldn't miss it. It's wonderful to see you! Let me introduce you to my husband, Arthur."

"Well met." I shake his proffered hand.

"Indeed. Ruth has told me all about you, how you rescued her and protected her. I owe you a great debt." Arthur drapes his arm around Ruth's shoulders and gives her a squeeze.

"I was so excited when Mother told me you and Ester were engaged to be married. That makes you my brother, right and true."

"It does."

"Isn't it wonderful? We always said you were our brother."

"And now I will be forever."

Ruth hooks my arm in hers and leans close to me. "You kept your promise."

"Did you see Blossom?"

"Mother told me you brought her back, but Blossom is your horse now. I want you to keep her."

"I promised I'd bring her back to you."

"Which you did. But I give her to you, all the same. Take her as your wedding present."

"No, I—it's..." But Ruth's eyes take on a dangerous gleam, so I relent. "You're too generous. Thank you. She saved my life more times than I can count."

"Mother told me. I'm so glad she was there for you. More than you know." The warmth of her affection soothes my skitterin' nerves.

Mary sweeps onto the porch, her wide skirts and curved bodice sparklin' with jewels, and her hair swept up on her head in golden curls. "We are about to begin. If everyone would stand at the bottom of the stairs, please."

Mary takes my arm and guides me to the porch while the guests congregate at the base of the stairs. Johnny takes his place behind me on the top step. The reverend steps to the center of the porch and Mary swings the front door open and scurries down the stairs to join the guests.

First, Elizabeth, lookin' very regal in a soft blue gown whose huge skirts billow around her, sails down the stairs into the foyer, waltzes out the door, and takes her place beside Johnny. I notice him eyein' her appreciatively.

Then Ester, dressed in a simple gown of pure white with a lace veil over her face and hair, glides down the stairway and through the foyer. She stops in the doorway for a moment and finds my eyes. An ethereal glow surrounds her as her eyes glisten with moisture.

My eyes fill in response, and I'm once again struck speechless in disbelief that this amazin' angel is marryin' me. This time, however, my certainty of God's love for me and His hand in our joinin' together as one fill me with gratitude and joy which bathes away the last vestiges of doubt. In her graceful way, she floats to my side, takes my hands, and turns to face the pastor.

My eyes remain glued to Ester. I hear the pastor speakin', but it sounds like the drone of a beehive in my right ear—I have no idea what he's sayin'. Ester consumes my thoughts. Then, I hear the name, "Martin Murphy" and know I'm supposed to say somethin', so I try to listen. "In sickness and in health, and forsaking all others, keep thee only unto her as long as you both shall live?"

That's my cue. "I will."

Ester responds in kind, and the reverend pronounces us man and wife. My tremblin' hands lift the fragile veil, but I don't lean down to kiss her as instructed. I want to soak her into me and let her fill me up to overflowin'. I want to absorb her like a sponge in water. I want to dive into her eyes like I used to dive into the pool at the base of the waterfall—to fall into them and disappear inside her soul. Ester reaches up and touches my face, and I become aware of tears streamin' down my cheeks as she brushes them away.

"My love." Her words are like silk against my skin, all shimmery and smooth, her smile rays from the risin' sun on a cool spring mornin'. I almost can't bear the ache of my love for her.

When I'm finally able to kiss her, everything around me disappears into a noiseless, brilliant white glow. Her pillowy lips, the smooth coolness of her skin, the cinnamon taste of her breath. We linger in the connection until the distant sounds of applause and echoin' cheers wake me from my dream. Our lips part, and I find the crystal blue of her eyes once more. I vow to never leave them.

Ester leads me like one might lead a dumb mule down the front steps to greet our guests on the lawn. A blur of handshakes, hugs, back slaps, and congratulations spin 'round me, but I'm still lost to this world, somewhere in the deep pool of her soul. I hear her voice as if through a fog, thankin' each person for sharin' our special day with us. I know I should be expressin' my own gratitude, but I can't make my mouth form coherent words, so I do my best to grunt my agreement as she performs the niceties.

Mary saves the day by callin' everyone to the dinin' room for finger foods and cake. We are swept up in the tide of our guests movin' indoors, where Willie and Mary have set out a beautiful table of all kinds of delicacies and rich desserts, includin' a tiered cake with swirls of icing. Ester and I stand to the side as our guests move around the lavish table to collect plates of food, then Mary places a long knife in my hands and points me to the cake.

I stand for a few moments tryin' to figure out what I'm supposed to do, until Ester places her hand atop mine and guides it to slice the cake and place a piece on a small china plate. She picks up the piece of cake and, without warnin', shoves it in my mouth. I almost spit it out in her face but manage to contain myself before it comes out in a spew.

Ester explodes in laughter, one hand flyin' to cover her mouth while the other drips icin' and crumblin' cake. My eyes narrow as I slice a second piece. "No, no—no you don't," she warns, but before she can scamper away, I grab her arm with one hand and the piece of cake with the other and shove it in her mouth. Good natured as always, she continues to giggle at the cake and icin' smeared across her face and dribblin' from the upturned corners of her mouth.

The room is abuzz with merriment, everyone chatterin' like a flock of jays and laughin' at us. I dump the squashed cake piece back onto the plate, pick up a napkin, and dab cake and icin' from her mouth and cheeks. With a lovin' smile, she licks the remnants of cake and icin' from her fingers, then uses another napkin to wipe the smears from my face and hand. Then, she cuts slice after slice to pass around to the guests.

My mind wanders back to the all-day weddin' ceremony that bound me to Flowing Spring—the drummers and dancers, the parade around the camp under the blanket held by the tribe's strongest warriors, the blessin' of the chief and the smokin' of the pipe, even my readin' of Scripture and Grasshopper's stilted translation into Lakota. I realize I miss the solemnity and symbolism of the ceremony, and a tinge of sadness colors the rest of the festivities for me. I wish I'd thought to read the verses I read during my marriage to Flowing Spring over this marriage, too. The wasicu weddin' ceremony seems basically a promise and a party but not much substance.

The prayer of the Lakota chief returns from my memory, and I, rather impulsively, decide to share it. So, I lift my hands and call for everyone's attention. Ester, her eyebrows raised with anticipation, beams as she waits to see what I will say.

"I would like to pray the weddin' prayer of the Lakota." An uncomfortable silence descends on the room. I glance at Ester, but she smiles and nods her encouragement to continue. "Great Spirit, you give life. The earth was cold, and the buffalo fled. But now we hear songs again. Your two children sing and make lighthearted. It is time for your children to make happiness together—time to build their nest. Time for pairing. Time of the eagle. Great Spirit, you are good. All creatures have a partner. You make us this way. Each wing needs a mate. Each feather needs a likeness. You make us this way. In secret, we carry the likeness of another close to our hearts until we meet, and your life starts in us. Your song sings in us. Your happiness comes to us. We praise you. He hechetu. Amen." I look around the room, aware of their discomfort but not carin' a lick. Then, I take Ester's hands. "Ester, you are the likeness I have carried close to my heart. Now, the Great Spirit has joined us together and made us one flesh, and now His life begins in us."

Ester, tears brimmin' in her eyes, wraps her arms around my neck and buries her head in my shoulder. I hear her murmur against my chest. "That's so beautiful."

I whisper in her ear, "I'm sorry if I've embarrassed you."

She leans her head back and gazes into my eyes. "I don't care what anyone else thinks. I love everything about you. It means so much that you would share the Lakota prayer with me."

It isn't long before the guests begin to take their leave. I can't help but wonder if my prayer dampened the mood and hastened the end of the celebration, but Ester assures me she's glad they've gone so we can finally be alone.

"But I don't have a home for us to go to so we can be alone." I think of walkin' into the tipi built by Soul of Moon, buildin' the fire, and waitin' for Flowing Spring to enter. I'm an utter failure. "I'm sorry."

"Don't be silly. Mother and Elizabeth are going out with Ruth and Arthur. They want to catch up. So, we will have time to be alone."

"Not in our own home."

Ester's brows knit together, and she presses her lips into a thin line. "Mac, does it really matter where we are? As long as we're together, I'm happy."

She's right. What's wrong with me, lettin' the past put a cloud over our present? "Of course, you're right. I need to listen to my own prayer."

"The time of the eagle. I like that." She closes her eyes and smiles. "They shall mount up with wings as eagles; they shall run, and not be weary; and they shall walk, and not faint."

"They that wait upon the Lord..."

"Shall renew their strength. That's right."

"Then we'll wait upon the Lord."

Ester lowers her eyes. "Well, we don't have to wait for some things." She gives me a quick glance and a crooked smile.

"No, we don't." I sweep her off her feet and carry her, gigglin' and squirmin' in my arms, up the staircase to Ruth's room—what is now our room, temporarily at least. "Welcome home, Mrs. MacAlister."

She punches me in the arm. "Technically, I'm Mrs. Murphy. According to the reverend, that is."

"You know what you need? A Lakota name. That'll take care of the last name confusion."

"Oooo, how exciting! What should my Lakota name be?"

It's my turn to close my eyes. I ask the Great Spirit to show me her wakan, and the image of a vast field of blue flowers blossoms in my mind—but it isn't the flowers that capture my attention, it's the gentle breeze causin' the flowers to ripple like the waves of the ocean. "Iyéchel Icáluzä Wáhwala." The warm approval of the Great Spirit touches my heart.

Ester whispers, as if speakin' aloud might break the spell. "What does it mean?"

"As gentle as the breeze."

"Teach me how to say it."

As I carry her into the room and into our bed, I whisper each part of her name, and she whispers it back to me. Our lips caress as she speaks the final word—"Wáhwala."

Later, as dusk darkens the sky to purple, we put on our regular clothes and sneak down into the kitchen to look for some leftovers of the weddin' spread. I'm ravenous. All I ate at the weddin' was a bite of cake—at least, the part that went down. But our surreptitious plans to enjoy some food in our room are thwarted when Mary hears us on the stairs and calls us into the sittin' room. There, we find Mary, Elizabeth, Ruth, and Arthur relaxin' after a long day.

"Come here, you two. I have a wedding gift for you. Elizabeth, would you look in the bottom of the secretary and pull out the big box, please?"

Elizabeth complies. "It's so heavy, Mother. Whatever could it be?"

"Open it, Mac."

I drag the heavy box the rest of the way out into the room and pull off the lid. Inside gleams stacks and stacks of gold coins. "What is this?"

"It's more than enough money to purchase back your family's land and rebuild your home—a home for you and Ester to share and raise your family there."

"I can't accept this."

"Yes, you can. I set aside gold for each of my girls, and when they wed, they receive it as their dowry."

"I got my portion when Arthur and I married," Ruth chimes in.

"Now, I'm giving it to you to fulfill your dream of buying back your land and rebuilding your family home. You'll provide my Ester a good life there, the kind of life she desires, a life of simplicity and peace. Everything you've told me about your land says it will be perfect for her, and I know it means everything to you. These little pieces of gold are a small price to pay to fulfill my loved ones' dreams."

"Oh, Mother. It's the perfect gift." Ester rushes to her mother's side and throws her arms around her.

"Promise me you will create the life you've always wanted, and you will love each other forever."

I step behind Ester and place my hands on her shoulders. "I promise I'll do everything in my power to make Ester happy, and to live a life worthy of the heritage you and Alex passed down to Ester, and my Ma and Pa passed down to me. A life filled with love and honor for each other and for God."

Chapter Thirty-three

A few days later, we are packin' up a new wagon, purchased with the money I earned workin' for John Willoughby, and hitchin' Blossom and Itowa to it. Itowa has never pulled a wagon, but he has pulled pallets filled with wood for tipis, so he adjusts easily to his new role.

Mary insists we take some of what she calls "basics" with us—cook pans, utensils, dinnerware, cups—"what civilized people use in their homes," is her final word on the matter. Those items, plus Ester's clothes, admittedly less than Elizabeth's but still quite a few boxes, take up most of the room in the wagon. All I own is my one suit I bought for the weddin' and two sets of work clothes, one of which I'm wearin', so it doesn't matter that I have little room.

Mary is flutterin' around like a mother hen. "Where will you stay while you build?"

"We can camp. Or I can build us a tipi. They are easy to build and quite comfortable."

Ester smiles. "I'd love to live in a tipi."

"What would your neighbors think?" Mary is aghast.

"Truth be told, I don't really have neighbors—not any that can see how we're livin'. Only ol' Mr. Johnson, and he won't care. If he's still there." I have no idea what we're gonna find when we get to Georgia. Will my land still be there for me to claim? Or did some Yankee carpetbagger snatch it up and maybe even sell it off in parcels to the highest bidder? I can't bear the thought.

Mary's hands keep pawin' at her throat. "I don't know about this. Maybe you should leave Ester here until you get your home built."

"Mother!"

"All I want is for you to be safe."

I stroke Mary's arm, understandin' her concern. Her daughter is goin' someplace she's never seen, someplace where there's no guarantee she'll have a place to live, someplace where terrible things happened to young girls. "I'll keep her safe, Mary. I promise you."

She pats my hand. "I know, son."

She called me son. I'm strangely touched. Perhaps I could call her Mother, like Ester? Maybe one day, I'll get up the nerve to ask her.

The goodbyes take forever, it seems to me, but I'm patient with it. Who knows when Ester will see Ruth again? And how long before we can make our way back to see Mary and Elizabeth? It could be next Christmas before we come back this way—assumin' I can buy our land. So, I stand beside Arthur and wait as the tears flow and hugs are shared between mother and sisters.

We spend a month on the road, stoppin' in towns with boardin' houses when we can, and sleepin' in the wagon where none are available. I'm amazed at the ease of our conversation. She wants to know everything about my life on the farm growin' up, about my time in the war, and about my life among the Lakota. I teach her some basic Lakota words and phrases and find her to be a fast learner, much quicker than I was under Grasshopper's tutelage. She's also fascinated by the principles the Lakota follow and their ceremonies and rituals and their meanings.

"We will need to bless the land as soon as we arrive, like a true Lakota family." Her eyes take on a dreamy cast, as if she's a hundred miles away, possibly imaginin' herself as a Lakota woman.

"Well, first we need to buy it."

She chuckles at herself. "Of course. Do you know any Lakota blessings for the land?"

"There are many ways we can pray for the land. I believe the one I'll choose is the prayer for the blessin' of my relatives and ancestors."

"Oh, that's perfect."

She shares what she remembers about her father and life before the war. But her stories of livin' with Cousin Marcus and Aunt Caroline cause the hair to rise up on the back of my neck. "It's a good thing I didn't know about the way he treated your mother and you girls when I went to his house to find you."

"I'm relieved Mother had the ability to leave as soon as she did. Imagine if he had gotten his hands on Father's gold."

Things would've turned out differently, that much is certain. I'm once again amazed as I see the providence of God at work, takin' the evil of man and turnin' it for good in the lives of His lovin' children. I whisper a prayer of gratitude that Mary escaped Marcus' clutches and made her way to Wilmington—that the Willoughbys came upon me when they did and not a day later only to find me dead beside the road—that Ester's heart compelled her to wait for me instead of marryin' Johnny Willoughby or some other young Wilmington boy—even that I survived the massacre of my tribe to receive this wonderful redemption He created for me.

My final thanksgiving leaves a hollow sadness inside me. As has become our custom along the road, I share my feelin's of sadness with Ester right away. Her sensitive and carin' response helps me talk through the reason for the deep ache in my heart—although I received God's redemption, I mourn the loss of my Lakota family, particularly Mato Waäylo, who took his own life. Does God not have a redemption for them?

"I believe He does," Ester argues. "I believe the Great Spirit would meet Flowing Spring and Súnkawakan Sápä and even Mato Waäylo in the moment of death and embrace them and invite them to come to heaven..."

"They call it Wanágiyata—spirit world."

"I believe a loving God would know Mato Waäylo's heart—why he did what he did. He would understand."

I take great comfort from Ester's assurances, along with the vision given to me by God of all my loved ones standin' together to bless my union with Ester. What she says must be true. It has to be. I grip that truth to my heart like it's a rope over a bog.

We also spend a great deal of time talkin' about God and Scripture. Her views are refreshin' to my soul. For her, God's love is an endless ocean with the tide ever risin', and everything God does flows from this body of love. I recognize I've not seen Him in this light, but I embrace her view, which better aligns with the whispers of the voice I hear when He speaks to me.

Ester is fascinated when I share about the quiet voice. "It isn't like that for me. He doesn't speak words to me. I feel things, almost like His Spirit presses knowledge into my heart like someone would press a seal into wax. That's how I knew to wait for you, that you were my one and only true love."

"I'm so glad He did."

When we reach the Blue Ridge mountains, Ester begs me to stop so we can look out over the rows of fadin' blue mountains and watch the mist flow like rivers through the valleys and the sunset color the sky coral and rose and purple behind the rollin' hills.

"It's beautiful, isn't it?"

"Mac, it's marvelous. Is this how your land looks?"

"Yes."

Ester moans with delight. "And we are going to live there."

All I can say is a whispered, "I hope so."

At long last, we arrive in Morganton. It's midday, so I go straight away to the bank to find out the status of the farm. Union soldiers remain there, still usin' the bank as a form of headquarters, but I don't recognize any of the men there. Still, in case they've heard of MacAlister, the deserter who killed his fellow soldiers, I introduce myself to the banker as Martin Murphy, former soldier with the cavalry in the western territories.

"What can I do for you, sir?"

"A fellow soldier who was killed durin' a battle with the Lakota Sioux asked me to reclaim his family's land for him should he die. In fact, he was fightin' out west to work off a tax debt on the land. He was to serve for five years. I wonder if you could tell me the status of his farm?"

"Certainly, sir. If you can give me the soldier's family name and the plat or parcel number?"

"MacAlister was the family name. It's a large farm atop one of the hills beyond town, parcel number 0562."

"Just a moment."

My heart races like a gallopin' horse chased by cavalry soldiers—the hoof beats pound against my chest. It isn't particularly hot, yet I'm sweatin' like it's July at noon. My fists are clenched, almost as if my body is gearin' up for a fight that I hope never comes. When the banker returns, his flat face gives me no clue as to what he found. He shuffles a few papers, pulls his glasses down on his nose, traces his finger along a list of numbers, turns a page, traces again, turns another page. I'm about ready to scream.

Finally, he sighs and looks up from his work. "I found the tax document. Unfortunately, the bank records show the tax remains outstanding. Now that your fellow soldier has died, the contract is null and void."

"Your meanin'?"

"The agreement he signed with the government was for five years of service to pay off the debt. All or nothing."

"I understand. I'm here to pay off his debt."

"The land belongs to the government now that he is deceased. They will, I'm sure, want to sell it for full value. Unless, of course, you and I can come to some arrangement."

"I'm here to fulfill his contract for him. They can't sell it if I fulfill the contract."

"That is correct. And may I ask, why, sir, would you do that?"

I scramble for something resemblin' the truth. "He—uh—he died savin' my life."

"I see. So, you are repaying a debt you owe to him."

"Yessir."

"You understand that taxes have continued to accrue each year."

"Yessir."

"With interest." The banker eyes my clothes with one raised brow and a bit of a sneer.

"I'm aware."

"And penalties."

"Yessir. How much?"

"The current debt is $425. Plus, my—fee—for allowing you to fulfill the contract in MacAlister's stead." He slides a scrap of paper with a dollar amount written on it.

"That's more than the land is worth!"

The banker frowns. "How would you know the value of land in this area. Are you from around these parts?"

"Nosir. But my friend told me, when he left for the war, the land was valued at $400."

"Things have changed a good deal since then. Be thankful I'm sympathetic to your situation, and therefore choose not to hand the land over to the government for them to auction the land at exorbitant expense."

I suppose he's right. His personal greed is workin' to my advantage. Once again, the hand of God stays the evil intentions of man. "I'll pay the full amount includin' interest and penalties—and your fees."

"The full amount?"

"Yessir. If you'll allow me to go to my wagon..."

"It occurs to me, if I were to sell this land outright, I might make even more money for myself."

"Nosir. You told me an amount, and that is what I aim to pay."

"A deposit, then, to entice me to hold the land for you."

"Sir, my wagon is just outside the door. I'll be back with your gold in less than two minutes."

"Gold, eh?"

"Yessir."

"Did some mining while you were out west, did you?"

"Yessir." It's easier to lie than explain, and he's more likely to wait for my payment if he believes I have gold.

"Do you have a piece to show me? To prove you have it?"

"Two minutes, and you'll have the full amount."

His eyes narrow. "Two minutes."

I race to the wagon, pull the box from beneath our clothin' and supplies, and count out gold pieces to $600 worth, all the while explainin' to Ester in ragged breaths what the banker is threatenin' to do to us. She lowers her head, and I can see her lips movin' in prayer.

I carry the bundle of gold pieces back inside the bank and drop them on the counter in front of the banker. He eyes them suspiciously, even bites on one, then counts each one, takin' his time about it. At long last, the man nods, pockets a number of the coins, smirks at me, and pulls out a deed labeled MacAlister.

"Where do I go to transfer the title?"

"We can do that here. There's a fee."

I sigh. "How much?" I'm grateful I have the money needed to cover the transfer from what's left of my few months of work in Wilmington.

The banker leaves again for several minutes and returns with a crisp new paper identifying the parcel of land formerly belongin' to the MacAlister family as the property of Martin Murphy.

I'm numb as I drift from the bank. A breathless Ester waits in the wagon, so I lift the new deed and say, "It's ours."

Ester claps her hands with glee but stops when she spies my somber countenance. "What's the matter?"

"I dunno. It feels—strange. I've fought and killed and almost died for this day. Why now does it feel so...?"

"Anticlimactic?"

"I guess that describes it."

"You'll feel better when you see the land. Let's go, straight away."

Blossom follows the familiar road from Morganton, up the windin' trail to our land. "Our land begins here."

As we make our way up the mountain, I point out the path to the waterfall and pool, I show her the fields, long fallow, and I point out the former location of our home, now nothin' more than a blackened scar and rubble upon the ground.

"May we please go all the way to the top? I want to see the distant hills."

"Of course, my love, but first, I need to check on something." I unhitch Blossom from the wagon and mount her. "Wait here. I'll be back very soon."

I follow the narrow path down the back side of the hill toward Mr. Johnson's ol' cabin. Once again, my breath shortens and my heart pounds as I approach the dilapidated structure. There's no sign of Mr. Johnson or any other life here 'bouts. To be sure, I knock on his door. "Mr. Johnson? It's Mac—Aidan MacAlister. Mr. Johnson, are you still here?"

I'm about to turn away when, to my great joy, the door creaks open on its rusty hinges and an ol' man with a bowed back peers out. "Mac? That you?'

"Mr. Johnson, am I glad to see you! I thought for a moment you'd moved on."

"Nowhere to go, son."

He's aged, his movements stiff and slow like his speech.

"I've paid the debt on the land. It belongs to me again."

"Mighty fine." He shuffles back from the doorway. "Com'on in and set down a while."

"I can't right now. I've left my wife up the hill alone, so I must return to her. I'd like to take you to meet her."

"Nawsir, I don't do much travelin' about these days. Just stay here mostly."

"Then I'll bring her down to meet you, once we get settled in."

"That'd be nice. Married, eh?"

"Yessir."

"Mighty fine. Com'on back and see me now, ye hear?"

"We will."

Seein' Mr. Johnson lifts my spirits, even though he isn't the sprightly ol' man I remember. He brings the presence of the familiar, a sense of normalcy to an otherwise strange and unsettlin' situation. I've heard the sayin', you can never go home again. I guess there's a truth to it. But Ester and I are buildin' something new—a new family, a new house, a new life—risin' from the ashes of my ol' one like Lazarus from his tomb.

As I ride Blossom back up the hill, I shake off the dullin' of my senses and focus on the new adventure before us. I see Ester as I round the last turn, the sunlight gleamin' behind her blonde hair like the halo of an angel, and joy blooms again in my heart like a sunflower stretchin' toward the sun. I nudge Blossom forward, and she trots the final few yards to Ester's side.

"Did you find what you were looking for?"

"Ol' Mr. Johnson. Do you recall my stories about him?"

She nods.

"He still lives in the shack at the base of the hill, older now but still the same kindly man."

"You're relieved." It isn't a question. The woman knows me better than I know myself.

"Yes, I am. Everything's changed—except he's still here, like he's been keepin' watch, waitin' for us to return. I'm glad to see him."

Ester reaches out and rubs my hand. "It's good to see you smile again."

"Let's go to the top of the mountain so you can see the ridgeline." I hoist her up in front of me, wrap my arms around her waist, and pump Blossom's reins. She gallops like the wind across the open field and through the trees, across the stream and up to the top of the hill. Ester's laughter rings across the hillside, reverberatin' through tree limbs and echoin' off distant hills, restorin' life to the empty shadow of what was once my home.

At the pinnacle, I jump down and gently lower her into my arms. Together, we stand in a tight embrace to watch the sun set behind the blue hills, lookin' for all the world like distant, rollin' waves approachin' our green shores.

Ester sighs in contentment as new colors streak across the sky. "I'd like to build our house here."

The impracticality of buildin' so far from the fields flashes before me, but I dismiss the thought out of hand. If my Ester wants to see the sun rise and set over the ridgeline every day for the rest of her life, so be it. "Then here we'll build."

We stand facin' the sunset, Blossom by our side, Ester's blonde hair glowin' with an ethereal, pearlescent light as the land is washed in shades of red and gold. Ester's whisper is barely loud enough for me to hear. "Bless the land. Here and now."

I raise my arms in imitation of the great Lakota chief and intone the words I remember to bring the blessn' of our ancestors and relatives upon the land.

"May our ancestors and relatives who shine like the sun linger at our call. May the sun find your soul among us, who knew the overflowin' river of riches in your spirits. May the warmth of your body heal the heart of the land. May your kindness shine light in the darkness. May you bless the rivers, clear and blue. May peace follow the river to where the green grass adorns the land. May you send your devotion where the winds and earth touched your feet, where the breath of life gifts us with new growth. May your warmth and your kindness heal this land. We carry the Great Spirit within us. Let us bow down and plow and plant our seeds with loving rays of light."

We stand in reverent silence to watch the sun complete its journey toward the hills. As the sun kisses the mountaintops, settin' them aglow as if fires burn along the ridges, and fan-like rays trace new pathways to heaven across the sky, I complete my prayer. "And Heavenly Father, before you, I promise we will live a life worthy of our ancestors and my Lakota family. We will love you with all our heart, with all our soul, with all our mind, and with all our strength. We will teach our children to love you and worship you in all they do. And we will honor the blessin' of your gift to us, this hallowed ground we call our home. He hechetu. Amen."

ABOUT THE AUTHOR

As an award-winning author, Christian counselor, spiritual director, and professor of counseling, I use my experience and professional insight into human motivations and personalities to develop complex characters and explore difficult psychological topics in-depth. My writings include fiction, nonfiction, professional counseling books, and children's books.

My husband, David, and I enjoy working and writing together. Our passion is to help others explore and deepen their relationship with Jesus Christ, and our work and our writings are geared toward that goal.

Our children are grown with families of their own. Our son, Hayden, is a teacher, married to Natalie, a nurse. They have two children, Coen and Petra, our precious grandchildren. Our daughter, Lindsey, is a veterinarian, married to Kyle, an electrical engineer.

Our youngest son, Cody, passed away at the age of seventeen from a degenerative neurological disorder. His life stands as a beautiful reflection of what it means to live in the Kingdom of God within. You can read more about Cody's story at https://codylanefoundation.com.

Please sign up to receive my newsletter at
https://thedoctorslane.com/sign-up
Each month, you'll get a brief devotion, updates on my writing and new releases from fellow authors, and special surprises.

OTHER BOOKS BY THIS AUTHOR

Fiction

The Interview
Sky Light Falls: Whisperers Book One
Sky Light Rises: Whisperers Book Two
Sky Light Ends: Whisperers Book Three
Time Forgotten

Nonfiction

Dwelling
Seeking Treasures
Strength in Adversity
Strength in Our Story
Wilderness Meditations
Restored Christianity

Professional

Please Share the Door: I'm Freezing—Creating Oneness in Marriage
Trauma Narrative Treatment
Gold Stone

How to Connect

Websites— https://thedoctorslane.com
https://restoredchristianity.com
https://codylanefoundation.com
Facebook— https://facebook.com/dr.donna.e.lane
Twitter—@Doctordelane
Instagram—@doctordelane

www.ingramcontent.com/pod-product-compliance
Lightning Source LLC
Chambersburg PA
CBHW030847030726
47495CB00005B/1414